FIRST
WIFE

ALSO BY SUE WATSON

HIS

FIRST

WIFE

SUE WATSON

THOMAS & MERCER

Text copyright © 2025 by Sue Watson
All rights reserved.

Published by Thomas & Mercer, Seattle

www.apub.com

Amazon, the Amazon logo, and Thomas & Mercer are trademarks of Amazon.com, Inc., or its affiliates.

EU Product Safety contact:
Amazon Publishing, Amazon Media EU S.à r.l.
38, avenue John F. Kennedy, L-1855 Luxembourg
amazonpublishing-gpsr@amazon.com

ISBN-13: 9781662523915
eISBN: 9781662523922

Cover design by The Brewster Project
Cover images: © Shutter-Man © levy © CeltStudio
© janniwet / Shutterstock

Printed in the United States of America

For Mum, who gave me a copy of Rebecca *when I was very young, sending me down this dark, twisty, wonderful path of writing.*

PROLOGUE

Have you ever met a stranger who accurately predicted your future? I have.

It was my first summer in Sicily, and I was standing on a lonely road after work, waiting for a bus to take me back to my apartment. The bus was late, my phone was out of battery, and dusk was slowly creeping in.

Then, suddenly in the silence, I heard a rustling behind me, and turned to see a dark figure in the trees.

'Hello?' I tried to sound calm, while inside I was freaking out. I tried to make out who it was – was it even human, or was it just the shape of the trees? But then I heard the voice.

'Lady, lady?'

Was it male or female? I couldn't tell; the sound was high-pitched, mean and scratchy.

'Lady?' the rasping voice repeated. I was terrified, and clutched my backpack to my chest. 'I tell your fortune?'

Despite the heat of the day still holding on, I remember shivering as the disembodied words emerged from the darkness. I really tried to focus, but it was impossible to see a face in the shadows of the trees.

'I tell you who you marry? Will you be reech, and happy . . . or sad and poor? Will he love you – or will he lie?'

Was someone playing a joke?

I was cursing myself for staying at work so late – for being in this area of the town in the dark and not considering my own safety. I looked around to see if I could hail a taxi or just run into the road shouting 'Help!' But everywhere was deserted, I hadn't seen a car for ages, and there was probably no one stupid enough to be walking through the wrong side of town at night. I was in flight mode, ready to run, but what if they ran after me? What if there were more of them hiding in the trees?

Where was the bus?

'You want to know if your love, he's true? Will he be your husband?'

A branch cracking, a shuffling sound, they were approaching. I braced myself, ready to make a run for it.

'Give, give.' The voice was much closer to my ear. I could now see the person was wearing a shawl around their head, concealing most of their face. Dread prickled my skin.

'Who are you?' I asked, keeping my eyes on the figure as I slowly opened my bag to take out what little money I had.

'I tell you your future. Your hand. Geeve me your hand. Come, come.' The voice was urgent, irritable. Long fingers beckoned. I reluctantly stepped forward.

'Your name?'

'I'm . . . Sophie.'

'And you are in the love, yes?'

I immediately thought of him, and a fire rushed through me. I felt my hand opening up.

'I show you . . .' Their grip was strong as they pulled me towards them, their face now down in my palm, a scratchy lace glove on my wrist, hot eager breath on my skin. 'I see a man, very handsome?' Gloved fingers pressed clumsily into the lines and swirls of my flesh, pushing and kneading.

'Oh?' My heart was pounding.

'Yes, a very beautiful man but . . . I see danger, dark secrets. You have to leave here.'

Shit. I tried to get my hand back, but the hand holding mine was surprisingly strong, pulling me in. I was about to scream when I felt a whisper close to my ear.

'Beware, *teste di moro*, too many dark secrets . . . someone lies and someone dies . . .'

That's when I ran . . .

I'll never forget the first time I saw him.

1

I'm drinking coffee at a pavement café in Sicily with an English girl called Abbi. We've been having a conversation about our plans to travel to Rome. Both too old to be backpackers, we have the kind of wanderlust that sometimes hits in your thirties, when you realise one day you will die.

Like me, Abbi is fairly new to Sicily, and despite loving the place, her job working for a car hire company isn't her idea of *la dolce vita*. I love my summer job teaching art, and took it in the hope that the university might extend the contract to autumn, but talking about Rome with Abbi has given me itchy feet.

The teaching work isn't as I imagined it anyway. My students consist mostly of the teenage offspring of rich Americans. They are fun and lively, but their interest in art is minimal and it is clear they'd rather have sex, smoke dope and party than learn to paint.

I enjoy the work, and love being in Sicily, but my life is a mess. Two years ago, at the age of thirty-four, I left my home in England when everything started to unravel. I had to get out. But running away is never the answer, and guilt etches itself on to your soul; it nestles in your organs and becomes part of you. The guilt I carry is like the freckles on my face – a fundamental part of me.

So, still seeking some kind of escape from the past, I talked about travelling to Rome with Abbi for a few weeks in the naive hope that another escape might finally exorcise the past. But today, as I sit at a pavement café drinking coffee, I suddenly see this man – and I can't explain it, something shifts inside me, so much so that I wonder if, instead of travelling all the way to Rome, I should stay here, on Sicily. I've never seen him before, but there is something about him, the way he walks, not swaggering, just quietly confident, strolling through *his* town. I assume he's from here; he has the dark, brooding good looks, the easy sophistication of the Sicilian male who knows where he's going. I smile at my own assumptions – he might not be like this at all – but something deep down tells me this gorgeous man strolling through town might just be the person to help me forget. For a little while, at least? Perhaps I simply fancy him, but it's weird, I feel drawn to him in a really primal way, like the stars have collided and created this bright flash of recognition, of familiarity: *Ah, here he is, this is who I've been waiting for.* After flailing around in the wilderness, I finally see a chink of light. I know it sounds crazy and weird to be mooning over a total stranger – and it is! And even as I'm drinking in his dark good looks, and well-cut suit, I'm inwardly reprimanding myself for being so stupid. Unable to stop looking, the sight of him gives me this overwhelming rush – I'm slightly out of breath and agitated. What's wrong with me? My tummy is swirling, and as much as I tell myself to stop being silly, I can't. I love the sensation, the sheer madness of this, and I'm already addicted.

I continue to watch from behind my menu as the object of my affection stops to gaze into the Dior window. Taormina, the town in Sicily where I'm living, is rich in history, but also shiny with wealth and luxury. Chanel and Versace compete for attention on the high street, while billionaires' yachts wait in the harbour, ready to move to the next Mediterranean haven when they grow bored of this one. But this is an island of contradictions, and the high-octane glamour and hedonism is always overshadowed by

Etna, the brooding volcano – waiting, threatening, unpredictable. It grounds me.

'So, I've planned our route,' Abbi is saying, as she unfurls an over-large map and waxes lyrical about the Pantheon and the Colosseum. I tune her out as I watch *him* wander into the designer boutique.

'Are you listening?' Abbi rips into my daydream. 'I said, I planned our route.' She brandishes her phone, with 'Be Kind' emblazoned across the case in gold lettering. 'I've kept all the receipts for the maps and stuff, so I'll work out how much you owe me.'

'Great,' I murmur, already having second thoughts about the trip. Abbi can be quite pushy, bossy even, and I don't always have the energy to stand up to her. 'Do we really need all those maps? I mean, it isn't the Victorian era, we have Google?' I suggest.

'Mind you don't spill coffee on this,' she says, ignoring my comment and unfurling the concertina of stiff paper on to the table, glasses on the end of her nose, like some despot planning world domination. 'The Basilica, Santo Stefano Rotondo, and, ooh, Chiesa di San Carlino alle Quattro Fontane,' she gasps. As my doubts about this trip and Abbi are growing by the minute, her ecclesiastical word salad isn't exactly selling it to me.

I gaze at the long, narrow high street, studded with achingly cool designer boutiques built into the ancient stonework. But having no savings, paying off debts from my previous life, and with only a temporary job, I always have my face pressed against the window of life.

'You have to be rich to be here,' I remark, staring at the wealthy tourists from behind the expensive coffee menu. Abbi isn't listening, too engrossed in her takeover of Europe, starting in Italy, one pope's tomb at a time.

The man is now emerging from the boutique with a white paper bag – 'DIOR' written on it in gold. I can only imagine what delicious designer gorgeousness is inside that hallowed bag. As he begins to walk up the high street and nearer to where we are sitting, I feel my tummy flip – he is even more handsome close up. His furrowed brow and expensive-looking jacket suggest class, and enough money to shop at Dior, and yet his shoes jar slightly. They are more like walking boots, dirty and worn. *How intriguing.* He has an air of mystery about him. I've always had a weakness for unfathomable men.

Abbi continues on about train times and student hostels, conjuring memories of cramped bunkbeds and the stench of overcooked cabbage. I'm suddenly distracted, my heart skipping a beat as the man wanders over to where we are sitting and pulls out a seat at a table close by.

'Imagine running your fingers through that dark hair, and unbuttoning that crisp white shirt,' I murmur, mesmerised.

'What?' Abbi has her finger pressed on the map, her phone in her other hand.

'Him – he's gorgeous!' I flick my eyes over to where he is sitting. For a moment, she drags herself away from dead saints to take a sidelong glance.

'Mmm. Good-looking, but isn't he a bit old for you?' She screws up her nose.

'I like older men.'

Her eyebrows raise momentarily before she returns to her map.

'*Un caffè e un cannolo, per favore,*' I hear him say to the waitress. His voice is like a warm summer by the sea, and my shallow heart thumps in my chest. I don't know this man, he could be anyone, I'm being silly, but when the waitress returns with his order, I see the way she looks at him and feel a tiny pang of jealousy, like a cocktail stick in my heart.

7

I think I may have imagined this, but when I catch his eye and smile, his eyes smile back, and I let my eyes linger a little too long on his.

Watching him take a bite of the crisp, sweet cannolo, I study his lips and wonder what he would be like to kiss. I also wonder if a man like that could erase the dark shadows that loiter in the corners of my life.

2

A few days later, I happen to see him again!

He's standing alone under a lemon tree at the University of Catania. It is pure fate, being where I work.

'Who's he?' I ask my colleague Lucia, as we walk through the sun-dappled trees to my class.

She glances over at him. 'Emilio Ferrante,' she says. Her Sicilian voice sings his name, bringing him to life for me. 'He is quite a high-flyer, a professor of volcanology.'

'Wow!'

A slow smile spreads across her face. 'You like him, don't you?'

'No . . . not like that . . .' I start, feeling myself blush.

'You do! I can imagine you two . . .' She is searching for the English word; she often does this. 'You are both *belli* . . . beautiful.'

'I'm not beautiful,' I reply. It embarrasses me when people say this.

'No, you need to have more of the confidence. He is, as you say, a hot-blooded Sicilian and *very* much would be interested.' Lucia waves a long finger at me, and before we say goodbye she promises to see what more she can find out about Emilio Ferrante.

◆ ◆ ◆

'A professor of volcanoes?' Abbi says when I tell her a few days later. 'That's a bit weird.'

'No it isn't,' I reply, disappointed by her reaction. I hoped she'd be more impressed. 'Only you could say someone who lives near Etna is a bit weird for being a volcanologist, Abbi.'

She shrugs. She really isn't on board with the idea of my dream man, but I'm not letting Abbi dampen my enthusiasm.

'I can't believe he works at the same university as me. It's fate, I'm telling you.'

'Fate? You haven't even spoken to him. You know nothing about him, Sophie.'

'I know enough. He's written tons of books and papers, and he's incredibly intelligent and highly respected in his field,' I announce.

'Straight from Google?'

'I may have googled a little,' I chuckle.

'Have you actually spoken to him?'

'No, but yesterday we caught each other's eye.'

'Oh, why didn't you say? Set a wedding date, have we?' Abbi rolls her eyes.

'You know what I mean . . . we both looked at the same time and there was a moment,' I say, recalling how we passed in the hallway, and as our eyes connected it felt like an electric shock. 'Then I turned around to see him when he'd gone past, and mortifyingly he was doing the same. I was a little embarrassed, but then he'd smiled. For the rest of the day I'd felt like flowers were blooming in my chest.'

Abbi shrugs. 'Don't get too involved, Sophie. You're still very fragile, remember?'

As if I could forget. 'He might be just what I need to move on from the past.'

'Or he might be some kind of playboy.'

'Hardly. He's a university lecturer.'

'University lecher, more like!'

'He's not like that,' I reply, my stomach jolting slightly as I recall seeing him chatting to a student the other day. They were standing outside in the quadrangle under a tree, and she looked up into his perfect face adoringly. She was clutching a pile of books to her chest, and rocking her hips slowly from side to side. Her body language was obvious – *take me now*, it said – but he seemed intent on conversation and I didn't get lecherous vibes. I was surprised at how irrationally jealous I was of her nearness to him, however. Then there was her youth as, let's face it, women in their twenties are beautiful, even when they're not.

'You're probably right, Abbi,' I say. 'Why would he look at a washed-up thirty-something like me?'

'Exactly.'

'Wrong answer.'

'Oh . . . I didn't mean that's what you are, I just meant they're all probably so young and fresh and willing,' she replies, digging a deeper hole for herself.

'I'm sure he has his pick of young students,' I agree, deflated.

'I don't know why you bother with men. You should get a hobby instead.' She sounds like my mother. 'I've joined the Taormina amateur operatic company, in the town. I'm the wardrobe mistress, I'll be sewing the costumes for the next opera, we're doing *Tosca*. Don't worry, it won't affect our Rome adventure, I just love sewing.'

'Oh good, that sounds fun.' But I'm only half-listening.

'Why don't you come along to the theatre and join the backstage team?'

'I don't have the time,' I say, which isn't strictly true. I have all the time in the world outside of my job, but I feel like Abbi is eating me up. She's kind and thoughtful, but so desperate for a best friend it makes her quite needy. I often find myself doing things I don't want to just to please her. Our planned visit to Rome is the prime example of this. I was originally quite keen, but am now forcing it, and the closer it gets to our departure date, the less I want to go.

I rent the apartment above Abbi's on a cobbled street just outside the town centre, and within an hour of me moving in, she'd invited me for coffee. Abbi was persistent right from the start, but having chosen to leave my friends in the UK, I really don't want a new friend asking too many questions. I need time to think – to be alone. So, for the first few days I avoided Abbi, until one night there was a power cut, and she came upstairs and knocked on my door holding a lit candle and a fully charged phone. 'I'm always prepared,' she announced. The flickering candle illuminated her face eerily and cast shadows on the wall. 'Us girls should stick together. We're two women in a strange country.' And with that, she virtually pushed her way into my apartment. I was surprised at this invasion, and slightly alarmed when she told me that the girl who previously lived in my apartment was a 'total bitch' who would never meet her for coffee.

After that, Abbi appointed herself as my friend and guidance counsellor. I just allowed it to happen, I guess I was lonely, and she was, after all, quite kind. She also speaks a little Italian, which is more than I do, so in time we have fallen into a friendship of sorts. She has my best interests at heart, but sometimes I feel her 'advice' is based on how something I want to do might affect *her*. This new crush I have is a perfect example of Abbi weaving her own self-interest into her 'advice'.

'I really don't see the appeal of getting tied down to a man,' she says. 'Before you know it, you're married and living his life.'

'You can be married and still be independent.'

'Were you independent in your marriage?'

'Yes, of course,' I reply, feeling prickly and uncomfortable. I'm not prepared to elaborate on my marriage.

'You like wine, don't you, Sophie?' she says suddenly, breaking the silence.

'Everyone likes wine,' I murmur, checking my phone for the calories in the Sicilian orange cake I just consumed.

'Great . . . there's an organic vineyard just outside town. I thought we might pay a visit at the weekend?'

'A vineyard?' I'm playing for time. I have no intention of allowing her to suck up my weekend. 'I'm sorry, I can't make it.'

'Why? You're not secretly meeting him, are you?' She frowns, wiping coffee froth from her upper lip.

'Who?'

'Volcano guy?'

'No,' I answer truthfully. 'I'd tell you if I was.'

'If you ask me, you really aren't ready for a new relationship yet, Sophie.'

'But how else will I move on? And please don't say sewing costumes at the am-dram opera.'

'Rude,' she huffs, only half-joking.

As always, she has a point, but Abbi is a pessimist. She doesn't *dream* about what might happen in her life, she *worries* about it, and her negativity is the last thing I need. I came to this beautiful place to forget, to escape my fears and worries, and rediscover the old me. I want to be carefree, happy Sophie again – the one who embraces life, falls in love and doesn't worry too much about tomorrow – even if, in my heart, I know I can never forget. I can run away, but the past follows me, and just when I think I've escaped it taps me on the shoulder, reminding me of what I've done.

3

'Hey Sophie, I haven't seen you for ages!' Abbi is waiting in the hallway for me as I come in from work.

'I saw you this morning,' I reply with a smile.

'Oh yes, I forgot. Do you fancy doing something this evening?'

'Sorry, I have to work. I'm working on some mixed media stuff with different textures.'

'I could keep you company while you work?' she says as I gently push past her towards the stairs to my apartment.

'I can't work with someone else around – but thanks anyway.'

'Will it take all evening?'

I can feel the tension in my chest. 'I don't know, Abbi. It'll probably take much longer.'

'Are you off at the weekend?'

'Yes, I always am,' I reply; as a teacher I never work weekends.

'I could take a couple of days off from the shop?'

I stop on the stairs and turn to her. 'Why?'

She seems a bit taken aback. 'I . . . well, our trip to Rome isn't for weeks. I was thinking we could go somewhere in Sicily for a couple of days, you and me?'

She's recently started to make these presumptions about my free time, like she has ownership over me. She rarely leaves me alone, and on days when I feel suffocated by her, I have to make excuses and disappear. I want to be alone with my thoughts, something she doesn't seem to understand, and there are times I pretend I'm going out when I'm not. But then I feel trapped in my own apartment, unable to play music or move too much in case she hears me. I guess we just have different expectations of friendship – she needs a best friend who is always available, and I'm not that friend, but I don't want to hurt her.

'Sorry, Abbi, I can't go away with you. I'm too busy. I'll be working on my project all weekend.'

I watch her face crumple, and immediately feel bad and obligated to offer some consolation.

'I know, why don't I go and do a couple of hours on my project, then we could get a drink later?' This is the last thing I want to do, but I can't leave her down there alone, feeling rejected.

Her face lights up.

'What about M Bar?' I say. 'It's supposed to be really nice inside, with great cocktails. My treat.'

She's thrilled, and I can walk away guilt-free – for now. I head for my room as she stands at the foot of the stairs watching me.

As always, I lock my front door, and once in my bedroom I open the wardrobe, reach into the back and lift out the cardboard box with all the photos in. I place it carefully on the table by the window, and stand for a while looking at it. I brought this box with me all the way from England, and I've been here a few months and still not yet opened it. If I want to rediscover the old me, I first have to find the courage to step back into the past and submerge myself in the painful memories held in this box. So I take a deep breath, lift the lid, and open up my world of pain and fear – starting with the first photo sitting on top of the pile. It's me as a teenager; I'm on a beach, in a bikini, laughing. Back then, I never realised how pretty I was – long dark hair, olive skin and the perfect body. It was flawless in the way only a teenager's body can be, my skin untouched by pain or time, like a brand-new dress – no creases or tears, still smooth and tightly woven. Back then, I thought I was ugly. Just one blemish on that perfect skin would send me into paroxysms of grief; a pound on the scales and I thought I was fat. All those pressures weighed heavily on my teenage soul, and it took me a while to emerge from my chrysalis.

Placing the photos on the table slowly, I also see the baby, the schoolgirl, and the twenty-something who grew into the woman I am today. I'm smiling to myself, immersed in happy memories, until I pick up a photo that gives me such a pain in my chest I find it hard to breathe. In it, I'm in the back seat of a fancy car, my face under a white veil. The next photo was taken outside the church. No one to walk me down the aisle, but that was okay, I'd soon be with him, and that was all that mattered. I can smell the roses from my bouquet, feel the happiness fizzing in my chest. That day I felt like the luckiest girl alive – after all, I was marrying my childhood sweetheart. I'd loved Simon since I was thirteen years old, entwined his initials with mine in my maths exercise book. My whole life was about him, after years of walking home from school together, holding hands in the cinema, and that first kiss in his parents' living room when no one was home. And now here we were all grown-up, him in his brand-new suit, me in my beautiful dress, amid the pungent scent of roses. This was my happy ending, or so I thought.

I continue to lay our wedding photos down on the table in the shape of a heart, tears springing to my eyes. We had such hope that everything was going to be just as we dreamed it would be, but I know now that life isn't like that.

I move on to later photos – the sadness, the false smiles, the pretend life we started to live, fooling ourselves and those around us. As I walked down the aisle to meet my husband-to-be, I had no concept of the agony and horror that lay ahead.

4

I work on my composition, using my photos, along with other memories and mementoes. Our first Valentine's card; a letter he once passed to me in class, telling me he loved me; the contents of a jar containing a hundred pieces of coloured paper, on each one a different reason why he loved me. That hits me hard, and I break down in tears, but minutes later Abbi is knocking at my door.

'I'm on my way,' I yell, the sound of urgent rapping grating on my nerves.

'Sophie, you okay?' Abbi gasps, apparently in panic because I didn't answer the door the moment she knocked.

'I'm fine, just a little tired.' I've been so involved in my art project I haven't had the time to change, but I don't care. I have little interest in myself, and opening the box has created a gnawing ache in the middle of my chest. 'You look lovely!' I tell her, trying to be kind, but emotionally exhausted from the excavation of my past and regretting this plan to go for drinks. But Abbi seems excited and has made such an effort in her new green dress, and she twirls at the top of the stairs, almost falling over.

'Whoa, be careful,' I warn, grabbing her arm, imagining the horror of Abbi crashing down the stairs, lying crumpled on the ground.

'You okay, Sophie?' she repeats.

'Great,' I reply brightly. 'You just gave me a scare.' I stand for a moment to gather my thoughts. My mind will never let me forget him at the bottom of the stairs, the staring eyes and twisted limbs.

On our way into town, two young men whistle at us as they pass, saying something in Italian that neither Abbi nor I understand. It's probably just as well.

'Wonder what they were saying?' she murmurs.

'Probably commenting on how hot you are,' I reply, trying to make her feel good about herself.

'Rubbish! It was you they were looking at. You're so pretty you could have anyone you wanted, Sophie.'

'I doubt it, but even if I could, I don't want just *anyone*.'

She groans audibly. 'Oh, you're not still pining for that guy, are you?'

'I haven't given up on the idea. It's good to have a goal in life.'

'Can I just ask, have we ruled out that he's not gay, or married? Hate to rain on your parade, but you know nothing about him.' Abbi *loves* to rain on my parade.

'Yeah, that had crossed my mind,' I say. 'Someone like that's bound to have been snapped up.'

'Yeah, and he's so old he's probably got grandchildren! Anyway, let's forget about him. It's a girls' night out, and we mustn't even *talk* about men.'

On arriving at the bar, we sit on two stools and she opens a cocktail menu, reading it out loud. Too loud really – the place is quiet, with low lighting and tasteful decor, and as I glance around, I suddenly see him.

Emilio Ferrante is *here*, just feet away from me! My mouth feels dry, and I wish I'd at least put some make-up on. He is sitting at a table, alone, a drink in front of him, a cigarette burning in the ashtray – and before I can process this, he sees me. My heart is pounding, and I don't know if it's my imagination, but the tension is as hot as that smouldering cigarette.

'Ooh, I love a mai tai,' Abbi is saying, still reading aloud.

Then she looks up from her menu, stares at me, and slowly follows my gaze. 'Oh, for fuck's sake, Sophie, he's over there. Have you set this up?'

Even in the dim light I can see she is flushed with anger, her eyes damp.

'No, not at all,' I reply honestly. 'I had no idea he'd be here. How could I possibly know?'

'Because you both planned it?'

'I wouldn't do that to you.'

She shrugs. 'I wouldn't put it past you.'

I roll my eyes. 'Forget about him. Come on, what are you having?'

'I'll have a pina colada,' she replies, grudgingly, still not happy about the situation. I'm not too pleased myself.

'Abbi, do you really think if I knew he'd be here I'd have this little make-up on and be dressed like this?'

She looks me up and down. 'I suppose not.'

I order a martini and a pina colada, and we sip them and chat. I try to forget he is there, because I'm here for Abbi. Still, I can't help glancing over at him now and then. He keeps looking at his phone, and by the time I've ordered two more cocktails, Abbi – who rarely drinks – is far more relaxed and in a much better mood.

'God, I don't know what you see in him. He's ancient,' she groans, breathing coconut and pineapple over me.

'He's not that old.' I discreetly glance over at him again.

'Yeah, he is, he's at least fifteen years older than you.'

'You're being ageist, Abbi. I think it's fate,' I say. 'I mean, what are the chances that he'd be here – tonight, the same night we turn up?'

'Er, he lives in this town, and so do we? And there's no such thing as fate.'

'Do you think there's such a thing as love at first sight?' I ask as our third cocktails arrived.

'No. It's just a chemical reaction – dopamine,' she replies.

'Trust you to ruin it with the science bit.'

'I learned it in psychology A level. I've told you before, love is just an idea. It isn't real, it's something to make us procreate.' She leans forward, resting her chin on her hands, and gazes into my face intently. 'Even if there was such a thing as love at first sight, are you even over your ex?'

I shift on my stool. I hate it when she does this; I wish I'd never told her I've been married.

'I see it in your eyes sometimes, Sophie. You don't even realise you're thinking about him, but I know. I know your pain.' She's like a dog with a bone.

No you don't, because I haven't told you everything. You have no idea what I went through that still keeps me awake at night.

'I took an online therapy course once,' she says, and then her eyes light up. 'Sophie, I could give you therapy?'

'No thanks,' I mutter. My eyes flicker over to see if anyone has joined him, but he's still alone. Perhaps he's waiting for someone?

'Is it because we're friends you don't want me to counsel you?'

'Yes, along with the fact you aren't a counsellor,' I reply, unable to countenance my horror at the thought of telling Abbi my deepest, darkest fears – and secrets.

'Mr Ancient is heading this way,' she suddenly announces, grumpily.

Is he coming over to me? Might he buy us a drink, engage in conversation? I hold my breath as he walks towards us, aware I have a silly, expectant smile on my face but unable to erase it.

He comes so close I can smell him: sandalwood and leather, a waft of heaven. I'm still smiling like an idiot, looking up into his eyes. And then, the crushing disappointment as he walks straight past us and out through the door. Without even a glance.

He hasn't even noticed me. He hasn't been smiling or catching my eye on purpose at work. He's just a nice guy. I am nothing. I don't exist.

'Did you think he was coming over to talk to you?' Abbi says under her breath.

'No,' I say vigorously.

But Abbi is shaking her head slowly.

'What?'

'Do me a favour and don't get involved with that guy.'

'Why?'

'The way he was looking at you.'

'What do you mean?' I try not to look too thrilled at this confirmation that he recognised me. 'He wasn't looking at me. He was staring into his phone all night,' I protest, which he was.

She leans in, looking genuinely concerned. 'I don't want to freak you out, Sophie. But he's a weirdo. From where I was sitting, I could see that he wasn't just on his phone. He was taking photos of you.'

5

I'll admit, I was a little creeped out at what Abbi said about Emilio taking photos of me in the bar. But it occurred to me that she might have told me that to put me off him, so I decide to take what she said with a pinch of salt. But when I literally bump into him in the coffee queue in the cafeteria at work the next day, I feel strangely exposed. He doesn't acknowledge me at first, but after he takes a tray from the pile for himself, he then takes another and hands it to me.

'Thank you.' I suddenly feel breathless.

Perhaps he has noticed me? Perhaps he did take some photos? Perhaps he's a weirdo, as Abbi announced?

After a week of glimpsing him from afar and catching his eye now and then, for him to hand me a tray feels huge. It's a direct acknowledgement, and I now need to reciprocate – unless, that is, he was simply handing a tray to a woman in the queue? I ponder this while standing close behind him clutching the tray to my chest as if it is a Ming vase, moving slowly with the line, knowing that this is a small window and once we reach the end of this queue, the window will close.

I don't care if he has taken photos of me. In fact, the more I think about it, the more flattered I am. I desperately try to think of something to say as we slowly move down the queue, his aftershave lingering behind him, allowing me to breathe it in like fresh mountain air.

Then, suddenly, he stops walking and turns to check out the open plates of food sitting in the cooler.

'Have you tried the arancini?' I ask, ridiculously. He's Sicilian, he's presumably been here long enough to try the university version of the deep-fried, tasty rice balls – a staple of Sicilian cuisine.

'It's not great here,' he mutters, studying a salad, then looking up. 'They do great arancini in town, on Via del Teatro Greco. Do you know it?'

He doesn't look at me, but I hear warmth in his voice, and I like the way the words are soft and rounded – a hint of Sicilian, but his English is good.

'I . . . er, no, I haven't been in Taormina long, just a couple of months, but that's near the theatre isn't it?'

'Yes. There's a place there with the best arancini in Sicily.'

'Wow, that's some recommendation,' I reply, unable to take my eyes off the slight stubble around his jaw, the smooth olive skin, the long dark lashes!

'You should, it's just before you reach the Teatro itself,' he says, referring to the ancient Greek theatre in town. 'It's quite beautiful at the theatre. Stunning views.'

'I've heard that, I must go,' I murmur, trying not to sound too obvious that I'd like to go there with *him*.

He gazes down the queue and, suddenly turning to me, says, 'We will go there.' Then he winks, and I wondered if he is teasing, but still the blood rushes to my face. I feel the physical shock of attraction, and it takes my breath away.

'Oh . . . yes . . . it sounds wonderful.' I smile. 'I'd love that,' I add, in the unlikely event that he missed me saying a big yes to his suggestion. I have to hold back, stop gushing, I sound like I'm begging.

23

'It would be my pleasure.' He is now putting a plate on his tray and grabbing a bottle of water. Oh, he did mean it?

I follow him along the line, taking a plate and grabbing a bottle, unaware of what I just put on my tray. The queue is moving quite fast now, and he is looking ahead, waving to a male colleague who seems to be waiting for him. I'm hoping he will suggest a day and time, or even just that we swap numbers, anything to pin this moment down. But now he is paying the cashier, and making a joke with her, then someone pushes into the queue and I'm out of his sightline. By the time I get to the till, he's joined his friend and has gone.

I'm devastated, bereft. But I tell myself he was just being friendly, passing the time of day, nothing more. I need to calm the fuck down and stop behaving like a teenager. He clearly isn't interested. I wander through the cafeteria with my tray, and to my relief see my friend Lucia, who is sitting with some other colleagues and beckons me over. I join them, smiling inanely, laughing at jokes I barely understand despite them kindly speaking slowly in Italian so I understand. The truth is I don't care; I have no interest in the food on my plate or the people around me, all I want to do is talk to him.

'Sophie teaches me English,' Lucia is explaining. 'We have coffee and the chatting, and I am so much the better for it,' she adds.

I just smile and bite into my arancino ball that I stupidly picked up while asking him if he has tried them. Since when has anyone used a ball of rice as a pick-up line? It's hard and tasteless and I want to abandon it and leave the cafeteria, never to return.

'She asks me for the gossiping. She likes a man and wants to know more about him.' She winks at me. Realising she is about to tell her smiling colleagues that I have the hots for Professor Emilio

Ferrante causes the blood to rush to my head. They might know him – this is so embarrassing, I have to get out now.

'I'm so sorry,' I say, looking at my watch, 'I have a tutorial with a student, I'd completely forgotten.' I stand up. 'Lovely to meet you all,' I garble. Blowing a kiss to Lucia, I walk quickly out of the cafeteria. God, how can I be so stupid as to discuss something so personal with a colleague? Sometimes I question my own judgement – I really have to stop oversharing.

I push open the doors of the cafeteria to leave, and begin to walk down the hallway, but have only gone a short way when someone appears at my shoulder. It's him, and he seems breathless. Has he been running to catch up with me?

'Hello again,' he says, attempting to sound casual.

'Oh, hi,' I reply, matching the low energy of his tone.

'I was thinking – if you would like we can go to the Teatro any time you are free?'

My heart is pumping; my mouth is dry. 'I'd love to . . .'

We stand in the middle of the busy hallway, I look up into his eyes, and everything else fades – there is no sound, no movement, just us. People rush past both ways, everyone dashing to be somewhere, but we stand like an island in the middle of a raging storm.

'Should I give you my number?' I hear him say, as he takes out his phone.

'Oh, yes, of course. Or we could swap?' I don't want to be the one to call him.

I tell him my number and he texts me, Hello, my name's Emilio.

I text back, Hi I'm Sophie I teach art.

He smiles at this. 'Ah, an artist?' he says, but before I can answer, he puts both hands on my shoulders and gently pushes me out of the way of three guys running down the hallway. I didn't even see them heading my way.

'Thank you,' I gasp. He is standing so close I can feel the warmth emanating from his body, and I have this urge to curl up and rest my head on his chest. Whether it's love or just pheromones, there's something about this man that makes me feel safe, as if while he is around nothing bad is going to happen.

Then, suddenly, his friend or colleague or whoever it is emerges from the cafeteria and slaps him heavily on the back, urging him to hurry.

'Look – I have to go, we have a meeting now,' he says to me. 'When are you free?'

'I can do tomorrow?'

'Perfect – I'll meet you at the Teatro at two?'

I nod eagerly, and he begins to walk away. He seems reluctant, backing up slowly, torn between staying and going. Then he suddenly disappears into the conga of people in the hallway.

Talking to Emilio is like hearing an old song that takes me back – echoes of the past, a quickening of my heart, something I thought I'd never feel again. But even as something blossoms inside me, I feel a warning chill, and just hope to God this will have a very different ending than the last time.

6

The sign outside the Teatro Greco indicating the waiting time says '2 hours'. It's blisteringly hot and there's a long queue to enter the ancient theatre's ruins.

I fan myself with a leaflet while waiting for Emilio. We arranged to meet at 2 p.m. at the Teatro entrance, but it's now after 3 p.m. Have I mixed up, or been stood up?

I find some shade by a tree to wait just a little longer, telling myself *ten more minutes and that's it.*

Then, suddenly, he appears as if from nowhere. 'Sorry to keep you waiting,' he says, offering no explanation as to why he's almost half an hour late. 'I bought tickets so we don't have to queue in the heat.'

I quell the urge to point out that I have been queueing in the heat for ages, but I'm relieved and pathetically grateful that he's actually turned up. So I just smile, surprised all over again at how handsome he is, and my stomach does a flip.

Silently, he guides me past the hot, disgruntled crowd, through the gate. Carved into a mountain, The Teatro stands high on a hill, and provides panoramic views of the Ionian Sea, and a simmering Etna in the distance. I follow him as we climb higher, into the ruins and then up the broken age-worn steps. The higher we go, the more the world beyond the ruins opens up to us, and at the top we stand together, looking out, each in our own world.

'I don't think I've ever been anywhere so beautiful,' I almost whisper, gazing up into a canopy of warm blue sky, then down at the sea.

He nods in agreement, unable to take his eyes from the horizon. 'Come,' he eventually says, taking my hand and leading me through the amphitheatre. He talks and points and mentions dates and events and influences and wars but I hear nothing. All I know is that he's here and he's holding my hand.

'You are too hot?' he says suddenly, stopping. No doubt he's noticed the sweat dripping from my upper lip and forehead. My hair's now flat and I'm sure my linen dress is damp under the armpits. I really didn't think this through; it wasn't how I imagined I'd look when I chose the dress from my wardrobe this morning and decided to wear my hair down.

'We will get drinks.' He's now looking at me with some concern. '*Andiamo.*' He manoeuvres me back through the crowded walkways. Despite the heat, being with him soothes me. I feel protected, like I can depend on him. He gently commandeers me down the steps and through to the theatre café, which stands on the edge of the mountain. 'Come, this way,' he says, and guides me through to a table outside. 'Sit here. I'll be back.'

I gaze out on to the most beautiful vista, and marvel at this wonderful place he's brought me to. Photos will never capture the beauty and drama, but still, I take out my phone and try to save the moment, snapping this perfect, warm, blue day, catching Emilio as he returns to the table. He's carrying bottles of water and lemon ice lollies, and moves away from the camera, like he doesn't want me to take a photo of him. I wonder why, and then I'm reminded of the evening in the bar with Abbi when she said he was taking photos of me, and when he sits down, I decide to ask him.

'Did I see you in M Bar earlier this week?'

He opens his bottle of water and takes a long drink. 'Yes, it was me.'

'You saw me, then?'

'Of course, how could I not see you?' He doesn't smile.

'My friend says you were taking my photo?' I look at him to see if he reacts, but it's hard to tell as he's wearing sunglasses. He slowly places his bottle on the table, giving a small, almost invisible headshake.

I feel slightly embarrassed. Abbi was obviously trying to creep me out, but asking him directly if he was photographing me has made it seem like I'm a bloody narcissist. He leans forward on his elbows. 'I remember the first time I saw you.'

'Really?'

An almost imperceptible nod. 'At the café in town. You were having coffee with the same friend I saw you with in M Bar.'

I feel a rush. 'That was when I first saw you too.' I hesitate before asking, 'What did you think?'

He sits back in his seat and pushes his sunglasses up on to his head, surveying me. 'I thought . . .' He ponders this. 'I thought, this cannolo is delicious.' He does a little chef's kiss with his fingers.

'I meant what did you think about me?' I giggle, reaching out my hand to bat his arm, a teenage gesture that makes me cringe as I do it.

'I thought you looked attractive of course. I wanted to talk to you, but I didn't know you.'

'You didn't know me yesterday, but you asked me out on a date.'

'Is this a date? Is that what this is?' he asks.

I feel stupid. Have I misinterpreted this? 'You asked me here, what do you think?' I try to stay cool, despite feeling a little unnerved.

'I think yes,' he murmurs, his voice low, intimate. 'I think I might have a crush on you, Sophie.'

His mouth is serious as he leans in, his breath on my face, and before I can say anything, his lips are on mine. The kiss is chaste, his mouth is closed, but it's so soft and warm. His hand moves to my back and then my neck, strong fingers gently caressing my warm, damp skin.

I go full-on Victorian lady, actually feeling faint at this man's touch, and reluctantly pull away. 'I'm so hot . . . it's right in the line of the sun here,' I say, praying I don't keel over.

'Are you okay?' He looks concerned.

All I can do is nod, unconvincingly.

'Your skin is warm. Is it . . . too warm?'

His eyes meet mine as he touches my skin, and an electric shock runs through me. His finger now caresses the soft inside of my arm, and he gazes into my face as if I were a fascinating specimen, something in a test tube he hasn't seen before. We sit in silence for some time, but silence scares me, and I'm compelled to speak.

'Your English is so good. Were you born in Sicily?' I ask.

'Yes, but my father was American, and he spoke English most of the time. He came from Chicago to visit a friend and met my mother. He called her his Sophia Loren.'

'That's so sweet.'

'When I was twenty-one I broke her heart and moved to the UK. I spent the next decade in England. I was a research fellow at Cambridge University.'

'Oh wow, no wonder your English is so good,' I say, impressed.

He looks away, towards the mountainside. 'I was born in a village north of here. My father and mother moved to be with her family when they married. He'd been a doctor in New York, and here he became the village doctor.'

'Quite a culture clash?'

'Yes, but he gave everything up for love,' he said admiringly.

'How romantic,' I sighed. 'So do your family still live there?'

He doesn't answer straight away. 'Family?' he mumbles, suddenly distracted by a woman walking past. She's stunning, with golden skin and long caramel-coloured hair. I also take her in as she sweeps past us.

'Your family are still there, in the village?' I repeat, unnerved by the way he's staring at the woman.

'Oh . . . er, no, my parents died years ago. I have no family . . . to speak of.' The woman disappears into the distance, and he finally looks back at me. I wonder if he's some kind of playboy as Abbi suggested?

'What about your family, Sophie?'

I look up into the sky. My childhood was difficult, but I'm not sure I want to share that right now.

'Don't feel you have to say if you'd rather not say.'

'I have no family now. I was an only child, never met my father. Mum died when I was sixteen.' I'm keen to move the focus away from me. 'Tell me about your work,' I say.

'It's nothing special. I lecture in between research projects.'

'Oh?'

'I travel quite a lot. I'm hoping for some time in the field again soon. Academia is wonderful; it gives me the opportunity to share knowledge, and ideas.'

But I don't really hear him. We're just gazing at each other.

'You are beautiful, Sophie.' His fingers reach up and push my hair behind my ear, then move to my neck, softly caressing the flesh.

We're getting closer and closer. I feel like I might explode. Then, just as I think we're going to kiss again, he pulls away. It's a slight move, but it ends the moment.

'I promised you arancini,' he suddenly says. 'The best arancini in Sicily, on the side of the road. You will join me?'

I don't answer. I'm adjusting to the gear change, and feeling very vulnerable, which he seems to misinterpret as reluctance.

'Are you sure about this, about me?' he asks. 'You have been hurt before?'

'Kind of . . . I was married.'

'Married?' He glances at my ring finger.

'Not anymore. He . . . died.'

'I'm so sorry.'

He must hear the tears in my voice, and doesn't push me to explain, but instinctively puts his arm around me. I instantly feel soothed and safe.

'You aren't alone,' he says.

I wait for him to say more, but like me he's obviously been hurt. There's so much I want to tell him, so much I'm hiding. It's the reason I came here, to escape the UK, to find somewhere I could be safe. And somewhere inside I feel this surge of hope, that Emilio might just be my salvation. He might be the one to click on the light – and kill all the darkness.

7

After leaving the Teatro café, we walk among the spectacular ruins of the theatre.

'To think it's been here for thousands of years. These remains date back to 300 BC,' he says.

It seems like the whole world is above and beyond us – the sea one way, the mountains on the other side. Everything is here and anything is possible.

'This would be perfect to paint,' I murmur as we look through an ancient archway, which leads to another archway, and on into infinity. I wonder if my future lies out there somewhere in all that warm blue.

Eventually, we leave the theatre, and he leads me down the Via Teatro Greco, a tourist trap of shops selling ceramic heads and fabrics decorated with citrus fruits. Along the way are food vendors offering Sicilian delicacies and ice cream in every flavour imaginable.

'Now, for the best arancini in Sicily,' he announces, and we continue along the street until he stops at a shiny silver food van.

'Take a seat and I'll order dinner.' He gestures towards a low stone wall, and while he orders the arancini, I take my 'seat' on the wall.

Within minutes we're eating the delicious fried rice balls, warm and pungent with herbs and spices.

'Good, yes?'

'The best,' I agree. 'When you said this was the place to find the best arancini – I assumed you meant one of the fancy restaurants around here.'

He stops eating for a moment. 'I have disappointed you?'

'No, I love this!' I say, holding up the foil-wrapped rice ball. 'Thank you.'

'Perhaps next time we could do something a little more "fancy"?' he suggests.

Delighted at the words 'next time', I tell him, 'I don't need fancy restaurants. I just need good food and good company, and I have both.'

'Agreed. But I don't want to disappoint you – or bore you?'

'It's the opposite, I'm having a great time.'

'But you're younger than me . . .' he says, revealing an endearing glimmer of self-doubt.

'It doesn't matter. I like older men,' I reply, dabbing my mouth with a napkin.

His face blossoms into a smile. 'But you don't know how old I am.'

'You don't know how old I am.'

He considers me, his eyes flickering over my face, my neck, my body. He gives little away.

'Are you twenty-five?'

I smile. 'I'm thirty-six, but thank you for your tact.'

'I'm forty-six, ten years older, are you okay with that?'

'I'm fine with that. I mean, it's not like we're getting married.'

I'm joking, and expect a smile, but he doesn't react, just looks at his watch. 'Would you like a drink somewhere, or . . . ?'

'Or?' I say this flirtatiously.

'We could go for a walk . . . or would you like to go home now?'

'Oh . . . not really, would you?' I'm disappointed that he's even suggesting this.

'No, I wouldn't. I'm sorry if I gave that impression. I haven't done this for a long time – dating, I mean.'

'Were you in a long-term relationship?'

He nods.

'It's difficult, isn't it? Especially when you're used to one person.'

He doesn't answer, so I don't pursue this, and it suits me because I don't want to talk about my marriage. So we sit for a while, watching the day people transition into night people heading for restaurants and bars. They're talking and laughing, and just enjoying each other's company. The wall we're sitting on is under a fragrant frangipani tree. The air is sweet, and clusters of tiny pink flowers have dropped at our feet like confetti, while a pink veil of dusk settles over Taormina. I want this night to last forever.

Later, he walks me back to my apartment, and we stand outside chatting, neither of us wanting to say goodbye. But out of the corner of my eye I see the twitch of Abbi's curtain from her apartment, which is directly under mine. I turn, and through the gaps in the lace fabric against the window, our eyes meet. She's watching us! Then she realises I'm looking right back at her, and there's a flurry of lace and she's gone. But it's too late, I feel exposed out here, and so I invite him up for coffee.

◆ ◆ ◆

Once inside the apartment, I see it through his eyes. It's shabby and looks unlived in. Despite having been here a while, I still haven't put down any roots. I can't, I have no idea how long I'll be here, how long I can stay safe in Sicily. In my other life I had a proper home, with my own furniture, and a set of lifetime ovenware. I miss that life, but I can't ever get it back – and besides, I sold it all, barely making a dent in the debts I still owe.

'Sorry, I don't entertain much and my seating arrangements are limited,' I apologise, handing him a cup of espresso as he sits on the only easy chair I have.

'So, how long have you been at the university?' I ask, sitting cross-legged on the floor like a child.

'You mean you haven't googled me?' He feigns surprise.

'No,' I lie. I have, of course, and it was interesting to see how brilliant he is and how many academic awards he's received and papers he's written. But he isn't on social media and his online presence is scant. It's mostly about his academic achievements rather than Emilio Ferrante the man.

'You should have googled me. I could be anyone,' he teases.

'Who are you then?' I hold his gaze.

He doesn't answer me. 'I presumed every young woman googles someone they're meeting for the evening.'

'Perhaps I like a little uncertainty in my life?' I offer.

His eyes flicker, but his face gives nothing away.

'Did you google me, Professor Ferrante?'

His smile is controlled; he won't give in to it. 'Yes, I did. You might have been dangerous.'

'Oh, I am.'

'I know, you're very dangerous,' he says slowly, and seriously. He leans forward, his hand reaches out, and he holds my chin delicately between thumb and forefinger. 'Very, very dangerous,' he murmurs, looking into my face like he's inspecting a work of art. His gestures are small, but thrilling.

'There's nothing to find out about me.' I giggle nervously. 'My only online presence is selfies and pictures of fancy coffees on Facebook and Instagram, so knock yourself out.' I've erased any potential issues from my social media, as I have from real life, as if nothing's ever happened to me. Essentially, I've wiped away my previous life. I've *had* to.

I reach for my bag and take out my phone.

'What are you doing?' he asks.

'I'm googling you.'

'Not now.' He tries to grasp my phone, but I'm clutching it to my chest. He stands up from the chair and kneels on the floor, then reaches for the phone in my hands. I surrender it immediately, and he gently places it on the floor out of my reach, but within his.

He leans closer, and I feel his heart beating against mine as he carefully lays me down and puts his mouth on my lips.

This time, he pushes his tongue gently in as every strand of uncertainty and fear that's wound around my veins loosens and unravels until I'm free.

I can't help myself, I want him, and sensing my urgency, he pulls at my dress until it's over my head, and I'm lying on the shabby carpet, naked from the waist up. I open his crisp linen shirt and one by one slip each button through its hole, slowly, controlling his building passion, keeping him on the edge. I want him to want me, so I keep him waiting. I want to be in control, and only when he's trembling with desire do I let him in.

And later, as we lie in a tangle of sheets and limbs, I hold on to him, knowing that Abbi was wrong when she said there's no such thing as love. What I'm feeling now can't be explained away by science – my heart's beating so hard I fear that a valve might tear.

As he sleeps, I run my fingers through his dark, wiry hair, then wrap myself around him and eventually drift off.

◆ ◆ ◆

When I wake just a few hours later, I remember, and say his name into the grey light between night and day. When there's no reply, I reach out, extending my palm inch by inch over to his side of the bed. All I feel are cool sheets, no warmth. 'Emilio,' I whisper again, as I sit up and turn on the lamp. To my dismay, he isn't there, and for a second, I wonder if I dreamed the whole thing.

I get up and pad to the bathroom, then to the kitchen and sitting room, but there's no sign of him. He's gone, along with his clothes, which were on the floor. There's no text, no note, not even the lingering scent of aftershave. It's as if he was never here.

I step out on to the balcony, just in case he's there, taking in the late-night air. No one's there. The street below is quiet, and empty. I'm now anxious, hurt. Why would he leave like that, without letting me know?

I stand on the balcony, in despair. What happened? I gaze across at the balconies of other apartments, most in darkness; just a few are lit, probably early risers starting their day, or night owls ending theirs.

Leaning on the balustrade, looking up at the scattered stars, I soon become aware of something else. There's a burning smell. I breathe in through my nose – the strong, woody odour of a cigarette. My eyes are drawn to the balcony opposite; the street is narrow, the houses close together, and I can make out a curl of smoke rising. In this thick silence, I hear the faint sound of breathing, and see the hot red tip of a cigarette. Someone is on that balcony sitting in the dark. Watching me.

8

More than a week has gone by since the night I spent with Emilio, and I haven't heard from him. No texts, no calls, and nor have I seen him on campus. I haven't told Lucia, my colleague in admin, because after having lunch with her and her friends I realised she would tell everyone. So I find myself confiding in Abbi, which is probably a mistake. We're having coffee and pastries at a café before work, and she's horrified yet delighted that he hasn't called.

'Have you called him?' she asks.

'Abbi, the guy walked out on me, I'm hardly going to call him. I don't want to look desperate.'

'Or like a psycho.' She pulls an awkward face.

'No, I'm obviously not going for that look.' I roll my eyes, wishing I'd never told her, but there's no one else and she's my most sensible friend here.

'He might be dead?' she offers unhelpfully.

I shrug, used to her lack of filter.

'Shame though,' she continues. 'You really liked him. I just don't understand why he didn't like you. I mean you're pretty and . . . if he found you boring or unimaginative in bed, why didn't he just say?'

I frown. 'Did you say you wanted to become a therapist?'

'Yes, I told you, I did that online course. Why do you ask?'

'Just concerned that after one session your more fragile clients might take their own lives.' I'm only half-joking.

'Sorry if you don't like what you're hearing, but as a counsellor, I'll take your insults on the chin. Honesty is key, and you might not like it, but there's a reason someone walks out straight after sex.'

'It wasn't like that . . .'

'Okay, we can continue this once we've ordered breakfast,' she says, disappearing behind the menu.

As always, Abbi does have a point, and I have to face the possibility that he left because he finds me repulsive or boring or awful in bed – or all three?

I see a curl of smoke rise from someone's cigarette on the next table, and my stomach lurches.

'The smell of that cigarette just triggered me,' I say.

'Yes. An aunt of mine used to smoke them. She was quite glamorous – always smoked Gitanes. She let me smoke them sometimes too.'

'A Gitane, is that what it is?' I lean forward, feeling a little vulnerable. 'Abbi, someone was smoking on the balcony opposite my apartment the other night. It was exactly the same smell; they must have been smoking Gitanes.'

She immediately looks up from the menu, horrified. 'Oh my GOD. Smoking on the balcony? All the soft furnishings and wooden furniture in our apartments? Shit, that's an inferno waiting to happen.'

'It was really creepy. They were smoking, and staring,' I said, wrapping my arms around myself, ignoring her health and safety concerns.

'The apartment *opposite* you?' She thinks for a moment. Abbi's been there longer than me and knows most of the neighbours. 'I think a family lives there, with a couple of kids.'

'Do they?' I feel slightly relieved at this – at least it's not a lone weirdo, a family lives in that apartment. 'Perhaps it's just one of the parents having some time out?' I offer hopefully, while aware this wouldn't explain why the smoker was directly facing my apartment. 'I never realised, but from that balcony anyone can look right into my bedroom if I have the shutters open. It's freaked me out.'

'Yeah, I guess they can . . .' She picks up the menu again, then immediately puts it down. 'I just remembered, that family moved out. I think Federico the landlord was looking for new tenants. Sounds like he might have found them. I'll ask him next time I see him.' She shifts in her seat. 'Could you see whether this smoker was male or female?'

'No, I couldn't see a face, just the outline of someone, a figure in the dark, very still except for the smoke,' I say, distracted by the fumes now coming from another table further along the pavement. It makes me wonder again who the smoker on the balcony was. *It could be anyone.* 'Were they trying to scare me? And if so, why?'

'Now I'm scared, you're creeping me out.' Abbi shudders. 'Was *he* still at your place when this happened?'

'Emilio? No, he'd gone. I was on my own.'

'You can always knock on my door if you're scared.'

'Thanks.'

'The best thing you can do now is to forget Emilio, and move on.'

'You're right. I thought he was different, though,' I sigh, feeling this compulsion to go over it like a detective with an unfathomable case.

'So what's so special about this one?'

'It's hard to explain, but before our date I knew he'd be pleasant, and charming, which he was, but he's hard to work out, like he's keeping something of himself back. I like that.'

'Weirdo,' she mutters.

'Lucia, who works in admin, told me he's brilliant, highly respected in his department, and he's also very private,' I say, refusing to stop talking about him.

'And he's old enough to be your grandfather!'

'He's not.' I laugh at her exaggeration. 'He's only ten years older.'

'You think that's a good thing?' she asks, doubtfully.

'Yes, I need someone older. I want someone to look after for me for once.'

She puts down her menu. 'And you think this guy will care for you, Sophie? He left you in the middle of the night, and he hasn't called since. I see a whole field of red flags waving.'

'I just want to know why he hasn't called. There might be a good reason?'

She's shaking her head. 'Like he's dead? Because that's the only explanation I'd accept.' She rests her elbows on the table, warming to her theme. 'Look, I'm calling it now, he's unreliable, and because he looks like a male model – an older male model,' she adds, pointedly, 'he's used to getting exactly what he wants, and you gave it to him.'

My avocado on toast arrives, but I have no appetite, so I just move it around my plate for ten minutes.

'Have you finished with that?' Abbi asks, having consumed her pancakes. I slide it towards her, untouched.

'This neighbour who was watching, I'm worried he might be a peeping Tom?' she suddenly says, starting on my breakfast.

'It could be.' I feel uncomfortable just thinking about it.

'Should we call the police?' she asks.

'No, it could have been nothing,' I say, not wanting to create a drama.

My phone suddenly pings, making me jump.

'Ooh, you on edge much?' Abbi chuckles, lifting her head momentarily from my breakfast. 'Who's that?'

It's from him, but I don't answer her.

I open up the message and devour every word.

42

Hey, Sophie. I was wondering if you'd like to meet for drinks sometime?

I place the phone down casually on the table. I'm not going to answer straight away.

'Who's that?' Abbi asks again.

'Emilio,' I reply coolly, trying to hide the catch of excitement in my voice.

'Oh?' She looks disappointed. 'Is he apologising?'

'Yeah,' I lie. 'Asking me out for drinks so he can make it up to me.'

'You aren't going to say yes?'

'I might.'

'But it's just a booty call, that's all it is.' She stabs her finger at the phone lying innocently on the table.

'I won't be sleeping with him,' I say, resenting the fact that I now have to explain myself.

'Okay, but don't come running to me when he breaks your heart, or worse. Just steer clear before it gets messy . . . and someone gets hurt.'

I'm suddenly reminded of the fortune teller from a few nights ago. *Someone lies and someone dies . . .*

I haven't told anyone, and I'm certainly not telling Abbi; she'll see it as far more significant than it is. After all, it was just some stranger. How could they know *anything* about my life?

Abbi's glaring at me, and in a low voice says, 'I have an instinct for danger, and trust me, I have a really bad feeling about this guy.'

The expression on her face tells me she's deadly serious, and the fear in her eyes chills my blood.

9

The day after Emilio texts, we meet for coffee at the campus café after work.

'I didn't expect to hear from you again,' I say, unsmiling. We're sitting at an outside table in the dappled sunshine drinking espressos.

I keep reminding myself that he disrespected me, but I can't take my eyes from his perfect face.

'Why didn't you expect to hear from me again?'

'Because I woke up and you'd gone, without even saying goodbye.'

He frowns slightly. 'We had a wonderful evening, you were fast asleep, and I didn't want to wake you.'

'But you could have left me a note, or texted.'

'I could have, I guess. I'm just not used to anyone wanting to know where I am, what I'm doing . . .'

Is he trying to say I'm too much? 'You haven't called or texted me in over a week.'

'I went straight to Catania the next day, and was there all last week – I didn't think you'd . . .'

'Mind being ghosted?'

'No, you're right. I'm so sorry, I'm just not used to . . . I should have called. I apologise.' He's smiling tightly. 'Sometimes I get so caught up in my research, work becomes more important than people.'

He takes one of my hands in both of his, and I'm reminded again of the last time we were together.

'I don't want a relationship that's just about sex,' I say to myself as much as him.

'Okay, no sex.' He isn't smiling, but his eyes might be – and I'm not sure if he's taking me seriously.

'I need someone who *cares* about me, Emilio, who doesn't just leave without considering my feelings.'

'I'm sorry, I'm a scientist. I guess I know more about volcanoes than the human heart,' he says, with a trace of regret in his voice. He hesitates. 'I lost someone I loved because I was clumsy with their heart. I can't keep making the same mistakes, Sophie. Can we start again? Let me take you to dinner and we can talk?' When I don't answer him, he touches his chest with the palm of his hand and says, 'After dinner, I promise I'll take you home, say goodbye on your doorstep. No sex . . . yes?'

'No . . . no sex,' I agree.

My battered self-esteem is easily flattered. This man is clever, respected, his students are in awe of him, his peers want to be him. And here he is, sitting at a café table begging to take me to dinner.

'So?' he asks, and I detect an edge of impatience in his voice. He probably isn't used to people saying no, particularly women. The silence weighs heavy, like a promise at the back of the throat, but I hold back, making him wait for my decision. He stares at me, unsmiling, waiting for my answer.

I drink my coffee and talk about the weather, and the longer I take to respond to his invite, the more tense he seems. I have no intention of saying no, but I won't make this easy for him, and after a little while, I finally let him know.

'I'm hungry.' I pick up my bag. 'So where are you taking me for dinner? I need to be home by ten.'

'I have a favourite place,' he says with a half-smile.

Then he stands up, offers his hand. I take it, and melt against him as we stroll to his car, then he opens the passenger door and I slide on to sun-warmed leather.

He gets in, but doesn't start the engine as I'm expecting. Instead he sits for a few seconds, perhaps even a minute, just staring ahead. It makes me slightly uncomfortable, and just when I'm about to say something, he turns to me with a tight smile.

'Where are we going?' I ask.

'Somewhere nice,' he murmurs. Then he turns the ignition, and as the engine starts, he slowly releases the clutch and we start to move.

'You okay?' I ask.

He gives a little shrug and I'm not sure what it means. I'm confused by him again. I realise that all his gestures are small; they give nothing away, and he's almost always wearing sunglasses. Is that because of the sun, or so no one can see his eyes?

We're soon driving on a high twisty coast road, both silent, in separate worlds. I try to relax and watch through the window as the evening sweeps past, turning from grey to navy blue. The drive is long, at least an hour, but it's quite beautiful; sea glitters beneath us as the road rises high above, and I hold my breath as we move further into the oncoming night.

◆　◆　◆

Arriving at the restaurant, we are shown to a discreet table overlooking the ocean. Emilio orders wine as the navy-blue evening slips into blackness.

He treats me as his guest, and recommends the pasta alla Norma, a Sicilian dish of pasta tossed in tomato sauce with fried aubergines on top. 'It's named after the opera by Bellini. Such a beautiful composer, he was born in Sicily,' he tells me.

'I'm not too familiar with opera. I love *Madame Butterfly*, but only because I saw it once in London. What's the story of Norma?' I ask.

'The oldest story in the world,' he replies sadly. 'Norma is the lover of Pollione, who falls in love with a younger woman. It's tragic, but quite beautiful. I will play it for you,' he offers. 'I have a Maria Callas edition, 1952 at Covent Garden – sublime.' He kisses his fingers. 'Wait until you hear it, she's an angel singing . . .'

I listen to him talk, and though he's perplexing and sometimes makes me feel a little unsure, I know he'll be good for me; he'll teach me, and heal me and soothe all the pain of the past.

'So, when was your last relationship?' I ask, a little later. I'm prompted by the sudden memory of the first time I saw him. He was carrying a Dior bag from the boutique. Was it a dress for a previous lover?

'My last relationship?' He seems to ponder this. 'It was some time ago . . .' he says. I think he's lying.

'Surely you have some idea.' I soften this with a smile. 'I mean, was it last year? Last week?' I lift my fork and hold it, waiting to put the food into my mouth. I want him to see that his answer is important to me.

'Sophie, tonight I want to give you all my attention. I don't want to talk about other women, as I'm sure you don't want to talk about other men – tonight, let it just be us.'

He lifts his glass as if to toast us, then drinks his wine without taking his eyes from mine, and nor do I take mine from his.

'I just think it can be hurtful, to talk about previous relationships,' he says, putting down his glass and dabbing the napkin on his mouth.

'I'm not jealous, you wouldn't hurt me by telling me about a previous relationship,' I say.

'Sophie . . . none of us know our own or another's capacity for cruelty. The one person you think you can trust, the one you give yourself to, can break you so easily.' He reaches for a breadstick and, still without taking his eyes from mine, abruptly breaks it in half. I see something so cold in his stare, it makes me shiver.

10

'The food here is good,' I say, wondering who hurt him, wondering why she hurt him. 'I love this . . . the sweetness of aubergines, the umami of tomatoes, salty capers and pecorino cheese – it's just yummy.'

'It's good, but not as good as my recipe,' he replies. 'I will make it for you, and you can decide.'

I imagine the two of us drinking large glasses of red in his kitchen while he works.

I've had the worst week – barely any sleep, just constantly wondering why he left – and now, all the uncertainty is gone and we're here in this beautiful place together having dinner. But not knowing has been emotionally exhausting, and I wonder if I have the mental stamina to be with Emilio. I sit across from him, listening to the sound of his voice, and when he reaches out our fingertips touch, and I know it's already too late to escape. I'm in. I remember this feeling from long ago – the same forever feeling, the same high I'm experiencing now.

Emilio is telling me about his childhood in Sicily, recalling summers spent with his grandparents in Palermo. I take it all in while watching his mouth and remembering his kisses.

'And you?' he asks. 'Where was your childhood spent?'

'Oh, I lived in the middle of the UK. No seas, no beaches, no volcanoes.'

'Ahh, is a place without a volcano even a place?' he asks in mock outrage.

We both turn to look at the dark shadow of Mount Etna.

'She's omnipresent, isn't she?' I say. 'Do you think her moods affect the moods of the people who live here?'

He smiles. 'Perhaps? Who knows? Etna has been here for more than half a million years, and will still be here in some form even when we are not. She sees everything.'

'Is she dangerous?'

'Yes. Like all of Mother Nature, she must be respected. People see her as harmless at their peril. She is a permanent, simmering threat to the city. She's quiet for now, but hard to predict.'

I gaze up at the huge dark shadow on the horizon and shudder inwardly.

'She makes me uneasy,' I murmur.

He nods. 'You're right to feel uneasy. I've seen the fire in her throat. We monitor volcanoes, gaze at the stars, and think we know what's happening under the earth's surface. But sometimes I wonder if we really know. Anything could happen at any time. We believe we have the tools and the capacity to predict the future, but do we even have a future?'

We both look out into the darkness. What he's saying is bleak – we're destroying our home, and who knows what we're leaving behind for our children, and their children?

'Are you superstitious?' I ask, changing the subject.

He shrugs. 'As a scientist I try not to be, but as a good Catholic I have been taught to believe some pretty crazy stuff.'

I wasn't going to say anything, I don't want to spoil the mood, but I'm intrigued to know his reaction to my encounter with the fortune teller. 'A really weird thing happened to me earlier this week. A stranger came up to me at a bus stop and started ranting about death and danger.'

'That sounds scary.' A small frown appears on his forehead.

'Yes, they said I had to beware. I don't know if they were male or female, young or old. They were dressed totally in black, their head covered up and wearing these black lace gloves. Honestly, so weird, like it was straight out of central casting!'

'So, what else did they tell you about your future, this crazy fortune teller?' He leans forward, looking at me intently.

'It was quite chilling. They told me to leave Sicily.'

He looks slightly perturbed at this. 'How could anyone leave Sicily?'

'Exactly.' I smile at his little joke. 'But I was terrified. They said there was "a very beautiful man" but . . . they saw "danger, dark secrets".'

I know it was just someone trying to make money, but hearing myself retelling the story reignites my fear and I feel uneasy again. I'd attempted to push it away until now, and was merely offering it as a funny story to see his reaction and amuse him over dinner. But it's giving me chills, and as much as I don't want to think about it, I find myself talking more.

'She said, "Beware, *teste di moro*."'

He raises an eyebrow. 'Beware, *teste di moro*?'

'Yeah, that's what I thought she said. My Italian isn't great but I know the *teste di moro* are the ceramic heads of the bearded man and blonde woman that people use as plant pots and ornaments here. I presume you know the story?'

He shrugs. 'Yeah, I think the guy lied to the girl, and she killed him. I can't remember.'

'In Sicilian folklore . . . the woman decapitated him with a sword and then planted flowers in the top of his head to make his head look like a plant pot, and hide what she'd done.'

'That's right. Most homes have them. My mother used to grow plants in hers.'

'How could you forget that story? Call yourself a Sicilian,' I joke.

He doesn't answer me.

'They must be on everyone's balconies,' I continue. My mind sees curling smoke in the darkness, an unidentifiable figure – and the ceramic heads. I hadn't made the connection before, but they were there on that balcony. Is that significant?

I feel someone walk over my grave, and shiver.

'Is the *testa di moro* the beautiful man in the story who has dark secrets?' I wonder. 'Or could that be you, Emilio?' I tease.

'I am flattered if you think I'm a beautiful man.'

'But do you have dark secrets?'

'Doesn't everyone?'

He waits for my response. But I remain silent.

'Well, *do* you?' he says. Waiting, his eyes on mine.

Panic slowly grips me like a hand around the throat, until he smiles, releasing me, and the dark plumes of smoke waft away from my mind's eye.

'It's just so creepy,' I say, fear tightening my chest. Moving his chair closer, his arm is now around my shoulders protectively. I like how it feels, and relax into his half-embrace, and we sit close, looking out on to the still-bubbling volcano. Etna's smoky breath slithers from her as she slumbers under a navy-blue blanket of stars.

After dinner, we drive back through the night, park outside my apartment, and kiss in the car. But the kiss blooms into something neither of us can resist and I ignore the rules I set for him and the promises I made to myself.

Within minutes we are in my bed, weeks of longing about to be sated, and I reckon my heart's lost somewhere in the mix too.

Being with him, feeling the warmth of his body, loving the physical closeness, I ask myself if I should just take this and not ask for more. I know I shouldn't have invited him in, but why punish myself? I can handle this, I can walk away at any time, can't I?

I turn over on to my side away from him, aware that I'm lying to myself. I know from the past that lovely moments aren't enough for me, and that raw, visceral need to be with him is already there – and inescapable. It's just like before, and I feel now like I did when I fell for Simon as a teenager. I still think about my life with Simon every hour of every day, though I hoped that in time I could move on. But falling for Emilio has reignited all the memories, good and bad, and brought the past flooding back. It's overwhelming, and I'm terrified that what happened with Simon might happen again in some way. But as I drift off to sleep, all I can hope is that, this time, things will end differently.

'When you go, at least say goodbye, won't you?' I whisper into the dark.

He doesn't answer.

11

Emilio and I have been together now for two months and three days, since that first date at the Teatro – not that I'm counting! Early on, he was attentive, kind, and considerate of my feelings, behaving more like a partner and less like a single man. I hadn't been happy like this since the early years with Simon. Just being in a new relationship was helping me work through the heartache of the last.

I was starting to feel like this could be something more, and having been offered an extension to work at the university indefinitely, I considered applying for a residence permit so I could stay in Sicily for as long as I liked. I even bought a second-hand sofa for my apartment, and started cautiously picking up the threads of life again. And when Emilio suggested we drive through Europe together next summer, I loved the unspoken assumption that we'd still be together a year on.

But over the past few weeks, things have changed. He isn't staying in touch throughout the day like he did in the beginning, and last week he didn't turn up to meet me for lunch as we planned. I understand when he's busy, but he didn't call or message to let me know, and I didn't hear from him until a day later, when he seemed really distracted. 'I'm so sorry, I forgot,' he said. I was hurt and confused by this. How could he simply forget?

I'm now concerned that he's been playing the caring boyfriend to reel me in. I've read about people love-bombing new partners, then retreating or even ghosting them to gain some kind of control or power. I'm driving myself mad trying to work out what's going on with him, and there's only so much of this I can put up with. Tonight he was due to come to my apartment at 8 p.m. for dinner. It's now ten past nine and there's no sign of him. I turned the oven off an hour ago, and now I'm pacing the apartment, my head whirling with anxiety and anger. I'm not calling or texting him; I'm seriously considering ending this. I hate the uncertainty.

Ten minutes later, he's standing at the door.

'Hey,' I say, unsmiling. 'I was wondering where you'd got to.'

'I'm so sorry, it's been a difficult few days.'

'With work?' I ask, and for a moment he looks doubtful, like he's considering this. 'What?' I'm slightly alarmed. I really think he's about to tell me something important. He looks troubled. 'You okay, Emilio?'

He nods, but doesn't speak. Emilio doesn't share easily, but tonight he seems even more guarded than usual.

'Okay, tell me what's going on.'

'It's nothing. I just . . . today, something came up that . . .'

'Oh?'

'It's fine. I'm good.' He closes down the conversation.

I doubt he'll open up, but I try. 'Is it me?' I ask.

'No, no, it isn't you.'

'You can tell me, Emilio. Whatever it is, I'll try to understand.'

He shakes his head; an instinctive reaction. He clearly has no intention of sharing whatever this is, so I let it go – for now.

'I made dinner,' I say, in an attempt to shake off this dark cloud he's brought in with him. 'I don't want to waste it. Are you hungry?'

'Yes, I am.' He doesn't sound enthusiastic, but perhaps he's just tired?

I go into the kitchen to resurrect the beef ragù.

'I'm sorry, Sophie!' he calls through from the other room.

This feels like an afterthought. His words seem empty, meaningless. I don't respond, just continue to stir the sauce, which heats and thickens along with the anger that is now swirling into the garlic and tomato-scented steam that fills the tiny kitchen.

After a few minutes stirring the sauce, I pour a glass of wine, drink it, and walk into the room where he's sitting with his head in his hands.

'What is it?' I ask.

He doesn't move. I walk forward, standing over him, and when he finally lifts his head there's a coldness in his eyes.

'Just talk to me,' I say gently. 'We're in a relationship. We should be able to share everything.'

'It's fine, really.' He can't hide the sting of irritation in his voice, which reignites my anger – *how dare he*. He's closed-off, secretive, and I'm being made to feel like a nuisance in my own place. Is this who he is? Because, if it is, I don't want this.

'No, it isn't fine! You turned up an hour late tonight,' I begin calmly. 'You haven't called or texted me much these past few weeks. You didn't even turn up for lunch the other day. Is this your way of ending things?' I feel shaky, resentful, and close to tears.

He looks at me, and I can't work out if he's angry, irritated or just sad.

'I don't want to end this . . .' he begins.

'But?'

'There is no "but". I care about you; I just have other . . . pressures.'

'What are they? Tell me.'

But he simply shakes his head.

'You keep everything so close, Emilio. I feel like there's a big part of you that I don't really know. And recently I've felt like you don't even see me. You come over here whenever you like, and . . .'

'Would you rather I didn't?'

'No,' I snap, frustrated with this obtuse response. 'But you often have this faraway look in your eyes, and you're just . . . absent. Are you distracted by work, or is it something else?' I hesitate. 'Or someone else?'

He doesn't answer me for an agonisingly long time, and when he finally looks at me I see guilt in his eyes. I'm fully expecting this to be a break-up conversation.

'I will be more thoughtful – I promise.' He reaches both arms out to me, and I move towards him, the prickles of anger and fear now soothed a little. Still sitting on the chair, he draws me into him, his arms around my waist. He rests his face on my stomach and I cautiously reciprocate, knowing I'm being drawn back in. But I can't help it, and I push my fingers through his hair, feeling the sudden warmth and passion between us. It's never far away, and soon I'm being swept back into the bubble. This is who we are, and these moments are worth fighting for. Aren't they?

'We're both new to this, and though we've avoided talking about past relationships, you told me that you lost someone, and didn't want to make the same mistakes again. Perhaps we should both open up?'

I'm scared to do this; I will be making myself very vulnerable. But I'm prepared to tell him everything about what happened with Simon – all the stuff I've kept secret for the past two years. It will be a risk, but worthwhile if it means he opens up too.

'Let's talk about the mistakes we've made – be really honest,' I say. 'We might be able to move forward instead of backwards, and save our relationship.'

He doesn't respond, just holds me even tighter, like he can't let go. I feel a little uncomfortable, but then he says, 'I want to share everything with you, Sophie, and one day I will – but tonight I don't feel strong enough to talk.'

I breathe a sigh of relief. I don't feel strong enough either. Not yet. And I can't bear the thought of losing him.

Was he like this with the woman he says he loved and lost? If so, did he hide things from her, and did she walk away because she couldn't understand him?

We hold each other for a long time, and as soothing as this is, my mind is racing. I'm confused and frustrated. What is going on here? Is Emilio the kind, charming, brilliant man I fell in love with? Or is he this dark, brooding man, simmering with untold secrets?

These thoughts make me pull away from him.

'I don't know if I want this,' I say into the silence.

His beautiful, guarded, unfathomable face stares back at me.

'I feel like I don't know who you are, and I'm not sure how to feel about that,' I tell him, then I hear myself say, 'I could handle not knowing you for a while, but I've realised tonight, just now, what I can't handle – that I don't trust you.'

After a few moments, he stands up, picks up his jacket and walks to the door. 'You'd be wise not to trust me, Sophie,' he says, and he leaves, closing the door behind him.

12

After he's gone, I go to bed, where I feel safe, and I sit for a while, clutching my duvet for comfort, with angry, hurt tears streaming down my face. Why can't I have a good relationship for once, with no issues, no drama, no loss? Why does love have to be so bloody painful? I tell myself it's for the best, and think about the problems with the relationship rather than the positive things. But I soon find myself thinking about the small but special smile he seems to only let me see, and the way he looks into my eyes like I'm everything. I love the way he talks about big things like climate change and nature. I love that he dragged me out of my small world of croissants and coffee with Abbi, and opened up the globe to me. Then I remind myself that, for some weird reason, it is obviously easier for him to talk about the shadows cast by a volcano than the ones darkening his personal life. I wonder again what he must be hiding – not that it matters anymore, I think it's over now. I can't trust him, and he agrees. What happened with Simon and me was traumatic, and I'm ashamed of what I did. But even so, I was prepared to share that with Emilio – so what happened in his relationship that was so bad he can't talk about it?

I have a busy day at the university tomorrow, but I can't sleep, it's hot and I'm overwrought, so I might as well do some work. I take out my art portfolio, spread everything out on the table, and climb back into my past.

It was the last good summer Simon and I had together, trekking in the sunshine, high above the bay at Kynance Cove in Cornwall. I sift through the photos, the memories sticking in my chest like huge great boulders of happiness. Grinning selfies taken together on white sands, or paddling in turquoise water peering into caves and rock pools the colour of emeralds. The greenish serpentine stone is said to embody the power of fertility, and in one photo I'm sitting on the rocks looking out to sea. I remember exactly what I was thinking in the moment Simon's camera clicked. I was making a wish that the next year might bring the baby we both craved. I find the appointment cards for the fertility clinic, and remember Simon's face, pale with fear and disappointment, and I have to put everything away and try not to think about the unexpected horror that lay ahead of us.

I zip everything up, back into the past. This piece will take a long time to complete, and tonight isn't the night for more sadness. I can't think about Simon, and nor can I think about Emilio – both make me cry for different reasons. It's all just so stupid and sad, and I wonder if perhaps I should have listened to Abbi, gone away to Rome with her, and pretended I'd never seen Emilio Ferrante. But from that first date I was lost. I couldn't even think of leaving Sicily and spending weeks away from him in Rome, much to Abbi's disappointment and annoyance.

Suddenly, I'm dragged away from my thoughts, and as my stomach jolts it takes a moment for my brain to process why. I can smell it again: the unmistakable stench of smoke just outside, slipping underneath my balcony door, creeping through the cracks in the walls. My blood turns cold, and I'm terrified to even peep through the shutters and see that figure, sitting in the dark, waiting, the fumes betraying their presence. But I'm also compelled to see it – to check that the threat isn't real, or that it's just a friendly neighbour who will wave and say 'good evening'.

I look at my watch. It's midnight, just like before. I stand up slowly, and reluctantly take the few steps to the balcony door. I stay by the slatted shutters, almost unable to look, but I have to. The smoke drifts over the balcony opposite and towards my apartment. The light of the cigarette confirms the figure in the shadows – silent, still, watching – and for a moment, the smoking seems to stop. I wait a moment, and suddenly I see small, almost perfect circles of smoke in the air, one after another. They're blowing smoke rings! Darkness shields them, but I don't need to step out for a closer look – I know they're looking straight into my living room. I'm frozen to the spot; whoever it is has moved closer to the edge of their balcony, and closer to me. And the cloudy rings feel like some kind of sick joke. Do they know I'm alone?

I have to step away from the shutters. I think about calling the police, but whoever is out there hasn't actually done anything. I think about the fortune teller, who warned me of a man with dark secrets and told me to leave Sicily, then tell myself not to be so stupid.

I stand back from the shutters, make sure the door is locked, and go back to bed to see if this time I can try and get to sleep. But the minute I get into bed I think of him, and of Simon and of the plumes of smoke sneaking on to my balcony.

The sound of my phone rips into the thick silence, making me jump. I check the name on the screen, *Emilio*, and a wave of hurt engulfs me. I hesitate to answer. What can he possibly say after walking out less than two hours ago, warning me not to trust him? I'm dreading this, but I have to find out why he's calling, so I reluctantly pick up.

'Hi, it's me,' he starts. 'I'm sorry I left so abruptly, not good. I was exhausted – and I find emotions . . . a lot.'

I don't speak; I have nothing to say.

'Don't put the phone down yet.'

'Okay,' I say coldly.

'I want to tell you that you're right, I've been locking you out. I am scared of opening up; I've been hurt and it's all about self-protection, which by its very nature is selfish.'

'I understand. We have to protect ourselves when we start a new relationship, but we also have to give a little too . . . I feel like just when we're getting somewhere and start to relax, suddenly you start being mysterious. It's unsettling, I feel insecure, and I'm not interested in someone who makes me feel like that.'

'I'm so sorry. I just couldn't deal with my own feelings. I'm still raw from what happened before, and I don't know if I'm ready for another relationship.'

'Wow,' I murmur. 'I wish you'd told me you didn't feel ready.'

'I don't know how I feel, I was . . . am still mixed up about my feelings. I sometimes think you're the same – and we both love two people.'

I soften; he knows me. 'Yes, I think you're probably right, that might be the issue here. Too soon?'

He pauses and I wait, holding my breath to hear what he has to say. 'I was cheated on – my heart and my pride were hurt, but I'm a grown man, I can deal with it – most of the time. But meeting you has reminded me of how I used to feel, including the hurt and betrayal and . . .'

'I understand. I'm going through something similar. Being in a new relationship often brings up memories of the good and the bad times with previous partners. It's the same feeling, but with a different person, and this time I want a different outcome.'

'What happened with you?' His voice is tender, caring.

'It wasn't like yours, I lost him in another way, but getting close to you makes me fear losing you too.'

'Your fears are mine. I don't want to lose you, Sophie.'

'I don't want to lose you either, but I'm not sure I've ever had you?'

'What do you mean?'

'I just feel like there's the life you live with me, and a much bigger one you never share. I've never been to your home, never met your family, I . . . I don't even know where you live.'

'Yes, I just felt it was easier to be together at your place.'

'Really? Is that the only reason I've never been to where you live?'

'Yes, it's nearer to work and the town, it makes sense.'

'Okay, so how far away is your place?'

'About ten miles outside Taormina. But you don't have a car.'

'I can Uber. I could come *now* if you like?' I hear myself say, like I'm in the final scene of a Netflix rom-com where the goofy girl jumps into a taxi and heads off into the night. Like I would be greeted at the other end by the love of my life, who has nothing to hide after all, and we'd fall into his bachelor bed.

'No, I have work tomorrow, it's late,' he says, and my heart falls to the floor. I'm not in a Netflix rom-com. This is real life.

'Okay. Goodbye, Emilio,' I say, ready to end the call.

'No . . . please. Don't go, I want you to come and see my home, and spend time with me there, but tonight it's just . . . I'm exhausted, I wouldn't be any fun. And besides, I need to clear the place up.'

I wait on the line, disheartened by this. Is he genuinely just tired and the time isn't right? Or is he trying to keep me away?

'How about Wednesday evening?' he offers.

'That's the day after tomorrow. Just how much cleaning-up do you need to do?' I half-joke, not believing him.

'I'm not there tomorrow. I'm staying in Catania as we're monitoring overnight. My partner Charlie and I have to take turns with the other scientists to do overnights, and tomorrow it's our turn.'

I don't believe a word he's telling me.

'I'll pick you up on Wednesday at seven and take you to my place. I'll cook dinner. Okay?'

'Okay,' I echo.

There's an awkward silence, like he wishes he could take the invite back. 'Great, I'm looking forward to it,' he says.

I put down the phone, not sure that I believe him, and still not sure that I trust him.

13

It's Wednesday evening, and I'm standing by my window looking through the shutters that I now keep closed most of the time.

I'm dressed in a new pair of white jeans and a thin lemon sweater, my hair loosely tied up. I'm looking for Emilio's car and hoping he turns up, but I'm worried he'll cancel on me. What's the real reason he's never invited me to his place before? Will I finally see his home tonight and find out who he really is? He's already ten minutes late.

Suddenly my phone rings, and I feel sick. He's cancelling, isn't he? I thought I'd be able to handle it, but the disappointment is crushing as I pick up my phone. He's only prepared to give me half of him, and that's not enough; I'm about to tell him this when a quick glance at the screen tells me it's Abbi calling.

I pick up. 'Hey Abbi!'

'Hey girl, are you ready for tonight?'

Shit, what's she talking about? 'Tonight?' I ask, desperately racking my brain to work out what's happening.

'Launch night at the new bar in town. Free drinks?'

'Oh God! Yes.' I remember now, but how am I going to break it to her that I'm not going?

'Shall I come up, or are you coming down?'

'I'm . . . I'm sorry, Abbi, but I'm seeing Emilio, I'd completely forgotten—'

'Him? You're seeing him tonight?' She talks over me.

'Yeah. I feel terrible, but—'

'But you and I were supposed to be going out. We talked about this last week!' She sounds almost tearful, and I couldn't feel worse if I tried.

'I'm so, so sorry . . . I feel terrible.' I try to take her into my confidence; she likes it when I do that. 'Remember you said that Emilio never invites me to his place, just turns up at mine at night?'

'It's called a booty call – and I didn't say it, he does it.'

'Yes, but guess what? He's invited me to his place tonight. He's going to cook. He isn't just using me, Abbi.'

'I wish I could say I was happy for you.'

'Oh, I wish you were . . .'

But she's already put down the phone.

I don't have time to call her back because a few moments later, to my surprise, Emilio's car pulls up outside my apartment.

'Sorry again about last night,' Emilio says as he opens the car door for me to climb in. 'Is it true, what you said about not trusting me?' he asks, once he's behind the steering wheel.

'Yes, but what did you mean when you said I was right not to trust you?'

He takes his eyes off the road for a moment. 'It depends on what you mean by "trust". I'm not sure anyone can be totally trusted. People look out for themselves first, even in relationships.'

'That's very cynical. I don't agree.'

'Well, that's my experience. I've had partners who've cheated on me, and I have them. I'm not even sure I can trust myself.'

'What?'

'I mean I wasn't ready for another relationship, I knew that, but I saw you and I fell for you and – I went against my own good advice, which was to wait. Therefore, I can't trust myself.'

'You're overthinking it,' I say, following the huge dark beast of Etna in my eyeline. 'In order to really love someone, you have to be able to trust them. I did things for my husband that weren't right for me. It caused me so much pain, but I did it for him, and he trusted me to do it.'

'Wow, that sounds heavy. I'm not sure I could do something for someone I loved that would cause me pain.'

'Perhaps no one's ever asked anything of you like that – have they?'

He seems uncomfortable. I've noticed he's happier talking in the abstract than the personal.

We don't speak for a while; he drives and I sit, Etna following me with her dark plume of smoke and ash. The sky is orange and misty from her small eruptions, which spit dust into the atmosphere.

'Not far now,' he says, as we drive down a potholed road, lined with Italianate villas and apartments. Some are beautiful and well kept; others are old and rundown with weed-smothered gardens, derelict or turned into flats. I'm finding it hard to imagine the kind of place Emilio would be comfortable in, but presume it will be messy with books and papers, huge volcanic charts pinned randomly on walls.

He turns the steering wheel to take a corner, and we drive through an iron gate into what seems to be a rather grand courtyard. Beyond is a beautiful old house, really big, with a huge duck-egg-blue door and window shutters in the same shade. He stops, turns off the engine and looks at me.

'We're here.' He gestures towards the house, which is so big it must be divided into separate apartments. My eyes skim the delicious blue paintwork, the perfectly shaped bay trees on either side of the door. I look up and with a jolt see a face at an upstairs window looking back at me. A young woman is glaring down, and as my eyes momentarily meet hers, I feel a stab of embarrassment. Like a peeping Tom who's just been caught, I smile, apologetically. She doesn't smile back.

'Who's that upstairs?' I ask.

'Who?' Emilio is leaning over and looking up at the window from the driver's seat. 'I can't see anyone.'

I look back, and she's gone.

Once out of the car, we reach the house just as the front door opens. The young woman I saw at the window is now standing in front of us. Still glaring. She's quite beautiful, with thick, dark hair and amber eyes, and is wearing what looks like a bikini under an open shirt.

'Sorry,' Emilio says, like he doesn't really mean it.

'What for?' she asks, folding her arms, her eyes dancing from him to me and back again.

'For disturbing you. I have no keys.' He leans on the door frame.

'You always disturb me.' Her face is close to his, she's challenging, but it feels quite intimate and I think his foot might be slightly over the threshold, against her leg. I'm very uncomfortable.

She gives me a sideways glance, presumably wondering who I am. Just as I'm wondering who she is.

'If you have no keys then you can't come in.' I think she's teasing him, but she tries to close the door and I realise that's why his leg is there, to prevent her doing this.

'You can't come in,' she repeats, her eyes laughing, the door pressing on his leg as she tries to close it.

'Then I'll huff and I'll puff . . . and I'll blow your house down,' he growls.

She gives a little squeal; it's childlike, and odd. I can't work out if she's flirting with him, or she means it. Either way, I feel very uncomfortable.

He continues to humour her. 'Let me into my house, little pig.'

'*Your* house?' She's not moving from the doorway, her arms are still folded, and she has a strange, twisted smile on her face. Emilio leans closer to say something to her; I can't hear the words, but as he's talking quietly, she looks over at me. Then her eyes slide back to his, and she looks at his mouth a little too long, following his lips as he speaks. She looks back at me, and the smile falls from her face.

'Sophie,' he says, beckoning me closer. 'This is Sabrina, she's staying here for a few days.'

'Or as long as I like,' she mutters, without looking at me. Her playful but wicked demeanour has been replaced by sulky resentment.

I'm confused. Does he actually live here – and if so, who is she?

'Sophie is my guest this evening,' he says firmly, making direct eye contact with her.

She's now glaring at me with barely concealed disgust. 'Your guest?'

'Yes, Sophie is my guest,' he repeats, smiling at me and then her.

She doesn't move from the doorstep, and nor does she smile back at me.

'Excuse us, please?' he says, making a move forward as if to step into the house. For a moment she seems to stand still and I really think she's going to try to stop him. They're close now, face to face and staring each other down, and it's tense. I can't work out the subtext.

Eventually, she steps back without taking her eyes from his. And Emilio ushers me in past her as she reluctantly holds open the door.

'Hi,' I say, awkward as hell. As she isn't moving, I am forced to smile weakly and squeeze past her, before following Emilio down the hall.

'I'm going out,' she calls.

'Okay.' His voice echoes with indifference. I'm deeply relieved. 'Come through here, I'll show you around.'

He grabs my hand and pulls me into a beautiful high-ceilinged room.

'Beautiful, isn't it?' he asks, but I'm too confused, and have too many questions about what just happened to appreciate this. Whose house are we in? Is it an old house that's been turned into an apartment block, are they both tenants here – and if so, are there others? Before I ask, I glance back to see if Sabrina's gone. She hasn't. She's still standing in the hall watching us as we disappear into the sitting room. And though she doesn't even know me, I can see by her face that she hates me.

14

'Sabrina seems a bit angry?' I whisper, trying to work out where this woman fits into Emilio's house – while hopefully being out of earshot.

'Moody.' He leads me to the window and I gaze out on the beautiful gardens.

'Is she a friend, or a tenant or . . . ?'

'Who?' he asks, like he's already forgotten her, but I wonder if he's stalling for time.

'Emilio, just explain to me the situation here.'

'What is there to explain? You wanted to see my house, and this is it.' Again that obtuse response. He obviously doesn't want to tell me about Sabrina.

'Do you live here alone, or in an apartment here?'

'I live in the house.'

'And Sabrina?'

He rolls his eyes. 'We go back a long way.'

'Really? She doesn't look that old to be going back a long way? Was she a student of yours?'

'Sophie, why so many questions?'

'Because a beautiful young woman seems to be living in your house with you.'

'Are you jealous, Sophie?'

'No, I'm confused.'

His eyes dart around, like he's working out how to explain this. 'She used to live here, and she turned up recently, needing somewhere to stay.' He shrugs. 'There are lots of rooms here, and she's a young woman, and Sicily can be a dangerous place for women.'

I don't feel like I can ask any more questions about her at the moment because I don't want him to think I'm a jealous woman who will question every female friendship in his life.

Perhaps he is genuine, and is simply letting her stay out of kindness. It doesn't make sense. If he's allowing her to stay in his home, why did she seem so rude and resentful towards him?

For now I have to give him the benefit of the doubt. She's just a friend – a beautiful, much younger woman friend. I can handle this. Can't I?

I keep thinking what Abbi would say if I told her, and seeing things through her eyes it doesn't look too good. I have an awful feeling she'd be open-mouthed in horror at the spectre of Sabrina. I hoped that seeing Emilio's home would ease my uncertainties, but Sabrina's presence and the way she behaved has made me feel even more insecure.

'Sabrina didn't seem too happy to see me?' I say, reintroducing the subject and trying to prod more information out of him.

'I told you, she's moody. Probably only just got out of bed. She parties all night and sleeps all day.' He manoeuvres me out of the room and into the next one. 'Now, come on, I want to show you the rest of the house.'

I try to forget Sabrina for now, and enjoy the beautiful rooms, all so stylish and classy, nothing like I'd imagined his home to be.

'What would you call this style? Eclectic Sicilian?' I ask. 'Is there such a thing?'

'Confused Sicilian?' he suggests, with a chuckle.

I gaze at the beautiful paintings, and the antiques placed alongside brightly coloured contemporary ceramics. Whoever decorated this house had a great eye for interiors; it's a clever mix of luxury and art and the odd beautiful antique that hints at old money. Is it Emilio's old money?

The thing is, I don't see anything of him here.

'Did you have a hand in this design?' I ask. We're in one of several sitting rooms. It feels bohemian, and fun, and . . . *feminine*. It shows no trace of what I know of Emilio's personality, and being an artist I have a feel for these things.

'I had *some* involvement in choosing the art, but an interior designer did most of the work.'

I nod. That makes sense.

'Is this a family home you inherited from your parents?' It's none of my business, but I'm so intrigued. A lecturer and researcher couldn't afford a place like this.

'Family . . . yes,' he replies vaguely, without elaborating. I can't quiz him anymore; it's bordering on interrogation. So, I wander the room, asking inane questions about the artists that painted the pictures or did the sculptures, and comment on 'the use of light' – something that fascinates me as an artist.

'Are these yours?' I try again, gesturing at the enormous canvases of pop art in vibrant colours dominating the wall. I wait for him to offer more, but he doesn't.

I love the gigantic frames filled with splashes and blocks of colour. The biggest canvas is a mosaic of dots, like computer pixels filling the space. Enormous sofas in bright orange and saffron shades line the huge room – such a clever design. 'These sofas look so soft I just want to lie on them,' I say, mischievously.

'Then lie on them,' he dares me, his eyes twinkling. I immediately allow myself to fall backwards on to a cloud of velvet and squishy cushions.

'Oh my God! I'm not moving!' I declare, as he walks slowly towards me. Standing over me, he slowly bends down and is about to kiss me when the door opens.

'Oh . . . there you are,' Sabrina's voice calls accusingly.

He moves quickly away from me; his hands going straight into his trouser pockets, he affects a casual stance.

'What?' he asks.

'I'm going out, do you want me to pick anything up for you?' She glances over at me as I scramble to sit up, but the luxurious softness affords me no dignity. I feel such a fool, struggling there in the velvet cushions, but no one else here seems to have noticed. They are now glaring at each other so intently I have to look away. Then, wordlessly, she turns around and leaves the room, almost slamming the door behind her.

'Oh . . . she's definitely pissed off about something,' I remark.

He shrugs, and I climb from the sofa and admire the wallpaper, waiting for him to explain how he came to live in the luxurious home of a multimillionaire, and where Sabrina fits in, but he offers me nothing.

'She seems very pissed off . . .' I repeat, pushing for information.

He rolls his eyes and walks to the other end of the room to another wall filled with pictures. It's then that I notice the cigarettes, and feel a chill go down my spine.

'Are these *yours*?' I pick up the box of Gitanes, the French cigarettes that smell just like the ones the watcher smokes. He looks at the packet as I hold it up to him. 'I didn't know you smoked?'

'I don't,' he says. 'They're probably Sabrina's. She likes the odd one, more for show than for taste.'

I'm now feeling very uneasy. Are they really Sabrina's? If they are, wouldn't she have taken them with her when she went out just now? I don't smoke, never have, so I don't know if she would. Perhaps she has more than one pack? As for Emilio, I've never smelled smoke on him, and I probably would if he did smoke, but they still might be his. How common is it for someone to smoke these cigarettes? Not very common, I'd guess – not outside France, anyway.

'Wait until you see my favourite room – that really is something,' he says, and taking my hand he leads me down a long hallway. The sign on the door says 'The Library', and turning the knob he opens the door on to a room that is floor-to-ceiling books. I lean in close and try to sniff him, but all I get is warm and woody sandalwood. It soothes me, and I lean my head against his shoulder. He responds by putting his arm around me, and I allow myself to relax. They're Sabrina's cigarettes, I tell myself, and she didn't even know me until a few minutes ago. She certainly isn't sitting on the balcony across from mine each night at midnight.

I gaze around the room; everything is here, from classics to modern novels to academic tomes about the earth, and of course volcanoes and stars. There's even a small ladder on casters that moves with the slightest touch, to reach the books on the top shelves.

'Oh, wow!' I spot his name on some of the books, and let my fingertips run along the spines of his work. 'You've written so many,' I breathe in admiration. He writes books, and travels the world giving talks – but it's academic work, I doubt it pays that well. He's not a bestselling fiction writer who can command millions. So how does he afford a home like this? Shopping at Dior, beautiful designer suits and expensive restaurants. Where has all the money come from?

'Look up,' he urges, dragging me from my thoughts. I do as he says and he turns out the light, plunging us into complete darkness. For a moment I'm confused, but looking up into the ceiling I see what seems like a million stars twinkling above. 'Welcome to my universe,' he murmurs, as we stand in the dark gazing up at the constellations.

'It looks so real,' I whisper.

'It's a film projection. Amazing, isn't it?'

'How did you even *think* of something like this, Emilio?'

He doesn't answer immediately, then he says, 'I guess I just wanted to see the stars without leaving the house.'

'What a lovely idea.'

Then he puts the light on again. 'Back to earth with a bump,' I say.

'Oh . . . I almost forgot, this is where I write.' He points to a beautiful, mahogany antique desk piled with papers and books. I walk over and touch the keys of a very old typewriter sitting in the middle of the paper piles and notice the photos on the wall above: black-and-white images of old Sicily.

'Are these people your family?' I ask.

'Mostly distant relations,' he says dismissively, he doesn't seem interested in showing me who's who and quickly moves to the typewriter. 'This was my father's. I dug it out of the attic only recently. I love using it; it's so much more authentic than a computer.'

'I couldn't imagine typing on anything but a computer, but it kind of fits who you are.'

'Really – in what way?'

I look around me. 'I can't quite put it into words, it's just a feeling. Old-fashioned . . . sturdy but stylish.' I laugh at my slightly clumsy description.

'I've never been called "sturdy but stylish" before.'

'It's not a literal description. This room makes sense, it's very you. But the rest of the house, and those . . . not so much.' I point to the Sicilian ceramic heads of the bearded man and blonde woman. I hear the weird, scratchy voice of the fortune teller at the bus stop months ago. *Beware, teste di moro, too many dark secrets . . . someone lies and someone dies . . .*

I try to push them from my mind. I'm trying to forget them and what they said, because my rational mind knows it meant nothing. But they won't go away; they're hanging around in my nightmares. I sometimes think I see them even when I'm awake, and alone in the dark.

I look back at the heads. The same faces sit on the balcony opposite my apartment with the watcher; they are everywhere, always present. They call my name, bang on my door, rattle my windows and demand my attention, like the other dark thoughts that fill my nights and some of my days. I hate them, with their garish, kitschy faces and cartoon eyes staring, watching my every move. Even now I swear I hear them whispering. *We know what you did, Sophie.*

'I'm convinced their eyes are following me around the room,' I hear myself say, approaching them cautiously, reaching out, allowing my fingertips to briefly touch the woman's smooth head. It's icy cold. I recoil slightly.

'I wonder why she killed him?' I say out loud. 'I mean, what did he lie about?'

'I don't remember.' He stares at the faces which stare solemnly back at us.

I'm not superstitious, but as the trees dance around the moonlight outside, their shadows cast through the window into the dimly lit room, I see the fortune teller. And on the breeze, I hear the gravelly voice echoing through the house, those words that will haunt me forever.

Beware, teste di moro, too many dark secrets . . . someone lies and someone dies . . .

15

I had the most wonderful evening at Emilio's last night. He cooked dinner for the two of us, and later he drove me home. It was like a proper date, and as we both had to work today, it made sense for me to sleep at my own place. And the icing on the cake was that there was no smoking action from the balcony across the way, which was a huge relief. I feel like my life is starting up again and everything is beginning to feel right – except with Abbi of course, so I call her when I get home.

'I'm really sorry Abbi,' I begin.

'I was so disappointed; I'd been looking forward to the bar launch all day. I'll be honest, Sophie, I feel like the stand-in. You only see me when he's away because you've nothing else to do.'

Ah, there she is, I think, complaining because she doesn't have all of me all the time.

To make it up to her I suggest we go for cocktails in town, and she grudgingly agrees. After a silent walk there, I buy the drinks and we settle on stools at the bar.

'Forgive me for letting you down last night, Abbi, I feel terrible.'

She's not happy, and from experience I know it will take at least three pina coladas before she is.

'I admit I felt slightly apprehensive about things with Emilio,' I continue, 'but now he's taken me to his home I feel much better. Oh. My. God. Abbi, it's an incredible house.'

'Really?' She's absently swirling her straw in her white pineapple-adorned cocktail, and whatever I tell her she's already decided to be unimpressed. I told myself I'd keep Emilio info on a need-to-know basis where Abbi is concerned, but I reckon she needs to know about his millionaire pad. So I begin with the stars in his huge library.

'I mean, this is no man cave, it's a whole universe, it's gorgeous.' I wax lyrical and go on to describe every nook and cranny of his gorgeous house. But each fabulous revelation – from the chandeliers to the starry indoor night – is met with a mere eyebrow raise or lip curl.

'The thing is, you were right, Abbi. After last night, I know he's been hiding his life from me – and I know why,' I say, in an attempt to include her in this, to bring her into my world.

'Oh, you do?' Finally a glimmer of approval in her eyes. 'So you know?'

I nod. 'Yes, he's been hurt in the past, and I reckon his previous partner might have been interested in his money more than him. Perhaps he just wanted to be sure of me before he showed me where he lived?'

'Is that what you think?'

'I do. He had to know that I want him and not what he's got, so he waited until he really knew me.'

'He might know you, but you still don't know him.'

'I know enough.'

'Do you know anything about his past relationships?'

'We've agreed not to talk about our previous partners until we feel ready to.'

'I find it really weird that you haven't discussed his past, and I'm sorry, Sophie, but I think he's stringing you along, mate.' She sits back; she wants to make a point.

'Abbi, I thought you were my friend. Why can't you just be happy for me?'

'I am your friend, which is why I don't enjoy seeing you get hurt.'

'I'm not being hurt. I know you care about me, but I'm a big girl, I'm fine,' I say gently.

'Are you sure?'

'I'm one hundred per cent sure. Now, let's change the subject . . .'

'I heard you arguing the other night.'

'I doubt we were arguing,' I say. 'We were probably just calling to each other from different rooms.'

'Oh yeah, cos it's such a huge apartment,' she replies sarcastically.

I hate the idea that she can hear us. We rarely argue, but when voices are raised the apartment walls and floors are so thin she can probably hear quite clearly.

I know she disapproves of Emilio, but she really needs to move on. I sometimes think she's a bit too interested in my relationship, and I wouldn't be surprised if she'd made herself a spy hole in her ceiling to watch us.

She purses her lips. 'I'm sorry, Sophie, but you're my friend and we're both alone in a foreign country. We have to look out for each other. I just sometimes feel like you don't check people out properly – like you're careless with your own safety. You think every man you meet is going to leave you like your ex did, and you grab on to them. You're doing it now with him. You've fallen for him and you're letting him walk all over you.'

'I'm not. It's called moving on and not staying in the past,' I say pointedly. Abbi spent a few weeks talking to some guy on a dating app, and she uses this experience to gauge all relationships. 'Abbi, you're such a hypocrite. At least I fell for him after I met him. You were planning the bloody bridesmaids' dresses before you'd even met Marco.'

'There's quite a difference,' she says. 'It didn't work with Marco because he had to travel for work.'

Poor Abbi – the one date she had with Marco didn't work out, and after one drink he put her on a train back to Taormina by 9 p.m. I imagine she came over as bossy and perhaps even a little boring with her stories from the car hire office. And I hate to say it, but her photo on the app was taken a few years ago in a good light, and she looks nothing like that now. Men can be so superficial.

'You need to heal. You're not ready to throw yourself into a relationship with anyone else. Especially an older man – it isn't healthy,' she's saying.

'Abbi, it's perfectly healthy,' I reply, irritated now. 'You obviously don't like him, but you don't even know him. *I* don't even really know him yet.'

'It's not that – you aren't telling me because you know it isn't right. When you first came here, you didn't mind me knowing your business. You were happy to tell me all about the dates you had with different guys here, and you hardly knew *them* either.'

'Yes, because back then you were supportive, but when I started talking about Emilio you shut it down.'

'Do you *blame* me? I don't trust him, Sophie.'

'Because you're scared, you're scared to death of men. Perhaps you should try dating sometime,' I suggest.

'I'm not scared of men, I just take it slow,' she retorts. 'I know you think I'm dull and just sit there waiting for you to come home, but it's not true . . .'

It so is.

'When I said you should try dating, it wasn't a criticism, I just want you to be happy,' I tell her. 'What about trying a dating app again? We could choose someone together?'

'Yeah, great idea, Sophie. It didn't work the first time, I'm hardly going to do it again. Besides, Italian isn't my first language, and I'm not prepared to risk life and limb with a stranger. It's not like I can rely on my best friend to look out for me either – because she'll be too busy with her lover to check on my safety.'

'Don't be so dramatic. You know if you needed me, I'd be there.'

'I'm there for you too, Sophie, but I think you've trauma-bonded with Emilio because of your previous relationships.'

Abbi's unasked-for psychological analyses are pointless, irritating, and straight out of *Psychology for Idiots*.

'We are more than our past relationships,' I say calmly, while sipping my Singapore sling.

'I disagree; I think they make us what we are. It's like second-stage nurturing after our parents. Our partners, lovers, friends – the people we meet along the way all play their part.'

I'm too tired to have a heated debate, so I sigh and take a handful of nuts from the bowl on the counter.

'Sophie, I know relationships, I've studied them. I know people too, and I don't trust him.'

Here we go again. 'And you've met him how many times? None! Yeah, you must know him very well,' I add sarcastically.

'I don't need to know him to know what he is,' she says.

'Abbi, just lay off me and my relationship, and while you're doing that, stop listening through the ceiling too.'

'I can't believe you'd think . . .' Her lip trembles, and she looks like she's about to cry. As much as she pushes all my buttons, I don't mean to hurt her, and she has this way of making me feel really guilty, even when I know what I say is justified.

'Whatever you think you might have heard, it isn't what you think. No one really knows what goes on in other people's relationships, even if they think they do.'

'That's hilarious. I know more about your relationship than you do.'

I roll my eyes at this. I'm tired of going round in circles. 'No offence, Abbi, but from now on let's just keep this subject out of our conversations. You don't know Emilio, and I'm not interested in anything you have to say about my relationship with him.'

She wipes her mouth with a napkin and stares at me, a half-smile forming. 'You're not interested in anything I have to say? What about . . . he's married?'

16

I stare at Abbi. I feel like my vocal cords have just been cut, and for a few moments I can't speak.

'He's not married. Why are you saying this?' I finally manage to blurt out.

She doesn't answer me.

'*Abbi*, what the fuck are you talking about?' I urge, desperate to hear how she can prove this, yet equally desperate to put my hands over my ears.

She leans forward, and her voice is soft. 'You said yourself he was keeping something back from you.'

'Yes, but that was in the beginning . . . and now I've seen where he lives . . .'

'Where *they* live . . .'

'NO!' I'm shaking my head, trying to stand up. I want to get away from the pain she's inflicting but at the same time I'm compelled to listen.

'He lives alone,' I say, thinking of Sabrina standing by the front door like the proprietor, and later storming into the living room to check up on us. Is *she* his wife?

'Where was his wife last night then?' I ask, defiantly, 'because I was there until well after ten p.m. It was just Emilio, me and . . . the lodger, but she went out.'

She shrugs. 'I've no idea where he was hiding her.'

'He wasn't hiding her, she doesn't *exist*,' I insist. 'Abbi, if he was married, I'd know. You can't hide something like that.'

'Well, you can, because he did hide it, and you didn't know!' She throws her hands in the air. 'Open your eyes, Sophie! He doesn't turn up when he says he will, he "works away" for days on end, "forgets" dates . . . and after weeks, months of dating, he *finally* takes you to his home . . . probably when she's away. He never took you there before; he had to make sure she wouldn't be there first. And you didn't stay the night, did you?'

I shake my head.

'You still haven't met any of his friends or family,' she's saying now, in between bouts of noisily sucking up the cocktail froth from the bottom of her glass.

'No, but his parents are dead, his friends are his colleagues, I don't *need* to meet them . . .'

'If you say so. I reckon it suits him to be the two of you in your little bubble – cosy nights in at your apartment, away from his wife and the neighbours' prying eyes.'

'So I haven't stayed over, or met his work colleagues. Doesn't mean he's married, does it?'

'Oh Sophie – he's *so* married.' She takes out her phone, and scrolls through while I wait to knock back whatever pathetic 'proof' she's about to show me.

She finally stops scrolling and looks up from her phone, then carefully places it down on the bar in front of me. All this time, she's watching my face for a reaction.

But I don't want to see; I don't want to even touch the phone.

'I'm not interested,' I lie, pushing it away.

'Sophie, you can't ignore it, you have to see this,' she urges, prodding the phone with her fingers.

So I take a deep breath and pick up the phone. It feels like something contagious, and I have this compulsion to hurl it across the bar, but against my instincts I slowly place it back down on the surface so I can see the screen. Abbi's left it open on an Instagram account, and I look at the name: Gina Caprini. I look from the screen to Abbi, puzzled. 'Is this who you think is . . . ?'

'His wife,' she confirms. 'Presumably she hasn't taken his name, she doesn't look the type – very much her own woman if you ask me. But they *are* married.'

'But . . . ?' I'm looking from Abbi to the Instagram photos and back again in disbelief.

'Just look through the pictures.' Impatience catches in her throat as she speaks.

I stare back at the screen.

'Check out her profile.' Abbi's eyes are intent as she watches me discover my lover's apparent treachery in the pixels on her phone.

Reluctantly I click on the screen, looking down at the tiny squares of someone else's life that, by their very existence, seem to cancel my own. I click and scroll and zoom to enlarge, and I'm soon swept into this woman's world. At forty-three she's a little older than my thirty-six years, with long caramel-blonde hair and eyes the colour of amber. In the recent photos on her grid she seems to be on holiday – drinking cocktails, walking on a beach, lunching with friends al fresco. She has an easy smile, and the kind of skin that turns golden in the sun. No sunburned shoulders or red nose for Gina Caprini.

I click on to Reels, where she's running in shorts, climbing rugged trails, and swimming in deep water that would terrify me. The video clips of her diving from high cliffs take my breath away, but she's screaming with delight; Gina loves the thrill. She moves unselfconsciously, like a young boy, and always seems to be laughing. I don't want to see any more; my heart is pumping.

I look up from the screen. 'She isn't Emilio's wife, I've gone back three months and he isn't in any photos with her.' I'm still trying to fight this.

'No, but she's wearing a wedding ring.'

'Still doesn't mean she's married to Emilio.'

'Keep looking,' she says, her face expressionless.

So I drag myself back to the screen. I feel like I've swallowed something whole and it's sticking in my gullet. Gina is now lying on white sand, climbing rope bridges, standing in the crater of a volcano. I feel dizzy.

'Have you seen it yet?' Abbi's asking, pulling me back into the present.

'That this woman's probably an accomplished triathlon competitor, and beautiful enough to be a model? Yeah, I see that. But I still see no link with Emilio.' I take a sip of my cocktail, keen to end this – to abandon the whole thing. But in the back of my mind, I hear jumbled words in a scratchy voice. *Beautiful man . . . Dangerous . . . Someone lies and someone dies . . .*

'Keep looking,' she says with such conviction my heart sinks. So, I go back in. She must know how painful this is for me. Is Abbi trying to mess with my head?

This woman clearly lives a wonderful life, and in the middle of all this life I see it – and I stop scrolling, wondering for a moment if I can scroll on. I look up and Abbi's eyes move hungrily from the screen and back to mine. I have to acknowledge this.

She's dressed in a long black gown, and receiving a prize. 'The Katia and Maurice Krafft Medal?' I read out loud from the podium behind her, my voice sounding puzzled. 'What's that for?'

'Awarded every four years to an individual who's made "outstanding contributions to volcanology through service to communities threatened by volcanic activity".' Abbi already googled it. Word-perfect. Classic Abbi. 'Apparently it's in honour of the Kraffts, who both perished under lava watching a volcano in Japan. He was forty-five, she was forty-nine. That's what happens when you play with fire, Sophie.' Her eyes widen in horror.

'Volcanology?' I don't know what to say, how to cope with this information. It feels like grief. Now dry-mouthed, dreading what I'm about to see, I plough on through the fear. My heart feels wedged in my windpipe.

I scroll and click, faster this time, aware I'm getting warmer and warmer, and Abbi's just watching and waiting for this volcano to erupt. I move quickly now back through the days and nights, weeks and months, of this woman's life, desperately wanting to look away, to abandon this charade.

But against every nerve, every sinew in my body, every message from my brain, my fingers continue to click through the acres of colour and sparkle and achievement.

There it is, the photo! A beautiful woman in a white veil, and a beautiful man: Emilio and Gina, the happy couple, posted on 26 June 2016.

They both hold glasses of champagne, toasting each other, standing by a familiar floor-to-ceiling book shelf, in his beautiful home. The two Sicilian heads smirking in the background. I was surprised when Emilio, a native Sicilian, hadn't been able to recall the reason why the woman had decapitated the man, but later I googled the story for myself and discovered exactly what he lied to her about.

A beautiful young woman falls for a handsome, older man she sees while tending the plants on her Sicilian balcony. He falls immediately in love with her, and the two of them begin a relationship, the girl hoping for marriage and children. But what she doesn't know is that her lover is already married with children, and he is returning to them after his sojourn in Sicily. She is devastated, and the night before he is due to leave, she kills him by cutting off his head while he sleeps. She then plants basil seeds in his head, so she can keep him forever concealed on her balcony, and he'll never leave her again.

17

I can't breathe, and I feel sick. But most of all I long to call Emilio and for him to say that it's not true, and that he'll jump in his car and drive to the bar, and I'll fall into his arms. We'll leave together, go back to his place, and Sabrina will have left forever, and we'll make love and laugh about Abbi's silly idea that he is married. Then he'll ask me to marry him, and we'll live in his big, beautiful house where he lives alone. Because in my world of make-believe, Gina Caprini, his beautiful wife, doesn't exist.

'What the fuck!' I mutter, my fingers clicking through, past the photo of them standing by the ceramic heads to the next one: a selfie of the two of them hugging; two perfect smiles, two perfect wedding rings.

I scroll on, and there she is, standing in the kitchen proudly holding a large bowl of pasta topped with fried aubergines, the same pasta we enjoyed together on our second date. Inspired by *Norma*, an opera about a married man who falls for a younger woman. The irony isn't lost on me; the clues were all there. Was he taunting me? Is this some kind of joke? I want to stop, but I can't, and I continue my deep dive into hell. Now she's sitting at his desk, his antique typewriter in the background, the Anglepoise lamp lighting her shiny hair and her slim, tanned shoulders. I read the caption: 'Thank you to my darling husband for this beautiful desk, I shall dedicate my next book to you.'

'If he tries to tell you it's over, don't believe him,' Abbi's muttering. 'Even in the most recent photos she's still wearing her wedding ring,' she adds, clearly finding it hard to hide the triumph in her voice.

'So he's been married since 2016?' I almost whisper it as I put down the phone. I look at Abbi, whose face falls as she sees the apparent devastation on my face.

'I'm sorry, Sophie, but I had to tell you.'

'How did you find out . . . how long have you known?' Why couldn't she just stay out of my business and leave me in blissful ignorance?

'I've known for a few days. I wanted to tell you last night, that's why I was keen to see you. I never trusted him,' she adds triumphantly.

I nod dismissively. I don't need Abbi to start listing the reasons why she doesn't trust my boyfriend. Again.

'A couple of days ago, this guy came in to hire a car, and taking his details he said he worked at the volcano hub in Catania. So I just said, "Oh, my friend's boyfriend works there." It was a passing remark,' she says, which I doubt very much. Knowing Abbi, it would have been less like a passing remark and more like a *searching* remark.

'Anyway, when I told him Emilio's name, he looked surprised, and said, "He's going out with your friend? I didn't realise he and Gina had split." I asked him what he was talking about and he told me about Gina Caprini. Apparently she's a volcanologist too.'

Shit, so they're not just both physically perfect, they're perfectly matched too. I can see my future swirling down a metaphorical plughole.

'I tried to find out more – discreetly of course. But he said he hasn't been at the hub for a few months, and doesn't know Emilio all that well. So he couldn't tell me any more, except he thought they were still married, and they wrote research papers together. Apparently they didn't make a big thing about being married due to their work – they didn't want to be seen as "a couple", rather two scientists with their own working lives. And when I found her Instagram it started to add up. In fact, she's posted a lot more photos in the past few months, so it looks like she's been away all the time you've been seeing Emilio . . .'

'That's how he's been able to hide it from me? She's away?' I want to throw up. My mind is desperately scrabbling for an explanation. But there isn't one; just the facts before me.

Abbi reaches for her phone, and points to a date on a photo. 'See, she was at the airport. That was just a couple of weeks before you started seeing him, wasn't it?'

I nod slowly. I can't bring myself to look as she talks me through the timeline.

'He'll know when she's due back, and I'm sorry, Sophie – but I reckon that's when your relationship will end.'

Tears are rolling down my cheeks. She's giving an advance announcement of the death of my relationship.

'It just doesn't sound like the man I know,' I say. 'I've been naive, stupid. He's lied to me, and he's betrayed her. I'm as bad as him for believing those lies and ruining their marriage – her life.'

'Don't you dare blame yourself!' Abbi grabs my hand. 'He's brainwashed you. I knew it all along, I knew he wasn't what he said he was.'

And as painful as it is, there's no other way of explaining that big white veil and their big white smiles.

'Ooh . . . I just realised something,' Abbi starts. I look up, hoping against hope she's about to say she's got it all wrong.

'What?' I ask, feebly.

'It's their tenth wedding anniversary this year. That's the tin anniversary!' she announces with no tact.

'That'll be his heart,' I murmur.

Back in my apartment, I feel numb. I check my phone and he's texted, asking if I'm okay, asking about my day, saying he misses me, all the stuff that usually makes me happy. But tonight it feels cruel. How could he lie to me like that? Not to mention the betrayal of his wife. What kind of monster is he?

I try to work through my devastation and stay rational. This is such a raft of hurt I'm not sure I can get over it – but I've been through worse, and I suppose it's better to find out now rather than when I'm in even deeper. I also suppose I should be grateful to Abbi, but I can't help feeling that she enjoyed being right.

I'm so disoriented by what I've discovered, I can't think straight. I can't eat, or even try to sleep. And weirdly, I even find the courage to peep through the shutters at the balcony opposite. I feel so raw that even the watcher can't scare me right now. I lift the wooden slats of the shutters of my fortress – a little hesitant, but still, not as scared as I usually am. To my deep relief, there's no sign of anyone; the balcony is empty, and the apartment is dark. Perhaps they've moved out? Or at least given up smoking and staring into my room each night? I tell myself that this could be a sign: the watcher has gone, my relationship with Emilio is over – it's finally time to say goodbye to everything and move on. I might even leave Sicily. I'm not sure I can stand seeing those ceramic heads mocking me every single day from balconies and doorways and shops.

I go to bed holding on to a little hope that everything will be okay, I just need time to get over this, and perhaps a change of scene? I can get over Emilio, can't I? He was fun while he lasted, I fell a little bit in love, but now I can forge ahead and find someone who's worthy of me.

I even manage to convince myself that the watcher may not have actually been looking at me, just contemplating life. Since I started seeing Emilio, I've been overthinking everything and becoming paranoid. So someone's been sitting on their balcony at midnight having a smoke? How narcissistic am I to think that it's all about me? I climb into bed and try to read a book, but then my phone pings. Another text from Emilio to ask if I'm okay. I don't respond, I might block him in the morning, but as soon as I turn off the light, he's there in my head, and I'm filled with this great big well of sadness. It fills me up and I can feel myself falling backwards, wondering if there's been a mistake. And I can't sleep, and . . . then it begins. The acrid smell of smoke invading my bedroom. I hold my breath, feel tense all over, and am vaguely aware I'm clenching my fists under the bedcovers. I'm lying in the dark, very still, because if I don't make a noise they might not realise I'm here. I daren't look outside. I'm terrified. So much for not being scared anymore. The unwelcome fragrance hangs around, becoming stronger, permeating my bedroom as the minutes pass. I lie awake, trying not to breathe in. But I can't stay here in the dark, I feel too vulnerable, like I'm waiting to die. Then I'm back with Simon, lying in the dark, he's saying disturbing things, and I'm crying. I have to get up now, so I grab my robe and go into the sitting room, but the smoke is already there, hanging in the air, heavy and bitter.

I don't want to look, but I'm compelled to; I couldn't stop myself if I tried. I press my eyes against the hard wooden shutters and face what I know is out there. But as my eyes make out the figure on the balcony, the shock hits my fingertips and my whole body tingles with fear. The figure isn't hidden in the shadows tonight – they're sitting closer to the edge, so closer to my apartment. Closer to me. I still can't make out a face; they're wearing a dark shawl or hood. I feel the smoke creeping slowly through the darkness towards me, and the hairs on the back of my neck stand up as they slowly lift their hand and wave.

18

The next morning I wake up, and for a few seconds I'm me, no watcher, and Emilio is single, until it comes crashing in, and my head is suddenly filled with it all.

I check my phone. There are several messages from him – 'good morning, how are you?' kind of messages, presumably his response to my complaints about him never calling or texting.

This time yesterday I would have been so happy to receive his texts about nothing; the wonderful, inane minutiae of our days that make a relationship. Reminders of each other popping up; little injections of dopamine, each message like a pixel in a photograph that, over time, builds the picture of two people together.

This is what's needed in a relationship. Finally, he gets it. But it's too little, too late, mate.

Apart from the obvious hurt, I feel such a fool. Abbi was right all along: it looks like I've simply been keeping him company while his wife is away.

I cried myself to sleep last night, devastated about what I'd learned, and also terrified about the watcher. The way they waved at me was shocking; they are so confident, brazen even – and that really scares me. So, in the middle of the night, I called the police. It wasn't easy to explain exactly why I was scared; my Italian is basic, and besides, you have to *be* there to understand how it is. I find it terrifying to look across my balcony to see a stranger watching me. It hasn't been every night, but it's usually around midnight, has become more frequent and they are literally getting closer and closer. I feel exposed and vulnerable. I don't know what they want, or what they might do next. Unfortunately, the officer I spoke to just didn't get it.

'He can smoke on his balcony if he wants to,' was the response. 'If it was your balcony he smoking on then yes, I send someone, but we have not enough men for this.'

'But they're staring at me. Last night they waved.' I realised as I said this that I sounded insane. 'Okay, just make sure this call is recorded,' I added into the silence, 'because if I'm found dead in my apartment this will be on your conscience!'

Obviously I couldn't sleep after the call – if even the police can't help me I really am alone, and this morning I feel scared and tired and hopeless. Meanwhile, it's only 10 a.m. and Abbi's already messaged me six times. She's demanding to know whether I've confronted Emilio about him being married yet, but I'm nervous because I know it will burst the bubble and end everything. I just want to stay in a state of suspension a little longer. But after a strong cup of coffee, I brace myself and text him.

> Hi Emilio, I know we hadn't planned to meet tonight but I need to speak with you. I'm teaching all day, so could you come over this evening?

I keep it simple – no kisses, no softening emojis, just a straightforward request. If I received that from him, I would guess this was something important and serious and message straight back. Emilio, though, is a different animal, and it's three hours later, when I'm teaching, that I receive his reply.

Hey, can we take a rain check tonight? I'm working until late
and I'm tired. Your fault for dating an old man. Xxx

Despite being in a classroom in the presence of eighteen
students drawing a bowl of apples, I feel like crying. Obviously I
can't just stand there in tears, so I make my excuses and run to the
nearest bathroom, hoping no one has noticed, but as soon as I click
the lock on the cubicle, I hear a voice.

'Sophie, darling, are you okay?'

Marian.

'I'm good, thanks, just a bit of hay fever.'

'Okay, my lovely,' she murmurs. 'I'll wait for you to come out
and check for myself.'

This almost makes me smile. Marian Darcy is lovely, if a little
eccentric, and at fifty-two she is the oldest in a class of students in
their teens and early twenties. She's short and chunky, and often
wears hats, which she says make her look taller, but they don't.
Everyone loves her because not only is she a brilliant artist, she's
posh and ladylike, but swears like a trooper. She also tells the most
obscene jokes, which is hilarious because it's such a surprise. As one
of the other students said, 'You don't expect that filth to come out
of those pursed pink lips.'

I suspect she's waiting for me now in the bathroom to impart
some wisdom. She's quite the agony aunt, and perhaps it's just what
I need right now?

After about five minutes, when I've wiped away my tears, I
head out of the cubicle. She's leaning against the sink, hands on
hips, and as soon as she sees me her arms open up. I walk towards
her, and as she draws me in to her ample bosom, I can't help it, her
kindness touches me, the floodgates open, and I start crying.

'Oh, my love, I know hay fever when I see it, and antihistamines
won't cure what you've got. Tell Auntie Marian all about it.'

I lean into her embrace, and she holds me for a little while, until I remember I'm at work. 'Sorry.'

'Don't apologise, my darling. We've all been there.' She hands me a wad of toilet roll, which I take from her gratefully and use to wipe my eyes.

'I don't want to burden anyone with my problems. It's just a man thing.'

'Isn't it always?' She smiles. 'Believe it or not, when I was a few years younger and a few stone lighter, I had man trouble too!' She chuckles at this.

I smile back. 'I'm sure you got over it.'

'Yes, and you will too. Just be strong, my darling, and tell him to bugger off! Unless of course he's good in the sack? In which case . . . ?' She holds out her hands.

I want to tell her everything, but I can't. It isn't ethical for teachers to discuss their personal lives with students, and the principal is very hot on it; she fired a lecturer not long ago for this. But I tell Marian my boyfriend may be cheating on me, which seems to give her a starting point.

'The absolute fucker,' she declares loudly in the King's best English. 'I hope you're going to kick him in the balls, then kick him into touch, dear!' she adds with an expression of genuine seriousness and concern, like this is measured and informed relationship advice.

'Oh, Marian, you do cheer me up,' I say, preferring her kind of support to Abbi's hectoring.

'It's my Scottish roots. I say exactly what I think,' she says in an exaggerated Scottish accent. 'You may have noticed?'

'Just a little.'

'My father cheated on my mother. They divorced when the latest mistress got pregnant, and Mum ended up going slightly doolally for a while.' She waggles her finger in a circular motion at her temple.

'I'm sorry.'

'She sent me away to boarding school in England where they starved me, beat the living daylights out of me, but taught me to speak French like a native – so every cloud and all that.'

'Oh, Marian, that sounds tough.'

'I blame my father. If he hadn't cheated, she wouldn't have sent me away and set me on a lifetime mission to hate men and eat everything in sight. Mother always said I was greedy, but it was so much more than that.'

'That's awful,' I say.

'Well, it gave me lots of tales to tell at dinner parties.'

'I can imagine,' I say, looking at my watch. 'Thanks so much for checking in on me, I do appreciate it. Perhaps we should get back to class.'

'They'll be fine. You need to think about you sometimes, sweetie. Us girls don't always put ourselves on top of the "to do" list.' She brushes my hair from my face and smiles. 'Look after yourself, darling, because no one else will.'

'You're right there.'

'Come on then, let's get those bloody apples drawn,' she says, slipping her arm through mine. 'God, if I see another sodding apple!'

'I'll just wash my face, try and make myself look presentable. Would you go on ahead and say—'

'Hay fever, allergic to apples?'

I smile. God I love this woman. 'Yes please.' I want to just throw my arms around her.

It's so soothing to be hugged. I guess never having much maternal affection and losing Mum young, it's extra meaningful to me. Talking to someone older, who's been through all the heartache and come out the other side, is wonderful. Marian doesn't take life seriously – unlike Abbi, who's so intense and makes a drama out of everything. Marian helps me put everything into perspective, and hearing about her childhood has made me feel less alone. When our fathers left, they set us each on to a path of destruction. They were different paths, but both still harmful.

Feeling stronger now, I text Emilio back, not even sure I believe that he's too tired to see me tonight – perhaps his wife's back? Well, he's going to have to make his excuses to her for once – for the last time.

I have to see you tonight at 8pm, my apartment. We need to talk.

I think about this – the older man, the younger woman, my need to be taken care of. How the past and present constantly collide, and how what happened before shapes who we become – and these thoughts take me back to Simon.

Later, once I'm at home, I take out my portfolio and work on my project – my therapy. If ever I needed to climb back into the past, now is that time. I find tickets to gigs, a weekend in Glastonbury when it rained so hard we lived in mud. I fall back into those days so easily; the early days with Simon were so glorious, and I giggle to myself at some of the memories, my heart swelling. Until I move into lockdown, the face masks, the isolation, and a faded scribble on a Post-it note.

Hospital appointment, Thursday 2.15.

19

I wait at my apartment for him to turn up, it's now 9 p.m. and he still hasn't texted or called. Why did I even start this with him? Why couldn't I just live my life and not invite uncertainty and complication? I came to Sicily to leave a messy situation, and now I've landed right back in another, and it's my own stupid fault.

The sky has gone from pink to grey to almost black, and at 9.10 p.m. I hear his car pull up outside my window. I stand on the balcony watching him in the dark. He doesn't look up; he can't see me.

Then I hear his footsteps on the stairs, but instead of running to the door and rushing into his arms as I usually do, I half-open it, my stomach in knots.

I've prepared myself for this conversation; I've worked out what I'm going to say. I just hope that, for once, he's honest with me.

'Hey.' He's smiling uncertainly as I open the door.

'You'd better come in.' I turn away from him and wander back to my tiny sitting room, where I sit in the chair, and he remains standing awkwardly by the wall. I feel like he's ready to run.

'I can barely see you,' he says, reaching for a lamp and turning it on. I've been here so long, my mind ticking over, I didn't realise how dark it is. 'What is it?'

I hear the sting of impatience in his voice. He's tired, and clearly isn't in the mood.

'Are you married, Emilio? And don't lie.'

He visibly slumps against the wall, and my heart follows.

I wait, my chest pounding, my mouth dry. *Please say no. Tell me I've got it all wrong.*

'Oh, Sophie . . . I wanted to tell you.'

'Just tell me, yes or no – are you married?'

'Yes.'

Silence. Despite all the evidence, it's still a slap in the face.

'I should have told you – I should have,' he says, his voice cracking with emotion.

'Why didn't you?'

'I couldn't bear to lose you. I didn't set out to hide my marriage. I really liked you, but had no idea if it would ever become more, so didn't see the point in telling you. But then I started to look forward to seeing you – I missed you and realised I was falling for you – so I put off saying anything. I just kept thinking, "Next time I see her, I'll tell her." But I couldn't, because by then we were closer, I should *already* have told you. I was scared you'd be angry and end things . . . and now you are.'

'You've hurt me so much, Emilio, and I feel a fool. I'm embarrassed that you've done this to me. No wonder you don't want to talk about your ex.'

'So many times I've been about to tell you. But I'm telling you now, when you and I first got together, my marriage was over.'

'Isn't that what married people always say to their lovers?'

He hesitates. 'Look, Gina . . . my wife, she wasn't happy, she met someone else.'

'But you're still married. Did you really think I'd never find out?'

'When I left it too late, I decided to start divorce proceedings, and *then* tell you. I hoped it would be less painful and you'd see

Gina for what she is – an ex-wife. When I met you in June, she'd already gone away.'

'Why should I believe you?'

'I don't know, but all I can do now is tell you the truth. We are still married, but not together. Neither of us have worn our wedding rings for months now.'

'But you live in the same house!'

'No . . . we don't. Well, we do, when she's back in the country.'

'Look, I'm not interested in a married man. As far as I'm concerned, I never want to see you again.'

He flops on to the sofa, his head in his hands. 'Let me just explain to you the situation; it's unforgiveable that I didn't tell you, but now I need you to know everything.'

'Fire away,' I say, feigning indifference. I wish I could say I don't care, but I do.

'We've been married almost ten years, we work in the same field, and until last year we were – I thought – happy together. There were ups and downs, but we respected each other. We were very different, but it worked – she'd never tried to change me, nor me her. I still loved her. But last summer things started to change. She spent more time away, and slowly, without realising it, we began to live separate lives. We kept our marriage apart from the work; we had our foundation, and our research, and we didn't want the disintegration of our relationship to impact on those things. But then, a few months ago, we were commissioned to write a research paper together on Icelandic volcanoes in the Reykjanes Peninsula.

'But just before we were due to go to Iceland, she was invited to work for NASA at the Hawaiian Volcano Observatory. This was bigger and far more prestigious than the Iceland research, and I was pleased for her, but equally I was disappointed. I'd harboured a vain hope that spending a few weeks together in Iceland might save our marriage. I suggested we go together to Hawaii, it was a huge project and would take many months, and I hoped we might use that time to rebuild our relationship, but she was adamant she would go alone. Unfortunately I didn't handle that very well. It was a real coup for her, and I should have been supportive and encouraging, but I wasn't because I felt rejected and let down. And then I discovered through a colleague that she was taking her handsome young research student with her to Hawaii. It suddenly occurred to me what was going on, and I was humiliated. The reason our marriage was in trouble was because she was having an affair.' He's shaking his head slowly. 'The last thing she said to me before she left was "He makes me happy, like you used to."'

'That's pretty brutal.'

He shrugs. 'It's who Gina is – a free spirit. She says what she feels, and that's what I loved about her, but over time I realised that freedom for Gina meant a lack of responsibility to others. Her "free-spiritedness" gave her permission to walk away, regardless of how much she hurt other people. And taking her lover to Hawaii . . . it was too much. I was angry, I felt like such an idiot, everyone seemed to know about her and this student except me. She made a fool of me both personally and professionally.'

This all seems quite plausible. Or am I just hearing it that way because I want to?

'So, where are you now, the two of you?'

'We are separated, and when she eventually returns we'll start divorce proceedings.'

'Are you in touch with her? Do you know where she is?' I ask this knowing that yesterday she posted a video of herself in Hawaii.

'Yes, she's in Hawaii, and judging by the photographs she's having some downtime. She'll probably go travelling – she's done this before, disappeared for weeks, sometimes months. She doesn't see it as her responsibility to communicate with anyone, even her husband.'

This might explain why Emilio has often failed to stay in touch with me. He actually seemed surprised after our first date when I asked him why he hadn't called me for a week – why he'd left my bed without saying goodbye. I guess if you're in a relationship without parameters, you're used to just doing your own thing, with no responsibility to anyone else?

'Gina texts me now and then,' he says. 'We are in contact, but she hates being "tied down", as she calls it. She had a rather bohemian upbringing – her mother took her to live on a commune after she divorced her father. I think that's why she's like she is,' he adds wistfully.

My flesh suddenly feels tender; might he still be in love with her?

'But what if she comes back tomorrow and says she wants to get back together?' I ask, trying not to sound hysterical at the prospect. I wait for his reaction; if he does still love her, he'd want to try again, surely?

'She won't.'

'But how can you be sure?'

'I just know her.'

'And you never told me any of this.' I pause. 'How could you not tell me? I don't know how I feel anymore,' I say sadly, my eyes filling with tears. 'Do you still have feelings for Gina?' I eventually ask.

He doesn't look at me, his eyes are somewhere else, and after some hesitation, he answers. 'Yes.'

20

This is another sharp, stinging slap in the face. I gasp, and tears spring to my eyes.

'Sophie, of course I still have some feelings for her. She's my wife, we've been through a lot.' He looks up at the ceiling, like he might find the words there. 'But whatever my feelings for Gina are – it doesn't lessen my feelings for you.'

'So you're happy to string me along until she comes back?' I have to be blunt; I'm angry and upset and I feel used.

'No, my feelings for you have grown, Sophie.' He moves towards me and holds out his hand. I take it, and stand up from the armchair, and he just holds me in the now-darkness. We stand together for a long time, and I think about my pain, and his pain, and wonder how she could just run away like that. I do feel for him, and when we finally come out of the embrace I can see tears on his cheeks. I touch them with my fingers.

'Are you sad, about your marriage?' I whisper gently.

He nods. 'I'm sad it ended. I thought marriage was supposed to last forever . . . but I'm more sad because I think I've lost you.'

I don't answer, I just sit down on the floor, and pat a space on the rug next to me, and he sits down. He takes my hand in both of his, and we kiss. It's warm and gentle and I'm flooded with relief that there's still something between us. I don't know what I'm going to do – whether to stay with him or not – but for now, I just want to be with him, and try to understand.

'How old were you when you got married?' I ask.

'I was thirty-six,' he says, looking into my face earnestly, like he's afraid he might give the wrong answer. 'I never imagined I'd ever get married, I was so obsessed with work. I thought volcanoes would be my fulfilment,' he continues. 'I met her at Etna. We were both there at the hub working and I remember seeing her across the room; she was laughing with a colleague. It was love at first sight. I asked someone who she was, they told me and I started chatting to her, and a few months later, on her birthday, we were married. She actually asked me to marry her – I told you she's a free spirit. She's instinctive, you know?' he says as an aside. 'Everyone was shocked that we were seeing each other, as we were so different. I was the straight one in the relationship.' He smiles. 'And when I told my colleagues she'd asked me to marry her, they were shocked, because they all wanted her. "You mean *the* Gina?" they said. "She asked you?" No one could believe that someone like her could fall for someone like me. I was quiet and studious, and she was the beautiful, effervescent party girl. I didn't believe it either! Couldn't believe my luck. Then, after a while, instead of our marriage making me happy, I felt anxious and insecure. I still loved her, and couldn't imagine being without her,' he says, with that faraway look in his eyes. 'Someone once told me she was my crack cocaine, and that's what it felt like – an addiction.' He's chuckling softly at the memory and enjoying the past too much for me to bear.

'But it didn't last – your marriage,' I remind him solemnly. 'You obviously went cold turkey.'

'Yeah, you can't live on a high like that for long; you soon come down with a bump.' The smile lingers, but sadness has seeped in. 'She's the real addict – always looking for new adventures, new

108

thrills . . .' The smile has fully faded now. 'Those colleagues who couldn't believe she chose me will say, "I told you she'd leave you for someone younger," when they find out she left me for someone else. I don't want to make the same mistakes again, Sophie. Please don't end this. I've never been happier than I have with you these past few months.'

This lifts me – perhaps there is hope for us – but I have to be clear. 'So if she does return, what will happen?'

'I'll move out of the house, and find myself a flat in town.'

'Really?'

'Yes, the house is Gina's, I was going to move before she came back, but she said there's no rush – and besides, I could feed the cat and keep an eye on things while she's away.'

'So the house? It isn't yours?'

He looks a little embarrassed. 'No, Gina inherited it when her father died. It's been our marital home for ten years. I'll miss it.'

'So Gina is the one with the money?'

'Yes, family money – all inherited. Her father is Bruno Caprini, of Caprini Martini, and her mother was from a wealthy property family.'

'Oh wow, she's a lucky girl,' I say.

'You'd think she was lucky, but like most people we think have perfect lives, hers hasn't been so perfect. Sadly her mother was an alcoholic, her parents split, and her childhood was lonely and unhappy. She always swore that when she had her own children, she'd make up for her mother's mistakes. "I'll love them to death" – that's what she used to say.' He stops for a moment, clearly upset. 'Gina's dearest wish was to have a child. She had everything anyone could want, except the one thing she wanted. We went to doctors all over the world, she had tests and treatments and went to hell and back – but no baby.'

'I'm sorry.'

'It wasn't meant to be, so we decided to accept our fate and get on with our lives . . . at least, that's what I thought we'd done.'

Suddenly, there's a knock on the door. I have visions of his wife standing on the doorstep in an evening gown, holding an academic trophy over her head, about to smash my brains in.

'Excuse me,' I say, opening the door to Abbi standing excitedly in my doorway with a bottle of prosecco.

'Have you kicked him out yet?' she says loudly. I turn to him, and mouth 'Sorry', and he tactfully disappears to the bathroom.

'Shh, no . . . he's still here,' I whisper back. I can't believe she's turned up like this. I know she listens in, so she must have known he's still here.

'What? I don't believe you. You're going back to him, aren't you?'

'I don't know, it's complicated,' I reply impatiently.

'No, it isn't complicated,' she hisses. 'It's simple – he's married and he didn't tell you!'

'Abbi,' I say quietly. 'Now isn't the time, can we talk later . . .' And I'm forced to close the door in her face. I feel bad, but we would have ended up arguing on the doorstep and I can only do one emotional confrontation at a time tonight.

Emilio soon emerges from the bathroom, and sits on the sofa.

'She really does like to get involved, doesn't she?' he says.

'She's just being protective.'

He hesitates for a moment, and reaches for my hand. 'I'm sorry, all this has impacted on you.'

'That's okay. All I want is a good relationship with no issues – but I never seem to get my wish.'

'Yes, the past is always there, isn't it.'

'Look, Emilio, I can't do this at the moment,' I say. 'I'm tired and I need some space. I'm sure you do too. We both need time to think about everything.'

He stands up from the sofa, looking crumpled and defeated; he reaches out with both arms and hugs me warmly. 'Take as long as you need, I'll be waiting,' he says into my ear, his breath warm, his voice thick with sadness. 'But promise me something – that whatever happens between us, one day you'll tell your story now I've told you mine?' he asks in a quiet voice, his breath on my neck.

But I can't promise that, because I don't know if I will ever be able to tell anyone my story.

21

I knew ending the relationship would mess me up, but the way it's affected me physically is quite shocking. As with Simon, it's a physical ache, an unbearable pain I can't escape from. Back then the doctor gave me medication, but I don't want to go down that road again, so I'm trying to distract myself with my art project. I know he's working in Catania for the next week, so there's no danger of bumping into him – I really couldn't face that. Meanwhile, I'm barely eating or sleeping, and I'm finding it hard to take an interest in anything, except one thing.

Gina – I am *obsessed* with Gina. I can't stay away from her Instagram; I google her in every possible permutation. I'm hungry to know all I can about this woman, who I don't know and who doesn't know me. Yet we're inextricably, invisibly bound, by Emilio.

Throughout this difficult time Abbi has, of course, been knocking at my door and messaging me. She's being kind, but I've told her I can't face going out anywhere, and when she suggested cocktails last night I felt sick. I said I needed to stay home alone and lick my wounds. But, classic Abbi, she turned up half an hour later with a bottle of wine and a box of brownies, which was sweet of her, but when I said, 'I want to be alone,' I didn't mean alone with *her*.

This morning is day three without him. It's Monday morning, and I almost called in sick, but I know from experience I can't just lie under the duvet and shut the world out. So instead I set off early, and now I'm in class readying myself for the students while doodling with a soft pencil, when I suddenly realise it's his face I'm drawing.

'Good morning, gorgeous!' Marian's cheery voice echoes through the empty classroom.

'You're early!' I say, glad to see her open, smiling face.

'Yes.' She lowers her voice and leans in conspiratorially. 'I like to get in early because the pastries are freshly made in the cafeteria. I'm always first in the queue – a minute after eight thirty and they're all gone!' She chuckles, waddling to her easel, breathless from the stairs. 'How are you, my lovely?' she asks, delving into her huge, brightly coloured carpet bag, which I always joke is just like Mary Poppins's bag, filled with all kinds of wonders.

'I'm good.'

She looks up from the bag, like something just occurred to her. 'You aren't usually in this early, Sophie.'

'I had . . . some things to do,' I say, forcing a smile. She closes the bag and scrutinises me. 'You look tired. I mean, you're as beautiful as always, but do I see a smidgeon of grey under your eyes, sweetie?'

'Just life, you know?' I reply awkwardly. 'I'm fine,' I add, reminding myself I shouldn't be sharing the details of my personal life with a student.

'No, you aren't fine,' she says, plonking her bag on the floor and marching towards me. 'You aren't fine at all. You can't fool me, my darling, remember I'm at least a hundred years older than you, so I've probably been where you are.'

I'd love to talk to her. I've had two days of Abbi saying 'I told you so', which isn't helping me. But what I love about Marian is that she cares, but can make light of the worst things. To Marian everything is a 'big hoot', and she lifts the darkest mood and has this lovely way of putting life into perspective. Only last week one of my younger students was in tears because she was missing home, and Marian just chatted with her, and she was soon laughing and so much more positive. That's what Marian does, she just shows you the bright side, and makes you realise there's really nothing to worry about. I'd love some of her magic right now, because she's a wonderful shoulder to cry on, and in her own wacky way gives good, solid advice too.

'Do you want to talk about it?' she asks, attempting to climb on to a stool and then giving up. 'Fuck it!' she's muttering, as she drags a chair over to where I'm sitting. Even this is making me smile; she's just bonkers and funny and I love her.

'You know on the rare days you aren't in class, I miss you, Marian,' I say. 'Everyone does, you bring the sunshine.'

'Do I, darling?' She leans in. 'I'll let you into a little secret, shall I? I'm as fucked off as everyone else most of the time, but I find warm sugary carbs help.'

I laugh at this.

'And if the carbs aren't doing it for me, I put on a bit of lipstick, flirt with *much* younger men, say filthy things and have a laugh.'

'So, should I start with the carbs or the lipstick and filthy things?' I ask.

'Carbs every time, my love – men have a tendency to be *arseholes*,' she says.

'Preach it, sister.'

'Indeed, sister,' she replies in her plummy voice. It sounds so wrong, but so funny.

Along with the sheer joy of Marian's company, being distracted by work and the students lifts me. I love helping them with their work, being surrounded by paints and pencils while chatting about anything and everything – other than my source of pain. Marian has us all in stitches talking about a 'rampant love affair' she had in the nineties, which I'm sure as the tutor I should have stopped before it got to the bedroom door, but there really is no stopping Marian.

But at the end of the day, as I wave them all off and prepare to leave, that horrible dread comes back over me like a dark veil.

I hate going home. I hate knowing I'm not going to see him tonight, or possibly ever again. And there's something else that's bothering me – the watcher used to turn up two or three evenings a week, when I was alone. They never appeared on consecutive nights, but it's two nights since Emilio stopped coming over, and the watcher has been there for both.

It's not a coincidence; I think they watch my apartment to see if Emilio turns up, and when he doesn't, they know I'm alone.

It's always around midnight, but now I've started making a note of the dates – not that I'd forget, but I'm going to see how it goes over the next few nights and then contact the police again. I don't know what else to do. In the meantime, I'm trying to make myself as safe as possible. As night falls, I close the shutters, lock the doors. I've even started to put towels around the windows and under the doors so I can't smell the smoke. But you can't lock it out; it always finds an opening to slither through. I'm aware I'm becoming anxious, paranoid, and instead of coming home and making dinner, I come home and build a fortress. Then I sit in the dark, just waiting. But the smoke is intangible, and like fear it wakes me in the night. I never see it coming until it's too late.

Should I just go out there and scream at them? But I don't even have the courage to open the shutters and go out on to my balcony. Last night, I took photos from behind the shutters, so if anything should happen to me, there's evidence on my phone.

Tonight, all I can do is sit in the silent darkness and wait for midnight and that first acrid breath. I check my watch – it's 9 p.m. I have three long, tense hours to wait for that first prickle in my nostrils, the fumes shuddering under the door. The anticipation is as agonising as the event itself, and I'm tense, like an animal waiting to be hunted.

And suddenly, into the thick, dark silence, *BANG, BANG, BANG* on the door. My nerves flare, and I'm short of breath. It will be Abbi, desperate for news, holding a tray of home-made biscotti as her passport into my apartment, and creeping in like the smoke.

But when I don't answer the door, she just keeps knocking harder and harder, until I can't stand it for another minute and have to let her in. *BANG, BANG, BANG.*

'OKAY, I'M COMING!' I scream into the darkness, close to tears. I will have to tell her to go away, but then she'll have that sad face and I'll feel even worse than I do now. I stand up and walk to the door. Abbi is as bad as the watcher; she's the echo. *BANG, BANG, BANG.*

I rip open the door, and I'm shocked to see a shadowy figure standing there. 'Emilio?'

22

'Can we talk?' he says. He looks terrible – his face is grey, there are bags under his eyes, he seems older. I let him in, and as soon as he's here with me I feel soothed, calm.

He sits in the easy chair, and this time I take the sofa. I offer him coffee, but he just shakes his head.

'Sophie, please, I know what I did was terrible, but can you see it in your heart to forgive me? Could we just start again – a new beginning? You know everything now. I think you want this as much as I do.'

He's right, I do want this as much as he does, but can I risk it, can I ever trust him? And if I need to ask myself those questions, I know my answer should be no – so why am I nodding, and why is he moving to the sofa, and I'm not stopping him?

'I can't tell you how terrible I feel for putting you through this,' he says, sitting close to me, almost whispering. 'I'm a coward, but the more I saw you, the deeper my feelings and the more confused I was. I wanted to tell you I was married and waiting for my wife to come back from her travels to get a divorce. But it sounds horrible, like a transaction, a swap – which of course it isn't at all.'

'I think I understand that, but it doesn't change the fact you hid it from me, and you're still married. And until she returns, that won't change.'

'I know. I've called her and called her, but she just doesn't pick up. I've also messaged her saying we need to start the process; I can show you the messages.'

'No, you don't need to do that.' I hope he'll insist, but he doesn't.

'Her response is always, "I'll be back soon, you can surely wait a few more weeks?"'

'If what you're saying is true, I guess she's right, there's no urgency. At the moment I still don't trust him.

'I just want everything back to how it was. What about you?' he says.

'I need time.'

'Of course, I told you I will wait. I'll wait forever.'

'That might be how long it takes,' I say, leaving an awkward silence to hang in the air.

Eventually he shifts a little, and says, 'Sophie, how did you know that I was married?'

'There were clues, mostly pointed out by Abbi, then she met someone who'd worked with you in Catania, and it came up. I figured being married explained why you never invited me to your home.'

He looks uncomfortable. 'I didn't feel it was right to bring my girlfriend into the house I shared with my wife. But I doubt Gina afforded me the same respect,' he adds, sadly. 'I've heard that she's often entertained her male students there while I'm away.'

I'm intrigued, and would love to know more about the indiscretions of his beautiful wife, but just as I'm about to get into it, my phone pings.

'Abbi,' I say, listlessly, glancing at the screen, with the message that starts: Have you spoken to him yet.

I turn the phone over; her interference is making me cross. I'm grateful she told me he was married, but now I need her to step away and give me a chance to sort it all out.

'I just wish she'd understand, and leave me alone.'

He gives a half-smile. 'I remember you saying she can be a bit of a stalker.'

'Yes, and she's not the only one. There's someone who sits on the balcony opposite staring at me. I don't know how much longer I can stay here.'

'Who's looking at you? What do you mean?' he asks, horrified.

'It sounds crazy, but at midnight, this person – I don't know if they're male or female – starts to smoke on the balcony. But all the time, they're staring at me.'

'Is this every night?'

'No, not at first, but now . . . I think it's becoming more frequent.'

'Have you told anyone?'

'I told Abbi, and I called the police, but they don't seem interested.'

'That sounds really weird. You sure you have no idea who it is? Do you have any idea *why* someone would do that?'

I quickly shake my head. I have a theory that they're watching me because they know what happened with Simon and they might want to blackmail me or scare me, but it makes no sense. I'm away from the UK now, and besides, how could anyone be aware of what I did?

'Would you be able to identify them?'

'No, they wear a shawl or a hood, it's hard to tell. They sit in the shadows, and sometimes all I see is the light from the cigarette. But recently they've started to wave at me if I look out through the shutters. They can obviously see me.'

'Let me stay with you tonight, and at midnight I'll sit on your balcony and wait for them. When they see me, they'll realise you aren't alone.'

'I don't know, Emilio, as much as I'd appreciate someone else being here, they've never done this when *you're* around, or when Abbi is over. It's like they *know* when I'm alone.'

'This has been happening a while then? You never told me.'

'I wasn't absolutely sure they were looking at me, but they are.'

'I feel even worse now – I've been neglecting you. I wondered why your shutters were closed and it was so dark in here.'

Glancing at my watch, it's just after 10 p.m. and I know I want him here with me. 'I was dreading tonight. In fact, I've been dreading coming home these past few weeks.'

'Well, let me stay. Let's see what happens if I'm here.'

'Okay,' I agree, and for the next two hours we both wait, the tension building as the clock moves forward and midnight approaches.

At 11.55 p.m., he opens the shutters, and goes out on to the balcony. I wait inside in the shadows for the smoke to come slowly in, like dread.

I can see the back of him, my knight in shining armour – a dim shadow waiting, and waiting. For once I long for those faint grey plumes to crawl on to my balcony and invade my home. I need someone else to see this.

He seems as tense as me, pacing the tiny balcony restlessly, every so often stopping and staring ahead, challenging the watcher to appear.

Eventually, he comes back into the apartment.

'Get your camera ready to film if he appears,' he says, assuming this is a man. 'I'm going to the apartment to see if he's there.'

'No, he might be dangerous!' I'm alarmed at this; it isn't something I've even considered doing.

'Stay here, and lock the door behind me,' he says, holding my arm firmly.

I do as he says, and wait behind the shutters with the video ready on my phone.

Perhaps this is his way of making it up to me? The only way he can think of to make me feel secure? It does make me feel protected, cared for, and as I wait for him, I'm scared something might happen, that he might get hurt. It panics me to think how much I care for him, in spite of everything.

After about twenty minutes, there's a knock on the door. My skin prickles with fear.

'Sophie, it's me.'

Opening the door, I'm so relieved to see him, I almost burst into tears.

'Are you okay? Did you see anyone?'

He shakes his head. 'I banged on the door, and waited a while stood under the window, but there's no light on, I don't think anyone is there. It looks pretty derelict to me.'

Impulsively, I hug him, and he reciprocates, folding me in his arms, my face buried in his neck. I breathe him in, and despite my fear and uncertainty, when he kisses me, my doubts float away through the shutters and out on to the street.

I pull away. 'One last look?' I suggest, and he immediately heads for the balcony.

'Nothing,' he calls back. 'Let's give it another half an hour.'

So he goes outside and I stay inside, both watching for the watcher, and eventually at 2 a.m. he's back inside the apartment and we close the shutters.

'We won't see them tonight,' I say, almost disappointed. I'm the only person who seems to have witnessed this, which is obviously what they want. But I need someone else to see. Abbi doesn't seem bothered, and the police think I'm mad. I really needed the watcher to be here tonight so Emilio could see them too.

'I've been thinking,' he says. 'You can't stay here. I could message Gina, tell her I'm seeing someone who needs a place to stay. I'd like you to move in until you find somewhere, and ask if she's okay with that. What do you think?'

The prospect of being alone here terrifies me. 'I don't know, it's all a bit . . .' I think about the alternatives. There's Abbi . . . or . . . Abbi. I have no other alternatives.

'If you think she'll be okay with it, I'd appreciate that, thank you.'

'I can ask,' he says, and I get the feeling he's unsure of what her response will be. 'After all, she messaged me recently asking me to stay on and keep an eye on the place, so she won't mind you being there too.' I feel like he's trying to convince himself.

I watch him type the message, and within seconds hear the ping of a reply.

'That was quick,' I say, expectantly.

He looks at the message, and a shadow crosses his face.

'What is she saying?'

He hesitates. 'She says it's okay.'

Unnerved by his reaction, I know that isn't what the message says, and he isn't volunteering to show it to me.

'Are you sure?' I ask.

'Of course.' I detect a little sharpness in his voice, then a deliberate softening. 'Gina says it's fine.'

23

In the morning, I pack some bags and go into work by Uber. Emilio left earlier, reassuring me that I can stay with him in the home he officially shares with his wife. I think I may have got myself into something very complex that I don't really understand. Does he still love her? Does she still love him, and hate the idea of his new girlfriend moving in? Was she horrified at his request and made that clear in her response? If so, I don't blame her – what if she comes back after months away to find me in her home? I don't care how many lovers she has, if she's said no to me staying then I wish he'd tell me. But the more I look at the alternatives, like staying with stalking Abbi, or remaining here with the watcher, being in my boyfriend's marital home is the better option. Which is a sad indictment of my life right now.

I stuff my overnight bags under my desk in the classroom, relieved I don't have to go back to my apartment tonight. In fact, I might never go back. On my way in I bought two dozen pastries for the whole art class, and though they're all appreciative, Marian is orgasmic.

'Oh my God, *this* is art,' she cries as she lowers a large cinnamon twist into her mouth in an extremely provocative way. She's so funny – and the class are hysterical at her antics. Who knew the power of warm pastry?

Later, when most of the students have wandered out for lunch, Marian comes over to my desk, beaming. 'Well, you're a different girl to the one we've seen of late,' she says, and comes round my desk to give me a warm and welcome hug. 'Glad to see you with some pink in your cheeks again, my lovely.'

'Oh, Marian, I wish you'd been my mum,' I say, sighing.

'Why, darling, was she a bad mummy?'

'No, but Mum didn't have the best life, and I always feel she blamed me. My dad was married to someone else when she got pregnant with me. It was all a bit of a mess.'

'Oh, that must have been difficult for you.'

'Yeah. He never divorced his wife, and he abandoned Mum before I was born. I think it made her bitter.'

'Life's too short to be bitter,' she says. 'There's so much we can be bitter about, isn't there. Life's a bitch – let's face it. So we just have to fight that bitch and keep our fists up, ready for her next blow.'

I smile as she holds up her fists like a boxer and punches the air clumsily with fat little fists.

'Ooh, that's enough exercise for me,' she chuckles, panting theatrically. 'I need another pastry now, I feel weak.'

I have a couple of pastries left, so offer her one. 'They're not as fresh as they were at eight this morning, but still . . .'

'Oh, who cares? I'm not as fresh as I was this morning either, but I'm *still* delicious.' She winks, sinking her teeth into the soft, sweet Danish. 'So, is everything hunky-dory now in Sophie's world?' she asks, dabbing her mouth with a napkin as she eats. 'I can't help but notice your bags under the desk – are you leaving him, or returning to him?' She looks at me steadily.

'I'm returning, we're back together. I'm going to stay at his for a while,' I say, wanting to tell her everything but knowing I shouldn't.

'That sounds like a plan.' She gives me a wink. 'So all good now, I hope?'

I shrug, then nod, like I'm six years old playing a confused game of charades.

'You don't seem completely sure, my love.' Her head is to one side; she's considering this.

'I am sure,' I say, aware I'm not quite feeling it yet. 'But how sure can you be about anything or anyone?'

'True – you just have to give it a go, otherwise you'll be left with what-ifs.'

'Exactly.'

'So, fuck it, go for it, and what's the worst that can happen? You embrace life, you're young and gorgeous and have an equally gorgeous boyfriend . . .' She pauses. 'I'm assuming he's gorgeous?'

'Very!'

She smiles warmly. 'Well then, enjoy! Who cares what happens tomorrow or next week, enjoy the now!'

'You're so wise, Marian. My friend Abbi says I'm doing the wrong thing, but I have to do what's right for me.'

'Oh . . . absolutely. I'm sure your chum is completely lovely and an absolute hoot. But she might *just* be a tiny little bit jealous.'

'Perhaps, but she's also being protective.'

Marian raises her eyebrows. 'But if she isn't *happy* for you, then is she a good friend? Remember this, my darling, *people pretend well.*'

I feel the hairs on the back of my neck prickle as she says this. She's right – Abbi's never happy for me, she stamps on my happiness and *pretends* it's because she cares.

'Gosh, you're very intuitive, Marian. I think you might be right.' Her wisdom blows me away.

'Well, I don't know the girl, but anyone who can't be happy for you can't be a friend as far as I'm concerned.'

'So true.'

'I can't tell you how much joy I felt walking into the classroom this morning. You were standing there with this big old smile, eyes sparkling. "She's back," I thought.' Then, looking at her watch, she says, 'I need to grab a sarnie,' and heads for the door.

'Marian?'

'Yes, my love?' She turns, one leg up behind her in a comedy pose, which makes me smile.

'Thanks.'

'Whatever for?'

'Being there, and being *you*.'

She blushes, blows me a kiss and goes, leaving me with a warm, fuzzy feeling.

I spend the next few minutes thinking about going to Emilio's tonight. He said in his text to Gina that I'd stay until I find somewhere, but I'm hoping that if things go well between us, perhaps when his divorce has gone through, we might move in together?

I wonder if his lodger Sabrina's still there, and my heart sinks a little. If she is, will she be more pleasant when she finds out I'm staying for a little while?

I'm still not sure what that friendship is about; she has the charm of a rattlesnake. I also think she has the hots for Emilio, which isn't exactly a good recipe for domestic harmony between the three of us. Then there's Gina, who sounds impulsive and easily bored, and if her fascination for the new boy toy starts to wane, she could be on the next plane back to Sicily. And that could be a very awkward homecoming – for all of us.

24

When I arrive at Emilio's, it's almost dusk. There are lights on inside the house, which feels welcoming, and when I ring the bell, Emilio answers almost immediately.

'I've been waiting for this,' he says, kissing me full on the lips, then taking my bags and guiding me into the hallway. But the moment I'm inside I glimpse through the open door of the library and the ceramic heads stare back, as if they're waiting for me. And suddenly I'm overwhelmed by an unexpected feeling of uncertainty, tinged with fear. What have I done?

I fake a smile, and follow Emilio into the large sitting room, where he puts down my bags before going into the kitchen, saying, 'You can unpack later. For now just make yourself at home.'

But this isn't my home. I'm a stranger here. Now that I know he's married, it feels different. I feel like an imposter with no right to be here, but what choice do I have? I sit awkwardly on the soft, squidgy couch that felt like clouds the last time I was here, but now feels like quicksand.

'I'm cooking dinner tonight.' He's walking back in from the kitchen, holding a glass with ice and lemon. 'Gin and tonic.' He places it down on a coaster on the low coffee table. 'There are books and magazines, feel free to flick through those and dinner will soon be ready.'

I smile uncertainly as he disappears back into the kitchen, leaving me alone in the room, like an alien who's just landed.

What am I doing here, on another woman's couch, in another woman's life?

I gaze at the huge canvas studded with millions of different-coloured dots. I was mesmerised when I saw it last time, and it draws me in again now. As an artist I wonder idly just how many dots there are, and how long it actually took to paint.

Is he only with me while he waits for her to come back?

I continue to stare at the dots. There's an image here, but I can't make it out. I need to adjust my visual perspective to try to see what it is. I stand up from the sofa, and while staring, take a step back, then another. Something is emerging from the canvas. I stop moving, frozen to the spot, and I hold my breath. I'm looking straight at the face of Gina Caprini. And she's looking right back at me.

She was here all along; it's as if she's in the room with me. The scent of vanilla and caramel drifts into the room. Her perfume? French, expensive, too sweet for my tastes. It sticks in the back of my throat like treacle, making it hard to breathe, and I suddenly get this weird sensation that I'm not alone.

Is she here? In the house?

Her eyes stare accusingly from the picture, and I imagine her angry voice echoing through the room, loud and empty in this huge cavernous space. She's telling me to 'STOP! Sophie, stop!' She doesn't want me here – she's warning me, telling me to go.

Terrified, I make for the door that leads into the kitchen, but the handle is stiff and as I try to turn it I feel like she's behind me, her perfume getting stronger. I don't turn around but I feel like she's touching me. I scream for Emilio, but he doesn't respond, and I scream again and again until eventually the door opens, and he's standing there.

'I'm sorry, I'm so sorry,' I cry, falling into his arms. 'I couldn't open the door, it was locked, I panicked.'

'This door can stick a bit, but mmm, looks like it was locked.' That shadow across his face again.

'But who would . . . ?' I'm close to tears.

'No one. It happens sometimes – old doors, old houses, they can be mischievous,' he murmurs, looking at me intently, stroking my hair.

I pull away.

'What's the matter?'

'I'm fine, I just . . . all the stuff that's been going on, I'm just a bit – jumpy, that's all.'

'I understand. Come into the kitchen; dinner's nearly ready.'

I follow him. The air is rich with the scent of garlic and tomatoes; it diffuses the stench of perfume and stops my thoughts from running wild.

'Whose perfume can I smell?' I ask as he stirs the pan of sauce.

He shrugs. 'I can't smell anything.'

I don't pursue this – it may be my imagination. But a voice in my head asks if it might be her perfume, lingering long after she's gone? Or is she *here*?

I immediately push this thought away and take a seat at the table. From where I'm sitting, I spot a Coke can and a dirty plate on the kitchen counter.

'You don't drink Coke and you never leave plates around when you're at my place . . .'

He looks slightly awkward. 'It wasn't me, they're Sabrina's.'

My heart sinks; I was really hoping she'd be gone. I spot a tiny ceramic bowl on the side with a couple of rings and a bracelet. 'Are those hers too?'

'No. They're Gina's.'

He doesn't elaborate.

'She must have a lot of jewellery to leave expensive rings behind, that's a big diamond,' I remark, referring to a ring that's been thrown into the bowl like a trinket.

'Your wine, madam?' He places a glass of red on a coaster in front of me, without acknowledging my query. I take a sip, and the rich warmth soothes my throat, takes the edge off, but not fully, something about Gina's jewellery unsettles me.

'Have you heard from . . . Gina?'

He looks at me like I've asked if he's heard from Jesus, then seems to realise this demands a response.

'No, I haven't heard from Gina,' he says vaguely. 'I called her, but the calls went straight to voicemail, which makes me think she's misplaced her phone again. She's always doing that. And then there's the time difference – and if she hasn't got a signal then . . . ? Anyway, how was your day?'

I'm a little surprised at the total gear change – but he's probably right, it isn't good for us to be talking about her.

'Good, they all produced good work. Marian is brilliant though, such a natural artist, and self-taught too. I don't know why she's in my class; she's a much better artist than me.'

'I doubt that very much,' he says. 'I love your work.'

'What about *your* day?' I ask, feeling more relaxed after the gin and tonic and now sipping on the wine. The kitchen's warm, the food smells good, Emilio is here – and Sabrina isn't.

'It's been quite a day,' he smiles. 'Charlie and I have been celebrating, Stromboli produced a predicted paroxysm today.'

'In English please?'

He chuckles at this. 'Okay, Stromboli is a volcano on the north coast of Sicily. A paroxysm is a kind of eruption, but the early warning system data told us this would happen and it did.'

'Wow! So you can tell when a volcano will erupt?'

'Yes, we've been able to do that for a while, but we aren't always right – this time we were.'

'I'm so proud of you,' I say, not quite sure how to continue the conversation. I know little about his work. I'm sure Gina would understand; she'd be able to add her own theories, share in their joint success. I really can't compete. And as I watch him chop tomatoes and add pasta to bubbling water, I feel like she hasn't really gone. I may not be here for long, but while I'm here she'll be with me – in this house, in the walls, a late firefly in the garden on these mild autumn evenings.

The faint echo of her perfume, her pictures, her jewellery sitting in a bowl waiting for her return, are all reminders to me that he isn't really mine. She was here before me, making coffee in their kitchen, hanging pictures on their walls, lying with him on their big, billowy couch. Am I really his new love, or will I always be the cuckoo in Gina and Emilio's nest?

25

'I'm so glad you're here, Sophie,' he says, wiping the countertops as the dish bubbles in the oven. 'I made the pasta we ate on our first proper date.'

'Lovely! I could only eat it with you. It wouldn't feel right alone or with anyone else.'

He smiles, and raises his glass. I do the same.

'So, how did Abbi take your leaving the apartment? Was she upset?'

This disrupts my calmness slightly. 'I haven't told her. I couldn't face telling her.'

'Then don't. Abbi doesn't have to know where you are and everything you do.'

'No, but she thinks she does. And if I don't tell her, she might send out a search party when I don't answer my door. I'll message her later and let her know that I won't be around for a while.'

He's about to say something in response to this when there's a sound in the hall, and Sabrina appears in the kitchen doorway, scowling. I wonder how long she's been listening to our conversation.

'I thought you were in France?' Emilio is clearly as surprised as me.

'Changed my mind.' She slopes in, drops her keys on the kitchen counter, and walks towards the table where I'm sitting. Then she grabs Emilio's glass of red and starts drinking it, as I watch, aghast at her rudeness. She's wearing a tight-fitting bandeau-style dress, and her hair has been done in waves. It's thick and bouncy, now more caramel than dark. She suits the lighter shade. I hate to say it, but she looks good.

'Enough there for three?' she asks, gesturing at the oven and slinking over to Emilio.

'I guess so,' he says with a sigh.

She's standing very close to him, too close, sniffing the warm garlic, and she reminds me of a little rabbit sniffing spring.

'Hello, Sabrina,' I say, refusing to let her ignore me.

Finally she lifts her head from the bubbling pot, and without taking her eyes from me, addresses Emilio. 'Have you told her who I am yet?'

He turns from her to me and back again, then hesitates before saying, 'I haven't had a chance, it's . . .'

'Complicated?' she offers, with a smirk.

I hold my breath, instantly on high alert, waiting for this revelation.

'Sophie – you've met Sabrina. She's . . . Gina's sister.'

'Oh,' I offer with an awkward smile. She's a lot younger than Gina, so I'd never have guessed. But now I know Gina from the photos, I see a vague likeness.

'So, he's finally told you that he's a married man?'

'Of course I have,' Emilio mutters as he grates Parmesan on the food with some vigour. 'I just didn't see any need to make a big announcement early on. I never lied about being married.'

'No, you just never mentioned it.' She accompanies this with a faint eye roll. I feel unsettled; I didn't realise he'd discussed it with her. A romantic dinner with the bitchy lodger is one thing, but she's his wife's vicious sister and she's now holding her plate out like Oliver Twist!

I want her to know that I'm also aware of what's going on in my relationship, and I'm not afraid to address the elephant in the room, as I'm sure she's about to. So I get in first, and putting down my glass, say in my sincerest voice, 'I'm sorry that things haven't worked out for Emilio and your sister.'

'No you're not,' she snaps. 'He wouldn't be with you if he was still with her.' Her eyes are all screwed up and she looks at me with such hatred, I'm taken aback. 'I bet you love being here, with him, don't you, Soph?'

It's going to be hard enough staying here, but if I let her think she can get the better of me on my first night, I'm sunk. But I'm a teacher, and I'm used to dealing with insecure, scared kids who lash out. And I see her. Sabrina's the skinny pretty bully at school, popular with boys and peers, but so angry and hurt, she's hell on wheels to the rest of us.

'Yeah. I love being here with Emilio. Why wouldn't I? He's a wonderful man, a wonderful supportive partner, and a wonderful lover. That's why I'm sad for your sister.'

Emilio looks horrified, and sweeps to the other side of the kitchen to tend to some pretend emergency involving the pasta in the oven.

Sabrina tries to be cool, but I think she's surprised.

'And it's always sad when a marriage breaks up and people split – whoever they are,' I add. Then I stand up. 'Shall I set the table for Sabrina too, is she joining us?' I ask Emilio as if she isn't even here.

He nods. He's uncomfortable, but his eyes are smiling. I imagine he's glad of some support in the verbal sparring with his sister-in-law. He must find her constant gladiatorial stance quite exhausting.

'So, you were planning to go to France?' I ask, taking cutlery from the drawer as she watches me. She's leaning lazily against the kitchen counter and barely moves for me to reach into the drawer.

'Yeah.'

'Why did you change your plans?' Emilio asks.

'I couldn't bear to be away from you,' she monotones, glancing over at him while sulking into her glass of wine.

Eventually Emilio has finished cooking, and we sit down to a steaming bowl of pasta topped with fried aubergines, tomatoes and Parmesan.

'I love this,' I say. 'You're right, you make it even better than the restaurant did on our first date.'

He smiles, and raises his glass to me.

While we eat, Sabrina makes a show of moving the food around her plate. Thanks to her, dinner is awkward, and as lovely as the food is, I'm finding it hard to swallow.

'Are you staying here for a while?' Emilio asks her, taking a sip of wine between mouthfuls.

'I don't know, are you?' This is a direct attack, and I feel for him.

I wonder why Sabrina is here; she must have other options. Is she simply waiting for her sister to return? Does she love the house, and when she's been away sees Taormina as home? There's a third theory forming in my head, inspired by the way she's twisting her pasta on to her fork without taking her eyes from her brother-in-law. Does she have feelings for Emilio?

I wonder fleetingly if there's a fourth option: she sees Emilio as a father figure. After all, her own father is dead, and she must only be in her late twenties.

'How old is Sabrina?' I ask Emilio later, when we're in bed.

'She's twenty-seven, I think. Yeah, that's right, she's sixteen years younger than Gina.'

'That's a big age difference for siblings.'

'Yes, but they're half-sisters. They have different mothers.'

'Are they close?'

'Yes. Gina's mother wasn't capable of looking after her, and being married to a Martini heir didn't do much for her alcoholism. So Gina's father wasn't happy about her living in a commune, and when she was about ten, he applied for custody, and she went to live with him and his new wife. Sabrina was born soon after and Gina says it was the happiest time of her life. They've bonded through trauma over the years. Sabrina's mum died when she was just a little girl, and their father died a few years back. Gina's like a mother to Sabrina.'

This explains why she's so at home here, and how, despite not officially living in the house, she comes and goes as she pleases. Like a daughter.

'She and Gina were both educated at the international school here, and spent a lot of time in America. Their father had a home there too. Their mothers were both Sicilian; and so was his family many generations ago.'

'You are half-Sicilian and half-American too.'

'Yes, we have a lot in common. Gina and I are at home in either country.'

I wince at the way he talks about her, like they're still in a relationship.

'It's kind of you to let her continue being here, especially as Gina's away.'

'Yeah, I wouldn't turn her away, though you may have noticed, Sabrina is pretty feral.'

'She's angry and insecure. I see it with my students. In the UK I taught at a senior school; she reminds me of those teenagers.'

'Yeah, she had issues with drugs when she was younger, got in with a bad crowd. She stole from us to get money for drugs and Gina put her into rehab. She paid her debtors off too. For a long time there were junkies on the doorstep demanding money. It was a really difficult time. We couldn't call the police because Sabrina was implicated, and they would have arrested her too. I kept a heavy fire poker by the front door for a long time, only moved it a few weeks ago when Sabrina threatened to use it on me.' He smiles. 'She was joking.'

'Or was she?' I say, feeling quite vulnerable.

'Oh, she's pretty harmless these days, but once a junkie . . . ?' he warns, switching off the light.

I turn away from him, wrapping my arms around myself, knowing I won't sleep tonight. I go over everything that was said, how she looked, the way she tried to goad me. And I wonder again why she's here, and why she hates me so much.

26

I wake up in a strange bedroom and suddenly remember where I am. I vaguely recall Emilio leaving early for work, and it feels strange to be here without him. I lie in the huge bed and look around at the Baroque-style chairs in blood-orange velvet, the beautiful bed linen, the floor-to-ceiling bedroom mirror. I should be happy, but I feel like an imposter in another woman's home. I feel her smooth complexion in the perfectly painted walls, smell her in the pear-scented handwash, and sense her standing behind me as I gaze into the mirror. Her mirror. I'm the cuckoo in her nest. I open one of my bags; my shirts and jacket look cheap in these luxurious surroundings. Like me, they don't belong here, and they make me feel ashamed.

Emilio and I are sleeping in the guest bedroom and I can't find any clothes hangers in here, so I tiptoe across to the master bedroom – which Gina and Emilio once shared. I tell myself it's just for hangers, but I'm compelled to see where they slept, see if I can get an idea of who she is – and what I'm up against. In truth, I'm a bit obsessed with Gina, and I want to know everything.

I assume Sabrina is in the house, so I open the big oak door slowly and quietly. It feels intrusive to be walking into Gina's bedroom, but I'm drawn to it.

I open the door on to a room of pure, sumptuous luxury. Beautiful Italianate furniture in pale ivory, thick cream wallpaper, and huge windows with floor-length chiffon curtains gently wafting in the light breeze. It's just as I imagined – tasteful, and expensive, in muted shades for sleeping. But I'm completely unnerved by the fact that the bed isn't made. It looks like someone slept in here and just threw off the covers. Apparently there's a cleaner, so presumably it wasn't left like this when Gina went months ago?

I walk cautiously towards the bed, and allow my fingertips to caress the cool cotton sheets and the caffè latte satin throw. It's then that I see a long caramel-blonde hair on the pale pillow, pick it up, hold it up to the light and sparks go through me.

Gina?

I imagine Emilio creeping into this room last night, finding her naked, wrapping her in his arms. The two of them reunited after her travels, clinging to each other in the darkness. Their marriage safe from intruders.

In my masochistic daydreams I've imagined this scene so many times. My heart's beating as I slip my hand on to my own breast, naked under my dressing gown. Her long limbs, tousled hair on the pillow, a slip of silk lying on the floor, syrupy lust dragging them both down under the covers.

Then I catch myself in the mirror, and recoil in horror at my arousal.

What is wrong with me? I feel like I'm losing myself. I sit on the bed, find my phone in my pocket and check her Instagram. Is she still in Hawaii with her lover? God, I hope so, because if she isn't, my disturbing fantasy may well have been reality.

I click on to her account, and there she is, climbing a volcano in tiny shorts. She has no fear, and clearly no cellulite. She is alone in the picture, but someone must be with her, because they've taken the picture from behind. The Hawaiian Volcano Observatory and

NASA are both tagged. Thank God she's still there, and isn't on her way back here – yet. With 600 likes, 36 kind comments, 153 crude comments, and 124 threats, I can see it isn't easy being beautiful online. I go through the other photos, now familiar to me, and watch her move across beaches, dance floors, on horseback, through swimming pools again. My heart thudding, mouth dry. Snapshots hit me like flashbulbs. Palm trees! Sunshine! Mountains! Golden skin! White teeth! Swishing hair! Gym-toned stomach! Gina's inside my head. She won't go. She wants me out of here. She hates me. She wants her husband back. I go back days, months, years; I sit with her as she watches the sunrise over an ocean, bathe in the pale pink light of Barbados, feel the chill of powdery snow on ski slopes in Gstaad, and listen to soft music under the stars in Mexico. My madness cools, my heart slows.

Apparently, she's in #Heaven having an #EarlyMorningSwim living the #BeachLife in #Hawaii.

I can't see her lover, but there are always young guys hanging out with her, and he must be one of them.

Will Emilio see her sun-drenched photo? Will he touch that beautiful face on the screen with his fingertips? Does he also look at the young guys in the background of her pictures and wonder which one took her away from him this time? Does he still love her and want her back?

I'm breathing deeply, imagining the horror of this when . . .

'What the fuck?'

'Gina?' I whisper, still in a kind of trance.

'No! Weirdo.' It's Sabrina in a towel, water dripping from her long hair on to the carpet, trickling between her barely covered breasts.

She's glaring at me, hands on hips, keen to make something of finding me here.

I put my phone back in my nightgown pocket, but not quite fast enough.

'Why were you looking at Gina's Instagram? Have you got a thing for her? Were you getting off thinking about a threesome with her and Emilio?'

'No! I . . . of course not . . . I came in here to look for clothes hangers, then I . . . I checked Instagram, her post came up.'

'Why? Do you follow her? You don't even know her, what's wrong with you?' God, she's angry.

'I just wondered how she is . . . where she is. I wanted to see if she was still in Hawaii because if she turned up here and . . . I'd hate to upset her if she came back here and found me . . .'

'Ew, so you're checking out her bedroom, and her social media to see where she is? You know there's a name for what you've got? It's called Rebecca syndrome, after the heroine in Daphne du Maurier's novel.'

'I'm familiar with *Rebecca* the novel, but wasn't aware of the syndrome.' I brace myself for the cruel remark that she's about to smack me with.

'Yeah, I saw it on TikTok, you've definitely got it, Rebecca syndrome is a really bad, pathological jealousy. An obsession with a partner's previous relationships.'

'I'm not *jealous* or *obsessed* . . . I just need to know where she is . . .' My voice fades. That came out all wrong.

'What are you, her *stalker*? She has one, you know,' she adds, like it's something to be admired.

'No, I told you, I don't want her to just turn up here and . . .'

'So I guess you're just hoping she stays away, so you can get on with trapping her husband?'

I turn to the wardrobe, reaching out to open it. 'Look . . . I just came in to find some hangers.'

She's smiling now, but it isn't warm; it's cold, and mean. 'I saw you touching yourself.' She's staring at me with mild amusement in her eyes.

I flush. She's making this into something and I'm mortified. 'You were getting off on my sister, weren't you?' I bet she can't wait to tell Emilio.

'Hardly. I noticed the bed had been slept in, and wondered who it was.'

'Well, Detective Goldilocks, it was me.'

I ignore her, open the wardrobe, and quickly start sifting through the clothes for spare hangers.

'Oh wow! Now you're going through her stuff? Really?' She's standing back, both hands out in mock outrage.

'I told you, I'm looking for hangers.' I'm flustered, aware that she's now walking slowly towards me.

'I know exactly what's in this wardrobe, so don't get any ideas about stealing her clothes,' she says.

'I wouldn't dream of it.'

'Yeah, well, you stole her husband.'

'I didn't . . . it wasn't like that.'

'Save it. If you tried to wear anything of hers, you'd only be reminding him of what he doesn't have.'

Tears well up in my eyes. I thought I could handle a young woman like Sabrina, but I can't. She's sharp, and has somehow picked up on my weakness, my fears. That I can never be Gina, that she's everything I'm not, and what's more, that she was here first, she'll always be first – and I'll always be second.

I can't let Sabrina see she's upset me – she'd enjoy that and poke at the wound – so I ignore her while continuing to search blindly for hangers. She's had her sport, and when she realises I'm not engaging with her, she pads back into the bathroom muttering and calling me vile names.

I then rush back to the guest room and lock the door. I don't understand her hatred of me, or what she wants. And what about Emilio? He moved me in here, but I'm still not convinced it's what Gina wanted, and he's put me in a horrible position.

I feel more vulnerable than I ever did in my apartment, even when the watcher was breathing smoke across the balcony and Abbi was banging at my door. I feel like an animal being hunted. But who is the predator?

27

I need to get a grip, and I contemplate the situation while I get dressed. Sabrina is, as I suspected, a mean girl who smells blood, but she's probably feeling as vulnerable as I am. Gina's not here, and her brother-in-law has brought a stranger into the house. In my teaching career I've got through to kids that are more difficult than her – even if she is twenty-seven years old. If I'm going to stay here, I need to be the bigger person, and try to reach out. After all, even she must have a soft side . . . mustn't she?

As I don't have a class until later, I can make time for breakfast, so I get dressed, go downstairs and put some brioche in the oven. Then my first challenge – which may be as tough as Sabrina – is to make myself a cup of coffee from the fancy machine in the kitchen. It looks so complicated I'm sure it could fly, and not surprisingly, on my first go, it spits stinging hot water on my bare arm. This hurts a lot, and already feeling battered I want to give up, but I refuse to do so, and I eventually manage to get it to work. The coffee's delicious, and tastes so much better than the instant powder I usually drink.

I breathe deeply and taste each mouthful. I need to savour every moment here because it's borrowed, and won't be forever. I'm here in this beautiful house with the man I love, and it's not perfect, but for now I'll make the best of it.

I look out on to the garden; the morning is lush and the smell of cut grass and sounds of birdsong waft gently through the open windows. I'll just breathe it all in, until I can't.

Sabrina's still upstairs, and I'm hoping she'll stay there until I go to work. As I'm alone, I take my phone out and continue to indulge in my new obsession: Gina's Instagram account.

I'd love to receive notifications on my phone every time she posts something, but in order to have that, I'd have to follow her, which obviously I can't do. She might not know who her new follower is, but I'm damn sure Sabrina would tell her.

I'm like a drug addict getting my secret fix; I woke this morning at 3 a.m. and took my phone to the toilet so Emilio wouldn't catch me poring over pictures of his wife in the dark. I'm sure he'd be horrified, and how would I explain it? Mind you, I might have to now Sabrina has caught me. God knows what she'll tell Emilio about finding me in the master bedroom. It will be completely exaggerated – *Emilio, I found that sick bitch pleasuring herself on the master bed while looking at my sister's photos.*

God, I'm going red just thinking about how she could spin it.

I know my need to check Gina's whereabouts every hour is not healthy. I just find it fascinating to create a mental picture of the person she is; I'm not just gazing at her like a wannabe teenage girl. I look at her followers too, but the only person I recognise is of course Sabrina, and sadly I can't lurk on her account because Sabrina has her settings on private.

I quickly click to see if Gina's posted since the last time I looked, about thirty minutes ago, just after my encounter with her vile sister.

This life of hers, counted out in boxes, is laid out before me, and however many times I've seen them, I have to look again. Is there something I might have missed? A flaw in her complexion, a clue in her captions? What is happening here? Who's that standing behind her? Is she really happy, can anyone's life be that perfect? I devour each photo, each cryptic caption, each comment, sipping my coffee while gobbling up her life in brightly coloured chunks. Until I suddenly get the feeling I'm not alone.

Sabrina's standing in the doorway, just as she did last night. I wonder how long she's been standing there. More worryingly, I wonder how good her eyesight is, and if she can actually see what I've been looking at.

'You scared me,' I say, as she saunters in.

'Not as much as you scare me,' she replies in a monotone, and wanders over to the coffee machine while I take a moment to recover, having quickly clicked out of the Instagram account and switched to emails. Did she see that I was looking at Gina's account again? I watch her discreetly as she makes herself an espresso with her back to me.

Thin and small, she moves like a little woodland animal – unseen, unheard until she's really close. RIGHT UP CLOSE!

I go back to my phone, hoping she'll make her coffee and go, and after the mechanical gurgle of hot water her espresso is delivered. But the sound of her tiny, bare, perfectly manicured feet padding across the floor in my direction makes me groan inwardly. Here's that harmless-looking, cute animal sniffing the air for trouble before pouncing and baring those sharp little teeth again.

She plonks her coffee cup on the table, and I have to acknowledge her now, so I look up; she's wearing cut-off shorts and a pink T-shirt, and her earrings are huge and intricate, studded with what look like diamonds.

'I like your earrings,' I remark, in an attempt to offer an olive branch.

'They aren't my earrings.' She flops down on the seat opposite me. 'They're Gina's, she bought them in Goa. Real diamonds,' she adds, smugly.

'They're beautiful,' I murmur, feeling so awkward at the mention of Gina's name after our conversation in the bedroom.

We both sit with our coffees, neither of us speaking, until she mounts her attack.

'She'll come back one day, you know,' she announces starkly into the waft of cut grass and birdsong.

'I'm sure she will.'

Then suddenly she leans forward. 'She's run away before. She always comes back.' Sabrina crosses her legs and blows on her steaming espresso. 'She won't be happy when she sees you've moved in. She's got a temper, you know?'

'I'm only staying a short time. If she comes back while I'm here, I'll move out.'

'You'd better,' she says, glaring at me.

Despite the age gap, and the fact Gina is several inches taller, Sabrina and Gina share the same impossible cheekbones and big, amber eyes. I doubt either of them have ever befriended a doughnut in their lives.

She's obviously dyed her hair too, and it's now a similar shade to Gina's. If I were as mean as she is, I'd point out that she's morphing into her sister.

'Does Gina message you, to let you know how she is?' I ask.

'Sometimes.' She wants to talk about her sister, but only wants to follow her own narrative.

'Sometimes' doesn't sound a lot for two sisters who are supposed to be close, but as Emilio keeps saying, Gina is a free spirit, so I guess Sabrina's used to it like he is.

'I imagine it must be hard, Gina just leaving like that. You must miss her, worry about her?' Now I'm really probing, but I stay with it.

'I don't worry about Gina.' Sabrina leans back in her chair, puts her feet on the table, crosses them at the ankles. Her trainers are Dolce and Gabbana, I can see the label, they must have cost a fortune. I wonder fleetingly if Sabrina has that kind of money.

'Do you worry about your sister while she's away?'

'No, she's a kickass, she'll be fine wherever she is.'

'If she were my sister, I'd be worried.'

She starts chewing her lip anxiously. I can see she is worried, but I'm not sure why. I suddenly realise what the problem is with Sabrina. Her sister is all she has – and she thinks she might lose her, and I'm the replacement.

Maybe she has no one to share her fears with; she's so angry and upset it's heartbreaking.

'Why should I be worried?' she snaps, clearly alarmed. 'I told you, she's kickass, no one can hurt my sis.'

So that's what she's scared of – Gina being away and coming to some kind of harm. That makes sense.

'I understand you must be worried. You don't hear much from her, and she does seem to go to dangerous places. But I'm sure she'll be fine,' I add.

She rolls her eyes. 'You really don't know her, do you? I told you, she's kickass, you don't need to patronise me, I know she's fine.'

She takes her feet off the table, and clearly uncomfortable she gets up and stands in front of me, stretching, her crop top lifting to reveal a taut tummy just like Gina's. She's pretending she's bored of the conversation and dismissing me, but her reaction tells me she's troubled. She hasn't heard from Gina; only the photos on Instagram. And that is concerning.

'Have you tried direct messaging her Instagram account?' I ask.

'Oh, Sophie, you are so very old. You really don't understand social media, do you?'

She's flailing around. I smile to myself at her naivety. She thinks she's the alpha here. Doesn't she realise that real alphas don't even have to think, they just are?

She wanders from the kitchen without saying goodbye, and it's some time later when I recall where I've seen her earrings before, and I'm straight back on to my phone and Gina's Instagram. I know exactly which photo I want to see, and open yesterday's selfie of Gina, on a beach, palm trees to the side, a rolling blue ocean behind her. But it isn't the stunning blue backdrop, or Gina's perfect smile, or even her eyes semi-closed in apparent bliss that draws me in. It's her earrings. Gina is wearing the same large, intricate earrings that Sabrina had on just now. She even told me they were Gina's. So how does that work?

Someone is playing games, and I don't know who or why, but Sabrina is definitely involved. What the hell is going on?

#Heaven #EarlyMorningSwim #BeachLife #Hawaii

28

Sabrina wasn't around when I got back from work this evening, so I tell Emilio about the earrings.

'But it doesn't make sense,' he replies between mouthfuls of salad. 'Are they the actual earrings, or just the same-style earrings? Perhaps she has two pairs? Isn't that what women do, buy two of something they like?'

'*Diamond* earrings? I doubt it.'

'Either way, I don't see it as significant.'

I don't know how, but I know it is.

'Sabrina was wearing the same earrings this morning that Gina had on yesterday in her photo,' I say. 'She said they were Gina's.'

'Sabrina says a lot of things, I don't believe most of it, and neither should you.'

'I'll believe what I want to believe.'

'Go ahead and believe it then, whatever it is. I'm still not sure what you're saying?'

'That there is one pair of earrings and two sisters are wearing them on two different continents at the same time! I've never understood what quantum mechanics is, but I think we're dangerously close to something otherworldly, or so mathematical it hurts.'

He shakes his head. 'Sophie, I have to say, I find it a little . . . odd that you are concerning yourself with all this.'

'Why?'

'She's . . . well, it makes me uncomfortable. I had no idea you were looking through Gina's Instagram. It feels intrusive.'

I'm embarrassed, I hadn't thought about it like this, but I suppose he's right. 'I'm sorry, I don't mean to be intrusive or make you uncomfortable.'

'I just wish you wouldn't look at her photos. It's as if you're spying on her.'

This feels like a whack in the face. 'You can't blame me for wanting to know about her. I'm living in her house, I'm in a relationship with her husband, and quite frankly I'm beginning to feel like your mistress!'

'Why do you say that?'

'Because it's like I don't exist, like I have no say in our relationship. I don't want to spend the next few years waiting for your wife to get back to you about whether or not she's ready to start the divorce.'

'It's as frustrating for me as it is for you, but what can I do? It's how she is.'

'And everyone else has to dance around her? I actually felt sorry for Sabrina this morning because I think she's worried something might happen to her, and you guys would never know. You say she's like a mother to Sabrina, but she rarely speaks to her.'

He takes a deep breath. 'Actually, I had a message from Gina today.'

'Oh . . .'

He rolls his eyes and gets up, takes the dirty plates from the table and puts them in the dishwasher.

'So what did she say?' I ask, hoping she's going ahead with the divorce.

'This . . . this is a bit difficult . . .' He pauses, and the look on his face gives me such pain.

'What did she say?'

'She's asked me to leave the house.'

'I'm so sorry, it's my fault, isn't it? She doesn't want me here?' I knew it. I feel terrible.

'It's all a bit awkward.'

'I understand, you don't have to spare my feelings, Emilio. She has every right to object to your girlfriend living in her home.' I would feel the same.

'Gina didn't object to you,' he's saying, still trying to defend her. 'She just pointed out that there are lots of valuable things in the house and . . . you're a stranger, and . . .'

'Wow! It's okay, you don't need to go on.' I'm hurt at the implication that I'm some kind of criminal. 'For such a free spirit, Gina sounds a little uptight,' I say, staring at the table, unable to look at him.

'I'm surprised too, it isn't like her. I never expected her to worry about valuables – she doesn't really care about things.'

'No, but Sabrina does, she prefers things to people.'

'It's got nothing to do with Sabrina. It's Gina who said this.'

'Yes, but Sabrina has probably been messaging Gina and telling her lies about me.' I think about her finding me in their old room this morning and blush. No doubt she relayed that scene to Gina in great detail. 'For some reason Sabrina hates me, which is a shame, because I really thought I might be able to get through to her. Even become friends one day.'

He shakes his head. 'I like your optimism, Sophie, but Sabrina's default move is to lash out. I'm so sorry you've got caught up in it.'

He sighs and looks at me with a mixture of sadness and guilt in his eyes. 'I have something to tell you, Sophie.'

'Oh?' My stomach tightens. What now?

'I've been invited to do some important research work . . .'

'Oh, is it in another country?' I can feel the rug being pulled hard from underneath me.

'No, it's in Catania, it's not far, about an hour's drive from here.'

'Yes, I know . . .' A little glimmer of hope twinkles. 'Perhaps I could come too, we could share somewhere in town, rent a place?'

He has that pained look on his face and I feel foreboding.

'I'm afraid I have to be based at the volcano, we'll be doing a lot of research all hours of the day, and much of the area is quite cut off.'

'I see,' I murmur.

'It's a great opportunity; the project will last for twelve months.'

'So you'll go and live there and work?' I ask as my world sinks.

Again, he winces slightly. 'It's something I can't turn down – I don't want to. It's an exciting time – I told you about the paroxysms, there's so much going on in Sicilian volcanoes right now. I've been waiting for the opportunity to get involved and be part of this research.'

'So you'll be moving into a house there?' I ask.

'Yes, basic accommodation, in the foothills of Etna, which is an unforgiving place. When it's hot here it's hotter there, and in winter the cold is unforgiving. There are no neighbours, and the nearest other humans are scientists.'

Scientists only. No Sophies allowed.

I'm such an idiot.

'When will you be going?' I ask, my voice almost a whisper. I'm trying not to cry.

'Soon, in the next few days.' He puts his head down. 'I'm sorry.'

'Wow. I've just been a distraction while you wait for her, haven't I?'

'That's not true.'

'And this is an easy way of ending things between us, leaving the coast clear for when she returns.'

'No. This isn't about Gina, *or* you and me. I've been offered the work, I *have* to go. The world is changing, Sophie, and it's *my* world, I have to be there. This happens once in a lifetime.'

'I thought what we have only happens once in a lifetime.'

'It does, and I care about you. But I just have so much outside of us to think about, and now I have no home.'

'Neither do I.'

'Will you go back to your flat?'

'No, I couldn't possibly, someone's stalking me. You *know* that.'

He looks helplessly at me, and as he didn't see the watcher himself it occurs to me that he thinks I'm mistaken or, worse, that I'm *lying*.

I can't bear another moment of this, so I leave the room, go upstairs, and pack my few still-creased belongings into my bags. I'm trembling as I walk down the stairs, longing to continue the intimacy of eating together, going over our days, thinking about what to do at the weekend, where to go on holiday. I just want a normal relationship with someone who can love me, but I have to cut my losses, because not only am I in another person's home, I'm in another person's life, and this is too painful.

Another time, in another place, we might have been good together, but we never stood a chance, because Gina is always with us, and Sabrina is waiting in the wings.

'I'll leave my bags here in the hallway. I'll get an Uber to pick them up tomorrow,' I say.

'Don't go like this, Sophie . . .' he starts, but I walk away, leaving my bags in the hall.

I'm about to open the front door, but before I go, I have to say something. 'She's always been here, she'll never leave – her clothes wait in the wardrobes, her jewellery hides in little glass dishes, her picture looks down from the wall, and her perfume fills every room. Emilio, I don't know what's happening here, but I think you're waiting for someone who will never truly be yours. You've put her on a pedestal, you mind her feelings when she doesn't seem to mind yours, and you've allowed her to live her life, but in doing so, she's destroyed yours. Perhaps you aren't ready yet to move on, but I hope one day you can, and when you do, I hope you find what you've been looking for.'

'I have, I've found you and—'

I reach out, and put my hand gently on his mouth. I smile. 'Call me in a couple of years if you still haven't got back together.'

He tries to say something, but I keep walking. I have to move on, if only to protect myself.

29

I leave the house, and walk quickly down the dark, empty street. It's late, no one is around, yet I hear footsteps behind me. My heart lifts – has Emilio followed me, is he going to say he can't live without me?

I slow down a little in case it's him. He'll tell me he's sorry, and that he only realised how much he cared for me when faced with the prospect of life without me. It focused his mind, and now he knows he loves me – and Gina's his past and I'm his forever.

I keep walking, and the footsteps are getting closer, and closer. I'm anxious, but also a little excited. But suddenly, something in the air makes my heart contract. Smoke. Like a snake it's curling around my nostrils, grasping me by the throat. I walk faster now. I can barely catch my breath as the footsteps increase their pace. Walking as fast as I can, I quickly turn to see a lit cigarette. They're closing in on me. It isn't Emilio.

I'm not thinking where I'm headed. All I know is I have to get away. The footsteps are gaining on me. And I start to run.

I've never run so fast in my life – but breathless with fear and exertion, I just keep pushing myself. I'm literally running for my life, and as I move, an image flashes through my mind of Emilio on the balcony waiting for the watcher. I felt so protected, so safe then. But now I only have myself, so I dig deep and propel myself forward again with a spurt.

My heart's about to beat out of my chest. My body can't push anymore and I feel myself slowing down. I can't hear the footsteps now, and turning around I can't see anything; the smoke seems to be fading too. But who knows? They could have thrown away the cigarette and be hiding behind a tree to leap out at any second. I take out my phone to try calling the police, but remember last time. What can I say now? That someone was following me while smoking, and now they've gone? I need somewhere to go, but I can't go back to my apartment – they're probably already there, waiting for me on the balcony, or even closer.

There's nothing else for it, and I reluctantly call Abbi. Even if she is pissed off with me, she's my friend, and she'll let me stay with her. I punch in her number and it says 'Calling Abbi' and rings and rings, but there's no answer. I try again, and it goes straight to voicemail. She knows I'm calling and she's sending it to voicemail.

Fuck! What do I do now? I continue to march on. I can't stand still in case they're watching from somewhere. Now I'm in full panic mode, but there's no way I'm calling Emilio. There's only one person I feel comfortable calling right now, and that's Marian. I remember her telling one of the other students that she was looking for a new lodger, as her old one had left. Me staying with a student won't go down well with the university, but who needs to know? I think about it – it's late, and I daren't go back to my apartment, because the watcher could be there waiting for me. I shudder at the thought.

I have no choice. So I find Marian's number in my phone and call her.

I let it ring, biting my lip, waiting for her to answer, but I have no luck there either. It's so quiet on the tree-lined road, and most of the houses are dark and set back, so I walk in the middle of the road where it's open and I have a chance to run if someone is hiding behind a tree. I listen hard for the footsteps, sniff the air for smoke, but there's nothing. So I walk a little further, then the first chance I get, turn a corner. To my relief there are lights in the distance, and I just keep running towards the safety of other people.

It takes a good ten minutes, but eventually I'm in the hubbub of Taormina, but wondering if the watcher is still near. I've no idea what they look like; they could be anyone. I look into faces as they pass, searching their eyes, the way they walk, but it's impossible. And so many people are smoking, walking past me, sitting at pavement tables, standing in doorways. I try Abbi again – it goes straight to voicemail. She must really hate me. I call Marian, and again there's no answer. I'm scared, vulnerable, and what few safety nets I had have disappeared: no Emilio, no Abbi, not even Marian.

This is really scary, and even if I could afford it, there are no hotels available. It's September and the town is still busy, accommodation is limited, and it's now almost 10 p.m. I have nowhere to go. What am I going to do? Panic rises like flames licking my throat and face, and I'm about to burst into helpless tears when my phone rings.

'Hello lovely, did you call, my darling?'

Marian! I almost cry with relief. She's returned my call. Never has a posh English accent sounded so good.

'Hi! I've got myself into a ridiculous situation.' I'm trying to sound flippant, like I lost my keys. I don't want to alarm her by announcing I'm suddenly homeless. 'I need somewhere to stay, and I was wondering, do you still have a spare room to let?'

She must be able to hear the tears in my voice.

'I do.'

'Could I possibly stay there for a couple of days? I'll pay you.'

'You will not! But of course you can stay, my place isn't too far from town, but I'm just having dinner at a friend's, can't leave just yet. I should be home by midnight. Can you come then? Grab a coffee or a glass of champagne or something and then head to mine. I'll be waiting with the kettle on!'

I arrive at Marian's just after midnight. I've barely knocked on the door when she whisks it open, and the small, stout, smiling figure stands in the doorway beaming. The first thing she does is open her arms and hug me, which is warm and soothing, and I just know everything's going to be okay.

She's wearing a glamorous floral dressing gown in coral, with matching bandana in the same silk around her head. It's pure Marian.

'Welcome to Chez Darcy,' she says, bustling me into the house and guiding me down a hallway into a large high-ceilinged room that smells of lavender and lemons. The walls are covered in big blowsy rose wallpaper, and the surfaces are dotted with various ceramics of cats, all dressed in hats and jackets – not my taste, but I'm sure they're heirlooms.

'I can see you've got your eye on my kitties?' she says.

'They're lovely,' I lie.

'They were Mummy's, worth a fortune, if only I had a daughter to leave them to.' The tinge of sadness in her voice makes me sad for both of us. I don't have a daughter either.

She sits me down on a pink velvet chaise longue and props me up with a big cushion, then waddles over to the sofa and brings a soft pink throw to cover my legs and stands back.

'There.' She smiles as she surveys me. 'Are you comfy?'

'Thank you, yes. I'm so grateful. I only need a few nights.'

'Whatever you need, it's here. Now, are you hungry?'

'I broke up with my partner,' I offer, feeling I owe her an explanation.

'Oh no. But it was all going so well, you've been so happy. Why can't the universe give you a fucking break!' she says, perching her ample bottom on the edge of the chaise.

'I was desperate. I had to call someone.'

'And I'm so glad it was me. I'm just glad I can be of help – women my age appreciate someone needing us now and then.' She moves towards me, and takes my hand in hers. 'We've all had our hearts broken, Sophie. I'm here if you need to talk.'

I smile, happy to be there, and so grateful. I take in the room, which is designed for comfort and colour – there's so much colour it's invigorating, even at this late hour.

'Shall I make us some tea?' Marian is now saying, standing in front of me, looking down at my face, so keen to make me feel at home I'm touched.

'That would be lovely, thank you.'

As she heads into the kitchen, I spot two paintings on the wall. One is of the back of a naked woman. She has long hair, long legs, a perfect body. The other is of the same woman, I presume, in a different position. But this time her hair covers her face, as if she's moving fast and her hair hasn't caught up. They are so good, almost like photographs, and the teacher in me can't help but admire the artist's work.

'Marian, did you paint these?' I call.

She appears in the doorway. 'Yes, they are of a very good friend. Sadly she isn't with us anymore.' She looks visibly upset.

'Oh, I'm so sorry. They're really good – the composition, the technique, the way you've captured the limbs . . . the hair, quite mesmerising.'

Marian beams. 'Why thank you, Miss.'

'I've never understood why you joined my art class. You're so talented, and obviously experienced. There's nothing I can teach you.'

'I'm not conceited enough to think I know it all, dear. I still have lots to learn. We all do – I think anyone who says they know everything should just lie down and die. Being alive is about learning, and if people won't learn then they don't deserve to live.' She makes this outrageous statement with a smile.

'Oh Marian, I love your dark humour.'

'Who says I'm being humorous? I mean it.' She giggles. 'My friends say I'm extreme, but I'd rather be extreme than boring.'

'I agree, but you could never be boring. And it comes through in your work. It's fresh and exciting, and your life portraits are outstanding.'

'I love the human face. Perhaps you'll allow me to paint you one day?'

'Oh, I'd love that!'

'Then we shall arrange a sitting. I would simply adore to paint that perfect face of yours. You have the most beautiful green eyes.'

'Thank you, they're a bit puffy from crying I'm afraid.'

'They're lovely. Mine are blue . . . shitty blue.'

'Oh, Marian, you have lovely eyes – pale, like the ocean on a sunny day.'

'You flatter me.' She can't help but glow at this. I doubt anyone compliments her about her physical appearance, or kisses her goodnight. I think about Emilio, a man who isn't about the grand gesture, or the frivolous compliment, but told me I was beautiful, and kissed me goodnight. My throat is choked with tears, and I wonder what my life will look like without him.

30

'Tea's up!' Marian announces as she enters the living room carrying a beautiful tray, with an art deco teapot in gold and green with matching cups, and a plate of biscuits.

'This is lovely,' I say, 'I'm feeling better already.' I discreetly wipe away the tears as she places the tray on the coffee table, then leans in, touching my chin with her thumb and forefinger. Her silent, motherly acknowledgement that she's seen the tears means she's here for me, and I'm grateful. Taking the easy chair opposite, she begins pouring. 'It's Earl Grey, I won't drink anything else. Would you like lemon, or milk?'

I go with milk and she offers me the plate of large cookies. 'Go on, they're delicious. I buy them from an American supermarket,' she urges. I take one to please her, but I'm so numb I barely register the taste.

'YUM!' she declares enthusiastically. 'Peanut butter and dark choc. I'm a slut for cookies.' She begins by nibbling the outer edges and works her way in.

I eat my cookie, finish the tea, and feel so tired I can barely keep my eyes open, and start to curl up on the chaise longue.

'Come on, my lovely,' she says, wiping crumbs from her bosom. 'You're physically and emotionally exhausted – let's get you up those stairs to Bedfordshire!'

I smile. 'My mum used to say that.'

'Mine too, it must be a prerequisite to being a mum!'

She takes my hand and we go upstairs, where she leaves me in the loveliest room, all pink and cream with a vase of fresh roses on the dresser. She's even left a nightie on the bed and a fresh towel. It's clean, warm, and reminds me of staying at my grandma's house when I was very small.

'This is a very welcome sanctuary,' I murmur.

'Sleep well, everything will be better in the morning,' she replies, stroking my hair gently as I fall asleep. This is what it must be like to have a good mother, someone who's there for you, and who drops everything in your hour of need. I may not have chosen to be here tonight, but I'm so glad I am.

I wake up early the next morning, and despite sleeping like a baby in Marian's lovely duck-down bedding, I feel horrible. The minute I open my eyes, I immediately remember last night, and I'm terribly sad. I'm also angry at Emilio's coldness. He'd already made up his mind to leave without talking to me, or even considering my feelings, not to mention my potentially homeless state.

My stomach is churning. I immediately take out my phone. I have three missed calls from Emilio and ten from Abbi, who's probably returning my calls from last night – but ten? Really? Abbi can wait, and Emilio can fuck off.

Like an obsessed stalker, I slide straight on to Instagram to check where Gina is. She's posted a selfie of her looking particularly beautiful from late last night; it looks like she was having drinks with friends. Her hair is down and she's wearing a deep-turquoise chiffon scarf like a stole around her shoulders, and it's the colour of her eyes. In fact, her eyes draw you to the photo; fine eyeliner sweeps across her lids, and she's looking right into the camera. She really is stunning.

Then I look at the caption underneath, and feel a prickle across my skin: 'I see you bitch.'

What a strange thing to post under her photo; she doesn't usually write cryptic lines. Then it hits me. Is this aimed at me? Is it a warning, a threat? But she knows I'm with Emilio and she's okay with that, so I don't understand . . . but then I realise, Sabrina must have told her I check her account. Is she letting *me* know that *she* knows? I suddenly feel exposed, and a little embarrassed.

Judging by that, it seems she wants Emilio back – and me gone. Well, she's got her wish. Hopefully Sabrina or Emilio will tell her we're finished and she'll back off.

I walk down the stairs feeling very raw, and just seeing Marian's smiling face makes me want to turn into a puddle of helplessness and tell her everything. But I resist; after all, she's still my student, and I must respect the tutor-student relationship.

'Tea?' she asks.

'Lovely,' I nod.

'Us British love our tea, don't we?' she mutters as she lumbers through to the kitchen. 'That's what I miss about being away from home – everyone in the rest of the world seems to drink bloody coffee!'

I follow her into the kitchen, which is as eclectic and quaint as the rest of the house, but less English, with a stone floor, red peppers hanging from the wall and terracotta paintwork.

'Marian, can I ask a favour?'

'Of course, darling.'

'I don't want to put either of us in an awkward position at the university, so would you mind not telling anyone that I stayed here last night?'

'Absolutely, my love. My lips are sealed. Does this mean you won't be wanting the room?'

'I'd love it, but the principal at the university is very keen on not overstepping student–tutor relations. I would have risked it, but feel perhaps it might cause problems for me. There are rules about these things,' I add regretfully.

'Well, I can see why. And rules are rules.' She rolls her eyes. 'Just know that you're always welcome here, and no one ever has to know.'

'I might take you up on that kind offer, but in the meantime, I will try and find somewhere. Sadly I think it's for the best,' I say, as she daintily puts teacups and saucers on a tray.

'Tea for two,' she sings once everything is on the tray, and I follow her through to the living room.

'I love the rose wallpaper,' I say.

'It's so bloody English isn't it?' she says. 'My little bit of home.'

'It's lovely, and I'm so grateful, I slept like a baby. I don't think I've slept like that for a long time.'

'Oh, I'm so glad, darling. Hopefully things will sort themselves out between you and him?'

'I don't think so, but we'll see. It's all very complicated.'

'Love is always very complicated,' she sighs. 'You just have to decide if he's worth all the heartache.' She plonks herself down on the easy chair. 'Thing is, my lovely, there are very few men who are worth the heartache. My last lodger left because some man broke her heart. She's gone back home to Sorrento.'

'I would have thought you'd have no trouble letting that room, it's lovely.'

'Well, I have advertised the room, but had some weird people turn up.' She pulls a face. 'And since I advertised, I had to let them in, and I feel like I've opened up a vent to hell.'

'What do you mean?'

'I can't quite put my finger on it. One of them . . . no, it sounds silly.'

'What?'

She looks thoughtful, and I see her more serious side. 'Well, I must have seen about ten potential lodgers . . . not everyone wanted the room when they saw it, but they were sent here by the rental agency, and they all had a good look round. It was pretty exhausting tramping up and down the stairs with strangers, I felt like a lady of the night!' She roars with laughter at this. 'But then I noticed strange things started to happen.'

'Like what?'

'Well, it started with phone calls. The phone would ring at all times, in the middle of the night even, and when I answered it there was just silence at the other end. And then last week, I came home from class, and I swear my ornaments had been moved around,' she says. I see fear in her eyes.

'Are you sure, Marian?'

'Well, yes, because I always have them in the same places, but then again I did some polishing the day before and there's a chance I may have moved them. Then there were the ceramic heads . . .'

'The *teste di moro*?'

'Ah, you know what I'm talking about – yes. I have a pair on the patio, and I came home from class and they'd both been turned upside down. They weren't smashed or moved; it wasn't random like that. It felt like . . . like someone was leaving me a message. But then the other evening . . .' She looks slightly tearful now and is wringing her hands. I've never seen her like this.

'Go on, Marian, tell me,' I say gently.

She takes a breath. 'I'd been to the opera with a friend, and this sounds really dramatic – but I was walking home and I thought someone was following me.'

'Did you see them? Do you have any idea who it might have been?'

'No, but I was going through the potential lodgers in my head, the ones that had viewed the room. I was trying to remember if any of them smoked.'

I suddenly feel my blood turn to ice. 'Why?'

'Because I ran in the house, and locked all the doors, then peeped through the window. And the person who followed me was standing in front of my house staring, and smoking.'

31

I feel like someone has walked over my grave. It seems that Marian has had a similar experience as me. She tells me about the strong cigarette smell, and the footsteps behind her.

'Something like that has been happening to me,' I say, and we both look at each other in horror.

'Do you think it's connected?' she says.

'I'm not sure, it could be a coincidence,' I say, and I explain all about the watcher on the balcony.

She's shocked. 'I mean it sounds very similar,' she says. 'I can see that a stalker would choose a beautiful young woman like you, but why would he choose a fat old bird like me?'

'Marian, don't say that about yourself. Anyway, it may not be sexual – it might be something else. I shouldn't really tell you this, but my boyfriend – well, my ex-boyfriend, as of last night – he's married.'

'Oh shit.'

'Exactly. I had no idea but it's all over now anyway, so doesn't matter. But it has crossed my mind that my stalker might be somehow connected to that messy situation.'

'Your ex-boyfriend is your stalker?' she says too loudly, putting her hand over her mouth theatrically.

'No – I just mean there may be a connection. His sister-in-law hates me.'

'But I don't know her, why would she stalk me?'

'I don't know – it may be that there is no connection at all,' I say, because Marian looks really scared now. But it feels like too much of a coincidence to me.

'I have to confess, Sophie, I'm quite frightened.'

'Me too. That's why I haven't gone back to my apartment.'

'Have you contacted the police?'

'Yes, but they were a waste of time. Have you?' I ask.

'Yes, but they didn't seem interested.'

We walk to the university together, and I leave Marian at the cafeteria checking out the freshness of the pastries. As my first class isn't for a couple of hours, I find a bench and give Abbi a call back. I don't really want to hear another 'I told you so', but it would be rude of me not to after she returned my calls from last night – ten times.

'Where the hell are you?' is her opening gambit.

'I'm at the university, I'm working.'

'I've been worried sick. Last time I saw you was earlier this week, when you were having a heart-to-heart with him and told me to go away . . .'

'No I didn't.'

'You slammed the door in my face, Sophie.'

'I apologise . . . Emilio and I were in the middle of a discussion and—'

'Whatever, but then last night you left voicemails really late saying you needed help, that you couldn't go back to your apartment, and you'd got nowhere to stay. I was in bed, your call woke me up, and I phoned you straight back, but then your phone was engaged, so I left a message . . . I left a few in fact.'

'I'm sorry, I called again. But your phone went straight to voicemail.'

'Yes, because I was calling you, then I waited a bit and called you again, and again.'

'I'm so sorry, Abbi, I was exhausted. I went to sleep, and my phone was on silent, I wasn't ignoring you—'

'I was awake half the night trying to get hold of you. The least you could have done was to leave me a message or just text to say you were okay.'

'I'm really, really sorry.'

'So, where did you stay last night then?'

'With a student from my class. She has a spare room . . .'

'A student? But you told me you aren't allowed to mix socially with students.'

'I'm not, technically. I mean, I could lose my job if the principal found out, but she won't tell. I called her really late – after I'd called you – and asked if I could stay there. I was so upset when I arrived, I banged on the door and was really panicking by then. When she let me in I just fell into her arms, then she made tea and then I almost fell asleep in the living room. She practically put me to bed.'

'Sounds cosy! Which student?'

'Marian, the English woman. I think I've mentioned her, she's so sweet and so funny . . .'

'The one with the filthy mouth?'

'She's very kind. Anyway, I'm sorry I woke you up last night, but I have to go, I have a class soon,' I say. I'm not in the mood for Abbi's petty jealousy about Emilio or anyone else I might choose to see instead of her. I haven't any other real friends here, and I cut ties with people back home because I didn't want anything coming back to bite me. Only I know what happened back home in the UK, and the real reason I'm here.

'I just think you treat me like shit sometimes, Sophie.'

I don't have the mental space or the energy for this. 'Look. I'm really sorry and I'll make it up to you.' I suddenly see Emilio walking across campus. I thought he was working away today; I can't face him, so duck behind a tree. 'Look, Abbi, I have to go, but I promise I'll call you.'

'Yeah, I won't hold my breath. Why don't you call your student friend instead and tell her all about your married boyfriend!' Abbi is just hurt and jealous, but that was vicious and at the moment there's no room in my life for Abbi – Marian was right about her, anyone who can't be happy for you can't be a friend.

I spend the next hour and a half in the library, sitting quietly, trying to work out what I'm going to do and trying not to think about Emilio. Seeing him gave me a real jolt, like a kick in the chest. It's far too soon.

Later, I leave the library and bump into Lucia, who hugs me. 'My English friend, we must meet for coffee soon, eh?'

'We must!'

'You still have the hots for the professor, Sophie?'

I smile awkwardly. I never told her I was seeing him, and now it's just embarrassing. 'I have my eye on someone else now,' I lie, to put her off the scent. I give her a fictitious name and she seems satisfied with that.

I head for the art room, ready to be greeted by enthusiastic student chatter. I must laugh along when they talk about who slept with who and how much they drank. So I put on a smile and push open the art room door. But to my surprise, there's no one in there. I check my watch, I was sure I had a class here today at 10.30, like I always do. Perhaps they've changed the room, and told the class but not me? So I go off around the art department to see if I can see my class, or ask if anyone knows. But after a lap around the whole department, I go back to my classroom and check online. It doesn't make sense; it says the lesson today is cancelled, the teacher unavailable.

There's obviously been a glitch in the system again; it happens all the time. But now all the students have disappeared thinking there's no class and everyone's time is wasted – plus, as a casual tutor I'm not sure I'll even get paid! I head straight to the principal's office, but she's in a meeting, so I tell her assistant what's happened and how cross I am.

'Isabella, I'm not hanging around, I have stuff to do in my lunch hour so I might as well go now,' I say.

'Don't worry, I'll let Angela know. She's been in a meeting with Paolo all morning, looks like something big has happened.' Isabella is always good for a bit of gossip, and I'm intrigued. 'The head of HR's in there, and they keep ordering coffee and now they're having sandwiches. I'm dying to know.'

'Me too, sounds interesting,' I say. 'I'll be back this afternoon.'

I walk into Taormina knowing I need to find somewhere to stay tonight. I might have to take up Marian's offer and go to hers for one or two more nights while I find something, but first I'll check out the hotel situation. All the decent ones will be full as it's high season, but some of the seedier ones might have rooms, and I only need a bed.

So I make a few calls, find a hotel, pay a deposit upfront for two nights, and head back to the university.

Just as I enter the gates, my phone rings. I pull it from my bag and look at the number. It's familiar, but not Emilio or Abbi's, so I pick up.

'Sophie, it's Angela Carullo, the principal. Isabella said you'd been to see me, sorry I wasn't available.'

'Angela, the system is all over the place. Today the online diary said my lesson was cancelled.'

After a moment's silence, she says, 'I'm afraid that's because your lesson was cancelled, and I'm sorry but all your future lessons have been cancelled too.'

'I don't understand.'

'I'm afraid a formal complaint has been made about you, Sophie. A very serious complaint – an accusation that you assaulted a student.'

32

Angela Carullo sits opposite me, her deputy at her side, a large desk between us.

'I don't understand. Who has accused me of assault? I'd never touch anyone, I'm not a violent person, Angela.'

She glances awkwardly at Paolo Conti, deputy principal. 'One of your students is claiming that you called at their home late last night and demanded to be let in.'

'That's not . . . yes, I did, but it wasn't like that . . .' There's obviously some confusion. Marian wouldn't say something like this. She was delighted to have me there . . . or at least I thought so.

'Apparently, you banged on the door so loud the neighbours were alerted, and when the student opened the door, you demanded a bed for the night. The student said she was' – she looks down at her notes – 'frightened, alarmed and intimidated, and when the student suggested you leave, you replied, "Go on, my boyfriend kicked me out, I have nowhere to go."'

She looks up from her notes, and takes off her glasses.

'That never happened! I didn't *say* that . . .' I think I might cry.

'You didn't go to the home of a student late last night and ask to stay with them?'

'Well, yes – I did, but out of context it sounds terrible. I wasn't aggressive, I called Marian first, and asked her if she still had a spare room. She said yes and welcomed me inside when I got there. I had to bang on the door because the knocker was loose.' I can't believe it, I'm so hurt to think that Marian would do this, I don't understand.

She looks back down at her notes. 'Then a witness saw you walking into the house, forcing your way in.'

A witness? 'No, I didn't! The student – Marian – welcomed me with open arms, literally!'

Did I completely misinterpret this? I was upset and tired. In my anxious state, did I push too far and make Marian feel *obligated* to take me in? No, I refuse to believe this, but that seems to be the gist of it.

'Did you then push past her in the hallway, almost knocking her over?' she asks now, irritated.

'No . . . no I didn't!'

She looks at me for a moment too long; she doesn't believe me.

Then she sits back, drops her pen on the desk. 'Sophie, why don't you tell us *your* version?'

I take a deep breath, try to swallow the tears that are threatening to start. 'It's true that I called Marian. I knew she had a spare room; my partner and I split up suddenly and I needed somewhere to stay.'

Angela folds her arms. 'Sophie, Sophie . . . you know that teachers should never stay with students. It compromises the teacher, and leaves both parties open to abuse and accusations like this.'

'I know, I know, but I had nowhere to stay. I could kick myself for being so stupid.'

'You put yourself in a situation I find hard to defend. You went to her home after eleven p.m. at night, and demanded to be let in.'

'No, that isn't how it happened.' I take a deep breath. 'I just don't believe this is happening . . . it's all been completely misconstrued. Marian wouldn't say any of this; she'd never say I assaulted her because it isn't true.'

'I will speak to Marian Darcy about this myself. The person that made the complaint on her behalf said she was too distressed to talk, but wanted the complaint to be registered . . .'

'Hang on, so you haven't *actually* spoken to Marian? Who's saying all this then?'

'The person who reported the incident called out of concern for Marian's welfare . . .'

'Someone is framing me, trying to get me fired,' I say.

'I doubt very much that anyone's trying to frame you. Sophie. The person who registered the complaint said they felt the need to call. They were concerned that Marian might be being taken advantage of.'

'By me?' The tears finally win, and I'm finding it hard to focus.

'I'm sorry, Sophie, I don't know what to believe at the moment, but until I can speak directly with Marian, Mr Biacchi is taking your classes for the time being,' she says, without looking at me.

'So you're firing me?'

'You are casual staff and officially contracted to cover on a short-term basis. As you know, we've been impressed by your teaching and you are a popular tutor with the students, which is why we were able to offer you more hours. But I'm afraid we ignore accusations like this at our peril. It's very much your word against theirs, and I accept that it may be exaggerated and not represent what happened last night. But as an educational establishment we can't risk continuing to employ someone after a complaint such as this.'

She is firing me, but covering it in principal-speak. I finally burst into tears, huge great sobs; it feels like a dam has burst in my chest and I think I might never be able to stop, as Angela and Paolo look on, embarrassed.

I'm aware my mobile is ringing, but I can't pick up. Angela is now handing me tissues, and looking concerned.

I stand up to leave, grab for the door and stagger out. I hear Angela telling me, 'Stop, calm down,' but I am running down the corridor until I reach the exit.

Once I'm off campus, I call Marian.

'Sophie, darling, I was worried about you. I got to class and your lesson was cancelled, said "teacher unavailable", but I'd walked in with you. What happened?'

I'm not sure how to broach this, but I have to ask her. 'Marian, did I in any way give you any reason to feel intimidated last night when I called and came over?'

'What? I . . . No, of course not, darling, are you okay?'

'No, not really. Someone has reported me to the principal, they're saying I assaulted you.'

'ME! Oh my God, that's terrible! How fucking dare they? Who are they and why have they done this?'

'I don't know, I don't understand . . . I've been racking my brains. I wondered if perhaps it might be a neighbour of yours. They might have heard me banging on the door very late and got the wrong idea?'

'But darling, my neighbours are all lovely people. They wouldn't report one of my friends!'

'They may have done it out of concern, because they wanted to protect you.'

'No, my neighbours are my friends, they know me. We have a neighbour WhatsApp, and if anyone had been concerned, they'd have messaged to ask if I was okay. So it definitely wasn't a neighbour. Oh lovey, this is too awful!'

'I know, I was worried I might have upset you in some way.'

'No, not at all. But I can't tell you how fucked off I am that someone has dared to try and get you into trouble, in my name! If I find out who it is, I won't be responsible for my actions.'

'If it wasn't a neighbour, I don't know who it is. I don't think I have any enemies,' I say. Then I think of Gina's amber eyes; 'I see you bitch' in the caption. *Is Gina somehow watching me?*

'Marian, have you said anything to anyone about me being at your place last night?'

'No, my love, you asked me not to, and I would never betray a confidence.'

'I know you wouldn't . . .'

'I'm so sorry you're going through this, darling. I feel responsible somehow.'

'Don't be silly, you were a true friend last night, but whoever has done this is no friend.'

'But who on earth would make a complaint like that, and especially about you? My God it's horrific!'

'I think what's upset me most is that Angela could even think I'd behave like that.' I pause a moment. 'Marian, can I ask a favour?'

'Anything, anything, darling.'

'Would you be kind enough to call Angela and tell her that none of this happened?'

'Of course, I'll do it now! Do you have a mobile number for her? I'll go direct to her and explain everything.'

'Thank you so much,' I say, sending the number to her mobile.

'Okay, now no more worrying, I'm talking to her now,' she says. 'Hold the line, my darling, I'll sort it.'

I wait for a few minutes, but it feels longer, then suddenly she's back on the line.

'Darling, she isn't picking up, but I left a long message to say you are devastated by this appalling lie – as am I. I've stressed it's a matter of urgency that she calls me back immediately!'

I'm so relieved. This will clear it all up and Angela will know all this is a big lie.

'Thank you so much,' I say as Marian clicks off the other line.

'If she doesn't get back to me I'll just keep trying. We can't have someone lying about you – this could be ruinous for you. I can't tell you how angry I am. If I could get my hands on whoever did this . . .' she spits, as angry and upset as I am.

'Whoever did it *knows* my boss has a thing about students and teachers mixing.' As I say this, a memory is triggered. I'm right back in the conversation I had with Abbi earlier today. *But you told me you aren't allowed to mix socially with students*, she said, aggressively. I remember telling her I'd called Marian very late and asked to stay overnight, and she seemed jealous that I'd found another friend to stay with. I gave Abbi the details that Angela knew – only, someone had added assault and that the student felt intimidated. Anyone who thinks Marian could feel intimidated has clearly never met her, and Abbi's never met her. But surely Abbi wouldn't make up a story like that to try to get me fired, would she?

33

I head to the hotel I booked earlier. At least I have somewhere to go. As I now don't have a job, I would rather not spend money on a hotel, but I have no choice. I would have preferred to stay at Marian's, but given the circumstances, it wouldn't be wise.

Arriving at the hotel, the lobby smells stale, the furniture is worn, and the curtains covering the filthy windows are grey with what looks like years of dust.

I go straight to 'reception', a small window with a man staring out, a cigarette hanging from his mouth. The smoke is in my nostrils and I'm immediately uneasy.

He looks up, no smile, just a nod, indicating that he's waiting for me to speak.

I give him my name, and he pushes a room key under the glass. I take it and walk towards the lift. He's shouting something: 'No elevator, no she broken.' He gestures to a staircase leading upwards. I check my key fob – I'm on the seventh floor.

So, my body already broken and my heart shattered, I start the long walk up. By the third floor, I have to lean on the wall and take a moment. It's then that I smell it – the smoke. This isn't the same smell as the cigarette the man was smoking at reception. This is the stronger, woody Gitane smoke that's now so horribly familiar to me.

Am I imagining this? Can I trust myself to know what's real and what isn't anymore?

I keep climbing, hoping I'm wrong, that if I don't acknowledge it, the smell will go away. But as I climb higher, the fumes reach out, smothering my throat, and I'm in no doubt.

Crawling up the stairs behind me, it's still faint, but there's the unmistakable acrid taste and smell that I now associate with one thing – the watcher. This smoke is ominous, and fills my chest with a darkness I can't escape.

And now I hear footsteps, two, maybe three, floors beneath me, but catching up, slow and heavy, as the smell of smoke gets stronger. I'm too far up to go back, and if I run downstairs I'd be running towards them, so I have to keep going, pushing myself up each step, my lungs aching, my chest wheezing. The smoke and the steps getting closer, and closer.

I'm trying not to make a sound, but if it's the watcher, they already know I'm here, and the thought of this pushes me on. I keep going, sweat on my upper lip. My thighs now on fire, as I push through the muscular agony of the mounting stairs. Once I conquer one flight, all I see is another up ahead, while behind me are footsteps, and smoke that catches in my throat. Floor six, and I'm going as fast as I can but it's like wading through heavy water; all I can do is force my body forward. I turn around, see no one, but the smoke is really strong now. The watcher is close, just beneath me, keeping a distance so at each turn of the staircase they stay hidden.

Finally I get to the seventh floor, and almost fall through the door on to a narrow corridor, I run down to find my room. Number 736, and the smoke is curling around the corner, reaching my nostrils as I push the key into the lock. I can almost feel the breath behind me as, coughing now, I ram open the door, slamming it behind me.

Once inside, I stand with my back against the door, tears streaming down my face, fear thudding in my head. Then I dare to turn around, and reluctantly lift the peephole cover, putting my face up to the hole. I hold my breath, blood racing, and force myself to look. I'm mentally bracing myself for an eye staring right back.

Nothing. Just an empty corridor. I turn back, rest my head against the door and wait for my heart to slow down.

Suddenly my phone rings, and I let out a yelp – is this the watcher? Do they somehow have my number? I pull the phone from my pocket, and his name flashes on the screen. *Emilio*.

'Hello.' The sound of his voice helps my heart rate to slow. What does he want?

'Hey,' I reply weakly.

'I've been worried about you. I left voicemails, you didn't get back to me. I was worried, Sophie. Where did you stay?'

'Why? You didn't seem to care last night.'

'I was, I am.'

'You didn't care enough to fight for me though. How could you let me go so easily?'

'Sophie, everything I touch turns to nothing. I mess things up and people get hurt, and I was protecting you . . . from me.'

'I don't need protecting from you or anyone else. Please, don't worry about me, I'll be fine.'

With that, I end the call. I sit on the bed, secretly hoping he'll call me back, and within seconds my phone is ringing again.

'Look, I'm okay. Please don't worry about me, I'll get over it. Goodbye.'

'No, no, please don't put the phone down on me. Sophie, I was upset last night. I want you and I want this work, but I needed time to think, to work out what to do.'

'Emilio, please, I understand that you still have feelings for your wife, it isn't over for you, and if she comes home you want to be there for her.'

'I will always care for Gina, but she is my past. She doesn't figure in my plans, I need to move on and I am. I just need time to adjust. You're more instinctive, you know what you want and you chase it, Sophie. But you have to wait for me, because I'll always be a few steps behind.'

In spite of everything, just having him on the end of the phone feels like a lifeline of hope; his calm, steady voice pulls me in.

'I've spent the last twenty-four hours awake and thinking, then I went to the university today and talked to my research boss. I think there might be a way I can work on the project and we can be together.'

'Look, you're going away, and I'm not young enough to spend a year waiting for someone to decide if he can commit to me. I want to know that my partner will be on my journey with me, not hankering after the past, or putting their career first. I'm not sure you're the one who can give this to me.'

There's a moment's silence, before he says, 'Listen to me, I can and I will give you those things. I'm asking you to trust me. Tomorrow I go to Catania; it's a bleak but beautiful place and I love it, but you . . . I'm not so sure. It's a difficult place, and I can be a difficult man, I know this. But having spoken with the project leader today, I have permission for my partner to join me . . . if you want to be there with me.'

My heart is slowly healing with every word he speaks, but I stay silent, just listening, drinking in his voice, his words.

'I still don't know if I can trust you.'

'Then take your time. Don't give me your heart yet, keep it for now. But come with me for a year to Catania, and in that time, let your heart decide.'

'I need to think about all this. I never expected to even see you again.'

'I knew last night when you left that I would see you again. I just had to work out what I could give you. Your life is here, and your work, I didn't feel it was right to take you away from that, but selfishly I found a way to make it happen – if you want it? I know your job teaching is something you love, and if you can't bear to walk away from that and your life in Taormina, I understand.'

I can't tell him about the drama at the university over my so-called student assault. It's too complicated to explain, and even though it's obviously a lie, now isn't the time.

'I really don't know,' I murmur. My heart wants to be with him, but there are so many issues around me agreeing to go. Can I trust him, for a start?

'I'd hate to make you leave a place you love and the friends you love . . .'

'Yes, there is that.' I almost laugh. I love Taormina, but apart from Marian I have no friends, and I won't be spending time with Abbi now. Was she ever even my friend?

'If you come with me, I'll support you. You've talked about your art project, how you can't find the time to really immerse yourself in it. You would be alone all day while I'm at work, and I might work long hours. You can use the time in Catania to do that? It's certainly very quiet, there'll be no distractions.'

I can't answer him. I just don't know.

'Why don't you come with me, take a break from work and Taormina and everything that's going on here. Stay a while, and if you hate it . . . or you hate me, then you just leave. We can be truly alone, there's no one there, it's like being on another planet . . . our planet.'

I hear him breathing on the other end of the line, desperate for my answer. But I can't give it to him, I'm too scared.

'Can I think about it?' I reply.

34

Arriving at the foot of Etna is like landing on the moon. The silver-grey landscape shimmers in the sunshine, and volcanic ash mists the air, giving the landscape an otherworldly feel. But the star of the show is Etna, six hundred square miles of simmering volcano watching over our lunar landscape, in the province of Catania. She's awesome, unpredictable, and potentially dangerous. Who knows what she's capable of?

But all I see right now is Etna's size, her majesty, and that this place is the ultimate escape. Having been at one of my lowest points ever, I said yes to coming here and living with Emilio for twelve months, with the proviso that I can leave at any time. And this morning, I'm arriving at my new home, marvelling at the strange, beautiful landscape as we drive through it in a battered old truck.

I glance over at Emilio's face as he drives; it's a study in concentration as he tries to avoid the boulders in our way. There are no roads as such, just tracks in the grey volcanic terrain.

'Only trucks can make it across here, especially in winter,' he says, as we go up and down, swerving and stopping now and then to look around us.

'This is our space buggy,' I joke, as the truck squeaks and rattles over the gravel ground.

He chuckles at this. 'I know it wasn't much longer than a day that we were apart, but I missed you,' he says, taking his eyes off the road momentarily.

'Let's never be more than a day apart again,' I say.

He reaches out and strokes my knee as we bounce along the ground, the truck and my heart both clattering. I've never been happier. We've done the hard times, been through hell, and now the universe has delivered our heaven. Our planet.

'I'm afraid it's quite a culture shock, being here,' he apologises, as we arrive at 'the cabin'. It's little more than a wooden shed, all on one level, with a couple of square windows. There's no garden; it's set in acres and acres of grey landscape, with a handmade fence. It's the only building for miles, and as we unload the truck carrying my sparse belongings, we are probably the only humans for miles.

'You won't believe how dirty it gets with the ash, and there are no real amenities. Even the bed is hard.'

'You're not selling it to me,' I say, standing before it, my palace on our new planet.

'It's only slightly better than that hotel we stayed in the last few nights,' I say. Emilio never left the horrible hotel, said he couldn't leave me alone there with the watcher on the prowl. So we stayed for a couple of days until I gave notice on my flat and he organised his twelve-month secondment to Catania.

'So you didn't like our five-star luxury hotel?' he asks sarcastically.

I roll my eyes. 'Yeah, I loved the fragrance of urine in the hallways, and the serial killer decor with a shower straight out of *Psycho*, and trust me, the guy on reception will kill again.'

He laughs, taking my hand and leading me from the truck to a small, dilapidated building made of old bricks. He opens the front door, and guides me through into a small vestibule, before opening a second door. He's stayed here for work before, so there are no surprises for him, only for me.

'Madam, here is the kitchen-diner,' he jokes as we walk straight from the gravel into a small room, a desk on one side, a small table, a couple of chairs and a makeshift kitchen.

'No oven?' I ask, looking at one ring to cook on.

'No, we don't need it, we have room service.'

A glimmer of hope sparkles as in my mind's eye a truck crosses the grey desert carrying silver-domed plates.

'That was a joke, there's no room service. No restaurants, no shops for miles.'

'It's literally like living on Mars,' I say.

'Yes, that's about the sum of it. I did warn you – but it's hard to capture the sheer bleakness in words.'

In another life I would have loathed somewhere like this – there's nothing here for me, no comfort, no shopping, no cafés and no friends. But right now, I'd rather be here with him than anywhere else in the world.

'Okay, now for the bedroom, with its king-size bed and silk sheets.' He swings open a heavy wooden door and I laugh out loud at the sight before me. A barely double bed, a rug, a bedside table, and a rusty lamp.

'So, this is where the magic happens?' It's so tiny, I walk around the room in six steps. 'I'm guessing the theme is sixteenth-century monastic?'

'No, the decor was inspired by the medieval peasant movement.'

'Ahh yes, I see it now. Inspired by the sheer poverty and frugality of medieval culture,' I add.

He lifts a carrier bag containing groceries. 'And don't forget, we have provisions, so there will be a lavish dinner this evening.'

'Mmm, I'm not sure "lavish" is the word.' I can't believe it but I'm weirdly excited to sit with him at that rickety table and eat pasta – for the next twelve months.

'I'm sorry it isn't the most romantic setting,' he says, pulling me towards him.

'I'm with you, and that's all that matters. For now.'

'Oh, *for now*?' he says, smiling.

'I don't want you thinking you've got me. You still need to work at it.'

'I will.' He kisses me, and I think of the hotel, the smoke curling up the stairs. I'm safe at last.

We move slowly to the bedroom, and once inside, he kicks the door closed with his foot and we fall together on the bed.

'It feels like forever ago,' I murmur breathlessly, as he takes off my clothes.

'It was this morning,' he reminds me, and we laugh, flesh on flesh, together at last. I've never known such longing, I'm hungry for him. I'm beginning to feel secure; he wants the same as me, and there's no Abbi or Sabrina or Gina here, it's just us.

Later, we have dinner and discover that the tiny table requires a folded napkin or beermat under one of the legs to keep it stable, a far cry from the state-of-the-art kitchen table and high-end cooking appliances at his and Gina's house.

'It's like being a student again,' I say. 'I already feel at home.'

'Home is where you're happy and the pasta is good,' he says.

I stand up to clear our empty plates, and as I bend towards him, my silk robe, so out of place here, slips off my shoulder. His fingers reach out and caress my flesh, his touch makes me sparkle, and I sit on his knee, slipping off his T-shirt, burying my face in his neck. Our lips and hands eagerly find each other, and though we're both exhausted, we make love again. Our need overcoming our weariness, we wrap ourselves around each other in a tangle of silk robe and limbs.

◆ ◆ ◆

'Thank you for taking me back,' he says later, as we lie in the tiny bedroom lit by the small lamp. His hand caressing my naked back soothes me, my eyes can barely stay open, and for once I might just feel safe enough to fall asleep.

'I just hope there are no more surprises,' I whisper.

'Talking of surprises, I heard from Gina. She's ready to start divorce proceedings.'

My eyes open, I'm suddenly wide awake. 'Did she say anything about us being together?'

'She was fine about it.'

'Fine? Really?' I say doubtfully, knowing he's not telling me everything. 'What did she *actually* say?' Emilio has a tendency to edit conversations, not in a sinister way, I think he just can't be bothered to tell the whole story. As a compulsive oversharer I find this extremely frustrating.

'She said "I'm pleased for you, but be careful."'

'What did she mean by that?' I'm immediately suspicious. 'Is she trying to warn you against me?' I'm angry at this. 'She doesn't know me, she hasn't even met me.'

'She just doesn't want me to get hurt.'

'How protective of her – as she lies on a beach in Hawaii with her lover,' I say.

He doesn't respond – how can he? I'm right.

Despite her rather unsettling response, I'm pleased that she's agreed to start the divorce at last. I'm not expecting imminent marriage, but I don't want to spend years as someone's mistress either. I'd like a future together without his wife in it.

'Being apart has made me realise something,' he says, breaking through my thoughts.

'What?' I lift my face slowly from the pillow and sit up, all thoughts of sleep evaporating in the darkness.

'I think I'm in love with you.'

I sink back on to his chest. 'You think?' I smile in the darkness and close my eyes.

I'll take that. There have been times when I thought this would never happen, but here we are in a dusty old cabin on the edge of the world, and finally, he thinks he loves me.

Emilio drifts off to sleep, but I'm restless with happiness. I just wish I could enjoy being happy, but for me there's always been a price to be paid for happiness. I mustn't spoil the good things with unfounded fears, but I can't help it – lying here in the dark, miles from anywhere, I'm filled with a sense of foreboding.

35

On my first morning at the cabin, I wake in that beautiful, horrible little room and want to sing and dance and call Abbi and tell her, 'You did me a favour losing me my job – and you were wrong about Emilio. It didn't end badly, it ended in paradise!'

But I have no intention of calling her. Marian said that anyone who can't be happy for you can't be a friend, and that's Abbi. She called me yesterday, and left a message demanding to know why I've moved out of my apartment without telling her. I can't have people like Abbi in my life; she's too dangerous, and far too possessive, and it's a relief to be away from her. My only concern is that she's the type to turn up on our doorstep late one night. Thank God Emilio's here with me.

We've come a long, long way to get to where we are now, but it's been worth the wait and the uncertainty and the pain – in fact, all those elements have merely intensified my feelings. I've made an impossible dream come true, and now it's just us, deliciously isolated, marooned forever in our silver desert. And there's no room for Abbi, Sabrina or his soon-to-be-ex-wife.

'I want to take you for a walk,' he says later, digging some walking boots out from a storage box in the kitchen, presumably left by a previous resident who worked at the hub.

'I love these, they have pink laces,' I say, trying to push my feet into them, but as hard as I try, they won't fit, they're too small.

I end up wearing a pair of his and we stuff them with newspaper, then he finds me an old weatherproof jacket, which is also pink.

'What a shame the boots didn't fit. This would have been quite a cute outfit,' I joke, as I slip it on.

Unlike the boots, it's so big he has to roll the sleeves up, and when I pull the hood up my face almost disappears. Whoever these belonged to was a tall woman with dainty feet.

'You're just a pair of eyes in bright pink whale skin,' he chuckles, as I stand before him, my face still hidden under the hood.

'I don't want to go out there, it looks cold.' I stand with my arms out, the stiff material like cardboard.

'It's a really cold day today, and it's only September, it will get so much colder. But it's beautiful through all the seasons. I want you to love this place like I do. I hope you'll decide to stay. I'd hate to be here without you.' He kisses my forehead.

This place has brought about such a change in him; he's never spoken quite like this before. I wonder fleetingly if this is how he was with her.

'You've changed,' I say. 'Being here, away from everything and everyone, you're much more open and . . . loving. Why is that?' I ask cynically.

'I'm in my favourite place with my favourite person.'

'Were you like this with Gina?'

He looks uncomfortable.

'Don't you wonder where she is, and what she's doing?'

'I don't need to wonder how she is, she messages me occasionally, and if I haven't heard from her, I check her Instagram,' he says.

This is a huge shock to me. I still check her Instagram whenever I can, but had no idea he was even *on* Instagram. 'I didn't realise you had an Instagram account. You've always been quite dismissive of social media,' I say, as he stands in the doorway, waiting for me to walk outside. Why am I constantly being surprised by him? And not in a good way.

'I opened an Instagram account when Gina first went away.' He's leaning in the doorway now. His tone suggests boredom at my questioning. 'If I can't get hold of Gina on text, and she isn't answering her phone, I direct-message her on Instagram. If she doesn't respond, at least I can look at her account, see that day's photos, and know she's okay. Obviously here the signal is in and out, so it's not so easy, but when there's a signal I can check.'

'Oh . . . I see.' *So he needs to 'know she's okay'?* The fact he still sees himself as being responsible for her safety makes me uneasy, but not as uneasy as it is to know he messages her. Then I remember that Emilio Ferrante doesn't follow Gina. I would have spotted that.

'What do you call yourself on Instagram?' I ask, desperate to deep-dive his account the minute he leaves the room.

'I'm . . . it's a bit embarrassing really – when Gina first met me she called me the "volcano geek", which was a bit rich coming from a volcano-obsessed woman, but that's what I am on Instagram.'

Why has he never volunteered this information before?

I understand that Gina's his wife, and she was in his life first. But *I'm* with him now, and it disturbs me that they have private messages with each other that he's never told me about. This suggests to me that they still have a sort of relationship. I wonder what they talk about? Will they always have private chats online that exclude me?

'So with your Instagram do you . . .' I begin to ask, and he grabs my hand.

'Come on, today I'm going to take you for a drive to my world,' he says, opening the front door.

I walk outside, blinking in the morning sunshine, still trying to work out what I'm missing here. He clearly doesn't want to address the Instagram issue, but it bothers me, and I can't rest until I know what's going on. Is it true that he doesn't text because she loses her phone – or does he DM her on Instagram so I can't ever see the messages, even by accident, like a text popping up? My head is filled with this, and I'm compelled to pursue this fresh hell. 'Do *you* ever post anything on Instagram, Emilio?'

'What? Why are you *still* talking about that? Sometimes you're like a dog with a bone, Sophie,' he says impatiently, turning away from me, staring out at the landscape from the doorway.

I want to yell at him about being secretive, cutting me out of parts of his life, but that would make me a hypocrite, because that's what I'm doing to him.

'Oh, I forgot my gloves,' I say, and go back to the bedroom to grab the gloves I'd deliberately forgotten, and lock myself in the bathroom with my phone. I know it seems mad, but I think I am just a little bit mad. I feel paranoid that he's hiding something from me, and I can only get peace by double-checking, which isn't good. But I'm driven to do it. So once safely locked in the bathroom, I click Instagram on my phone to look at Gina's followers. And there he is – Volcano Geek. His profile picture is of course a volcano, and I'd totally missed this – so what does this mean? I really don't know. I should just leave it all alone and trust him.

I couldn't have gone out walking with this playing on my mind, and now I have to believe him, because the alternative is tortuous and making me a little too crazy. So I breathe deeply, put a big smile on my face, and dash out of the house to join him.

'Come on, the truck's parked and waiting,' he's saying, grabbing the petrol can from the little shed next to our cabin.

'The walk will be fun,' I say. I know I'm becoming slightly obsessive, and I try to clear my mind and enjoy the bleakness and beauty of the grey, glinting landscape. We set off walking, and soon my concerns over Gina and Emilio's Instagram accounts fade.

'Infinity,' I murmur, as we push on through the cold, two insignificant ants on our very own glittering silver planet.

Crunching across the gravel, he guides me through the terrain, taking lumps of volcanic dust from the ground, telling me how it forms, the science behind nature. After about twenty minutes trudging through this brittle landscape, I'm a little worried we may not find our way back.

'It all looks the same,' I say. 'You could abandon me here and I might never find my way home.'

But he doesn't answer, just keeps ploughing on through the grey until eventually the truck emerges in the near distance.

We climb into the vehicle, and I'm surprised to see a couple of coats in the back.

He opens the passenger door and moves a coat and a bag of sweets on to the back seat before I climb in.

'Are they Charlie's sweets?' I ask.

'Yeah. Take one if you like.'

I'm about to answer when I see something at my feet, a small cylinder. I can't see what it is, and can't reach it with my seat belt on.

Emilio starts the truck and off we go, through the rough terrain until the land seems much firmer. Slowly the landscape changes, and within half an hour we're arriving in a town.

'Where are we?' I say. My eyes have been so used to volcano gravel and nature that perfectly proportioned stone buildings now seem alien to me.

'We're in the city of Catania. It's the hub where I work,' he replies.

'Ahh, you've brought me to your workplace, that's sweet.' I kiss him on the cheek.

'I want you to see why I've given up a year of my life to be here. It isn't just dust and gravel, Sophie, it's life and death. Volcanoes have been around far longer than we have, and they hold all the secrets. Just look at her there.'

In spite of this new, man-made landscape, Etna still looms over us, demanding our attention. 'She's blowing smoke rings,' I say, pointing at the rings of white smoke emerging from the top of the volcano.

He smiles. 'They're called vortex rings – just gases and water vapour – but they're magical, aren't they?'

As Etna sends perfect circles of white smoke into the cold blue sky, he watches with all the wonder of a child at a funfair for the first time. For me, the smoke rings have a different connotation, and I'm back in Taormina on my balcony while a stranger watches and sends pale grey smoke rings into the night sky.

I climb from the passenger seat, and as I do, I notice the small cylindrical object in the footwell again, and my mouth goes dry. It's a lipstick.

36

I slip the lipstick into my coat pocket, and don't ask Emilio about it, because I need to process this. Besides, I'm not sure he'd tell me the truth. I guess I still don't trust him after all.

'So here we are,' he's saying excitedly. I look up at the sign, which tells me we're at the Catania hub of the National Institute of Geophysics and Volcanology, a beautiful building in the Piazza Roma, Catania.

'There are over a hundred of us here,' Emilio explains as he walks me through to the control rooms, where a friendly scientist shakes my hand and tells me about the hub and how proud he is to work with Emilio. I'm soon swept into the world of volcanoes, as Emilio guides me through the building. 'Gas emission detectors, seismographs, and heat-sensor cameras all send information in real time to us here,' he says, pointing at the huge screens dotted around.

'It feels like a cross between a space station and a war room,' I say, smiling and taking it all in.

'We're having some quite alarming stats at the moment, and the maths shows signs of a bigger eruption than usual on the way,' he says, while machines that look like lie detectors scribble away. As we walk through, he introduces me to more of his fellow scientists, who all greet him fondly and welcome me. 'Professor Ferrante is the amazing Volcano Man,' one of them says. 'He is *the* man!' another corrects him. We all laugh, and I'm so proud and impressed at how respected he is, and how complicated and vital his work. To learn more about this side of his life helps me to feel like I'm part of it, because being here now, seeing what he does, meeting his colleagues, I realise I didn't really know him at all. I hope that now he's finally opening up to me. I want to hold his hand, and show how proud I am to be with him, but of course that wouldn't be appropriate. So I just stand by his side and simmer with admiration and pride.

'And now, my office.' He smiles, walking towards a lift, pressing the button. 'The underground laboratory,' he says as we take the lift down into the bowels of the building, and he walks me through into a small room where a woman is looking through a microscope.

She lifts her head on hearing us enter, and turns around and smiles at him. 'Hey.' Her voice is warm, intimate, like she just rolled over in bed.

Standing up to greet us, I'm dismayed to see how gorgeous she is – long dark hair, long legs, a knockout smile.

'Hey, I brought Sophie to meet you – wanted to show her where it all happens,' he replies, and I note his tone is warm, but more formal than hers.

'This is my work partner. You've heard me talk a lot about her.'

'We do get into some scrapes.' She smiles. 'And I apologise for keeping him late so many nights.'

I'm alarmed and a little confused. I thought his work partner was a guy called Charlie.

'Sophie, meet Charlie,' he says, beaming at her, while I attempt to hide my dismay with a smile. 'I thought you were . . . I didn't realise you were a girl,' I say, recovering quickly.

'I'm Charlotte – Charlie to my friends. It can be confusing, but I just hate the name Charlotte – so stuffy! So please call me

Charlie!' She shakes my hand just long enough for me to check her bare ring finger.

'How are things looking?' he asks.

'Not good. If the primitive magma continues to rise to the surface, a lateral opening could form.'

He takes a sharp intake of breath. 'Flank eruptions?'

'Exactly,' she replies, and I see the sparkle in her eyes as they continue to chat. I suddenly feel excluded – not for the first time today. They are both using words that are almost meaningless to me, like 'magma' and 'fractures' and 'lateral eruptions'. They might as well be speaking another language. Her accent is Italian, so I guess they're using English for my benefit. While they talk, I try to smile and appear chilled while trying not to imagine them alone together every day in this cosy, subterranean love nest. In my discomfort, I put my hands in my coat pockets and feel the tube of lipstick. Is it hers? Did she leave it in his truck? Then I remember him saying he dropped her off home last night, and I feel my world tipping slightly. I take some discreet breaths, and silently talk myself down.

I'm being ridiculous. It's just that Emilio has mentioned Charlie once or twice, and he seems fond of his colleague. But now I'm going back over those few remarks and seeing them from a completely different perspective. 'Charlie's the best teammate I've ever had.' And, 'Charlie's cool, and so brilliant, just understands volcanoes, you know?'

So, here's another beautiful woman in Emilio's life that I didn't know about, and like Gina, she also shares his passion for volcanoes. I feel the lipstick in my pocket, and my stomach churns. After what I've been through in the past, I'm unsure, fragile. And now this roller coaster with Emilio is making me question everything. From finding out he was married, to discovering his house was their marital home, to him suddenly leaving me to come here before changing his mind and asking me to join him. It's made it difficult for me to trust, and that's why I'm finding this situation with Charlie so uncomfortable. They seem so close, and I feel like the one who doesn't belong.

We set off on the drive back, and Emilio explains his concerns about the lava flow down the sides of the volcano.

'It opens up fractures on the low-lying mountains, which is a risk to the cities below – we could be in for a big one,' he warns. I try to look concerned while wondering if he and Charlotte ever have lunch together, and if she feeds him. This is so ridiculous, and I almost laugh at myself. I really need to get a grip.

'There's been a lot of ash too, more than usual,' Emilio is murmuring, almost to himself, while I wonder idly if they ever work late together when no one else is there? And how she dropped her lipstick on the floor of his truck?

'There she is,' he smiles, pointing to Etna as we drive along. 'At every turn she looms.'

I watch her towering above us, a shadow topped in clouds and dust, shrouded in her own mystery, smoke hovering over the crater like a secret.

'Wherever you go, she's here,' I say, 'like an old friend who's always on your mind.' Or a beautiful woman who's always in your life.

He stops the truck, gets out and looks up; our hands are entwined. 'What has she seen, what does she know?' he says, with a heavy sigh.

I stand by him, looking at the smouldering volcano, and hear the echoes of that strange woman's voice. *Beware, teste di moro, too many dark secrets . . . someone lies and someone dies . . .*

37

We've been living in the foothills of Etna now for almost three months. We arrived in late summer, and now it's the end of November. Emilio was right, it's beautiful throughout the seasons in different ways. Our first few weeks were spent watching the distant forests turn from green to gold to bare, and snow has now fallen, covering the crater, transforming it into a huge iced Bundt cake, round and deep with a hole in the middle.

Emilio spends long days at the hub, but sometimes works from home, and those days are my favourite. We wrap up warm and take long drives through snowy forests, and he monitors the volcano, testing and measuring to determine the threat of eruption, the effect on the landscape and climate.

'She's angry today,' he'll say, watching from a safe distance, while Mother Nature's witchy cauldron spews her killer fire up into the air, sparks flying.

We recently went on a boat to see Stromboli. She's a smaller volcano than Etna, and located off the northern coast of Sicily. We watched her erupt constantly from the middle of the Tyrrhenian Sea. 'She's as angry as Etna,' I said, feeling safe from the flames, wrapped in his arms, the boat bobbing smoothly on the glass-like water.

'She's known as the Lighthouse of the Mediterranean,' he whispered in my ear, as I relaxed, protected from the wrath of Stromboli; and as she spat and hissed, flames flickering through the smoke as we both watched, I turned to see the wonder in his eyes, like it was the first time.

I think I'm finally beginning to understand Emilio, and what draws him to this dangerous, fabulous place.

'She holds secrets to our past and our future,' he says of Etna, as he takes measurements, samples, and sometimes goes a little too close and risks his life for answers. And I know he'll never stop until he finds out her secrets.

The more I understand the landscape, the more I understand him. I love living here, where there are no other people, no ghosts, and the only shadow is Etna looming over us, a constant reminder that we are always at the mercy of nature.

There seem to be shadows, though. I'm never completely sure, never fully secure with him. Is it because of my past, or because of Gina? Who knows? But at the moment, my fears also centre around Charlotte, Emilio's beautiful colleague, with whom he's very close. He was late from work this evening because 'Charlie needed some help with a magma flow'. *I bet she did*, I think as I chop carrots aggressively for dinner.

I wish I didn't have to suffer this horrible insecurity; it colours everything for me, and feeling like this has brought Gina's shadow back. She's laughing at me in the steam as I boil vegetables, dancing in the flames of our cosy little fire, and when I look in the bathroom mirror I'm sure she's giving me the middle finger – or the Italian version.

If we were married, I'd feel different, more secure, but how can we get married when he can't get divorced? Having promised to start divorce proceedings months ago, Gina hasn't done a thing, and I'm secretly worried she's changed her mind. Emilio messaged her a while ago to ask if she'd appointed a solicitor, but she just said no, she was too busy. So a couple of days ago he messaged her again, and I've been aching to ask him if he's heard anything from her yet. But I've held back, because it seems the minute her name is mentioned, he becomes cold, I get upset, and we argue.

Tonight, I'm really anxious, and I promise myself I won't ruin another night by asking if he's heard from Gina. But within seconds I'm fighting with myself, because now he's here I just have to go there.

'Have you had any messages from Gina . . . or anything?' I ask, like I'm merely musing. He's been home about seven minutes, so I held on as long as that.

'Actually no, I haven't, and neither has Sabrina, which is odd.'

'Oh?' I'm on full alert. 'You never said you'd spoken to Sabrina,' I say. This is part of the problem, his head is so full of bloody volcanoes he forgets about real life.

'She called me yesterday, said she was worried about Gina.'

'I've always thought that Sabrina's secretly worried, but she's all about bravado.'

'Yeah, and I didn't worry because I assumed Gina was regularly messaging her, but she thought Gina was messaging me. It was only when we started talking that we both said, "Hey, I haven't heard from her for a while."'

'Are you worried now?'

He bites his lip as he considers this. 'Yes and no. As I've said, she's done this before; she's like a magpie, and sees something glinting in the sunshine, wants it and chases it. The last time this happened and she didn't call, it was 2018 – the Volcán de Fuego had erupted in Guatemala. It was huge, people died, but she jumped on a plane and headed out there. When she arrived, she offered to help the team, and they immediately took her on of course.'

'Yeah, of course,' I say in a monotone. I wish he wasn't still so impressed by her.

'I mean, she's an internationally renowned volcanologist,' he adds proudly. 'Who wouldn't want her on their doorstep begging to come in.'

Me, for one?

'But talking to Sabrina has concerned me because it turns out neither of us have had any contact with her for a couple of weeks now. I wish she'd get in touch,' he adds.

'Has she left Hawaii?'

'Sabrina's making some calls today to try to find out.'

I'm already aware that Gina hasn't posted anything on her Instagram for a couple of weeks, but that doesn't mean she hasn't messaged.

He shrugs. 'I would have thought she'd let me know if she'd left Hawaii.'

'Why?'

He looks at me, puzzled, for a moment. 'I guess you're right – why would she? We aren't together anymore.'

Finally he gets it!

'I know it's hard to let go. When you've cared for someone for a long time, it's the most difficult thing to say goodbye.'

'You understand, because you've been there too,' he says. 'Did it take a long time to let go?'

'It did, and I still feel incredible sadness. We had so many plans – we wanted to travel, and Sicily was on our list. That's why I came here, I think I felt I could do it for both of us, but that wasn't helping me move on – meeting you helped.'

'It's the same for me. Meeting you made me realise what I could have. Gina and I both want different things, and it's hard to admit, but we weren't meant to be forever. She's moved on and so have I. And even if she did have second thoughts, she knows I'm with you now.'

We have dinner, and as he worked late he's tired so soon goes to bed, leaving me to work on my art project. I've been focused on this more often recently, and discovered something that is probably quite obvious – the happier I am, the easier it is to be creative.

My memories with Simon aren't all sad and they aren't all happy, like most relationships. So in my artwork relating to this project, I use gritty, real-life words like 'disappointed', 'devastated' and 'empty', and juxtapose them with words like 'honeymoon', 'first date' and 'flowers'. I want to show the journey of a relationship, the ebbs and flows, ups and downs, the beginning and the end. I paint these words in different colours, and next I'll place them on a black background full of stars.

I finish around 1 a.m. Time flies when I immerse myself in my work. Before I go to bed, I instinctively grab my phone and do a quick check of Gina's Instagram. She hasn't posted for over two weeks, and as this is the longest gap between posts, I'm a little concerned. Is she heading back to Sicily? Or is she already here, ensconced in her lovely home? Looking through her Instagram now, I go looking for clues in old photos, zooming in, seeing who else is with her, if I can spot any landmarks or something that would give me a bigger picture. And it's then that I see it – in her most recent post, Gina is wearing her wedding ring. How did I miss this? I feel sick. There are lots of close-up selfies where her hands aren't visible.

Neither of us have worn our wedding rings for months now, Emilio told me when I first found out about Gina.

So why was she still wearing hers just two weeks ago? Did she forget her marriage was over? Or was Emilio lying when he said he'd told her about me and their marriage was no more? Have Gina and I *both* been played and she's wearing her ring because she thinks she's still married?

38

When I finally go to bed, Emilio is fast asleep. I try to wake him gently by saying his name, but when that doesn't work, I decide it's best to let him sleep. Being woken in the middle of the night by me demanding to know why his soon-to-be ex-wife is still wearing her wedding ring might not be the most tactful approach. He'll be annoyed that I've been looking at her Instagram too, so I have to work out how to broach this in the morning. First, I need to be sure that he has told her about me and he isn't lying about that. Then we need to find out why she thinks it's okay to keep her wedding ring on in November, when they apparently agreed not to wear them months ago!

Emilio gets up at 6 a.m., and despite not having had a wink of sleep, I get up with him and put on a pot of coffee. I need to discuss this wedding ring thing before he goes to work. I can't sit here all day ruminating.

I pour him some coffee as he makes toast. His hair is thick and unruly from bed, and his face bristly and unshaven. 'I'd like to take you back to bed,' I murmur as I put his coffee on the table. He stands behind me, puts both arms around me and kisses my neck softly.

'You'll have to stop that, because if you don't I won't let you leave for work today,' I say.

I turn and face him and he's looking at me with such love, I don't want to spoil the moment with confrontation or questioning, so I kiss him instead. It's a few minutes later, when he's eating his toast and I'm drinking my coffee at the table, that I embark on the conversation I need to have.

'Can I ask you something?'

'Of course.' He takes a bite of toast.

'Do you think that Gina is accepting that you guys aren't married anymore?'

He looks at me with eyes I remember from before, cold and impatient. 'Sophie, what's this now?'

'Nothing, I just wondered. I mean, she hasn't done anything about the divorce, has she?'

'I don't know. I'm not even sure she's read my most recent messages yet. The signal here is so unreliable.'

'It's just so frustrating.' I try not to sound angry, but can't help my feelings. I hesitate slightly but decide to go for it. 'Look, I checked her Instagram and she's still wearing her wedding ring.'

'Sophie, Sophie,' he repeats, clearly exasperated. 'Why are you still torturing yourself with this?'

'Am I torturing myself, or you?'

'What are you talking about?'

'This is obviously uncomfortable for you. But someone needs to keep an eye on your wife's Instagram because she's still wearing her wedding ring, which is a complete contradiction to your narrative.'

I stand up, and storm into the bedroom, slamming the door so hard it nearly falls off.

I sit there for a few minutes just boiling, and I'm so angry and sleep-deprived I have to go into the bathroom to throw up.

'Are you okay in there?' I hear him as I'm retching over the bowl.

'NO!' I yell back angrily.

'Sophie, I'm sorry,' he's saying as he walks in, and he kneels next to me, wiping my face with a damp towel. 'You mustn't keep looking at Gina's Instagram. All it does is upset you.'

I turn to him. 'It upsets you too.'

'What do you mean?'

'Her photos aren't lying, but *you* are. You told me you'd agreed to take your wedding rings off, and you weren't wearing yours when I met you – if you had I wouldn't have even gone out with you. So why is she still wearing *her* ring?'

He flops on to the floor, and lies down looking up at the ceiling.

'Why, Emilio? You can't answer me, can you?'

'No – because I'm not in Hawaii with her right now to ask, but I can message her. She probably won't respond, but I'll do it here now if that would placate you?'

I look at him; I don't need to say anything.

'Okay.' He takes out his phone, and clicks on to Instagram, and starts typing. And when he's finished, to my surprise, he hands me the phone.

'I don't need to see it,' I say, refusing to take the phone off him.

'No – you do, because you don't believe me. You don't trust me, Sophie, so you need to see this.'

I take the phone from his hand and read the message he just sent.

Hey, hope all is good with you. Sabrina and I are a little worried that you haven't been in touch, let us know you're ok, she worries about you. And I just wanted to ask – are you still wearing your wedding ring? It's just that I thought we'd said we would take them off now. As we're both in new relationships I feel it's the kindest thing. Love E x

I read it. Twice. It's definitely been sent to her account.

'Feel free to see our other messages,' he offers.

I shake my head and give the phone back to him.

'There is one I'd like you to see,' he says, and starts scrolling, then hands the phone back to me.

Hey, Remember I told you that I was dating this art teacher called Sophie? Well, I think I like her, really like her you know? I still haven't told her I'm married, am scared of putting her off. I think I might, and in the first instance take her back to the house one evening, make dinner.

He's standing up, starting to wipe the sink and toilet as I sit there, and while he cleans up, I check he isn't looking and shamelessly scroll through to the next message.

She just sends a thumbs up to this, which is better than nothing I suppose. He's now pouring bleach down the sink, so I quickly skim the next message.

Hey, Sophie came back to the house, she loved it. She's such a funny, kind person, really sweet too, I think this one might be the one. Only trouble is Sabrina was here when we arrived and gave her a really hard time, I can't see them ever being friends. Sophie said she seems like a real bitch.

'Are you feeling any better?' he asks as I hand him the phone. I bet Gina hates me for saying that about her sister. But she didn't seem to react, just the thumbs up, so the good news is he's been telling me the truth the whole time.

'I'm okay now, thanks. I'm sorry.' Standing up, I put my arms around his neck. 'I just feel really stupid, and really tired,' I say, leaning on him, enjoying his physical strength and the way he's holding me.

'I'd better call Charlie,' he says, pulling away.

'Why?'

'I need to let her know I'm going to be later than I thought. We have a breakfast meeting.'

'Who with?'

'Each other. She brings croissants and we work out our plans for the day.'

Why does he tell me these things? If I didn't know I wouldn't fret about it. But it's like when he's talking about Gina and how wonderful she is and the great times they've had. I'm dying inside, and he doesn't seem to realise.

'You get off, it's obviously important. I'll just stay here and vomit some more,' I say, pretending I'm joking when I'm actually not. I want to mention her lipstick, the one I found in his car, but I've left it too long – I'd sound like even more of a psycho than I already do.

'If you are sure you don't mind me getting off to work?' he asks, but doesn't wait for my answer, just kisses me on the top of my head and minutes later he's gone.

He just doesn't get it, and probably never will.

I get into the shower to wash away the horrible vomit smell and scrub away at the grey dust on my skin. Volcanic ash has accumulated in my pores and is now collecting in the plughole. I spent last night unable to sleep because of Gina, and now he's set me off again about his beautiful work colleague who only has eyes for him. I can see how Gina might have felt neglected, and unloved. He just doesn't think before he speaks. Emilio is catnip to women; even his sister-in-law can't take her eyes off him. He's a charming, good-looking guy, but the really attractive thing is he's unaware of it or of the effect he has on women. He sees them as friends and colleagues, but Charlie was all over him in their laboratory – where, apparently, 'the magic happens'. And now he's rushed off to work early to enjoy her warm croissants. Ugh.

I turn off the shower, and I'm about to leave the bathroom (naked and still damp) when I hear a clatter in the kitchen. It must be Emilio. So, he's realised that rushing off to breakfast with Charlie has pissed me off and he's come back to make sure I'm okay?

'Emilio,' I call as I grab his robe from the bed. 'Have you come back to make it up to me?' I ask softly. He doesn't answer, and I know he would; he always announces his arrival. 'Emilio!' This time I shout it into the silence and it almost bounces back. I suddenly feel a bit jumpy, because he probably didn't lock the door when he left. I'm in a small house on the slopes of Etna, the nearest village is more than a mile away, and no one would hear me scream. I hear another movement in the kitchen. A cupboard door opens and closes.

If he's not here in the house – who is?

39

I pick up the rusty old lamp from the bedside table and wait silently by the bedroom door. There's definitely somebody here, I can hear them moving around. So, clutching the lamp, I take a deep breath and step out of the room. 'Hello?'

It's only then I smell the sweet stench of vanilla and caramel, sprinkled with brown sugar. Her perfume.

I can barely put one step in front of the other. I want to cover my eyes. I want to scream. But nothing will help me now; she's here. She's standing in my kitchen waiting for me.

'Hey, Sophie.' The soft American/Mediterranean rich girl voice – Emilio told me the sisters were educated in California. I'm frozen to the spot. She's standing in the dark little kitchen, the light from the window behind her. I can't see her face, just the long caramel-blonde hair.

'Gina?' I almost whisper.

She throws back her head and laughs, stepping slowly forward, her face emerging.

'It's me, it's Sabrina. Don't tell me you've forgotten me already. It's only been a few months.' She turns to the kitchen area, opens a cupboard and takes out the bag of coffee. Then she bends down to the cupboard under the sink and takes out two cups.

'Coffee?' she asks, clicking on the heated ring and putting the coffee pot on. I stand, frozen in shock. What is she doing here? And how does she know where everything is in the kitchen. How?

'Er, yes, thank you,' I say, trying to regroup. 'I didn't expect to see you,' I offer, hoping this will be enough for her to explain. 'Does Emilio know you're here?'

'Well, let's put it this way, he won't be surprised to see me.'

'Oh?'

'I have to speak to him. We've been in touch but I always think it best to discuss important things in the flesh, don't you?'

'How . . . did you find us?' I say, assuming her question was rhetorical, or mischievous – either way, I'm not playing her games.

'The cabin? I've been here loads of times. I often came here when him and Gina were working.'

I had no idea, I thought this was our place. I thought coming here would erase her from our relationship – but Gina's been here all the time. I suddenly remember the outdoor boots in the boot rack, the ones with pink laces that I tried to force my feet into. They must be hers – I feel like an ugly sister to her Cinderella.

'I jumped on a train and took a taxi from the village,' Sabrina is saying, running her fingers through her hair. It's longer than it was the last time I saw her. She's obviously had it restyled and dyed, the cut and colour are exactly like Gina's now and her make-up is subtle – softly rouged cheeks and a tawny nude on her full lips. She looks stunning, and so out of place in her soft Chanel cowl-neck in pastel pink. She seems incongruous in this setting, like Paris Fashion Week is being held in a mud hut.

She splashes scalding coffee into two cups, and hands one to me.

'So why do you want to speak to Emilio? Is it about Gina?'

'It is,' she says, and for the first time, she looks slightly uncomfortable. 'Shall we sit down?' she says, like she's a hostess and I'm a guest. I imagine that's how she sees me – merely as a guest in their lives. Perhaps I am?

She takes a seat at the rickety table, immediately bestowing it with a shabby-chic glamour it doesn't merit. Meanwhile, I sit opposite, with wet hair, wearing Emilio's big old towelling robe in dirty brown that's too big and trails along the floor. Yesterday this robe felt warm and cosy, and I thought I looked cute. Now, I feel like I just crawled off the set of *Lord of the Rings*.

'Yeah, I wanted to talk to Emilio about Gina. I'm worried about her, haven't heard from her for weeks.'

'Yes, Emilio mentioned that. He said you were both concerned.'

She gives me a doubtful look. 'When she first went missing, Emilio said we mustn't call the police, but I'm not prepared to just sit there and hope she'll get in touch.'

'I find it hard to imagine Emilio actually saying you mustn't call the police?' I feel a prickle of unease.

'Well, start imagining, because that's exactly what he said. "She's fine, she'll come back when she's ready," he kept saying. "Just leave it, Sabrina." But she's not posted anything on her Instagram for over two weeks.' She's looking at me intently, then looks away. 'But then you'd *know* that.'

I don't take the bait, even though she stops talking for a couple of seconds to see if she can ignite something. But I'm not sparring with her today.

'So, anyway, I called the police.' She finishes her coffee.

'Okay, and what did they say?'

She pulls a face. '"Do you know how many people go missing in Seecily each day?" She says this in an exaggerated Italian accent. '"Mees, you 'ave to understand, if shee in another country we don't have resources to look, we send note to Interpol."' She holds out her hands in despair. 'They'll send a note, can you fucking believe it?'

I have this image of a Post-it note sitting on a desk at Interpol, with papers piled on top – lost forever. I shake my head while Sabrina continues her rant. It hasn't gone unnoticed by me how pleasant she's being, but I'm waiting for the hate.

She's now warming to her subject. 'Then they said, "Has eet occurred to you that she may not want to be found?" I was just so crazy by now, so I said, "No, but eet's occurred to me that you're all lazy bastards who should be fired!"'

I smile at this, her total disrespect even for authority is mildly amusing. Or am I just so starved of female company that she seems more entertaining than she is?

'Perhaps you and Emilio need to do some investigating?' I suggest.

'Emilio isn't interested.'

'He is, I'm sure he wants to find her just as much as you do,' I say, though I'm not sure of anything anymore. 'Look, I have to get dressed,' I say, looking down at what feels less like a robe and more like a costume.

'Yeah, what the fuck are you wearing?'

I laugh. 'I came here with a silk robe, but it's so bloody cold I abandoned it in in early October. It's Emilio's.'

She's looking at it in horror. 'I *knew* I'd seen it before, I remember it now.'

I'm sure she doesn't mean anything, but the suggested intimacy of her remark hits me right in the chest. I have to assume she saw Emilio in his old robe when he was with her sister and she stayed here.

I dress quickly and return to the kitchen, where she's looking at her phone.

'Hey queen,' she says, smiling as I walk in.

She's made more coffee, and the rich, welcoming fragrance mingles with the vanilla notes of her perfume.

215

'I love your perfume,' I say.

'Thank you!' She smiles, and I think she might mean it.

I sip on my coffee, breathing in the scent. I haven't worn perfume for months, or smelled it. I've been starved of anything feminine here. 'That jumper's gorgeous too,' I add. 'Sorry, I sound like a ten-year-old girl meeting Taylor Swift for the first time.'

She giggles at this.

'Since I came here, I don't bother with make-up, and just wear whatever's warm and comfortable, which was fine until I saw your new hair and gorgeous jumper.'

She touches her hair self-consciously. 'Yes, it's a very masculine energy here, isn't it?' She shudders slightly. 'I don't know how you put up with it. This place is grey outside and grey inside. You need some colour in your life.'

I nod. 'I think you're right, that's exactly what I need.'

'Okay.' She stands up, pulls her sweater over her head and hands it to me. I see a glimpse of old track marks on her forearms and remember what Emilio told me about her drug problems in the past.

'Try it on,' she says, standing over me in a lace bra, cream silk against her winter tan.

I feel like we're bonding, and she's being friendly, so I do as she says.

'Wow! You look better in that than I do,' she enthuses.

'Oh, you're very kind, but you're ten years younger and slimmer and—'

'Keep it.'

'Oh no . . . it's too much, I couldn't.' This is awkward. 'It must have cost hundreds of euros.'

'The colour suits you better than it suits me, and if you don't keep it I'll just throw it in the garbage.'

I believe her.

'Well, if you're sure?'

'Yeah absolutely.' She delves in her handbag, brings out a bottle of scent, and before I can say anything she's sprayed it all over me. 'Honestly, I don't think I've ever seen you look or smell so good. Keep it on, and as he walks through that door, watch Emilio fall in love with you all over again.'

'You're sweet, and thank you. I'm touched.'

She wafts her hand dismissively. 'Gina and I used to swap clothes and perfume – this smell makes me feel like she's close.'

Me too. And not in a good way.

But I feel a warmth towards Sabrina today, partly because she's just given me her Chanel jumper, and also it's this place. Here in the cabin nothing feels real, it's so quiet and peaceful, the noise of the world is shut out – and I think it's even made Sabrina pleasant to be around.

'Emilio told me the other day that you've been married before. I never knew. So many secrets Sophie.'

Oh, forget that – apparently she wasn't being pleasant, she was lulling me into a false sense of security.

'I don't keep secrets from Emilio,' I lie.

'Really? Because he keeps secrets from you.'

40

'Etna's angry today,' Sabrina says, standing up and gazing through the window.

'Emilio says there's a chance of a big eruption quite soon,' I reply, knowing she wants me to ask her what secrets Emilio is keeping from me, but I won't give her the satisfaction.

'Yeah, she's simmering isn't she, you can just feel the tension in the air.'

She moves away from the window and begins pacing, but the room's too small to pace, so she sits down, then stands up. Then she's sitting down again. She's restless, like a caged lion. I see echoes of Etna, a simmering impatience, like she's about to blow. I wonder if she's using again?

'Are you okay, Sabrina? You seem agitated,' I ask eventually.

'Fine, fine.' She sweeps her hand across the table, and turns back to the window. 'Do you know, I haven't actually spoken to Gina since she left, it's only been messages,' she says, and turning away from the window, she looks at me for a reaction.

'Emilio says that's how she mostly communicates when she's away – by Instagram message. He says she rarely calls to chat, and never responds to texts.'

'Yeah, well, I don't know about him, but she's always made a point of calling me at least once every couple of weeks when she's away. "I need to hear your voice," she says, "I have to check you haven't been kidnapped and the kidnappers are using your phone."' She smiles at this. 'She's a bit paranoid. We both have trust funds, you see, from our dad. She's much richer than me. She was his favourite, so he left her more, and she has her mother's too.'

Is that resentment I hear in her voice? 'Do you think if something happened to her . . . it might have something to do with her wealth?'

'Yes, that's exactly what I'm worried about. Is she being kept somewhere against her will? Kidnapped?'

'But then there'd be a ransom, wouldn't there?' I offer, feeling like we're now in make-believe territory.

'I don't know, but her bank statements might show something – has she spent any money, and if so, where?'

'Do you have access to her banking?'

She shakes her head. 'The only person who knows about her money is Emilio.'

This hangs over us as she lets it sink in. I'm not sure how to respond – I never considered this, and I'm uncomfortable with the way she's studying my reaction. And the implication of what she's just told me.

'I told the police my theory,' she continues, 'but as I said, they didn't seem interested.' She suddenly seems agitated. 'I need to speak to Emilio. Any idea when he'll be back?'

'No – it depends, volcanoes are notoriously unpredictable.'

'Mmm, so is Emilio,' she murmurs.

I'm uncomfortable now. I don't like where I think this is going. I don't understand why she's here. Is she here on serious business to cause trouble and imply that Emilio knows more than he's saying about Gina's disappearance? Or is she here purely for pleasure and is going to blindside me with some devastating information about Emilio? Or Gina?

Then there's also the slight possibility that she's telling the truth, is genuinely worried, and as she can't get any information from the police she's come to see Emilio for advice.

'None of it makes sense,' Sabrina's saying, leaning forward, lowering her voice conspiratorially. 'I came back to Sicily all the way from Cali, and couldn't wait to see her. I arrive home and Emilio's there on his own, says she's gone to Hawaii on some work trip with some guy she's hooking up with. Yeah, I know she *does* shit like that but . . .' She's shaking her head. 'Meanwhile my bro-in-law isn't losing any sleep, and he turns up later with a younger model – you – and with lightning speed, he moves you in! I mean, what the *fuck*?'

'I can see that was difficult for you, but it doesn't mean he isn't concerned about your sister.'

'You think?' She's glaring, waiting for my response.

'Why are you saying this? I thought you were fond of Emilio?'

She shifts in her seat. 'Do you want to know what I think?'

I shrug, genuinely not keen to hear this, but I reckon she's going to tell me anyway.

'Someone else is posting on Gina's Instagram.'

I'm shocked, but also – why hadn't I *thought* of this? 'What? But *who*?'

She shrugs. 'I don't even like to think it, but if someone's hurt her, or they're keeping her locked up . . . they might just be doing it so we think she's still alive, and the police think she's gone by choice.'

'That's a bit mad, isn't it?' I smile indulgently at her, not sure where she's going with this.

'Nope, it isn't. And I've got a theory as to who might be doing it.'

'Who?'

'I'm not sure I can trust you not to tell.'

'Of course you can. I probably don't even know them.'

'Oh, you *do*.'

My stomach is suddenly in knots. Sabrina and I only have one person in common.

'Emilio,' she announces triumphantly.

'No!' I say firmly. 'He just wouldn't *do* that, only somebody who's crazy would . . .'

'Exactly!' She rests her chin on her hands, amusement in her eyes. 'Sophie, think about it, he's the only one who'd have reason to do it.'

'Rubbish, what reason?'

'A new girlfriend.'

'He hadn't even met me when Gina went away.'

'No, but you work at the same place, he might have *seen* you, set his sights on you. So he bumps his wife off and needs to pretend she's still alive, so keeps her social media going.'

I almost laugh at this, but the seriousness on her face is quite disconcerting. She really seems to believe in her mad theory.

'But he hasn't a clue about social media,' I say. 'He only has an Instagram account so he can see where Gina is. She's the only person he follows.' My voice fades on the final word. I just heard what I said.

She almost stands, then sits down again. 'He only follows *Gina*? That's it right there.' She slaps her palm on the table, delighted, believing she's caught him out. Now she can make some real trouble for him. She'll now take this and run with it – straight to the police.

'Oh. My. God. What the fuck, Sophie?'

I could kick myself for saying anything, as the real Sabrina emerges like a phoenix from Gina's ashes. Is this what the new-found friendliness act was about – a way of teasing information from me so she can use it to condemn Emilio?

'But Gina had already met someone else,' I announce, relieved to have something to kill her ridiculous theory. 'It was a student at the university. She told Emilio about him before he started seeing me.'

'Oh my GOD! There's another motive right there. What if it was a crime of passion? Emilio loved Gina so much that when he found out about the other guy he decided if he can't have her no one else will? Puts a whole different spin on things . . . doesn't it?'

She's starting to scare me, I don't want to think about it, let alone say anything else to Sabrina, but I *have* to defend him.

'No, Emilio wouldn't. That isn't the man I know.'

'Sophie. No one is who we *think* they are. We're all hiding in plain sight.' She slowly puts her finger to her mouth, and my blood turns cold. What if Emilio *was* upset about his wife leaving him for another man? Taking her new lover to Hawaii in her husband's place would surely be humiliating, and upsetting? But enough to kill?

Have I missed the red flags because my feelings for him are so blinding, so all-consuming? My love for Emilio is like nothing before, it coils inside me like a snake, unfurling quickly at the prospect of danger, alert to all threats. He will always be a mystery, and that's his charm. I suddenly realise that the thrill of being with someone who keeps something back, who never quite gives himself to me, is what keeps me here. An echo of the shadowy figure of the father I never knew.

But that isn't how love should be – always holding something back, keeping secrets. And what if . . . what *if* Sabrina is right?

41

Sabrina spent the afternoon out on a long walk. I offered half-heartedly to accompany her, but she was keen to stress how well she knows the terrain around Catania.

The minute she left the cabin, the tension lifted. She brings such toxic energy with her, and she blows hot and cold. She unnerves me. But she's been gone for hours and I'm starting to wonder if she's okay; there's a blizzard starting to whip up. She was stupid going out really, but as usual so determined I didn't try to stop her.

I distract myself by making dinner, stretching the lasagne ingredients to make a dish for three.

I reckon Sabrina probably just came here to stir things up, and it's worked. She saw how happy I am, and played the friend, then threw all her poison at me knowing her suspicions would make me question Emilio.

I wonder if she's genuinely worried about her sister, or has she simply landed on our planet for sport? I go back to my comforting theory that she's bored and wants to introduce some uncertainty into our perfect life. I'm her captive audience in this dark little house, now surrounded by snow, miles from civilisation.

Suddenly the door seems to blow open and she dashes in out of the weather, looking pretty wet and windswept.

'You were ages,' I say, 'I was starting to worry.' This isn't strictly true, but I read from the expected script.

'I walked for miles.'

I nod in acknowledgement. 'It's bleak but beautiful.'

'No, it's just *bleak*,' she corrects me and leans on the kitchen counter watching me clean up after cooking. 'That sweater looked so good on you,' she says. 'Why did you take it off?'

'I was cooking, didn't want to get lasagne near it.'

'You don't like it, do you?'

'The sweater? Yes, of course I do, I love it!'

She looks a little hurt, which surprises me, so I go back into the bedroom, take it from the wardrobe and carefully put it back on. It's beautiful, and I've never worn anything so expensive. I stand in front of the broken mirror on the wall and admire myself. It's amazing the difference clothes make. I actually like myself a little – I haven't felt that for a long time.

'This has lifted me,' I remark as I walk back into the room. Smiling, she looks up from taking off her boots, the ones with pink laces. Gina's? I don't ask, don't want to know about their tiny matching Cinderella feet.

'Yeah. You look different, Sophie. That sweater's put colour back in your cheeks.'

'Thanks,' I smile.

'I don't know how you stand it,' she suddenly says.

I feel my smile fade, and brace myself for what she's about to say.

'I mean, you've given up *everything* for him. I wouldn't even give up a manicure for a man!' She wanders over to the bumpy old sofa, and lies down, gazing at her nails.

'I haven't given up *anything*.' I say firmly. 'I've gained a lot though. And it suits me to be here too, I'm working on an art project.'

'I can't imagine it's very inspiring for an artist out here.'

'Quite the contrary – it is.'

She slowly sits up on the sofa. 'Promise me something, Sophie.'

'Anything – within reason,' I add, remembering who I'm saying this to.

'Don't become as grey as the landscape out there. Gina stayed here a whole winter with him once and almost disappeared.' She hesitates. 'You know, in many ways you remind me of her – you're warm and funny and . . . be careful, Sophie.'

My stomach lurches, but I refuse to let her see how her comment shakes me, and change the subject back to her sister.

'I hope Gina's okay. I feel like I know her.'

'She would like you. I think you'd be friends.'

Perhaps Sabrina sees me as a replacement big sister. Does Emilio also see me as a replacement for Gina?

'So, have you thought any more about Emilio being the phantom Instagram poster?' She's smiling, clearly loving the mischief.

'I haven't, and I won't,' I lie. 'And it isn't that easy to pose as someone else online, if someone was doing it, they would need her password to get into her phone.'

She suddenly opens her eyes wide. 'Emilio knows Gina's passwords. He used to tell her all the time to change them – she's had the same ones for years.'

I try not to react too much. Knowing Sabrina, the more I say it *isn't* Emilio, the more she'll push in that direction.

'Well, if her estranged husband knows her passwords, there's a good chance her new lover will too,' I point out. 'And this younger boyfriend might be jealous, and insecure. Have you considered the possibility that *he* might be the one using her phone?'

She looks at me like a sulky child, reluctant to concede that there's an alternative to Emilio. 'I guess,' she murmurs.

'Until she's found, everyone's in limbo, it's the not knowing that's the worst,' I say gently. 'I hope she's okay – you and Emilio are both going through hell over this,' I add to make my point.

She shrugs, defeated, while inwardly I breathe a sigh of relief. Any hint of her ridiculous theories repeated to the police could ruin him. If Emilio thought for a moment that Sabrina was intimating that he'd hurt Gina he would be devastated; it isn't who he is. She's invaded our world again, coming here with her poison, trying to ruin everything.

'So, the wanderer returns!' I hear Sabrina's voice and look up. We can see Emilio through the window, tall and handsome, climbing from his truck into the snow, and seconds later, opening the door. My instinct is to run over and hug him, apologise for shouting before and tell him how much I love him. I wouldn't dream of doing that as we aren't alone, but Sabrina has no inhibitions, and she jumps up and hurls herself at him, like a child would to a father they hadn't seen for a long time. I sit and marvel at this display from someone who just a few minutes ago was virtually accusing him of murdering his wife.

'Hey, I would have tried to get back earlier if I'd known you were visiting,' he says. I'm not sure if he's pleased to see her or not. I can't read him.

She immediately turns to me and winks. 'Have you been working late at the office with Charlotte again?'

I feel like a bullet just hit me in the chest. How the hell does she know Charlotte? Even more concerning, how does she know I'm insecure about Emilio's close relationship with his work colleague? I think about the lipstick I found in his car. It had to be Charlotte's. I hid it in a drawer, I don't know why. Perhaps one day I'll confront him? Perhaps I won't? I want to throw it away, but not yet.

'So . . . *have* you been working late with old Charlie?' she asks again.

Emilio appears cool. 'Sabrina, don't tease, or I'll send you home,' he says, like a big brother to his little sister.

'I'm not teasing, you always liked working with Charlotte. It used to drive Gina mad. You were always working late, hanging out with Charlotte.'

Emilio is about to say something when he suddenly seems to remember I'm in the room, and registers my sweater.

'Why are you wearing that?' He isn't smiling.

'I . . . Sabrina gave it to me.' I search his face.

He looks from me to her then back to me. 'Please take it off.'

'Ooh, I told you he'd love it – get a room,' she smirks, but I only see his eyes, cold and staring.

'That's enough, Sabrina,' he snaps.

I look from his fury to her feigned nonchalance.

'I don't understand, it's a gift, she gave it to me?' I croak, realising I'm in the middle of something else here.

'Just take the sweater off and give it back to her,' he says. 'It *isn't* a gift.'

'Why? I don't understand.'

'You wouldn't, because Sabrina probably didn't tell you. That was Gina's sweater, I bought it for her. You smell like her too.'

42

My eyes are filling up, I am an idiot, I can't believe she did this to me, but I refuse to stand and cry in front of Sabrina. So I run to the bedroom and shut the door. Seconds later, the door opens and she walks in.

'What the fuck, Sabrina?'

'God I'm *so* sorry, Sophie.' She pauses, gently closing the door behind her, and sits next to me on the bed.

'I should have told you,' she whispers. 'But if I had, you wouldn't have worn it.'

'No I wouldn't! I thought you were being kind, I thought we were finally friends?' I whisper back, angry, confused.

'I was and we are, I promise. It's just that when you tried it on, you reminded me of Gina, and as much as I wanted you to have the jumper, I wanted him to see you, and remember her.'

'But why would you do that? You sprayed her perfume all over me too. It's hurtful for him and for me, why do you get so much pleasure from other people's pain, Sabrina? Don't you think he's been through enough? And it's been no picnic for me either. I've spent the last few months with a man who's been tormented by the past and seemed incapable of loving anyone ever again.'

'I'm sorry.' She sits there tapping her toes on the stone floor, her head down. 'You have to admit, his reaction to you in that sweater was weird.'

'No it wasn't,' I snap. 'If anything, his distress shows how much he still cares about your sister.'

'Or he doesn't want to be reminded of her for some reason?' she says slowly, for impact.

There's a knock on the door. Emilio walks in, and for once Sabrina is sensitive enough to leave.

'I'm so sorry,' he says, taking her place next to me on the bed. 'I overreacted. I saw Sabrina, then that jumper, and I just knew she was playing games.'

'I think she's feeling mixed up. She's worried about her sister and she's scared. She's just lashing out,' I say, trying to be charitable.

'That's no excuse. She has a wicked tongue and an issue with the truth.'

We hug for a few minutes, but then I pull away, feeling uneasy with Sabrina around. I imagine her listening at the door, or sniffing around our things like a nosy little fox.

'Come on, I made dinner, let's eat,' I say, my heart heavy. We go back into the living room, and in silence I take the lasagne from the oven, while Emilio puts three plates on the table.

The atmosphere is tense. I've felt it now for a couple of days, like we're waiting for an eruption. I put the pasta on to the plates and place Sabrina's in front of her, but she doesn't look up, and Emilio seems to be ignoring her. She'll be here for another few hours at least and I can't stand it, so I try to smooth the friction by speaking.

'Sabrina's spoken to the police,' I tell him, once we're sitting down.

'I did, not that they were any help,' she mutters.

'The problem is, she's in another country,' he says, standing up.

'Exactly, that's what they said to me. I think because she's in Hawaii, the police here see it as a Hawaiian problem.'

Emilio takes a bottle of red and three glasses from the cupboard, and places them on the table.

'Ooh, drinkies.' Sabrina claps her hands like an excited child; suddenly the police and her sister are forgotten.

'I hate to be that girl, but should we be drinking wine?' I ask. 'It feels a bit celebratory, and this isn't a celebration.'

'Oh, you're so English, Sophie – us Sicilians drink wine any time, any occasion, don't we, Emilio?' Sabrina looks at him for confirmation and he nods half-heartedly, and offers me some wine.

'No thanks – I'm English, remember?' I say.

He smiles at my little joke, while she lifts her glass to his, saying '*Salute!*' and takes a huge mouthful.

'Sabrina came all the way out here to talk to you about Gina,' I say, pointedly.

'Oh, she came to talk to me about Gina, did she?' He takes a sip of wine, and looks at her. 'I thought she might be here to make mischief.'

'I can do both, if you like?' She's leaning back in her chair, wine glass in hand, observing him like he's prey.

Not on my watch.

After dinner, Emilio clears the plates, and grabbing the bottle of wine, Sabrina refills both their glasses, and I wonder if all this worry might lead her back to her addiction problems.

'Look, I'm sorry about earlier, Sophie. You were right, I've been avoiding the issue, putting other things first, but I'm just burying it because the prospect of anything . . .' He sounds tearful. 'The thing is, she was messaging me, so I wasn't really worried, but I'm glad you contacted the police, Sabrina. I think I should call them in the morning, add some more weight to it.' Emilio sighs, and I can see this is quite sobering for him. 'It's an admission that something isn't right, that she might not be safe. I find that hard.'

'Me too,' Sabrina says, and I see the tears in her eyes. She does have feelings, it's just that other side of her that can't help but cause hurt. I wonder fleetingly what her relationship is really like with her sister, and if, when she's scared, she hurts Gina sometimes too.

I walk over to Emilio, putting my arm around his waist and my head on his chest, and he instinctively puts his arms around me. And I can see her watching from the corner of her eye.

◆ ◆ ◆

Three more glasses of wine and Sabrina is getting louder and more lairy. And I hold my breath when Emilio asks if she'd like to sleep on the sofa tonight.

'God no, I've booked myself in for a couple of nights at the Asmundo di Gisira, the Bellini suite – remember it, Emilio?' she asks, with a twinkle in her eye.

'Yes.' He smiles awkwardly, then looks at me. 'Gina and I used to stay there sometimes.'

'The suite has its own piano, very romantic,' Sabrina says with a wink.

Emilio looks up. 'Why would you need a romantic hotel room? You're staying there alone, aren't you?'

'Who says I'm alone?' she smoulders.

'Do you know, I can't work out who Sabrina came to taunt tonight, is it me or you?' I say to Emilio, while Sabrina rolls her eyes.

'Well, Sophie, I reckon she's going for a double tonight. Being toxic is her oxygen; she has no friends so she's come all the way out here to practise on us.'

'Aren't we the lucky ones?' I say.

I love this – finally we're working as a team, and as much as Sabrina hates being teased, she takes it.

'Aww shucks, you guys love to indulge me,' she says with a sickly smile.

This might just be the way to deal with her – address her behaviour openly and laugh with her about it. She's like a naughty teenager who needs to be aware that her clumsy trouble-making is hurtful and fooling no one.

'Hey, I forgot.' She goes to her Tiffany-blue Osprey weekender bag, and produces a bottle of Ginacria gin.

'Your favourite.' She hands it to Emilio, who seems to accept it gratefully.

'I love this, thank you. It's made from botanicals picked from the slopes here. Volcano gin,' he says to me, before pouring them both a drink and they toast to the future and 'Finding Gina!'

'Oh God this is good,' Sabrina says, 'like lemons and oranges. Are you sure you don't want any, Sophie?'

'No thanks, gin gives me a headache.'

'There's liquorice root too,' Emilio says. 'It tastes like Sicily.'

'Is there any music in this hovel?' Sabrina asks. 'I know the Wi-Fi is useless here, we tried to play music before but no go,' she says, taking the gin bottle and pouring more into each of their glasses.

'There are some CDs?' I offer.

'Okay grandma, get the CDs out,' she jokes, good-naturedly. I dig them out from a drawer and put them into the player.

'What the hell is this?' she asks as the music starts.

'It's Emilio's band – from university.' I glance over, and he smiles at me.

'I didn't know you were in a band,' she says.

'Oh, there's a lot you don't know about him.' I'm tapping my fingers on the table.

'Come on then, let's dance to your music.' She grabs his hand and forces him to stand up. Emilio doesn't like to dance, and she must know this, but rather than cause a drama, he reluctantly agrees. I sip my water and watch them, her arms around his neck, her hips swaying, his awkward shuffling. And I can see how obvious it is. Sabrina is in love with him.

43

Sabrina's taxi arrived late last night, and she left in a flurry of kisses and sweet perfume. I was glad to see her go.

Her presence brought an energy that now sits between us at breakfast, and her little barbs and whispers still float through the house, catching me sharply as I make the coffee. The hurt and fear is suddenly heavy at the back of my throat, as I recall her familiarity with Emilio's dressing gown, the way she asked about Charlotte like she knew something I didn't. And the dancing, Sabrina pressing into Emilio, her face in his, her adoring eyes, will forever be stencilled on my brain. Sabrina is a butterfly; she flutters around like a pretty accessory. But I *see* her, I know exactly what she's capable of – because I'm the same. We are both damaged people who know how to survive.

But today, I'm free of her cruelty, there's a wintery sun pushing through the clouds, and she's gone. So, with Emilio at work, I'm giving some time to my project, and I'm back with Simon. I'm still creating a montage from photographs, amongst other things. The project is evolving, with memories, feelings, love and endings. I'm just being driven by emotion rather than any grand plan. I have paintings I did of Simon, and the souvenirs of our lives together. I'm calling my project *After the Wedding*, because invariably that's when relationships really begin, and you get to discover the person you married.

It's painful, but healing, and I go into a state of calm when I'm working, and the hours fly by, and when I stop and realise I've been working for four hours, I heat up some soup for lunch. But when I pour it into a bowl I really don't want it. I haven't eaten much for days; I haven't fancied food, which isn't like me. I'm always happy to lose a few pounds, but this is a little worrying.

I shiver with cold and try to eat some soup, but it makes me feel sick. So, I do what I always do now when I'm feeling low or worried – I call Marian, who's always delighted to chat.

'Hello, gorgeous!' she sings down the phone, and I'm immediately warmed up, feeling like life is being injected back into me. She tells me about her new opera obsession, and how she's learning to sing. 'I joined a little opera group, we're doing *Tosca*!' she says.

Marian never went back to the art class after I left. 'How could I?' she said when I asked. 'They treated you like absolute doo-doo, darling. Besides, there isn't an art teacher in the country who's a patch on you.'

I appreciate her loyalty. I know how much she enjoyed the class – it can't have been easy to leave.

'So, how is life on the moon?' she asks.

'It's great, Sabrina came to see us, but now I feel really rough,' I tell her.

'Is it connected to the fragrant Sabrina's visit? From what you tell me, that one could make anyone feel rough. I'm sure she's the last thing you needed.'

'Yes, she came to talk to Emilio about her sister – remember I told you about his wife Gina, who's gone travelling?'

235

'Oh yes, the beautiful Martini heiress! Oh darling, you mix in such glamorous circles. What I wouldn't give to cling to the hem of your gown as you drag me down a red carpet.'

I laugh at this image. 'You do cheer me up, Marian.'

'Why, are you sad?'

'A little, I don't feel well. I keep being sick, I don't know what's wrong with me.'

'Sweetie, it's probably just a bug and you'll be fine in a few days.'

'I'm sure you're right.'

'I know I keep saying I'll come and see you, but I promise I will, very soon,' she says.

'I'd love that. Come any time.'

'I'll wait until you're feeling better and we'll make a date. Ooh, talking of dates, I'm being whisked away on a man's mega-yacht.'

'Oh, is that a euphemism, Marian?' I tease.

'You are so naughty!' She giggles like a schoolgirl. 'Yes, an old chum from Palermo got in touch – he's in his seventies, far too old for me, but he's my sugar daddy, has a huge yacht and plenty of lolly. Anyhoo, he's invited me to cruise the Med on his big one!'

I giggle at this.

'I had to tell him – I won't be putting out, I'm not one of those girls.' She chuckles to herself. 'Anyway, it's November, won't be that warm, so he won't be seeing me in my skimpy beachwear – good job, it might inflame him, and at his age . . .'

'Marian, you are outrageous.' As happy as I am here, when Emilio is working long hours it can get a bit lonely, and her phone calls just lift me. She's kept me going.

'Well, as my lovely mother always said, if you don't laugh you'll cry, and we can't have any of that. So, I'm setting off the day after tomorrow for a month around the Med, all expenses paid!'

'I'll miss our chats. Don't think I can go a whole month.'

'Oh we'll stay in radio contact, my darling. If and when I get a signal I'll call or text.'

'Yes please. I'm sorry, I feel a bit nauseous, so I'll have to go, Marian.'

'You're not preggers, are you, darling?' she asks, suddenly sounding serious. For the first time in our friendship, we're both unusually silent, and I see this shaft of light come through the window. The grey landscape suddenly has a silvery sheen.

'I don't think so,' I say, 'but I hadn't even considered that.' Then we say our goodbyes, and I run to the bathroom to be sick. After retching for a few minutes, I can't be sick, but I have to sit in there for a while until the feeling passes, and when it does, something occurs to me.

I dig out my suitcase from under the bed that I still have old stuff in from before I came here. And after much searching, I eventually find what I'm looking for in the bottom of a small toiletry bag. It's been there for several years, and it might not even work anymore, but it's worth a try.

Emilio returns from work exhausted, but is still sweet enough to take an interest in my artwork, which is piled on my desk – the photographs, wedding invites, significant dates and tickets, the souvenirs of a life together.

'Using your old laptop, I've worked with digital images, pixels and strategically placed dots, and if you stand back you can see Simon's face,' I say, gently guiding him backwards.

'Wow, it's made from tiny photographs of his life from a baby, and all kinds of other stuff . . .' He's screwing up his eyes, really taking it all in.

'Yeah, school days, the football team, our wedding, significant train tickets, sweet wrappers, our tickets for Glastonbury. I used to keep stuff like this, Simon always said I was a hoarder, but now I'm glad I did. I brought it with me from the UK in my luggage. I couldn't leave it behind.'

Having lost my dad at an early age, I didn't want to lose anyone or anything else. All my life I've preserved memories. I find it difficult to part with the smallest thing.

'I don't know a lot about art, but I think you should try and exhibit this project when you've finished.'

I shrug. 'Thanks, but at the rate I'm going it won't ever be finished. I'm finding it so hard to focus at the moment, there seem to be no certainties right now.'

'I know, I feel the same. I called the police – I felt I should add my voice to Sabrina's. I called the observatory in Hawaii too, left a message. I just need to know she's okay. It's time to find Gina and get on with our lives,' he says.

'What did the police say?'

'They took down details, and asked if I thought she "wants to be found". I sometimes wonder . . .' he adds.

'Yes, it'll be good to know she's okay, living her life – and we can then live ours.'

'Exactly, she'll turn up.'

'I hope so. You need that divorce – being Catholic.'

He looks at me, puzzled.

'Isn't it a sin in your church to have a child outside marriage?'

'Yeah, it's a bit old-fashioned, but I guess so,' he's saying, then he suddenly looks at me. 'What?'

'It's not a game changer for me, but it would be nice to get married before the baby comes,' I say, holding my breath for his response. *How will he take this?*

He's looking from my stomach to my face. For a moment, I really don't know how he's going to react. 'Are you telling me we're having a baby Sophie?'

I'm nodding, my eyes filling with tears, and his face lights up as he wraps me in his arms. The old pregnancy test I had in my suitcase from a previous life produced a strong blue line swiftly and clearly.

'I know we didn't plan this, and I'm as surprised as you are, but you're okay, aren't you?' I ask.

He looks at me, holding my face with both his hands. 'Sophie, I've dreamed of this, but I never thought it would happen for me.' He guides me to the sofa. 'We have to be careful with you. We're miles from the nearest hospital and this is so precious. You sit down, relax, let me cook dinner,' he says.

'I think I'm going to like being pregnant.'

'You mustn't do anything too strenuous,' he's saying. 'From now on, I lift everything. Don't even lift a cup, I'll put it to your lips,' he jokes.

We lie together on the sofa for the next few hours, talking about our baby, what they will be called, how we'll bring them up, who they will be. All the practical stuff about whether we'll stay here or go back to Taormina we can save for another day. Tonight is about our dream coming true and the universe handing us the greatest gift ever. I am delirious; I feel so lucky and happy. I've never felt closer to anyone, or more in love. But after everything that's happened, I'm almost scared to be happy, because in my experience happiness is often followed by something bad waiting just around the corner.

44

Yesterday was one of the best days of my life. It started grey and cold and I felt like I was drowning in ash. But then a little sunshine forced its way through the clouds after taking the pregnancy test. I just wanted to see his face – and as long as I live I'll never forget his smile; it was wonderful.

This morning, he's very attentive, insisting I stay in bed, making me promise to take care and rest.

But I get up. 'I'm not sick, just pregnant,' I say. I planned to do some work today – sketches of Simon, some from memory, and some from photographs. The point is to see how I remember him compared to how he was. I think being in a new, different relationship gives me perspective.

Before he leaves for work, Emilio looks at the piece I started working on earlier today. It's a large charcoal sketch of Simon I ripped into several pieces then stapled together again.

'This is interesting, it gives me chills,' he says.

'It's meant to. When he emerged from one of many operations, he told me he felt like he'd been ripped apart and put together again.'

'Does it bother you, to work with photos of him?'

'It makes me sad. We started out so happy and hopeful. People take too much for granted,' I say sadly. 'How does it make you feel, to know I spend all this time poring over the past?'

'I see it as something good coming from something bad.' He gazes at the sketch, rests his fingertips gently on the staples that jut out of the smooth surface, the soft charcoal.

'It was brutal,' I murmur. 'But see, in the background, look closely.'

He leans into the picture. 'Is that a butterfly?'

'Yes, it's a reminder that life continues – it went on before us and it will go on after us. I'm trying to inject some positive light into these pieces. I'm going to paint the butterfly in vivid colours, but keep the rest in charcoal.'

'I think it's brilliant. It speaks to me. It says, "Live your life, don't focus on tomorrow or next week, just grab everything precious and hold it to you. All we have is now."'

'Yeah, that's exactly it.' I smile. 'And I want what we have now. I just feel guilty sometimes that I'm so happy.'

'Don't be. You were a young widow, Sophie. He wouldn't have wanted you to spend the rest of your life alone.'

I glance at the memories scattered in squares on the desk. My eyes rest on a photo of Mum, pregnant with me, with no partner to hold her hand. I know my life will be different.

'You're so precious,' he says as he kisses me goodbye and puts his palm on my stomach. 'Bye baby, be good,' he whispers to my belly, which as yet shows no sign of what's to come. I wave from the little window as he sets off in his truck, and wonder at life and all its shocks and surprises. Who'd have thought that I'd be having a baby with the sophisticated designer-clad man I saw walking out of Dior that day? And who would have known then that he had an alter ego – the unshaven, volcano-obsessed scientist, walking around in dirty boots and frayed old jumpers. I love whichever one he chooses to be. Waving him off from the little window, my heart is filled with so much happiness my face is in a permanent smile.

◆　◆　◆

Emilio returns from the hub this evening, and opening the door to greet him, I see his face and my world goes dark.

From the moment he walks in, I know something's wrong.

'How are you?' he says, unsmiling. 'Are you feeling okay, darling, no problems?' he asks, looking at my tummy.

'I'm fine . . . we're fine,' I add, looking into his face for a clue, but he's impossible to read.

'Good, good . . .'

My heart sinks. He seems preoccupied, far away. *Has the pregnancy freaked him out after all? Has he had time to think today and feels differently now?*

'How was your day?' I hear myself croak, wondering what the hell is wrong now. I was so happy just seconds ago.

'It wasn't good. It's Gina . . .' He plonks himself down on a chair, rubbing his bristly chin with his hand. 'The observatory in Hawaii called me back today. You might remember I left a voice message? I could kick myself for leaving it to Sabrina. She has no idea – she's an idiot!'

'What . . . what do you mean?'

'About three weeks ago, just before Gina seemed to go offline, Sabrina said she'd called the observatory, but couldn't get through.'

'So . . . what . . . ?' I can't imagine where this is leading, but judging by his ashen face, it's not good. I walk slowly towards him, kneel down beside the chair and touch his hand, and he lifts his other hand and puts it on mine, gently stroking it.

'Well, you know I was starting to worry. It was odd we hadn't heard from her and so I called them just before I left today. I had to wait because of the time difference, so someone would be around. I spoke to a guy I vaguely know, and asked if Gina was okay, as we hadn't heard from her . . . and could he get her to call us . . .'

'And . . . ?'

'He said she never turned up. Sophie, Gina never even arrived in Hawaii.'

45

Emilio is struggling with the news about Gina. He's spoken to Sabrina, who is upset; he's been back on to the police, checked with the airlines and called his friend at the observatory to ask again about the email she sent them. He didn't sleep much last night; he spent a lot of time on his laptop, and I know this sounds mean, but I'm pregnant and selfish – and feel like she's taking him away from me again.

'Perhaps she was having mental health issues?' I suggest over breakfast. 'Perhaps the pressure of work, or her new relationship, sent her to the edge, and she's gone somewhere to lick her wounds? Who knows what torment people feel?'

'Perhaps. But surely she'd have told me . . . or Sabrina?'

'But, hang on, the Instagram photos were all posted in Hawaii.'

He's shaking his head. 'I looked through them all last night. They're mostly close-ups of her, no landmarks, just an ocean or a mountain in the background. She could be anywhere.'

'Wow! So you think she just dumped the NASA offer and went off somewhere with her lover?' I ask.

'Who knows? The police are trying to locate him at the moment.'

My mind is blown. There are so many possibilities and permutations. 'If she has just disappeared without telling the people that care about her, it's incredibly selfish.'

'She can be incredibly selfish,' he says distractedly.

'Perhaps the police are on to something, asking if you're sure she wants to be found?' I sigh. 'I just don't get it.'

'Neither do I,' he says. 'I'm going to work. I need to think about something else, it's driving me mad.'

I spend the morning working, but I can't really concentrate, my head is so full of Gina. If I'm completely honest, I'm not sure I care that some beautiful, spoiled, rich woman has decided to give up her job and take to the seas with her young lover, or whatever. Good luck to her, I say, but unfortunately this is going to slow the divorce down, and if they don't find her soon and start divorce proceedings my baby will be born to a man who is married to someone other than their mother, just like I was.

Anyway, a mug of hot chocolate warms me and cheers me up a little. My mood is raised further by a hilarious text from Marian about her travels involving her 'sugar daddy' and 'his enormous vessel'.

I am actually giggling when my phone rings, until I pick it up and see Abbi's name on the screen. In my first few weeks in Catania I received lots of calls and messages complaining that I'd gone without saying goodbye. She talked about me 'throwing away our friendship' – but she was the one who did that when she reported me to the university and said I'd assaulted Marian. I almost don't pick up, but now I'm pregnant I want to tell everyone, and there aren't many people here to tell – I will enjoy telling her how happy I am and how perfect my life is here with Emilio.

I'm very cool when I pick up.

'Hello, Abbi,' I say.

'Hey, Sophie, are you okay?' She sounds concerned.

'Yes, I'm great. No thanks to you.'

'What do you mean?'

'You know exactly what I mean – you got me fired!'

She feigns surprise at this and, when I explain, she of course denies telling my boss I assaulted a student.

'Honestly, Sophie, I wouldn't do something so evil,' she says. I'm not so sure.

'Whatever, you could never be happy for me. Anyway, Emilio and I have moved to Catania, on the slopes, in a little cabin. It's wonderful and we're very happy, thank you,' I say coldly.

'You're still with Emilio?'

'Of course,' I snap. The days of listening to her criticism, leaving me doubting everything I do, are long gone.

'Oh . . . I'm surprised you're still with him, given what's happened?'

'What are you talking about?' I ask wearily. Here we go again with the criticism.

'You don't know?'

'I've no idea, Abbi,' I say. Why does she have to drag it out and get the most drama out of everything?

'Have you seen the news this morning?'

'No, I'm busy.'

'Looks like his wife's been found.'

'Whose wife?' I ask. But I know. *She's back!*

'Gina of course!'

'How do you know?'

'It's all over the news! I'm WhatsApping you now. Brace yourself, Sophie.'

What the fuck?

My phone pings, and everything starts to spiral.

The body of a woman found in the Valle del Bove in Sicily is believed to be that of Gina Caprini, volcanologist and heiress to the Caprini Martini empire.

Police helicopters began the search where Ms Caprini was last seen after the family reported her missing when they hadn't heard from her for over two weeks.

Ms Caprini, who hasn't been seen by family and friends since May, had been offered a prestigious NASA research post at the Hawaiian Volcano Observatory. However, a spokesman for the world-renowned institution said the volcanologist never arrived in Hawaii. 'Ms Caprini was due to arrive to take a senior research post in June, but emailed us just hours before to say she'd changed her mind and would be staying in Catania to do important work there.'

Award-winning volcano expert Gina Caprini, 43, was married to fellow volcanologist Emilio Ferrante, 46. The couple, both respected academics who last year celebrated ten years of marriage, were well known on the Sicilian party scene. Also praised for their charity work, in 2021 they set up a foundation, Past and Present, to focus on how the study of volcanoes can inform, and potentially save, the future of the planet.

A police spokesman said: 'We are waiting for the forensic report, but it seems that the body may have been here for several months, but I can't yet confirm. The death is currently being treated as suspicious.'

No formal identification has taken place, but police say the family of Ms Caprini have been informed.

I stare at the screen on my phone. *Fuck!* I don't know what to think; I can't begin to process this, and I read it again. I'm genuinely in shock, and immediately think of Emilio, and Sabrina too. I guess I hadn't faced the possibility of Gina being dead. What does this mean now? My mind immediately goes to her young lover. I wonder if something happened between them?

'Are you okay, Sophie?' Abbi is saying. 'Talk to me. I need to know you're okay?'

'Yes, I'm fine,' I snap, as irritated by her as ever.

'You have to admit it's really dodge, Sophie. I mean, he was seeing you, and his wife suddenly goes missing.'

'I started seeing him after she left – and she wasn't missing, she was abroad on a trip,' I say in a monotone, refusing to match her hysteria.

'Well, I'm watching the news now and they're saying she never left Sicily. She hasn't been anywhere. She might have been dead since *June!*'

'We don't know anything—' I start.

'Sophie, are you still in denial? I knew he was gaslighting you – and now we know why.'

I feel nauseous. I have to get her off the phone.

'I told you this would end badly – I knew it! I'm really worried for you. Men like him get bored easily; she was some kind of heiress,

248

and she looked like a model. If he can get bored of someone like that, he can get bored of you – no offence.'

'Offence taken.'

'Sophie, listen to me, get out while you can. Leave him now, or you'll be next!'

I press the end call button and take deep breaths.

Time has passed, I've no idea how much. Minutes, an hour, two? I'm breathing, but tears are streaming down my face. I never expected this, I never in a million years thought she'd be dead.

Suddenly, my phone rings, making my heart leap. If it's Abbi, I'm not picking up. Ever again.

I glance at the screen – it's Emilio. My heart is racing, and I might just burst into tears when I hear his voice.

'Darling, it's me, have you seen the news?'

'Yes. I'm so sorry, Emilio, none of it makes sense.' I want to say so much, but he talks over me.

'The police left me messages, but I didn't get them until I went back to the hub. Charlotte and I are working out on the north side. It's desolate there, the signal comes and goes. There's not another soul, it's so, so quiet.'

I'm trying not to envisage the two of them completely alone in the beautiful wilderness of Etna.

'That's heartbreaking. Can't you come home? Leave work, you can't work with all this going on.'

'Yes, I'll come home, but first the police want to interview me . . .'

'Oh!' My heart is in my throat; I feel sick again.

'It's fine, only an interview. I'm the husband, of course they'll want to interview me. I imagine they'll see Sabrina too.'

'I hope she doesn't say anything.'

'What do you mean?'

'She was just pointing the finger a bit when she was here. I didn't say anything to you because I didn't want to upset you but she said she thought you'd been posting stuff on Gina's Instagram. I'm only telling you now in case it comes up with the police.'

'Oh God,' he groans.

'She said you know her passwords.'

'Yes, this is true, but I'm sure Sabrina knows her passwords too.'

'Yeah, well, I guess she was worried and just looking for someone to blame. But now I'm thinking – the police are saying she may have been dead for a while, so it looks like *someone's* been impersonating her on social media.'

'It would seem that way,' he sighs.

We say our goodbyes and I put down the phone, worried about Emilio. If the police interview Sabrina she'll say all kinds of things – she's just a liar, and I'm beginning to wonder if Gina was the same?

I'm horrified, and sad about her death, but I'm not devastated, and I feel guilty but I can't grieve for someone I never knew. As Sabrina pointed out, I only know her through Emilio's eyes. And now I'm having unwanted thoughts about his part in all this. What really happened in their marriage? Was Emilio genuinely convinced she was fine, and in Hawaii – or did he know something? Has Emilio known all along that his wife never made it to Hawaii?

46

I barely have time to even think about my conversation with Emilio when my phone rings again.

'Have you heard?'

'Sabrina, I have. I'm so, so sorry.'

'I can't stop crying. My heart's just breaking, Sophie, what will I do without her?'

'I know, I know, and all the time we thought she was in Hawaii with her beloved volcanoes. It doesn't bear thinking about.'

'When the police called this morning to tell me, I just screamed down the phone. How can I go on without her? My life will never be the same.'

Only Sabrina could make the discovery of her sister's body all about her.

'I always knew there was a chance she'd come to harm,' she's saying. 'She took risks, she loved the thrill of life, you know? I just can't get my head around the fact she's gone!'

'It's impossible to comprehend, I didn't know your sister, but I feel like I did,' I tell her.

'I knew it was her the minute the police told me what she was wearing. Who else would be wandering the craters of Etna in the middle of May in a vintage Chanel ski jacket in winter white?'

I'm exhausted; my head is whirling with so many worrying scenarios, but also I'm wondering how all this will affect me, the baby and Emilio. I remind myself that this is about Emilio and Sabrina's grief, and whatever happens, I must support them both.

Sabrina's obviously distraught. 'I just keep thinking about her body, twisted and mangled at the bottom of that crater. She's been there for more than six months you know.'

'How has no one spotted her?'

'There are almost three hundred craters on Etna, and police say it was a crater on the east side that no one ever goes to. Only someone with knowledge of the area would know it exists. It's a thousand metres down; she would have landed heavily from that height and was probably submerged in volcanic dust. The jacket would have absorbed some of the dirt, which camouflaged her, and then later, when the snow came . . . she stayed hidden.'

'That vintage Chanel winter-white ski jacket,' I hear myself murmur nonsensically as I shake my head.

'I know. I told her she should have bought the cropped pink and purple puffer – if she had, she might have been spotted sooner. It may have saved her life.'

'She didn't survive the fall, surely?' I ask, horrified, imagining her lying there with broken limbs, dying of hunger and thirst. A slow, painful death, her broken body unable to sustain life.

'The police said to assume she didn't survive the fall, but I think they were just saying that to stop me screaming. I guess the post-mortem will tell the story.'

'Do they know why she was there?'

'No . . . she seems to have gone off-grid once she reached Catania. The thing is, we should have reported her missing sooner – but Emilio kept saying she was fine.'

My heart sinks. So she hasn't given up on this? 'He thought she *was* fine. He was messaging her and she was messaging back!'

'That's what he says! But now I ask again, what if he was pretending to be her on Instagram? He didn't see her for months, and he did nothing, Sophie.'

She still seems determined to point the finger at Emilio, and now a body has been found she has something more solid to go on. I'm really worried for him, and my hand instinctively rests on my abdomen.

'Have you told the police about her student lover?' I ask, trying to distract her. 'Perhaps *he* knows what happened?'

'They're looking for him, but he had no reason to kill her.'

'You don't know that. He must have wondered where she was. Why didn't he report her missing early on?'

'Why didn't her husband?'

'Why didn't her sister?' I reply softly. I hate myself for being so mean, but she needs to see that Emilio isn't the only one with a target on his back here.

'He was her husband. He's next of kin, he's the one responsible for her safety. Stop being so horrible, Sophie, I'm grieving!' she says, like a little girl.

I make one last bid to shut down her conviction that Emilio is responsible for Gina's death. 'Do you know what I think? That the press is going to turn this into a crime story – a beautiful heiress, her handsome husband, both rich and successful. They might even have photos of the lookalike sister and consider the part she played in all this. They might ask if there was sibling rivalry, if the younger sister was jealous of her big sister's beauty and success . . . they might find someone who says you had a crush on Emilio, for example?'

'I do not!'

'No, I wasn't saying you do,' I lie. 'But just like you're saying Emilio is guilty because of a, b and c, I'm sure someone else could come up with just as many motives for *you* to be Gina's killer. After all, she was the heir, you're the spare, and we all know how that plays out. Bitter, jealous, resentful – and hell-bent on revenge.'

'Wow! That's nasty.'

'I didn't mean to be nasty,' I reply in a sweet voice.

Silence.

'If you want my theory as to what happened,' I start, though she clearly doesn't, 'your sister was probably holed up in a gorgeous hotel in Catania with her new lover. She may or may not have been going to Hawaii, but that was her story so she could spend time away from everyone, and just be with him. They went for a long walk together, and she stepped out on to the edge, and fell. And I hope I'm wrong, but they might discover his body down there too one day.'

'I find that difficult to believe.'

'We may never know what happened, but you and Emilio are always saying how she didn't like rules, she wasn't scared of things. She flew too close to the flame – she probably danced on the edge of the volcano,' I add gently. 'Perhaps she died as she lived: young, beautiful and reckless.'

'That's horrific, but quite lovely, I might use that in the eulogy if it's okay with you?'

'Knock yourself out,' I say. She really is a psychopath.

'But despite your lovely storytelling, the police are treating her death as suspicious, so I'm not buying her fall.' She hesitates, then goes back into grieving mode. 'I'm upset and scared . . . she was like a mother to me.'

'I feel for you. Emilio's struggling too.'

'Emilio, struggling? I don't think so. Oh, I guess you don't know?'

'What?'

'Turns out Gina never changed her will, so on her death, he gets everything.'

This is not good news. It puts him right into the frame.

'Your boyfriend is now a very rich man. If he can stay out of prison. Do you still think he's innocent of murder, Sophie?'

When I put down the phone, my heart is so heavy. She was saving that bit for last, the jewel in her twisted crown.

Do you still think he's innocent of murder, Sophie?

Why didn't I know about the will? He's never mentioned it – but why would he, we didn't know she was dead. At least, *I* didn't know she was dead. Perhaps Sabrina is right and *he's* behind the posts on her Instagram? *Someone* had to be if the police are right and Gina died months ago. Perhaps Sabrina's the only one with her eyes open, and I've been so blinded by love I haven't seen it? I thought the messages he showed me between the two of them were proof they'd been in touch. But he was messaging whoever was operating her account – and therefore maybe messaging himself? Perhaps the way he talked about not using social media was all an act to put me off the scent?

No. No. No. I have to believe he's innocent, that the police will find that someone else did it or their investigation opens up another possibility. It might have been suicide, or a tragic accident, or an unnamed, unknown lover who never appeared again? It can't be Emilio!

But the universe is cruel, and as I glance at my phone, a breaking news story reveals the worst possible thing has just happened.

47

I see the words *uomo arrestato per omicidio*. My Italian is still dodgy, but I know this means a man has been arrested for murder. I use Google to translate the story.

> A man was arrested today on suspicion of the murder of Gina Caprini, heiress to the Caprini Martini fortune. The body of Ms Caprini, a volcanologist and Research Professor at Taormina University, was discovered yesterday in the base of Valle del Bove, a volcanic crater, on the eastern side of Mount Etna.
>
> The area is considered to be dangerous and unpredictable, with an extremely deep valley, and no shelter. Hikers are advised only to attempt walks here with an experienced guide, at times of safety and on recommended routes. However, as a volcanologist, with many years' experience, and familiar with the terrain, Ms Caprini may have taken a different, and potentially dangerous, route.
>
> This is a breaking story.

For a few minutes, I tell myself it isn't necessarily Emilio. Perhaps they've found the lover? Or they've arrested a stranger who happened to be walking past on the day it happened, and pushed her? There's the drug angle too, with Sabrina's 'little problem' being managed by Gina. Was she paying off drug dealers and putting herself in danger for her little sister?

But within the hour, I've received a call from the police informing me that Emilio is in custody and the police are now inviting me to the *stazione di polizia* for an interview, and a car is on its way.

I'm so nauseous, I have to get out of the house, so I open the door and run out into the cold air. But this seems to make me feel worse, and within seconds I'm vomiting hot, bitter liquid into the snow, the acrid taste making me cringe as I spit out the remnants of vomit. Grabbing a handful of snow, I put it in my mouth to take away the sourness, but now all I taste is ash. I stand for a while, and try to remember the good times here.

When I first arrived, our planet was a silver sanctuary, diffused sunlight turning the ash into glitter and the sea into pure platinum. I thought we'd landed, that after all the hurt and sadness, other people's judgement and noise, we had finally found home.

I saw Etna as shelter – a permanent, comforting presence standing over ten thousand feet high, always there, a smouldering keeper of secrets.

With Emilio I've learned so much about the natural world; we've hiked along paths made from lava stopped in its tracks, frozen in time. 'In the past are our clues to the future,' he always says. Sometimes, at home, he's called me to join him outside and we watch firework displays of orange lava shoot into the night sky.

But today the sky's turned black, and it feels like the calm before the storm. I stand small in the shadow of Europe's most dangerous volcano; activity is increasing, and the eruption rate climbing by the day. This is no sanctuary, I'm not safe here anymore; something is happening that I have no control over. The ground trembles, and I feel the warmth of his breath as he whispers in my ear: 'This is how continents are made, darling.'

I suddenly see a vehicle in the distance, and know this must be the car that will take me to the police station and back to reality.

◆ ◆ ◆

I assumed that my visit to the police station would be a formality, but the mostly male officers who I encounter in the first few minutes put me on my guard. They don't smile, and their voices seem angry as they deliver me to a bare room, with just a table, a couple of chairs, and a few posters on the wall. The stale smell of cigarettes hangs over me like a cloud, and I'm immediately triggered, recalling the watcher. Who were they, and what were they trying to do?

I try to distract myself by translating the posters, most of them demanding *ATTENZIONE*. If I wasn't scared before, I am now.

Eventually, the door opens and two detectives walk in. One nods at me, while the other studiously ignores me.

It's soon apparent that their English is no better than my Italian, so *il colloquio* – the interview – is halted for an hour and a half, until a translator arrives. She's the first person to smile at me, and she feels like my only friend in the world right now. She immediately confirms that Emilio is the man who's been arrested for murder. I knew it, but I'm in shock, and I'm almost sick again.

During the course of a very confusing set of questions, it's established that I'm Emilio's partner, and they now want details. They're asking about the times and dates of when we met, if he ever told me he hated his wife, had he ever given me any reason to feel scared? Just so many questions, my head is buzzing, and I don't know how best to answer, but it seems that the more I plead

Emilio's innocence the less they see me as the innocent girlfriend, and more an accomplice! My stomach is churning, and my heart is beating so fast I think I might faint. The looks that pass between the two men are tense, knowing, and the questions are probing and personal. But when they ask me if I hated Gina, if I wanted her dead, I have to hold on to the table. My eyes turn to the translator, pleading with her to help me, but she isn't a lawyer, and I feel I'm in deep water.

'Surely, it would be in your interests for his wife to be dead and the inheritance in your lover's hands?' she translates. Christ, the inheritance. I smell Sabrina's influence.

I can't hold this off a minute longer, and ask for a lawyer, which seems to annoy the lead detective, who informs the translator that it won't be necessary, they are now concluding the interview. They clearly don't have enough evidence to detain me any longer, and I almost cry with relief, but it's bittersweet because I'm leaving Emilio here.

'Can I see Emilio?' I ask the translator. 'Or speak to him by phone?' She asks, and the response is that he's being interviewed.

I leave the room, realising I haven't helped get him home – in fact it's quite the opposite, and what I've said has made him look even guiltier. I told them the dates we started seeing each other because I wanted to be honest about that, but the fact he had a girlfriend so soon after Gina went missing now looks very suspect. And what's more, I might now be implicated in Gina's death too.

I head for the exit, where at my request the officer at the front desk orders me a taxi. And when it eventually arrives, I walk out into the cold afternoon to where a horde of people are gathered, one or two with cameras, others clutching microphones and recording devices.

What the hell?

'Sophie, Sophie, did you help your lover kill his wife?'

'Sophie, were you jealous of Gina?'

I'm frozen to the spot. More and more faces seem to be coming at me; I hear Italian voices speaking English, all saying words like 'murder' and 'lover' and 'money'. Inside, I'm screaming. I never asked for any of this, and now, just because I fell in love with someone, I've landed right in the middle of this hell! And as they jostle me, thrusting cameras and microphones in my face, I'm frightened for my own safety. I run back into the police station, where the desk officer looks up, like I've forgotten something.

'Paparazzi,' I say, knowing he'll understand. 'I need help to get to the taxi.'

He looks bored, and for a moment I think he's just going to refuse and I'll have to fight my own way to the waiting car. But he calls over a couple of other officers, and they escort me outside, and through the now-growing crowd of press.

I jump in the car, feeling tearful now.

'You want to go back to your home?' the driver says in broken English.

'Yes please.'

'I saw on the TV news just minutes ago. It's the same there. *La Stampa*, they wait for you outside your house in trucks with cameras and microphones.'

'They're at my home, near Etna?' I ask, despairingly.

He nods. 'You might want to go somewhere else.'

But where else can I go? Marian is away with her friend on a yacht, and I refuse to see Abbi, so the only person I can think of is Sabrina. I know she's still at the house in Taormina. But can I trust her? Do I have any choice?

The skies are darkening. I'm returning to a desolate house alone with all my fears, and the added horror of journalists peering into the windows trying to get a photo.

I can see how this looks – the handsome husband, the rich dead wife, and the younger mistress, it's a great story. I should have known this would happen. Being here was supposed to be my escape, but now I'm involved in an even bigger mess.

I punch in Sabrina's number.

'Hey queen,' she says.

'Hi Sabrina, I need a favour.'

'What do you want?' She sounds dubious, like she isn't sure she wants to help me.

'Thing is, I have a few problems?'

'Wow! Understatement? Emilio's been arrested for murder and the newspapers have christened you as the biggest slut this side of the Med!'

'That's not helpful, Sabrina. Look, I'm in a taxi right now, and I wondered if I could lie low at the house with you for a while?'

She seems to hesitate. 'Okay, queen. So, you finally realised what he is, what he's *done*?'

'No, I still don't believe he's done anything to Gina. But I can't go home, because the press are there.'

'Oh gosh, how glamorous.'

'Hardly.'

'Well, so much for standing by your man, eh?'

'I believe he's innocent,' I say, though now I'm not as sure as I was. 'Thing is, I need to stay somewhere where I can be safe and calm, and not get too stressed.'

'Good luck with that.'

'No, I mean it. I'm pregnant.'

'Oh shit, no!'

'Thanks, we're thrilled,' I reply sarcastically.

'I don't believe it.'

'I was surprised. Obviously I'm happy, but I am concerned it might not be the best timing.'

'His wife's dead and his girlfriend's pregnant? No, not the PR dream, is it?'

'Sabrina, please don't tell anyone.'

'Me? Tell anyone?'

48

I'm in the taxi on the way to Sabrina's wondering if I'm driving to a safe haven, or straight into hell. She was clearly not happy about my pregnancy – her reaction was horrible.

I still can't work her out. Is she just moody, or is she knowingly manipulative? Sometimes I think I feel genuine warmth towards her, and she seems kind and funny. But if her mixed messages to me are confusing then the way she is with Emilio is even worse. Her flirty affection towards him contradicts her desperate need to constantly point the finger at him regarding Gina's disappearance . . . and now her death.

But right now, I have no choice but to throw myself at her mercy and stay with her for a while, because it isn't just about me anymore. The emotional stress of all this is bad for the baby, and I can't risk being physically accosted by photographers and reporters too. I feel like I'm between the devil and the deep blue sea, because I'm putting our lives in Sabrina's hands.

It's dark, cold and raining by the time I arrive at Sabrina's. I pull my jacket around me, and pay the taxi driver with the only coins I have left. I was in Catania as Emilio's partner, he was supporting me, and now he's been arrested, his bank accounts have been temporarily frozen. I'm going to need Sabrina until he's released. And he will be, I have every faith.

I step out on to the pavement. The house is in darkness, and it occurs to me that Sabrina might not be home, but I dismiss this fear and walk up the steps to the front door and knock. Waiting at the door, I think back to the first time I came here. Sabrina was gazing from an upstairs window, then standing in the doorway almost barring us from entering. I'm filled with foreboding as I knock again, dread taking little bites at me as the seconds go by. There's no light springing on inside, no sudden rattling of locks and Sabrina shouting 'Hey queen!' as she opens the heavy wooden door. I go down a few steps and lean across to the window, banging hard on the shutters, but whoever's inside the house can't hear me, or is choosing not to. I check my watch. It's 11 p.m., early for Sabrina, but what if she's had a drink and fallen asleep, or worse, taken drugs? Emilio reckons she's been clean for years, but it would be just my luck if she relapsed tonight.

It's cold and raining harder now; I can't stay out in this weather. But I have nowhere else to go. I can't even think about a hotel in case someone recognises me as the scarlet woman who lured Emilio from his perfect marriage.

Defeated, I plonk myself down on the steps. Sabrina isn't here – did she *ever* intend to be? Is this another one of her mean tricks? I think about the sweater she gave me; she seduced me into putting it on without question. Then there were the nasty remarks, the sullen expression on our first meeting. The fleeting warmth – was it just that, fleeting? Was it even real? Emilio and I are both in a very vulnerable situation. I gaze ahead absently, working out what to do, where to go. Then something materialises opposite me. My whole body tingles with fear. Someone is standing across the road in the rain. Very still. Just staring. Watching.

I hear myself groan quietly. I feel like a trapped animal. Are they back?

I'm sure it's the watcher. I'd recently questioned if the watcher even existed, wondering if it was all part of my feverish imagination while falling in love, before Emilio loved me back.

Now I know this isn't in my head; this is real, too real. Standing up, I steady myself, ready to run, compelled to escape . . . but where to? And if I run, will they simply run after me? I step backwards, pressing myself against the door – the only solid thing in my life right now. I keep my eyes on the now slowly shifting figure, praying they won't leap out. Shit, are they moving this way? The rain seems heavier, sharper; it stings my face as a cold wind moves down the street. Suddenly, they move, and I see it's a young man, in a black hoodie, he's meeting his girlfriend on the corner, they kiss. It isn't the watcher at all. *I'm going mad.*

I slide down the door, sitting with my head resting on my knees. It's growing colder, but the rain is lessening slightly, and I stay there for a long time.

My mind wanders to where it always wanders when I need comfort. I think of Emilio, and how this should have been one of the happiest times of our lives. Tonight we should be sitting by the fire together, the rain lashing down outside. I'm desperate for him to share this pregnancy, to feel the new life growing inside me. But he's locked in a cell at the police station, our home is being stalked by reporters, and our lives have been smashed by the death of his first wife. *She's here again.* Gina always turns up in some form, and even now she's stomping through our happiness. The woman who haunts me, stands behind me at the mirror, whispers in my ear when Emilio and I make love; she watches me as I work, and now I hear her tinkling laughter as her husband sits in a jail cell.

I look up, and for a moment I think she's standing over me, the street light a halo behind her, but it's Sabrina.

'Hey queen?' Sabrina is standing there – red lips, leather biker jacket over a glitzy mini skirt – smirking.

'You should have said you were going out,' I say. 'I wouldn't have insisted on coming here.'

'I didn't know I'd be out. The police contacted me just after you called. They wanted to talk to me down at the station.'

She's unlocking the door as she tells me this. 'They asked *so* many questions.' She pushes the door open and steps inside.

'About who?' I ask, following her in, my feet squelching water, my hair dripping around my face.

'Everyone! Emilio, Gina, *you.*'

'It sounds like they don't have enough on Emilio if they're asking about us,' I say, then go cold. 'You didn't say anything about the baby?'

'That you are pregnant? Yes, of course.' She's standing in the hallway, looking at me like it was the most innocent thing.

'I *told* you not to tell anyone.'

'Babe, when the police ask questions, I answer! I don't want any more trouble with the police,' she replies. 'Besides, everyone will know soon enough when your belly pops.'

'It's about the timing, Sabrina,' I say through gritted teeth. I'm so angry with her, but at the same time I need her.

Taking off her jacket, she stops to look at me. 'So, he bumps his wife off in May, starts dating you in June, and now it's December and you're pregnant. He's totally fucked. He didn't think this through, did he?'

God, I wish I was anywhere but here, with the resentful, unpredictable Sabrina, who's just taken off her jacket to reveal a full-on sparkly mini-dress more suited to a nightclub than a police station. Was she really with the police this evening, or is she lying about that? Can I believe anything she tells me?

'But don't be too disappointed, Sophie, if he can avoid a murder conviction and stay out of prison, he'll be a daddy *and* a multimillionaire – looks like you hit the jackpot!'

I wonder if she cares as much about her sister as she does about the multimillion-euro inheritance she stands to gain if Emilio ends up in prison?

I close the front door behind us and, walking through the hallway, I glimpse the stairs leading up to Gina's bedroom. Only she knows the secret of her death, only she knows who pushed her down into that crater, in the shadow of Etna, the only witness to her killing.

The fortune teller told me to *beware, teste di moro, too many secrets, someone lies and someone dies . . .* and now I know who dies, but to tell my *own* future, I need to know, who *lies*?

49

I follow Sabrina into the kitchen. 'Help yourself to whatever you want.' She flops on a chair while I take a glass from the cupboard and fill it with tap water.

'You won't believe this, but the police asked if we were a throuple!' She chuckles to herself at this.

'Hardly,' I snap. She found out today that her sister's dead and the brother-in-law she seemed so close to has been arrested. How can she laugh at *anything*?

Suddenly I hear a noise outside; it's probably an owl but it freaks me out. 'That noise made me jump,' I say. 'Did you hear it?'

'Oh, that's just Gina, she knows you're pregnant, she's come to haunt the shit out of you,' she chuckles. Again. Is she *insane*?

'That's not funny,' I reply, unsmiling. 'The last time I saw you, you told me Gina and I would have liked each other.'

'Yeah, but that was before I found out she was dead and you were pregnant – with her husband's baby.'

'Look, Sabrina. I need to stay here for just a few days, I would appreciate some kindness.'

She rolls her eyes. 'Kindness? That reminds me, one of your weirdo friends turned up this afternoon. She had a phone case with "Be Kind" on the front.'

'Abbi. What did she want?'

'She said she thought you might be here. She's going to call back at some point. She said you'd know what it was about.'

'Yes, I do, and she'd better not come anywhere near me,' I reply. Abbi's left about ten messages since we spoke this morning, I listened to them in the car on the way over here. 'I'm so sad for you, I'm here if you need me. Shall I come to Catania or are you coming back to Taormina? I've missed you so much Sophie.' Ugh, I can't even.

'She's not happy with you, said something about you promising her you'd go with her on a trip to Rome, and she never understood why you got together with Emilio.'

God, will she ever move on? I don't have the headspace to even think about Abbi, but the idea of her coming here creeps me out. 'Mmm, she probably thinks I dumped Emilio within hours of his arrest. She must think I'm young, free and single, and dying to go to Rome to fetishise some monuments with her.'

'Ugh, spare me that. I've seen her, remember, and that revolting image of her *fetishising* will live rent-free in my head now.'

'I'm tired,' I say. 'Do you mind if I go to bed?'

She leads me upstairs and to my surprise turns right, in the direction of Gina's room that she once shared with Emilio.

'Here we are. Thought you should have the best room, given that you're expecting,' she says, pushing the door open.

Shocked, I reluctantly follow her in, but I don't want to stay in here. This is the bedroom where Gina and Emilio used to sleep.

'But I thought you were sleeping in this room?'

'I was, I felt closer to her here, wearing her clothes, using her stuff. Before we . . . found her, I felt like I was somehow keeping her alive, but now there's no point.' She looks into my eyes for a moment too long. I don't respond, just allow the tension to hang in the air. She's testing me; she thinks I know something.

'So, there's plenty of space in here,' she suddenly says, releasing the tension. 'It's the comfiest bed, and there's a lovely big standalone bath,' she adds, turning on the bedside lamp. 'Sleep well, queen,' she sings breezily, moving quickly out the door. I turn to ask if perhaps there's another room I could stay in, as this feels inappropriate. But she's gone.

I plonk myself on the edge of the huge bed, surrounded by Gina's things. What just happened? Does Sabrina realise how uncomfortable this is for me, or is she genuinely trying to be kind by giving me the best room? Somehow, I doubt it. She must know how being here will make me feel, and putting me in Gina's room is a bit much. But she's letting me stay here at the house, so sadly she's in charge, and if I object, it could create the drama she craves.

Gina's jewellery is scattered all over the dressing table; necklaces hang from the mirror. The matching earrings that Gina was wearing on Instagram are here too.

Several fat jars of expensive face cream sit there expectantly, and a bright tangerine lipstick lies waiting to touch her lips one last time. She was so beautiful, so alive, and being here with her creams and cosmetics, I feel the tragedy of her death. She had all this glorious, luxurious life waiting for her, and she never came back.

I take one of her necklaces and place it around my throat. Then I push a bohemian flower hairpin into my hair after gathering it together in a loose topknot – just like I'd seen her hair on Instagram.

I imagine what it was like to be Gina Caprini, wife of Emilio Ferrante, heiress to the Martini millions. Picking up the tangerine lipstick, I put my lips where hers once were, and gaze into the mirror. I'm expecting to see her stare back at me, but when I look in the mirror, all I see is a cheap, Gina Caprini tribute act.

I press the lipstick hard on to the mirror, and write 'SOPHIE' in angry weals of orange.

◆ ◆ ◆

Jealousy stalks me as I walk from the bedroom to the bathroom.

I haven't seen the bathroom before, and it takes my breath away. It's filled with swathes of pink in every shade, and encased in candy-pink mosaic tiles. A large vanity unit made of pink marble stands against one wall. I caress the smooth stone with my fingertips, my eyes devouring the blush tones and rich burgundy veining of the stone. And right in the middle of the room, the jewel in the crown: a huge, shiny, rose-coloured bath, with flamingo feet in the brightest pink.

Gina's tastes were classy, and expensive – but also wild and fun, and sexy, with a sense of humour. Yes, this room is her most intimate self; it's who she really was, but I had to go through a private door, beyond the pale elegance of the bedroom, to find her.

Beautiful bath oils and lotions in every shade of pink line floating shelves in large glass bottles, next to tubs of French body polish and skin creams as soft as butter. I lift the lid off a tub of cream, dipping my hands into the slippery satin lotion, instinctively lifting my top and gently massaging it into my belly. The gentle rush of tuberose and lavender soothes me, and my mind drifts off, my eyes closing as I caress my tummy. I'm in Gina's bathroom, using her creams on my baby belly, something she never got to do. I feel this huge, unexpected well of sadness open up inside me. I'm here now, enjoying all the things she never will again. I wonder if she's watching me? As I rub Gina's Crème de la Mer into my cheeks, I see something move behind me in the mirror. But when I turn, there's no one there. I put the pot back down, and screw on the lid. I can't do this. I can't take over another woman's life.

Sabrina put me here deliberately to unnerve me, to make me see Gina and compare myself to this woman. Her effervescence, intelligence and beauty were a hard act to follow when she was alive, but now she's dead I can never compete. Like an insect captured in amber, she will always be young and beautiful, perfectly preserved for him to love forever.

Naked, I walk back into the bedroom and open the wardrobe to find a beautiful silk robe, and I drape it around me. It moves over my skin like angel hair, and I gaze at myself in the full-length mirror. Am I morphing into Gina? I'm not sure who I am anymore – do I even exist? Am I the second choice, the pale imitation of his first wife? Is it me who's been the ghost all along?

50

I'm so bone-achingly tired. The anxiety, the pregnancy and late hour are pummelling me, but as exhausted as I am, I can't even close my eyes. Lying stiffly on Gina and Emilio's old bed is weird. Dim light allows shadows to form in all corners of the room, and I long to turn off the lamp, but I'm scared of the dark.

I lie there for a long time, my eyes burning with tiredness, but my head is so jumpy I know sleep won't take me tonight. As I came straight from the police station, I have no clothes of my own and I'm having to wear Gina's stuff. It feels so intimate, wearing her underwear, fabric that once touched her skin now touches mine. The *man* who once touched her skin now touches mine. It's too weird to even think about.

I take a nightdress from the chest of drawers, and as I close it, something rattles. I know I shouldn't go looking, but my curiosity gets the better of me, and I open the drawer further. At the very back, sellotaped to the side, is a mobile phone. I suddenly feel very uneasy, and my scalp tingles as I gently, quietly, pull it away from the wood. I feel hot as I hold it in my hand.

I know I should simply put it back where I found it, and try to forget it's there. But how can I sleep near it all night, knowing it might hold answers. But what if I find something terrible? Will I have to confront Sabrina, then have to tell her I looked at a phone hidden in her sister's room? Should I turn it on? What will I find? Do I really want to know? I go straight to the en-suite bathroom; I need to be safely locked away. Sabrina could walk in on me any minute, and I don't want her to see me looking at the phone. I know it's wrong. But why was it taped to the back of the drawer?

I turn it on, and Gina and Sabrina come to life – a photo of the two of them taken about ten years ago. I'm fascinated, but frustrated, because there's so much potential information in my hand. It may provide some answers, and might even help Emilio, but to get any deeper, I need a passcode. Just six numbers. Random numbers? Or birthdays? Or the year someone was born? I sit on the side of the bath, and think. What passcode number would Gina choose? What means the most to her? I think hard. Emilio said they married on Gina's birthday, and she was three years younger than him, I know they married in June. So I look around the room and find a photo of their wedding, which I'm sure wasn't in here before. I imagine Sabrina put it on the wall seconds after I called her earlier to ask if I could stay. No doubt it's there to remind me that they were happy once – she must know how uncomfortable that makes me, especially now Gina's dead. Anyway, I take it down, and as I'd hoped, someone has written their names and the wedding date on the back. I can see it's the 26th of June, so I try Gina's birthdate – which would be their wedding too, so I punch in 230683. Nothing. Then I try Emilio's birth date, 080980 – and there it is, the world opens up and I'm giddy and scared. So, Emilio's birthdate is a significant number for Gina? The question is, am I brave enough to open up the Pandora's box now sitting in my hand?

I have everything here in front of me, but as I begin to navigate my way around the phone, it strikes me as odd that there aren't any text messages or contacts. Apart from Instagram, there seem to be only the very basic apps that come with an iPhone on here. This is weird. So, I open Instagram. The profile picture is of someone who looks like Gina, but her hair is in her face, like she's shaking her head and the camera has caught her mid-action. I can't wait a second longer, and go into the DMs, where I hit the jackpot – and find the messages.

Emilio's name is at the top. Her most recent message is from him; that's so weird. *Please, please talk to me*, it says.

Feeling uneasy, I click on their message thread – I need some context. I wait a moment, and consider the moral aspect of looking into someone's phone. But I can't ignore it, I can't tuck this phone back where I found it and pretend I never saw it. I have to open the door on to a world I'm not meant to see.

I need to know what's happening, I need clues to Gina – the past, the future, and what her death means to Emilio and me. So I click on direct messages, but there are only messages from Emilio to Gina and from her to him. I can't see any messages from Sabrina, which surprises me. The first one I read is from Emilio.

We need to talk, where are you? I'm sorry things have turned out this way, you seem to be rejecting me. If you're home, come and see us in Catania. Love always x

If this was sent after Gina's death, but before her body was found, was it a message from Emilio to Sabrina? What the fuck?

Is *that* why she turned up in Catania and caused mayhem? Because Emilio *invited* her? Have I been fooled all this time? Were they together before I was even in his life? Did Gina know?

My world tips upside down as I try to work out what's going on. But I have to throw up first, and when I've finished, I take the phone back into the bedroom. I need to lie down. I need to stay calm. If Sabrina should walk in on me, it seems like she has more to hide than I do, I tell myself as I lie on plumped pillows, bracing myself for the next onslaught of messages. I go back to the message thread and look at the recent exchanges, which may tell me the most. But what I see floors me.

Emilio, I never wanted to leave, I wanted to LIVE!

Gina I don't understand . . . ?

Oh I think you do Emilio. I couldn't understand why you wanted me dead – now I do. You met someone you love more than me, you have discarded me like garbage. Perhaps with her you will finally have the child you always wanted, not to mention the money you always wanted. I'm scared of you, I know what you're capable of.

Who is this?

Emilio sounds confused. This messaging is between Emilio and Gina, just before she stopped contacting him or Sabrina and before Gina's body was found. But it obviously can't be, and this message looks like someone's rather childlike way of framing Emilio. There are no messages from Sabrina, and yet she said she was messaging Gina all the time, and Emilio said she also knew Gina's passcode. Sabrina wouldn't bother messaging someone if she already knew they were dead – would she?

I'm breathless, can't take this in, it doesn't make any sense to me. I look for more messages, more clues, and realise that Sabrina knows her sister's passwords and has been using this burner phone to log into Gina's Instagram account.

Wow! All this time she's been trying to blame Emilio, saying he knows Gina's passwords, and he's trying to pretend she's fine when she's not, but in fact it's Sabrina who's been doing just that. And that's why Gina was still wearing her wedding ring in the photographs, it's why Sabrina was wearing the earrings that Gina must have left in a trinket bowl at home. The posts are old pictures, old holidays, all put on Instagram to make it look like she's living her best life – when all the time, she was dead. Now I'm really scared. I'm in this house, pregnant, with nowhere else to go – and downstairs there might be a killer.

51

All the time it was Sabrina. It turns out Gina's little sister has been manipulating evidence, telling lies, and sticky-taping secrets to the inside of a drawer. But why would she do that? Was she trying to catch Emilio, or frame him to take the spotlight off herself?

Most of the messages from him are just asking if she's okay, and she sends the same. Then there are volcano messages, using technical terms, which Sabrina sometimes responds to – probably with help from Google.

I read some more of the messages, but it makes me uncomfortable and I feel like a voyeur. I can't believe that Sabrina would do this. She was receiving messages from Emilio, and answering as Gina. It's obvious she hasn't a clue what he's talking about when he uses technical terms, but she tries to get a dig in about me now and then, which Emilio bats away.

I've screenshotted as many as I can with my phone in case I need them, but I'm so uneasy now in this house with her. And I need to get this phone to the police as soon as I can, as I think this might help Emilio.

So, in the morning, I put the burner phone in my handbag, and head downstairs to confront her.

'Hey queen?' She looks up from her phone. She's sprawled across the sofa, and watches me walk across the room. I take a seat in the armchair under the huge canvas of Gina's pixelated face.

'Sophie, I have to tell you, I'm going to fight this inheritance tooth and nail,' she starts, before I even open my mouth. 'He's not pushing my sister into a crater, then walking away with everything,' she says angrily. 'Until she married him, she left everything to me.'

I see a loophole and jump in. 'So if Emilio was convicted of her murder, the will would revert to the previous recipient, and you'd get everything?'

'Yeah.'

'So you have a strong motive for trying to frame Emilio?' This is beginning to make a kind of sense.

'I have nothing to hide.'

'Oh, but you do.'

She flushes at this, and fiddles with the many rings on her fingers.

'Sabrina, I found the burner phone you use to access Gina's account. What were you going to do? Pretend to find the phone, then blame Emilio? Were you planning a second visit to see us so you could plant it in the cabin, then call the police?'

She's shaking her head. 'You've got this all wrong.'

'Did you know Gina was dead?'

I watch her face as it pales and her mouth opens in horror. She's genuinely shocked. 'What are you saying?'

'Why would you pretend to be your sister if you thought she was alive?'

'It wasn't me. I think Emilio left it in that drawer.'

'I never mentioned finding it in a drawer.' *Gotcha.*

She seems to shrink before me. 'Okay . . . okay. I admit, I was . . . trying to smoke Emilio out.'

'Really?'

She nods, like a child who's been caught stealing sweets.

'Do you realise the harm you've done Sabrina? All that time her Instagram was active, everyone thought she was fine. So nobody looked for her!'

'I know, and I feel stupid.'

'You weren't helping Gina or smoking anyone out – you were simply buying time for whoever killed her.'

I'm still not convinced of her innocence – was she buying *herself* time? She sits up. 'I just know it's him. He had some kind of weird influence over her, and I wanted to scare him – I mean, if he killed her, it would freak him out that she was now online. I knew they talked on Instagram, and I wanted to see what he was saying, and for him to slip up. To say . . . "who is this?"'

'But he didn't?'

'No. But he has the *motive* – he'll get *all* her money.' She pauses. 'I called my lawyers yesterday and all I get now is some trust fund that I can't actually access until I'm forty – and what use is that to anyone? I'll be too old to enjoy it then,' she says sulkily.

'You've already spoken to lawyers about Gina's will, on the same day her body was found?' I'm shocked.

'Don't look at me like that, Sophie, I'm trying to stop an injustice here.'

'But Emilio was her husband. It isn't unusual or *unjust* that she'd leave most of her money to him,' I say, astounded at her sense of entitlement.

'What about me though?'

'You have your own family money, don't you?'

She takes a deep breath, like she's bored of explaining this to someone not clever enough to understand how terrible life is for millionaires.

'Yeah, I have money. When Dad died I got some Caprini money, but Gina got the lion's share. Just because I'd dabbled in a few drugs he didn't trust me,' she spits. 'And she already had money from when her mum died. She was so fucking rich, Sophie.' I hear the deep resentment in her voice. Here she is – the jealous little sister who wanted to be as beautiful and rich and clever as her sibling, but never quite made it. I wonder how that manifests itself in her. Is she resentful enough to kill?

'Anyway, I'm convinced that when Gina changed that will to leave everything to him, she signed her own death warrant,' she's saying.

'No! Emilio isn't driven by money and things. He cares about people, the environment, he's happier living in that little cabin with nothing than I've ever seen him before. If he had money, he'd give it away.'

'Wow! He really has brainwashed you, hasn't he?' She leans forward. 'Sophie, you can say all this fairy-tale stuff about him hugging trees and hating wealth, but look at the evidence!' she says emphatically. 'He adores this house, the luxurious rooms, the artwork, his library with the starry ceiling.' She waggles her fingers in the air. 'Gina was his golden goose, the ticket to a life he'd never get as a research scientist. So when she met someone else, he wasn't giving this up lightly. Getting rid of her was the only way he could keep the house and the money.'

'You ever heard of divorce?' I ask.

She shakes her head. 'He signed a prenup. He was never going to divorce her.'

This shocks me. I'm worried that what she's saying is starting to sound plausible. I try not to show a reaction, but I'm disturbed. Emilio has never talked to me about Gina's will, or the house or even a prenup, and I assumed that was because he isn't money-oriented. But what if he is?

But it's what she says next that chills me.

'Emilio just needed a new, fertile Gina to put in his palace, and here you are, princess.'

52

I'm trying hard not to let Sabrina's revelations, or her cruel words, sink in and take root inside me.

Emilio told me that as a child she had no regular family home life, no parental guidance or love, just a big trust fund to blow on drugs, which she dutifully did. She will spin her stories, and conjure all kinds of accusations and lies. She's dodgy and flaky as hell. And if I can show the police her burner phone and make them realise that there's an alternative suspect, it might help get Emilio home and free.

'I need to pop out in a minute,' I say.

'Where are you going? I might come with you.'

'Oh . . . nowhere special, I'm meeting a friend for coffee,' I lie.

'Oh, not that awful one with frizzy hair who has "Be Kind" written on her phone?'

'That's the one.'

'Ugh, no thanks, I'd rather stay home and stick pins in my eyes.'

Which is exactly the reaction I was hoping for.

'I'll just have something to eat before I go.' I'm still having morning sickness, but I need to eat, so I head for the kitchen.

I open the fridge to see beer, a chocolate bar and a bottle of vodka. I find a box of old chamomile teabags in the cupboard and boil some water, and sit at the kitchen table alone. I keep checking my phone to see if there are any messages from Emilio or the police station in Catania. I'm also checking for news, because if he's been charged, I might see it there first. My stomach is churning; this isn't good for the baby.

'That smells a bit off.' Sabrina wanders in, holding her nose.

'It's chamomile tea.'

'Smells like dead grass.'

She grabs the chocolate out of the fridge, starts ripping it open, then joins me at the table. She's so skinny she can sit cross-legged on a kitchen chair and there's still room.

I gaze around the kitchen. It isn't the same without Emilio at the oven, pouring wine, but there's something else that's different too.

'There are loads more photos on the walls than there used to be,' I say. At least twenty photos of Gina are now filling one wall in a big square. 'I noticed that in the bedroom too – there were loads more pictures.'

'Yeah, I want her with me, around me, you know?' she replies touchingly.

When I finish my tea, I walk over for a closer look and, as with her Instagram feed, I'm soon swept into Gina's perfect world. The beautiful bride, sunshine behind her, running barefoot through a huge garden. I turn to look through the glass doors, and see the garden that's in the photo. I look back to see Gina laughing, her head back, enjoying a joke with some girlfriends at some glitzy cocktail party.

'Her bridesmaids,' Sabrina says, standing next to me.

'Oh . . . none of Emilio?'

'No, just Gina in here. He's in the bedroom,' she murmurs.

I ignore this; I'm sure she's said it to make me feel insecure, but I'm more interested in the photos. And as I'm looking I step forward and bang into what must be a large photo or painting propped against the kitchen island.

'What's that?' I ask. It's covered in a paint-splattered sheet, which to an artist is very interesting.

'Oh, it's a portrait of Gina,' she says. I find it fascinating the way rich people have their portrait painted in the same way the rest of us have a photo taken.

'Wow, what a luxury, I'd love to have mine done. Can I have a look?'

'Yeah,' she says, shrugging, clearly not interested.

I carefully lift the protective sheet, and gasp. There she is – Gina, looking so real, so lifelike, I feel like she might just step out of the painting.

The style is like that of the Old Masters, and she looks like an aristocrat in a crimson silk gown, but there's a freshness about it, a contemporary edge, because despite the formality of her gown, she's sitting cross-legged. Her hair is loose, framing her face in deep, caramel waves, ripples of hair snaking around her decolletage. And her perfect face. Matching crimson lips and big, big eyes with huge fake eyelashes.

'Beautiful,' I sigh, mesmerised by the brushstrokes, the light playing on her hair, the shiny fabric of her dress. 'It's so good, it looks like a photograph in a certain light.' I move around, studying every aspect like an art critic. 'Is this an Eloise Aitken?' I ask.

She shrugs again.

I look more closely and eventually see the letters EA. 'It is! It's an Eloise Aitken, look her mark is here. She's a British artist, buyers clamour for her work, but she's a recluse, no one knows much about her, except that she's very talented. She's painted film stars and royalty. This painting will be worth quite a lot of money.'

Sabrina glances over, vaguely interested if it's worth something.

284

I continue to look at the rest of the photos on the walls – the parties, the holidays, the awards. Gina was everything to everyone, and had a dress for every occasion. I'm just resenting the way her dress clings to her perfect figure when someone in the back of one of the photos catches my eye.

'Do you know that woman?' I ask Sabrina, and she looks closely as we both scrutinise the photo.

She shakes her head. 'Never seen her before,' she says dismissively. 'She's just staff, isn't she? A waitress or something?'

'No, she isn't dressed like a waitress. She's in an evening gown.'

I look again at the woman gazing lovingly at Gina.

'Do *you* know her?' Sabrina asks.

'Yes,' I say, surprised by this unlikely connection. 'But I didn't realise she knew Gina, she's never mentioned her.'

'Who *is* she?' she asks, absently.

'She's one of my students, she's great fun! I've never seen her looking quite so glamorous, though. Her name's Marian Darcy.'

'I'm going to have a nap,' Sabrina says, bored of this now.

'Okay, I'm popping out in a bit,' I say, my eyes flickering to my handbag where the phone sits. 'Before I do, though, I'm calling the police in Catania. I'm worried about Emilio, I still haven't heard from him, and I'm hoping there might be news. I can't rest until I know he's being released.'

She shrugs. 'Well, don't get your hopes up. I saw on the news today they're planning to do a dig around his cabin out there. They think he may have buried some clues or more bodies or something . . .'

'That's not funny, Sabrina,' I mutter, desperately searching for the story online, and seeing a picture of the lovely little cabin surrounded by police tape.

I call the station, but there's no response, the phone just keeps ringing and ringing.

I wait a few moments before trying again and take my mind off it by looking again at the photograph with Marian in the background. I take a photo of it, and enlarging it on my phone, I see she's looking up at Gina and Emilio adoringly. Sabrina's there too; she's also in the background watching the couple, but the look on her face is anything but adoring.

53

I try the police in Catania, but again have no luck – it just keeps ringing – so I head off to the Taormina police station with Sabrina's spare phone in my bag. I have so much on my mind I barely notice that I'm back here in town, among shops and houses and people. I'm concerned about Emilio, I'm desperate to speak to him, but there's a slight shadow over me after what Sabrina said about money being everything to him. I know it's not true, and I have to keep the faith and try to get him home, and the first step is to take this phone to the police so they can see that Sabrina was impersonating her dead sister online.

On the way to the station, I pass the bottom of Marian's road, and it sets me wondering about that photo in the kitchen. Did Marian just happen to be there, or did she actually *know* them? And if so, why has she never mentioned that?

Once I left the university and all the student/teacher rules were gone, I talked openly with her about my relationship during our regular conversations. I didn't hide the fact that Emilio's wife was Gina Caprini and that she mixed in glamorous Taormina circles, so I wonder how Marian didn't pick up on that? I wish she was here in Taormina now and not sailing the high seas with her sugar daddy. I could call in on her, drink Earl Grey and tell her all the gossip. She recently became obsessed with true-crime podcasts, so I know she'll have a theory on Gina's murder, like everyone else in Sicily.

But, just as I'm about to cross the road on the way to the police station, I hear someone calling my name. I turn around, and to my sheer joy, there is Marian in bright pink floral with a matching turban, waving both her arms at me manically.

'Darling!!!!' she's calling, as I walk briskly towards her, my heart lifting and a smile taking over my face. 'I thought it was you!' Her face is beaming, her arms wide open.

We grab each other and embrace. She holds me so tight that I feel the love, which is wholly reciprocated.

'What happened to you riding a big one on the Med, Marian?' I tease.

'Oh, my sugar daddy went down with fucking Covid! That's the trouble with old bastards, their immune systems are on the blink, not to mention their prowess between the sheets.' She winks. 'Do you have time to come over to mine, drink tea and catch up?' She looks up at me. Her lips match the bright pink of her dress and turban.

'I have a little errand to run,' I say.

'Oh, sweetie, please! I've *missed* you.' And the pleading in her eyes makes me think I can drop the phone off later – an hour won't make any difference. I guess it won't do any harm, because if Sabrina is the killer she's already killed. Her next victim is probably Emilio, who is at least safe in custody. My heart drops as I think of him.

'Oh, Marian, we have so much to discuss,' I say, putting my arm through hers as we stroll along the tree-lined road to her house.

'I've seen the news,' she says, and for once she resists making light of something, for which I'm grateful. 'I wanted to call you, but I assumed you were up to your neck.'

'It's been horrific.' I want to say more, but I think I might cry. She's sensitive enough to pick up on this, and with my arm still through hers she reaches with her other hand and pats mine.

'Is Emilio still in police custody in Catania?'

'Yes, unfortunately. I have no idea what's happening, the police aren't keeping in touch. When I did get through and asked to speak to Emilio they said he was in an interview. I thought he would be allowed a phone call?'

'You need lawyers, my darling.'

'Yes, I'm trying to find out where we are with that, but until I speak to the police . . . by the way, I think you know them – Gina and Emilio?'

'Yes, well, I think everyone knows of them.'

'It's just that there's a photo of you standing near them at a party. It's on the wall in Gina's kitchen.'

'Oh really?' She stops and touches her chest theatrically. She does everything theatrically. 'I'm deeply flattered to be gracing their hallowed walls.' Then she nudges me. 'Well, I'll let you into a little secret. I've been in their company and indeed I've painted Gina Caprini on more than one occasion.'

I'm amazed. 'I had no idea you'd painted her—' Then I stop dead in my tracks. 'You aren't . . . you are, aren't you? That painting of Gina . . . the red silk, the hair?'

She's looking up at me, a huge impish smile on her face.

'No . . . you're not Eloise Aitken?'

'I am. But *you* can call me Marian,' she says as we arrive at her door and she starts tugging at the wonky lock. Then she pushes it open, gesturing for me to go first. Walking back into her house feels like going home – there's that waft of lavender and soft lamplight even though it's the middle of the afternoon. But as it's a winter's afternoon, it's cosy to come into from the chill outside.

I'm still in shock at her revelation. 'But you're so famous, yet no one knows who you are. I read that everyone you paint has to sign an NDA, even celebrities. Is that true?'

She raises her eyebrows. 'Yes, even the Kardashians, but I didn't ask Charles and Camilla – took them at their word that they'd keep schtum.'

We both chuckle at this.

'I love your work, but I've often wondered why, in all these years, you haven't revealed who you are.'

'In the beginning, as a young ingénue, I welcomed the attention, loved the limelight. But then it became more about me and less about my art, and I just got so bored of the fawning. I had no real friends, just the sycophants, and men who wanted to bed me – and I'll admit I took up some offers, especially from the handsome ones.' She giggles. 'But I discovered that, to create good art, I had to live my life freely, without interruptions and interference. But I was starting to feel like a bloody one-woman corporation, darling – buyers and critics waiting for my next piece, galleries on the phone, the press literally camping outside my door. Consequently, with all that noise, my art suffered. Their expectations put me under so much pressure, I had a breakdown, swanned off to Sicily, didn't tell a soul and continued to paint in my own time, on my own terms. Now this is a secret, Sophie. No one in the art world knows I live here, only my agent. Just think of me like a female Banksy, darling. I sweep in, undercover, do my thing and leave.'

'I promise, I won't tell a soul . . . but who are you? Eloise or Marian?'

'As I said, you can call me Marian, but neither of those is my real name. I think when I was born my mad mother called me Mary, or Audrey, or something equally tedious, but at six years old I called myself by other, more interesting and exotic names, usually after actresses or pop stars. You should have known me in my Angelina years,' she laughs. 'My Madonna years were wild.'

I can only imagine.

'But Marian . . . or Madonna?' I say with a smile. 'Why did you join my class? I couldn't teach you *anything*.'

'I've said it before, darling, we're on this earth to learn, and when we stop learning, it's curtains.'

'With all the horrible things that are happening around me, to discover my friend is a world-famous portrait painter is a lovely thing to happen today. Thank you.'

'Ahh, you're going to make me cry.' She reaches out and gives me a hug, then offers me the pink chaise longue, and the moment I'm seated she arranges a pink, woollen throw over me. 'Now, you relax here, put your feet up, I'll make tea and toasted teacakes, and we shall catch up.'

'Thanks, Mum,' I joke as she bustles out of the room chuckling. I put my feet up, stretching them along the chaise, which I wouldn't dream of doing in anyone's home but my own. But Marian has this way of making you feel like you're home. She's the mother I never had, and I want her in my life – and my baby's. I just hope my baby's father will be there too.

Minutes later, Marian is trundling back into the room with a tray and the beautiful art deco teapot and cups and saucers. 'So, start from the beginning . . .'

She's loaded a plate with hot buttered toasted teacakes and a bowl of strawberry jam with a silver spoon, and we eat and talk. I feel warm and easy, as all my problems slowly fall away from me.

'Gosh, my love, you're really going through it,' she says after I've told her all about the arrest and Sabrina taking over Gina's Instagram. I tell her my suspicions, and we talk through all the permutations. 'I never thought I'd have the chance to solve an actual true crime,' she says.

Then, reaching over from her easy chair and resting her hand on mine, she says, 'My darling, Taormina is a small place, and there's a lot of talk at the moment – silly rumours, ignorant people of course. But as your friend, I have to tell you that there is a strong feeling here that Emilio killed his wife for the money.'

54

'Try some of my home-made strawberry jam, I grow the berries myself in the garden,' Marian says, as she spoons the bright-red strawberry conserve on to both our plates with a tiny spoon. 'I made the teacakes too, you can't get them here. As much as I love Sicily, there are things I miss about home.'

'Me too,' I say, wistfully.

She plumps a cushion and sits back in her chair. 'So who killed Gina? We must explore all possibilities, and use the evidence plus instinct to reach our conclusion. Evidence plus instinct,' she repeats for emphasis. 'I heard that on a podcast.' She nods, taking a large bite of teacake.

We talk about the fact Emilio *might* have the biggest motive – certainly bigger than Sabrina's. 'She has money, you see, he doesn't,' Marian says gently. 'And playing devil's advocate, one can never underestimate the power of money where human beings are concerned. I know you believe he's innocent, and I'm not arguing with that. I'm just saying you have to step back a little – because my darling, we don't always know other people like we think we do – even those we love.'

Her words chime so much with me. 'My biggest fear is that I will fight and fight only to discover that he was guilty all along,' I say, before adding, 'but my instinct tells me he isn't.'

'And we have to trust our instincts, my love. If we didn't, where the fuck would we be?' She pours more tea, and gasps in horror as we discuss Sabrina's behaviour.

'Do you think she killed her sister?' she asks.

I take a bite of teacake, covered in strawberry jam. I pause to finish chewing. 'I think Sabrina is capable of murder, but I wouldn't like to say. If I had to choose between her and Emilio I'd choose her every time though. I mean, she should be the one who's locked up, not him.'

'But apart from those two, who else *has* a motive?' she asks.

'There's the lover, a student that was supposed to be going to Hawaii with Gina, but she never went?' I offer.

'Oh yes, there was something in the *Giornale di Sicilia* about him this morning, good-looking boy, can't blame her for having the hots for him. But according to the newspaper he has an alibi. He was in South America around the time she died, they'd had a falling-out or something. Gina may have been beautiful, but she didn't have luck with the men,' Marian says, standing up. 'More tea?'

'I would love that, but as much as I'd love to stay here for hours, I need to take Sabrina's Instagram phone to the police station.'

'Oh, and we're having such fun – stay for another cuppa!' She leaves the room, taking the tray to replenish the tea.

I take out my phone and access the website for the *Giornale di Sicilia*, and soon find the story about Gina's student lover. His name is Brad, and he was one of her geology students, who at twenty-two was twenty-one years younger than her. I guess when you're as beautiful as Gina, age doesn't matter. He's saying that Gina had an invitation to go to Hawaii and asked him to go, just as Emilio told me. But before they were due to leave, she sent him a message to say she'd changed her mind, so he went off to South America instead.

'Judging by the photos of him with his new girlfriend, I don't think Brad's losing any sleep,' I say to Marian as she comes back in from the kitchen. She is limping slightly and it takes a while for her to walk across the room, but she won't hear of me taking the tray off her.

'I'm looking after you!' she says.

I'm still holding my phone, and reading the rest of the article. 'What this guy – Gina's student lover – is saying is that, like Emilio, he thought she was fine because she was responding to messages. And like Emilio he knew she had a reputation for taking off at a moment's notice, and as far as he was concerned, she'd simply gone without him. This is why Sabrina faking the Instagram is so vital to Gina's murder investigation,' I say. 'Sabrina's stupid little game stopped everyone from asking where she was, which gave the murderer a head start. What a little idiot she is.'

Marian raises her eyebrows. 'Yes, absolutely! Are you okay, my love, you look a little pale?'

'I'm just tired. I could go to sleep right here under this throw. Your house is so cosy and warm.'

I wonder if it's my pregnancy. The first trimester is supposed to be the worst as far as tiredness and sickness is concerned. I can't wait to get through this.

'Snooze away, my darling, in your condition you need all the rest you can get.'

This surprises me. 'How do you know I'm pregnant?'

She stands back, surveying me. 'You don't get to my age and not know when your chum is preggers,' she says, her face beaming. 'I noticed how your cheeks have filled out. And that awful tiredness that pregnant women suffer from, it shows around the eyes.' She perches on the end of the chaise. 'To be honest, I was a little hurt you hadn't told me.'

I feel awful. 'Oh Marian, I'm sorry. I wasn't *keeping* it from you. I was planning to tell you, but I wanted to *wait* to tell you . . . with Emilio.'

She smiles. 'Of course, I understand.'

'I might as well ask, you know. I was going to ask if you'd be godmother.'

At this, tears spring to her eyes, and she's silent for a few moments, but when she speaks, her voice is thick with tears. 'No one has ever asked me to be a godmother before, or a bridesmaid – or a *wife*, come to think of it.' She rolls her eyes and laughs a hollow laugh. 'Thank you, Sophie, I didn't expect that.' She's wiping her eyes with the back of her hand. 'I'm a silly old sausage, aren't I?'

I'm glad she's so pleased, and reach out my hand and squeeze hers. We're both too choked up to speak.

Then she stands and reaches for a tissue from a box covered in antique lace that's on a bookshelf near where we're sitting. But being in an emotional state and not the most agile person, she overreaches and almost falls over, knocking several things from the shelf. Despite her protestations, I leap up to help her. I'm worried she might hurt herself.

'You sit down, I'll pick them up,' I say, but while gathering up the books and a stray cat ornament, I spot something that surprises me.

'I didn't know you smoked, Marian?'

I'm on the floor, holding up a packet of Gitanes in the iconic blue packet. Suddenly the mood in the room seems to shift.

'Occasionally,' she says. I wait for the hilarious remark to accompany this, but it never comes. And I can see by her face she's uncomfortable; her whole demeanour has changed, as if a light has gone out. I put the books back on the shelf, aware she's watching me, but not in the loving, motherly way she was just minutes ago.

55

I stand up, handing her the stray cat ornament, and try putting on a bright voice, like I haven't noticed the Gitanes are the same kind of cigarette I think the watcher smoked.

'Are you okay, my darling? You seem a bit peaky all of a sudden,' she asks, unsmiling.

'Yes . . . I'm okay, I just remembered I need to get that phone to the police.'

'Oh, calm down and relax, sweetie. Take a seat, you need to rest.'

I'm confused, and suddenly uneasy about being here.

She looks at me. 'Sit down, darling, you're driving me mad, pacing around.'

'Was I? Sorry, I didn't realise.'

'Is it the Gitanes?'

'What? Yes . . . I'll be honest, seeing them just triggered me.'

'It's perfectly understandable. I remember you telling me you had that terrible experience.'

'Yes, I was terrified, and seeing them brought it flooding back,' I reply honestly. I need her to go back to being Marian, to making me laugh and being warm and kind, but she seems stiff, frozen. I've never seen her like this before.

'Gina smoked them, they must be hers,' she offers, but I'm not convinced.

It's too convenient for the cigarettes to be Gina's – and besides, she's been gone since May, and if Marian doesn't smoke, then why would she keep them here? Is it too much of a coincidence that I was being stalked by someone who smoked this quite unusual brand, and I find a packet here in my friend's house?

I've gone from feeling comfy and welcome to suddenly feeling trapped. Panic is rising in my chest, and I don't know if it's hormones or sheer disappointment that Marian might not be *Marian*. I want to cry.

She's unusually quiet; she seems to be thinking.

I really need to get out of here, so I stand up.

'You okay, darling?'

'Yes, Sabrina will be wondering where I am.'

'I wouldn't pander to Sabrina, my love, she won't be worried about *you*! Less than half an hour ago you had her down as a murderer.'

'No . . . she's mixed up – not a murderer.'

'I miss her so much,' Marian suddenly says, like she's having a different conversation in a different room.

'Who?'

'Gina, of course. We were very close, shared all our secrets. She'd come here often.' She gestures towards the two paintings of the naked woman on the wall. I admired them the last time I was here, but I didn't see then what I'm seeing now.

'It's Gina?' I walk over to the paintings for a closer look. I'm still shaking, not sure what the hell is going on, but I'm playing along.

'She was my muse.' Marian moves closer to stand by me as we both look closely at the pictures. The long, silky hair, the sensual body, long-limbed yet curvy. In one picture her arms are lifted, her fingers run through her hair. Her eyes are steady, staring, captivating.

'Always looking for a thrill, she was. "Come on, Marian, let's go on an adventure," she'd say, and off we'd go – cocktails in Palermo, nightclubs in Taormina, dinners *à deux* everywhere. "Are you ready for a roller coaster ride, Marian?" she whispered excitedly in my ear one evening. I of course said yes, and we got into my little car and I drove her all the way to Palermo. I didn't realise why we were going until we arrived, and this gorgeous, young, blond hunk was waiting for her on the beach, in the sunset. I have to say I was a little miffed. "I thought *we* were having the adventure, darling, you and me," I called as she ran along the beach and into his arms, but she just laughed. "I'll ask him if he has a brother," she called back. But apparently he didn't,' she says sadly.

This is so weird. I don't know what to say, how to react. Does she mean it? Or is she suddenly going to step out of character and say, 'Only joking?'

'Of course, Emilio didn't deserve what she did to him. He's such a lovely man, he's handsome and amusing – well you'll know,' she says, like she suddenly remembers my connection to him. 'I did wonder what she saw in the younger man when she had a mature man at home, who seemed smitten I have to say. But that was in the early days. I think Emilio became disillusioned with her, she hurt him with her dalliances, he didn't deserve that,' she says more soberly. 'But he can certainly charm the birds off the trees, as you well know,' she adds, a sparkle in her eyes. 'Anyway, having a gorgeous husband didn't stop Gina playing away. I used to drive her off to see lots of different men, then drive her back, and her hair would be all mussed up, lipstick kissed off. She'd get in my car and I'd have to drive her home and lie to Emilio's face about where we'd been.'

'So you drove her and covered for her?'

'Yes, I didn't mind, sometimes she'd invite me in for coffee and Emilio would pour me one of his lovely red wines and she'd fall asleep while we discussed art and volcanoes.'

I find it difficult to hear Marian talking about Emilio. They both belong in different compartments in my head, and the idea that they once had a friendship is surreal to me. She clearly had a very close relationship with Gina too, and hearing her talk she sounds obsessed with her. I just feel this is all a bit off; she has this weird attachment to Gina, even now, that I can't quite grasp. Was she in love with her? Did she want to *be* her? As an artist I know one can often get close to subjects, but this feels unhealthily close. And Gina was obviously using her, which is sad, but, despite my unease, now she's started talking, I'm keen to hear more. And something tells me I might be wise to record what she's saying. So I take out my phone.

'I just want to let Sabrina know that I'll be late. I told her I'd only be half an hour.'

I pretend to text, then hit record, and put the phone face down on the coffee table next to me.

'I miss our shopping trips the most,' she's saying, smiling to herself. 'Gina and I would go into town or drive into Palermo and she'd fill my little car with all her shopping bags. "You should get a bigger car, Marian," she used to say. But I love Diana – she's my VW Beetle, named after Princess Diana. Gina loved that car . . . she and Brad would often borrow it, her own car was too obvious, it had a number plate that everyone would know. And as she said, "Marian, me having a cute blond twenty-something boy in the passenger seat might set tongues wagging."'

'I can imagine, Taormina is a small place,' I reply, realising that Gina was obviously using Marian and her car to facilitate her affair.

'Gina was the most beautiful woman I ever met, and painting her was a joy,' she sighs.

For all her ribald comments about men, I'm beginning to wonder if Marian loves women and had a huge crush on Gina, along with the rest of Taormina. 'I know your mother was rather controlling, and probably wouldn't approve, but if you are gay and you loved Gina, you shouldn't feel you have to hide it,' I say gently.

'Oh, Jesus Christ, get a grip, my love. I'm not a lesbian, I *adore* men – big, strong, handsome men. And you know what? I get them too. There are so many men in the art world who admire me, and would give anything for a night in my bed, and sometimes I let them – as long as they sign an NDA in the morning.' She roars with laughter at this. 'I know I'm like a fucking film star to men like that . . . Oh no, my darling, I loved Gina, but not like that. I'm in love with Emilio.'

56

She's standing opposite me, and this suddenly feels gladiatorial. I don't understand how someone could change so quickly. It's like all her powerful positive energy has suddenly turned bad. Gone are the winks and the smiles and the 'darlings'; suddenly it's as if she's a robot and she's been turned on.

'I had no idea you felt like that about Emilio,' I say. 'All the conversations we had about him, when I told you about our life together when I was in Catania – that must have been difficult for you.'

'Damn right it was. He'd still be with me if you hadn't come flouncing into town with your flat stomach and come-to-bed eyes, darling.'

This isn't Marian. Where did all this bile come from?

'You needn't look so surprised, he's closer to my age than yours. I'm fifty-two, not a hundred and four – he's only six years younger, darling. But nobody takes women my age seriously, do they? We still want love and sex and relationships, just like you thirty-somethings. We're human too, you know.'

'Of course you should have love, whatever your age,' I say gently.

'And I *had* the chance of love.' She's wringing her hands. 'I'm telling you, Emilio and I were meant to be together. We mix in the same circles darling. Emilio and I would have long, meaningful talks. I could see he felt the same about me.'

'I'm sure he thought you were wonderful, as I do . . . perhaps as a friend?' I offer.

'Don't be patronising, darling. I'm old enough to know when someone *wants* me!'

She's pacing the floor now, fidgety, on edge – I wonder if she is on medication and hasn't taken it?

'Anyway, whatever you may think, I know for a fact he had feelings because Sabrina told me.'

'Sabrina didn't even recognise you in a photo, Marian. She doesn't *know* you.'

'She does, Sabrina and I are good friends. She has her faults and foibles, as you've pointed out this afternoon, but she's a good egg. One night we were all at a party, and she leaned over and whispered in my ear, "My brother-in-law told me he's in love with you."'

I gasp, horrified, because this sounds very much to me like Sabrina was making fun of Marian. Emilio is a kind and charming man, and someone like Marian – who probably doesn't get an awful lot of male attention – mistook his kindness and polite attention for something more.

'Marian, I understand how you feel, and I'm not sure what happened before I came along, but Emilio isn't free. He's my boyfriend and we're expecting a child—'

'He was my first real love you see,' she's saying sadly, taking a tissue from the box and twisting it in her fingers. It's like I'm not here. 'Mother never let me have boyfriends; she said I had to stay home with her, and that's when I started to paint. When she died a few years ago, I was relieved, and I started dating, I was a complete slut.' She chuckles to herself. Then her smile fades. 'But once I met Emilio . . . there was no one else for me.'

I don't know how to respond, so I stay silent.

'I know you don't believe your boyfriend could want someone like me, but he did. He told Sabrina he was thinking of breaking up with Gina for me.'

'Did Emilio tell *you* this too?' I ask, knowing he didn't.

'Are you jealous, my love?'

'A little . . . perhaps?' I lie.

'Well, you *should* be, because a slick of red lipstick and a sultry smile and they just fall into my bed – well, they used to. But no, Emilio didn't tell me directly, he spoke with his eyes and only told Sabrina how he felt. Gina didn't mind, she said I should give it a go, but by then it was more about me taking him off her hands so she could be alone with Brad. Sometimes, at Gina's request, I would spend the evening charming her husband. To others it may have seemed like small talk, but it was so much more.

'"Eloise, you can always make me laugh," he used to say. That's the trick, Sophie – laugh them into bed. He's a lovely man, inside and out, even Sabrina used to try it on with him, but he only had eyes for me.' She stops talking for a moment and looks me up and down. 'Don't get me wrong, darling, I love you to bits, but I've always wondered what he sees in you. I mean, you're lovely, but an art teacher? It's a bit provincial, isn't it, darling? It's just so fucking sad, Sophie. I'm six years older than him, and he's *ten* years older than you – women over fifty aren't the same as men over fifty, are they, sweetie?'

'I'm sorry I came along and spoiled everything for you, Marian.'

She shrugs. 'I'm no competition for the likes of you. Most men want vapid schoolgirls in short skirts with nothing to say.'

'Thanks,' I reply.

'I wasn't talking about you – don't flatter yourself, darling, you're no schoolgirl.' She chuckles to herself at this.

Marian has gone from my child's potential godmother to my worst nightmare in a matter of minutes.

Was she just a joke to Sabrina and Gina, or was she genuinely part of their social set? I imagine she was a novelty – the international artist who was also quite funny and possibly delusional.

'You were such good friends with Gina and her crowd I guess you know everything about them – Emilio too,' I say. She's sitting now, relaxed, enjoying reliving the good times and telling me all about it. 'They must have trusted you with everything.'

'Oh yes, Gina would strip off and let me paint her, and she'd tell me all about Brad, what he was like in bed . . .'

'What do you know about Gina's death, Marian?'

She looks at me with eyes that turn my blood cold.

My mouth's dry, my eyes are on hers. I'm afraid to move in case it stops her talking.

'*Everything.*'

Blood rushes through my head, and my heart is pumping.

'Do you know . . . who did it?' I ask quietly.

She hesitates, then looks around to check no one's listening. 'Yes.'

57

'Marian, tell me who killed Gina?'

She sits down, settles in her chair and begins to talk. 'There was a party – my party actually,' she starts, and I know it's likely to be a long, drawn-out story. All I want is a name, but Marian squeezes every drop of drama out of her stories, so I try to quell the tension in my chest and listen.

'I'd spent a few weeks in the Middle East painting a sheikh who'd paid me more money than I will ever spend. So I thought I'd treat my chums to a champagne-fuelled evening with fabulous food at Country House Villadorata hotel, this fabulous sixty-two-acre summer residence. Luxury rooms, gardens with olive groves, almond trees, a vineyard, infinity pools, spas. It was *divine*. I hired the whole place for three days and invited everyone I knew – but there was only one person I wanted there, and that was Emilio. Gina told me she wouldn't be coming because she was spending the weekend with Brad. "I'm going to insist Emilio comes alone," she said. "Will you look after him for me?"

'Then she winked, and Sabrina said, "You won't need to insist he comes, Gina, because he's just dying to get Marian alone."'

All I could hear was a story about two mean, spoilt sisters having fun at someone else's expense.

'I was thrilled of course, and on the first night, everyone arrived in groups or alone or in couples, and I waited and waited for him. The champagne was flowing and I was in bright blue silk, fitting my curves – and though I do say so myself, I looked absolutely ravishing, darling,' she adds as an aside, and I see a flicker of the Marian I thought I knew.

'But then I spotted Gina and Emilio walking through the citrus grove in the dusk. I'll never forget it, the sky was pink and they were holding hands. They were together and Gina clung to him, they were all loved up, and I thought my heart might break. I took her aside. "I thought you were with Brad this weekend," I said, but apparently Brad was with someone else. He used her as much as she used everyone else. I was quite furious, I'd planned this wonderful, romantic weekend, bought fabulous outfits, lingerie, even a swimming costume in case Emilio wanted to take me swimming. And she fucking ruined it!'

'So, who killed Gina?' I am desperate to know.

'Steady on, darling, all in good time. So, there I was, in tears. The setting was perfect – the gardens, the food, my bed was covered in rose petals. I'd thought of everything, and Gina had even given me her blessing to be with him. Yet she turns up by his side, at *my* party, bold as brass. I could never forgive her for that, my darling, and abandoned my own birthday weekend. I was so devastated I asked my driver to take me home. I'll never forget Emilio standing on the steps outside, a drink in his hand. She was all over him, but as he watched my car drive away, I saw the sadness in his eyes. I realised then that we could never be together while Gina was around.'

Oh God. I know how this ends.

'So . . . who killed Gina?'

'I'm about to tell you – patience, my darling,' she chides, and takes a sip of cold tea. 'So, Emilio was away, I knew she was alone,

306

so I called her and said I had some news about her painting, the one with her hair down in the red silk dress. I told her a TV company wanted to make a documentary about it called *The Lady in Red*, and the director wanted to meet her. "He wants to meet very early in the morning, so I've booked for us to stay overnight in the Asmundo di Gisira," which is a luxury hotel in Catania. She, of course, jumped at this, and I asked her not to tell anyone because it was top secret, which made it more fun for Gina, so I picked her up that night at ten p.m. I told her I'd been delayed, but really I wanted to pick her up in the dark so no one saw us as we set off for Catania. She was so excited about meeting the director. "Do you think they'll cover my life story?" she was saying, like it was all about her. I have to tell you, darling, by then she was getting on my last nerve. She was such a bloody narcissist, thought the documentary was "Gina's story". I was getting so cross as I was driving and had to remind myself there was no fucking documentary. I'd just made it up to get her there.' She laughs heartily at this, and I try to get her back on track.

'So you went to the hotel?'

'Did we *hell*, darling, I'm not stupid! The plan wasn't to get her a frangipani body wrap, it was to get *rid* of her. Thing is, my love, she'd never taken me seriously, and Sabrina said she made fun of me privately. She actively encouraged my relationship with Emilio, but apparently when they were alone, she turned him against me.'

She is so messed up.

'So, I told Gina I wanted to stop at Valle del Bove on our way to the hotel to get some photos of her. "I want to give the film director a vision to work with," I said, "so we need photos of you in the moonlight on the edge of the crater at our breakfast meeting, darling." I also said I was going to paint her, and the National Portrait Gallery had already agreed to include the painting in "Women of Our Time". It was all lies, of course, but she lapped it up – I'm pretty smart and she was pretty vain.'

She stands up from her chair and walks towards me. I'm leaning on the back of the sofa, too scared to sit down, feeling very vulnerable.

'So we arrived at the crater, and I took a few snaps, then approached her saying, "I need you to stand more like this," and she let me manhandle her.'

Marian has approached me now and is holding me by the shoulders to illustrate what she's saying. I can feel how Gina must have felt. I feel sick with fear.

'Then, before she realised what was happening, I pushed her hard, and she screamed. It made a horrid echoing sound, I still hear it sometimes. Anyway, within seconds, it was all quiet and she was gone . . . it was too easy really.' She's shaking her head. 'One push, and a whole life ended. I can't believe the detachment, the absolute lack of any feeling.'

'You don't know if she died on impact or . . . suffered?'

'It was pitch-black, darling, I haven't a clue.' She shrugs dismissively. 'So, I went back to my hotel room, where I was booked in as Scarlett Johansson.' She smiles at this and gives me a little wink. 'I ordered dinner through room service. Listened to the latest *Motherkiller* crime podcast, cleaned my teeth, and went to bed dreaming of Emilio Ferrante. The very next day I invited Emilio to a private art exhibition, and he came along and we chatted, and flirted and made plans to see each other at an event the following week. He didn't know it then, but I knew he was single, and he'd soon realise she wasn't coming back. But I always knew there was a chance I might lose Emilio – he's so good-looking and charming and . . . so I kept an eye on him, and one day I saw you both at the university, in the canteen. I can tell when someone is interested, and he was definitely interested in you, probably because you were gazing at him so intently in the coffee queue. I remember thinking, "She might be trouble."'

Now I'm terrified.

'I wasn't going to hurt you, I just wanted to scare you off . . . that's when I decided to join your little class. I was a latecomer, but everyone including you made me feel so welcome.' She wanders over to the bookshelves and, taking a cigarette from the box, lights a Gitane.

'Did you . . . it was *you* who was smoking on the balcony opposite me?'

'Yeah. I borrowed a hooded cloak from the opera society. You might recall I joined them to learn to sing. I met a lovely girl there, she was the wardrobe mistress, told me all about her friend Sophie and what was happening with her latest relationship.'

Abbi!

'So I was able to keep an eye on you in class, and get a lot of intelligence from her. She's such a leaky bucket, sang like a canary, darling. Of course, "Be Kind" Abbi knows me as Eloise . . . we keep in touch.' She throws her head back and starts to blow smoke rings into the air.

I have to do something.

'Excuse me a moment, I just need some water,' I say, slipping my phone into my pocket and heading for the kitchen.

'Let me get it for you.' She's moving from her chair, but by the time she's up I'm already in the kitchen.

'I'm only getting a glass of water, don't bother yourself,' I call, pretending to find a glass. But I hear her lumbering across the room, bringing the tray we had tea on, it's rattling closer and closer.

I reach out and feel for a kitchen knife in the drawer. I need some protection; this isn't just about me anymore, I have my baby to think of.

I grab my phone from my pocket and text Sabrina.

Please help I'm a prisoner at Marians Salita dei Gracchi 11 Taormina

I quickly put my phone away, but when I look up she's standing in the doorway.

'What are you doing?'

'Water . . .' I say, feeling my throat close up with nerves as I drop the glass on the floor. As it lands with a smash, I slide the knife under my trouser leg and into my boot.

'Clumsy girl, you'll never be a ballerina,' she says. I imagine that's her mother's voice, which explains a lot.

I clear up the glass with a dustpan and brush, while she continues her story. She really is enjoying this.

'It wasn't long before we were friends, and I knew if I played with your mind, I could weaken you and you'd soon give in. I wanted you to think it was him on the balcony, so I told the landlord I had to have that room and I would pay him whatever he wanted for it. He took the piss, but I paid it and he evicted the previous tenants.'

'You scared me to death,' I said, standing up and throwing the broken glass into the bin. I'm light-headed and have to lean on the kitchen counter for a moment.

'What are you doing now?' she asks impatiently. She's keen to get on with her story, and I follow her from the kitchen, letting her talk, while desperately trying to see where her front door keys are – I know she locked it when we came in. I need to grab them and get out of here, but I can't see them, so have to go back to the chaise, where she's holding the pink throw, waiting to 'tuck me in'.

'Do you know I loved that smoker-stalker role,' she says as she sits back in her easy chair, head back – remembering how much fun she had, no doubt. 'I really should have been an actress.'

I just listen, terrified; my mind is plotting my escape, but my body's too weak to run.

'Then you turned up on my doorstep that night, and I thought it was a gift from God. The next day I was straight on to the college

310

to complain, pretending to be a friend, and got you fired, I thought it was my finest hour, but it backfired and sent you right into his arms. The next thing I know you're all loved-up in a cabin in Catania, and I thought all was lost. But now you're back, my darling.' Smiling, she pats my leg under the throw and I recoil.

'None of this has been in vain after all. And don't worry about Emilio, I'll look after him. The internationally acclaimed artist Eloise Aitken will abandon her life of seclusion to marry the renowned volcanologist Professor Emilio Ferrante.'

She is unhinged. I need to get out of here.

'Gina and Emilio were a golden couple, and he can have that life again with me. He could never have had that with *you,* darling.' She looks at me with such pity, I feel exposed.

I'm suddenly really tired and quite disoriented. I'm not even sure what she's saying now – her mouth is moving, but I can't focus on a word. I feel extremely vulnerable, and despite the mists now forming in my head and the heavy weight of my limbs, I attempt to stand up.

'Now, dear, you mustn't overdo it,' she's saying, rushing to my aid. But is she? Is she trying to help me, or is she pushing me down? She is – she's pushing me down on to the sofa!

'My baby' is all I can say, and all I can think. I gather all my strength and try to extricate myself from her surprisingly strong grip. I pull away, lashing out at her with my arms. I have little coordination, but I'm able to land some strikes. I'm thinking only of saving myself and my baby – that's all that matters, my baby is all that's ever mattered.

I stagger the few paces to the front door, fully expecting her to rugby-tackle me. Flinching as I make my way, waiting for the weight of her to land on me as I reach the door, but when I do, all I hear is her laughter.

'Did you . . . Marian . . . did you give me something?' I hear myself slur.

'My home-made strawberry jam, darling. Takes away the bitter taste of the diazepam. I didn't have any myself, just put some on both our plates. It's very useful when you want to shut someone up – sometimes forever.'

I lunge at the door, start trying to turn the knob from the inside, but it doesn't move. I put all my strength into it, and twist as hard as I can, but nothing is moving. I can hear myself whimpering with fear as I turn to see her right behind me. She has a poker – a sharp, metal poker – and she's holding it over my head.

'If I let you go, you'll ruin everything for Emilio and me, just like Gina did. I told you everything because you can't leave here. I have this plan. I got away with murder once, I can do it again. This time I'm going to make it look like suicide. I can push you off my bedroom balcony; you're distraught because you just found out your lover is a killer and you're having his baby. Come on now, darling, let's go up the wooden stairs to Bedfordshire.'

She pushes me into the hallway, and I grab the banister rail and hold on with both hands while she tries to shunt me up the stairs with her chunky little body. I'm feeling weaker every second; the diazepam is really taking hold now. I can't let her do this to me, and I slump down and pull the kitchen knife from my boot.

'Oh darling, you can't be that woozy yet, I didn't put a lot of sleepy pills in your tea, just enough.'

I can barely keep my eyes open, but something urges me forward, and it takes everything I have to lift the knife and plunge it hard into her chest. Her mouth opens in shock and, clutching her chest, our eyes meet for a horrible moment before she falls on her back, and just lies there, a crimson ribbon trickling from her mouth.

◆ ◆ ◆

By the time Sabrina arrives I'm sitting in a pool of blood, sticky and red. It will take a long time to wash all this away. She's banging on the door, but I can't get up. I try to attempt to lunge forward, but I'm weak and drugged and keep landing back in the slippery blood. The slick of red holds me down, like Marian's still here, pulling me back, making me stay. Her body is close to me, her eyes staring; this will be in my brain forever.

Sabrina's shouting now, and I hear the panic in her voice as she calls my name. I can't speak, I'm so sedated I can barely move, and I just lie there covered in my victim's blood. It seems Sabrina is making so much noise that neighbours have come out of their homes. She screams and calls for help, and when they hear her, they batter down the door with their bare hands.

'She killed Gina,' I say as Sabrina hugs me and wipes the blood spatters from my face.

'What are you saying? You've been given something, you don't know what you're saying.'

'She drugged the tea . . . the baby,' I manage to blurt, as I sit in the red lake rocking backwards and forwards, my hand over my belly.

58

Eventually the police arrive, along with an ambulance that takes me to the hospital, where I'm given fluids and medication and kept in for a few hours' observation. The following morning, Sabrina and I are taken to the police station, where Emilio is waiting, his arms open.

'Is the baby okay?' he asks, his face melting into a smile when I nod in confirmation. 'I can't believe what you've been through,' he says, pulling me to him. 'The police told me you got a confession.'

Thank God I thought to leave my phone on to get her story. It's all there.

Marian seemed like a mother to me. But all the time she brought the light, she was actually bringing the darkness. Watching me, causing trouble, turning my life into chaos. Scaring the hell out of me. She saw Gina as the obstacle to a life with Emilio, and she saw me in the same way. I could very easily have been next.

I will never forgive myself for taking a person's life. If I wasn't pregnant, I don't think I would have pushed that knife into her chest. I was saving my baby, and I found the strength to get rid of the threat.

'You must never blame yourself or feel bad about what happened,' Emilio says, with tears in his eyes.

I take his hand and hold it on my tummy.

'You saved yourself and our baby, and if you have to blame anyone, blame me. If you hadn't been with me, none of this would have happened. From the moment you met me I've caused you nothing but trouble. I'm so sorry, Sophie. All the pain and worry and I just want to go home with you, forget about everything.'

'I just want it to be the two of us, it's all I've ever wanted, just me and you and our baby, that will be my happy ever after.'

Later, I make a full statement to the police, with Emilio and Sabrina by my side.

'I wish things were different, I wish Gina was with us now, but at least we now know what happened the night my sister died,' Sabrina says. She turns to Emilio. 'I'm sorry I thought you were involved, but I was desperate. I couldn't rest until I'd found out what had happened to her.'

The police have the recording of Marian's confession, and the forensics team will confirm that I killed her in self-defence. The forensics regarding Gina's death will always be difficult to establish due to the fact her body lay there for so long. The quality of DNA has reduced drastically, especially because the body was exposed to heat and the elements during an unusually hot summer. But the confession is enough to close the book on Gina Caprini's death.

'I completely misread Marian. She seemed like a kind, decent woman, and I trusted her,' I tell Sabrina.

'I didn't know her all that well,' she says. 'But she used to follow us around, a hanger-on who never let go. I will never get over my sister's death, and as long as I live, I can't forgive Eloise for taking her away from me.'

'But Marian . . . or Eloise . . . was led to believe that if she removed Gina from the picture, Emilio would be hers. I wonder why she thought that?'

She shrugs. 'Who knows? Deluded bitch.'

Clearly Sabrina isn't going to acknowledge her own part in manipulating Marian, and speaks about her as if she hardly knew the woman. Had the sisters not toyed with Marian's rather naive idea about love, Gina might still be alive today. Emilio and Gina would be divorced, and Sabrina would have been back in Gina's will, inheriting everything. I guess Sabrina got what she deserved: nothing.

◆　◆　◆

We had a meeting today with Gina's lawyers, and Emilio will inherit most of Gina's wealth as her will stipulates. Sabrina's fear that she gets a modest lump sum when she turns forty is correct, but with the proviso that she stays clean and has regular drug tests. Gina knew her sister well; she was concerned about Sabrina's past addiction, and leaving her everything would surely tempt her back into that life.

Emilio will inherit the house, where we will live, as the foothills of Catania aren't the place to bring up a baby, but we plan to return there from time to time as a family. Meanwhile, Sabrina isn't too happy about Emilio's inheritance and has decided to go travelling – we breathed a huge sigh of relief when she said she was leaving.

As Emilio pointed out, the money she has won't last, the way she spends it. We just hope she can stay off the drugs.

Tonight, as Emilio and I sit on the huge sofa in Gina's old sitting room, I finally dare to feel happy, but there's just one thing.

'Shall we change the pictures on the walls?' I ask, as, along with many other images, the huge pixelated image of Gina's face still looks down on us. I hope by removing her images, we'll finally be able to exorcise the ghost of his first wife, but just as I say this, my mug of hot tea falls from my hand, splashing me with boiling liquid.

I look up at the picture and we stare each other out – and it occurs to me that Gina might never be ready to leave here.

59

THE FOLLOWING SEPTEMBER, AT THE CATHEDRAL OF SAN NICOLA, TAORMINA

It's a beautiful September day in Sicily, the sky is bright blue, and children dart around the square as we emerge from the cathedral into the blazing sunshine, and I take a snapshot in my head of this moment. Life doesn't get any better than this.

Beatrice Ferrante was born in July weighing a healthy seven pounds, three ounces. She's now three months old, the light of our lives, and today – our wedding day – we've become a family.

It's all I've ever wanted, it's been a rocky old road getting here, but it's all been worth it. I was the girl without a family, and then a wife without a husband, and finally Emilio and Beatrice have made me whole. This is what I've been waiting for all my life.

◆　◆　◆

I stand in the doorway of the church. The photographer is taking pictures of Emilio and me; we're holding Bea in our arms and looking into each other's eyes. It's a picture I've held in my head for a long time, from the early days, when Gina haunted my waking hours, to the time Emilio was being held by the police. I just focused on this picture, kept the faith, and the three of us are now a family.

Though his parents are dead, most of Emilio's relatives are here to celebrate with us today. I was concerned that they might compare me unfavourably to Gina, but their greetings have been warm and kind, and I think they approve. She's still around, and probably always will be, but I think she's taken a step back recently. I'm confident in my relationship with Emilio, and it's given me the strength to resist her whispers of doubt in my head. I won't let anyone or anything come between Emilio and me ever again.

Sabrina couldn't make it today. She's thousands of miles away on her world travels. I keep an eye on her Instagram just as I did Gina's. There are no volcanoes there, only tropical beaches and nightclub wastelands. I feel only pity for Sabrina; she lived all her life in the shadow of the volcano that was Gina. I wasn't the only one who felt diminished by her presence. Gina was a hard act to follow, as I know only too well.

I wave to Abbi. Yes, she's here. Once the dust was settled, I called her and told her that I appreciated her as a friend, and I was sorry if I hurt her feelings, abandoned her, then accused her of reporting me to the university principal.

Once Abbi finally accepted Emilio and saw how genuine he is, she was happy for me, and insisted on helping me plan the wedding. Her notebook has been permanently in use, and she's organised the flowers, helped choose the venue and the catering companies. She's been in her element, but most of all, she's totally falling for Beatrice and has been a huge support to me since she was born.

I still see Abbi's flaws, as she sees mine, but the difference is, after my experience with Marian, that I know Abbi is a *true* friend.

She might be a bit bossy at times, and she doesn't always approve of my choices, but at least she's not a psychopath or a murderer – I hope.

Talking of which, Marian aka Eloise Aitken – the late, internationally renowned artist – now also goes by the moniker of the Crater Killer, and you know, I think she'd be okay with that. Marian always wanted to be considered different and quirky. Her biggest fear was to be boring, and she certainly wasn't that. Even after death, her memory will live on as a rather colourful, eccentric and brilliant artist – and killer.

There's been so much written about her, and the public can't get enough. She's the new *Baby Reindeer*, and there's talk of a Netflix film and a Broadway musical. She's also a big pull in the weekly guided trip for tourists – the Killers of Sicily Ghost Tour. Visitors lap it up, and the tour's fully booked two years in advance. And it's not the Mafia hitmen, or even the woman who used her victims' bodies to make soap that the tourists are seeking – no, they all want a piece of Marian.

Whoever could have guessed that the hilarious, well-spoken, sweary woman in my art class harboured such darkness, and was capable of something so desperate. Sometimes I feel the pain of her sadness – that unrequited love, laughed at by Sabrina and Gina, was as real to Marian as my love for Emilio is to me. Thinking about that makes me cry for her, and my guilt is sliced open, bloody and raw all over again.

Meanwhile, my own artwork, now called *Go and Make Memories*, the project detailing Simon's life and aspects of his death, has been a critical success, and bought by an art investor.

Obviously I haven't told the whole story in the art project – no one knows that, and no one ever will; I'll take it to the grave with me. But I'm glad that through art I've been able to revisit my time with Simon, and bring him back into the world again. He deserves to be remembered, and I had to do that, for both of us.

If Emilio and Sabrina give their permission, I hope to do another project – this time about Gina's life and death. My artist's eye can see all the images, the possibilities of something special – a testament to her life, to her work. Born in the shadow of a brooding volcano, Gina was the girl from Caprini Martini, who every man wanted, and every woman wanted to be. How tragic and ironic that the poster girl for volcanoes met her untimely death in a volcanic crater, where her body lay for months.

I shudder, just thinking about that horrific event, and remind myself that today is my wedding day, and I need to enjoy the *now*. I look out on to the square where Emilio is chatting with family and friends. He's holding Beatrice close, and I see the happiness on his face; the closed smile is open at last.

We are both finally free from the past, and the ghosts of those we loved before don't creep around in our present quite so much. When I came here to this beautiful place, I was fleeing from the fear of getting caught, of someone finding out what I'd done. Sicily was my sanctuary, until I met Emilio; then a new fear took over, and the watcher began to haunt me. I thought they knew my secret and wanted to punish me for what had happened with Simon. The dread smell of strong cigarettes, followed by a plume of smoke, and staring eyes made me feel seen – and not in a good way. Thank God the watcher died with Marian; there are no more wisps of fear under my door, and I can finally sleep at night.

Just thinking about the watcher fills me with dread, and in my mind, I smell that horrible smell. But then I breathe in. Is it only in my mind?

It must be. It's just my mind playing tricks, knowing that any happy days I have are paid for with bad days. Am I simply expecting something bad to happen because I'm happy?

But then I actually see it. A curl of smoke emerging from behind the church, just around the corner from where I'm standing. I think my heart might just stop. Surely it's a guest having a sneaky cigarette out of sight, hoping no one will see?

The smoke is twining into rings of grey clouds, mocking me. *Beware, teste di moro, too many secrets, someone lies and someone dies* . . . I still feel that kitchen knife going through her breast bone and right into her heart. The whimpering squeal as she slumped. Is she now at my wedding, is the ghost of Marian joining the ghost of Gina? Their whispering is now a hissing chorus in my head, and it's getting louder and louder.

Still standing by the church, I'm unobserved by my wedding guests who are chatting and laughing, while anticipating the wedding breakfast in the beautiful hotel high in the Sicilian hills. I see Emilio smiling at me through the people, and he lifts Bea's tiny hand so it looks like she's waving, and instantly the ghosts in my head cease their whispering. Peace.

I'm soothed for now, but as he's drawn back into his family, I'm drawn back to the smoke.

I know it's in my mind, but still I slowly begin to follow the smell, and when I get around the corner, I can't believe who's standing there.

60

She's standing around the side of the church, where she can't be seen by the guests.

'Sabrina, I thought you were on the other side of the world?'

'You mean you *hoped* I was?'

'No,' I lie, horrified that she's turned up now, on my wedding day. 'Why are you here?'

She steps out, and gazes over at the small crowd milling around a few hundred yards away.

'I need a favour.'

'What?' My heart sinks.

'Money. The fucking family accountant says I'm going through the allowance that my father left me, and I can't have any more until next year.' She sucks the last bit of life out of her cigarette and, dropping it, she grinds it into the ground with her shoe.

'I can't help you with money,' I say.

'But you're rich. *He's* got all Gina's money.'

'Yes, it's not *my* money.'

'Damn right it isn't your money, and it's not his either.'

'Not this again.' I turn to walk away, but she reaches out and grabs me by the wrist. 'Sabrina, you're hurting me.'

'I don't care,' she says through her teeth.

'This is my wedding . . .' I start.

'I don't care about that *either*.' She continues to hold my wrist tightly, but holding it down so no one can see.

'Sophie, I need you to see this little piece of artwork I noticed while I was in *the artist's residence* in Catania.'

'What are you talking about?' My heart starts thumping.

'There you go.' She hands me her phone, which I take with trembling hands. It shows a photo of one of my diary entries from when Simon was poorly. I want to be sick.

'You took this picture in Catania,' I say. 'I wondered why you turned up out of the blue like that. You didn't come to see us because you were worried about your sister; you came to try and find something on me or Emilio that you could use to destroy us.'

'Everyone has a secret they'd kill for, Sophie.'

'You went through my stuff . . . my *private* stuff.' My voice breaks as tears stick in my throat. 'And the smoke . . . was that you too?'

'No, that wasn't me. That was Marian and her sad little pantomime.' She chuckles to herself. 'Yeah, I knew the crazy bitch was doing it – she couldn't wait to tell me all about it. She was furious because you now had *her* Emilio. Hilarious, really.'

I feel violated. 'Yes, and it suited you for me to be terrorised. You didn't want me anywhere near him either.'

'I may have resented you at first, but I wouldn't take your sloppy seconds now.'

'You are so fucking sinister,' I hiss, 'and I won't be blackmailed with this.' I thrust her phone back into her hands.

'Calm down, queen,' she says, rolling her eyes. Smiling and waving at someone she obviously knows in the group of guests a little further down the hill.

I'm trying desperately not to cry. If Emilio sees me crying, he'll be straight over here. I don't want that; he can't ever know.

'Sophie, let me read to you, and let's see how you feel about not getting the money to me after you've heard this story.' She starts reading my diary entry in a whiney voice.

'"My husband is thirty-three, we've been married for three years, and we've just been told he has terminal cancer. He hasn't been well for a while, but when the consultant called us in today and told us he has stage four cancer we both almost collapsed. It's such a shock, we can't take it in. I am writing this down so I can read it, so it goes into my head, because I can't believe it." No dates, not like a proper diary,' Sabrina observes, before continuing with a later entry. '"We are devastated, but Simon is adamant that he isn't going to let this take him. I'm now buying only organic foods, I'm making him healthy meals, and trying to make him smile, but he doesn't eat or smile much these days."'

She pulls her face down into a fake sad expression, before continuing. '"Simon's not been good this week, the chemo is taking its toll."' She turns to me with a mocking sad face. '"But I keep repeating positive mantras – 'we've got this' and 'fuck cancer'. But some days I feel like cancer's fucked us." Nice play on words there, Sophie,' she smirks.

I glare at her in disbelief. I knew she was cruel, but this is beyond anything I imagined her to be capable of. I want to run away, but I'm rooted to the spot, frozen with grief. How could she do this – and how is she still smiling?

She looks back down and starts to read more in that same whiney voice. '"Simon fell down the stairs this morning. I heard him, and ran to help, but he lay there on the ground, deathly still, his limbs twisted. I thought I'd lost him but then he opened his eyes, this disease tears through its victims at such a pace, like film speeded up. We both cried for the strong, fit young man my husband used to be – only months ago."'

She pulls another sad face. I want to slap her.

'"Yesterday we were told that the chemo hasn't worked, and Simon asked the doctor, 'So, what next?' The doctor didn't need to say a word, the expression on his face told us all we needed to know. There is no next. The prognosis is vague, but we've been told it's months, not years. The consultant's parting words to us were 'go and make memories'."'

'You're sick,' I say, and start to slowly move away. I don't want her yelling at me and making a scene. No one can know.

'If you walk away, I'll just read the rest louder so everyone can hear it,' she says loudly. I stop dead in my tracks.

'Poor Simon,' she murmurs, sarcasm oozing from her voice. '"Today Simon said, 'I don't want to die in hospital under heavy medication. Let me go in the garden, on a warm afternoon, sitting in a deckchair with a glass of red wine, Sophie. Please?'" Shall I go on?'

I have to stop myself from knocking her to the ground. I clench my fists and hold them by my sides.

'"It's just three months since the diagnosis, and the cancer has all but taken him. He can't walk, can barely speak and he's in constant pain. Today was his birthday. I baked him a cake, but it's still here in the kitchen, wrapped in tin foil. As I dressed him this morning, I heard him say, 'Today.' Despite knowing it was moving towards us, the pace quickening with each day, it felt so sudden, so blunt an ending. I know we'd talked, but there would always be something else to say. 'It's a beautiful morning,' I said, 'wait a little while longer.' But he looked at me, big eyes in his gaunt face, pleading. 'If I stay until this afternoon, you'll beg me to stay tonight, and then it will be tomorrow. I don't want to wait until the cancer chooses – I want to make one final decision about my life, Sophie. I've left it too long as it is, I can't even get the pills myself because I'd never make it to the bathroom. I'm sorry to put this on you but . . . give me back my dignity.'

'"So, a little later, I gathered all my courage, and with a breaking heart, moved him into the warm, syrupy sunshine. He closed his eyes while I went back inside, ground down the sleeping pills, and sprinkled them into a large glass of his favourite red wine. Then I took it out on a tray, sat on the deckchair next to him, and trembling, I held the glass to his lips. He drank slowly, struggling to swallow, but as he closed his eyes, a smile spread across his face – and that's how I remember him."' She glares at me, completely unmoved, her face like stone. 'You don't mention any of that in your artwork.'

'What kind of monster are you, Sabrina?' I say, choking on tears.

'No wonder you didn't want to talk about your marriage when I asked. I just *knew* you were hiding something, and boy were you!'

'Of course I was hiding it, but I had no choice, he didn't want to die in pain and—'

'Oh, you can dress it up in all kinds of shit and use words like "pain" and "dignity" . . . but the fact is, you killed him, queen. He said it himself – he was too weak to go upstairs and grab those pills, he needed you to do it, and you did.' She steps closer to me, and whispers in my ear, 'You murdered your husband, does your *husband* know?' She nods her head in the direction of Emilio. I'm terrified.

'It wasn't *murder*. Surely you know by reading that diary.'

She's shaking her head. 'You might as well have stabbed him in the chest . . . I mean, that's your signature move, isn't it, *queen*?'

I see the knife sticking from Marian's chest, the trailing ribbon of crimson, and retch.

'Playing at being squeamish now? You are a "hoot", as Marian used to say.' She steps back, and looks me up and down, 'You've killed *two* people, Sophie. You are a danger to society, there are prisoners serving *life* for doing less than you have.'

'I killed Marian in self-defence.'

'*Whatever,* I'm bored of your whining now. Look, I want you to convince Emilio to give me fifty thousand euros by next week. I need the money in cash, no banks involved, and I need it by Wednesday. If not, I'm putting in a call to the police to tell them you killed your first husband in the UK, and you murdered Marian because she got you sacked.'

'But that's not true.'

She shakes her head. 'You don't get it, do you? It's not about *truth*, it's how it looks, and trust me, anyone can be made to look guilty. Assisted suicide is illegal in the UK, and I have proof that you broke the law right here.' She waggles her phone. 'You would be extradited back to the UK, and the fact you have since been involved in another killing . . .' She lets the threat hang as it sinks in. 'I mean, one is careless . . . but two? We're talking Sophie the Serial Killer.'

She is a monster, and her lies could tear apart everything I hold dear. She has proof of what I did for Simon, and is happy to lie to the police about Marian. If I don't get that money, she will ruin my life.

61

'I can see the headlines now,' she says. '"Wife of Caprini Widower went on Killing Spree!" Oh gosh, I doubt your handsome groom over there would find you quite so endearing. Self-defence is one thing, but euthanasia wouldn't go down too well with Emilio's Catholic values, would it?'

'I told you, there's no point in blackmailing me. I can't get hold of the money, it isn't mine.'

'You can get it. And I want fifty thousand euros.'

I am exasperated, tearful, I don't know how to handle this, or handle her. 'I'm not being difficult, Sabrina, but Emilio would want to know why I need fifty thousand euros.'

'Lie – it wouldn't be the first time,' she smirks.

I'm just shaking my head in despair. I don't know how to appeal to her – she has no conscience, no soul, she's just mean and nasty and dangerous.

She leans back against the church wall inspecting her nails, then looks up. 'And of course, there's Beatrice to consider.'

My stomach drops. 'Don't you dare, this has *nothing* to do with my child.'

'Er, it has a lot to do with her. Even if you miraculously escape a prison sentence, I doubt Emilio will let his daughter anywhere near you. I mean, let's face it, Sophie, you'll never see either of them again – the bodies are piling up!'

Her eyes slide over to Emilio, who is mingling with the guests.

After everything we've been through, I won't lose Emilio, or my daughter, the most precious thing in the world. But how can I stop her?

'Think about it,' she says. 'We'll catch up later.' She starts to walk, then turns around and looks at me. 'Congratulations, by the way.' And with that, she continues downhill towards the wedding party, greeting Emilio with a smile and an elaborate hug.

I wipe my eyes as I watch her. I *know* I did right by Simon. It was an act of love – something Sabrina knows nothing about.

From the short distance, I watch Sabrina chatting and laughing with my new husband, and words pop into my head from nowhere. *Someone lies and someone dies.* It was *her* the strange fortune teller warned me about – *she* lied to Marian about Emilio having feelings for her, and that lie was the catalyst for her sister's death.

My encounter with the fortune teller was early in my relationship with Emilio, just before the smoker, but around the time Marian appeared in class. I suddenly hear echoes of her voice in my head: 'I borrowed a hooded cloak from the opera society. You might recall I joined them to learn to sing . . .' The fortune teller was short, with a croaky Italian accent, and Marian was the consummate actress – it was Marian all along, trying to scare me off. Threatening me with lies and death. I'm shocked at the lengths this madwoman went to in order to stop me from being with Emilio. But even though Marian's dead, it will never be over, because now Sabrina is manipulating me. She's also threatening my happiness and my marriage, albeit in a less theatrical way.

I now know what I must do. Walking away from the church, I approach the wedding party, and pull her aside. 'I'll get you the money,' I say quietly in her ear.

'Yay! I knew you'd see the light, queen.' She touches my face and I recoil.

'But if I get you the money, I want something from you.'

'Oh?' Her face drops.

'I'm hoping to do a new art project about Gina, but first I need your permission.'

She shrugs; she doesn't care.

'And also – I want to take some photos of *you*.'

'Why?' she asks, suspiciously.

'Because this project about Gina, whether I like it or not, it's also about you. You're her sister, the only remaining blood relative.'

Her face lights up. 'Me? You want photos of me in the project?'

'Yes, you look so much like her,' I continue. 'I want to capture you, in your youth and beauty, the same way artists captured her.'

She is loving this, and can't wipe the smile from her face.

'Okay queen, but perhaps I should be asking for more than fifty thousand for photos of moi?'

'No, no way. That's it.'

'Okay, calm down, it was just a joke. I'll do your little project.'

'Great, let's meet up next week, in Catania. It's beautiful there right now, the weather's mild, and the crowds have gone so it'll be quiet. I can get some lovely shots, and some sketches too – and then I'll hand the money over without anyone seeing us. You mustn't tell a soul about our meeting because Taormina's a small place, and my husband mustn't know.'

'Sure, your secret's safe with me.'

It isn't, though, is it?

'So the money is your silence, okay?' I say under my breath.

'Sure, so what kind of clothes should I bring – for the shoot?'

'Bring whatever you feel good in. I'd like to do some really moving stuff around the crater . . . if you can handle that? It might be a lot for you?'

'I'll be fine, I'll do it. You'd just better make sure you have that money.'

'Oh, I *will*. I'll meet you there, at the crater. So, next Thursday, about six p.m.?'

She nods and I move through the guests, stopping to chat to people and give them directions to the wedding breakfast. Eventually, about ten minutes later, I spot Emilio and go to join him.

'Darling, there you are,' he says, enveloping me in a hug.

'Where's Beatrice?' I'm smiling, and looking around.

'She's with Auntie Sabrina,' he says, and my heart jumps. 'Where, *where* is she?' I ask, rigid with sheer panic.

'I thought she was there,' he says, pointing to a group of people, but there's no sign of Sabrina.

'I can't see her, Emilio, how could you let her—'

'It's okay, she's over there,' he says, relief in his voice. He obviously doesn't trust her with our child either. Sabrina's standing nearby, holding Beatrice and smirking at me.

I rush over, and take my baby from her.

'Hey, don't be mean, I'm getting to know her. We were just having a little chat about her mummy.' She grimaces, then turns to Beatrice, who is gurgling in my arms. 'I was telling you all about your mummy's *adventures*, wasn't I, Bea?'

I look away from her cold, calculating eyes, and down at my sweet little girl, and, if I had any doubts about what I'm going to do, this moment has convinced me it's the right thing for all of us.

◆ ◆ ◆

Next week, I will meet Sabrina in secret at the crater where Gina fell. I'll tell her how beautiful she looks, take out my camera and ask her to pose. Like her sister, she loves the attention, is easily flattered, and I'll just click away pretending to 'capture her youth and beauty'. And when the time's right, when no one is around and she's teetering on the edge of the crater, too wrapped up in herself to be aware, I'll push her, just as Marian pushed Gina. And if ever her body is found, I'll remember how she never got over the death of her sister, and talked about joining her one day, which is true.

But right now, I smile, wave to my guests, and Emilio helps me and my long dress into the car. I clutch Beatrice to me, and once we're seated, I watch Sabrina climb into another car with people I don't know; we're all heading for the wedding breakfast. I just hope she doesn't stay long, because while she's around nothing and no one is safe. I watch Emilio talking to Charlotte, his colleague, the beautiful woman I thought was a man – and I still feel uneasy about her. I have her lipstick still, and I might just throw that in the crater with Sabrina. It wouldn't be enough to charge her with murder, but questions would be asked, and shadows would be cast, and it would wipe that smug smile from her face for a while. As Sabrina just said, 'It's not about *truth*, it's how it looks; *anyone* can be made to look guilty.'

Emilio is smiling into Charlotte's face, and I wonder how it would feel to be *rid* of her. Is it true that after you've taken one human life, it becomes easier? Is this how serial killers start their careers? I'm horrified and thrilled to imagine a world where problems like Sabrina and Charlotte can be eradicated. Excitement and anticipation tingle through me, as I turn to my gorgeous husband now climbing into the car and sitting next to me.

'I can't believe we're finally married. I love you, Mrs Ferrante,' he says, kissing me as the car pulls away. 'Just a few months ago, I'd never have thought this happiness was possible. I'm a different person. Life holds such darkness, but also some amazing surprises.' He's looking at me with such innocence and tenderness that tears spring to my eyes.

I nod in agreement, the voice of the fortune teller in my head – *someone lies and someone dies* . . . it's about to happen again. Only, this time, *I* will be the person who lies, and Sabrina will be the one to die.

I look out of the window, and as the scenery goes by, Etna remains constant in my vision, rumbling, waiting, foreshadowing the darkness to come.

'It's been a strange time,' I agree. 'Gina's death was tough, but Beatrice's birth was the best thing that's ever happened to me.'

'Me too.' He smiles. 'Life is light and dark, isn't it?'

'Yes, and so unpredictable. If I've learned anything from this past year, it's that you never know people,' I reply, thinking of Marian. 'Everyone has their secrets, their reasons, and sometimes good people do bad things, and, given an impossible choice, a decent person can turn to murder. A potential killer could be sitting right next to you . . . and you'd never even know.'

AFTERWORD

This story has been wandering around my head since I visited Sicily a couple of years ago. We stayed in Taormina, the town where the book is set. It's one of the most beautiful places I've ever been. Smooth and shiny with wealth and luxury, Chanel and Versace compete for attention with the billionaires' yachts waiting in the harbour, and at first glance, this was heaven. But the beauty here is overshadowed by Etna, the dark, still-live volcano – threatening and unpredictable, a constant reminder that we aren't in control, that fate and nature are our masters, and they're marking our diaries.

I imagined a mysterious, handsome Italian, a man with secrets whose moods reflect the volcanic landscape. I wondered what would happen if he met a woman who also mirrored the beauty and darkness of this place, and had her own dark secrets. Immediately, I thought of Daphne du Maurier's *Rebecca*, and that was the spark that lit the flame. I had to write this book. I later shared this idea with Victoria Haslam, my editor, and together we worked it into a dark and twisted love story.

Writing this book has been a joy, mostly for the sheer pleasure of living with Taormina in my head for months. I was back there, with the chi-chi restaurants, the shadow of Etna, the lunar landscape at the foothills, and the fancy houses where the eyes of the star-crossed lovers see everything . . . and say nothing.

ACKNOWLEDGEMENTS

This book was inspired by my visit to Sicily, but also *Rebecca* by Daphne du Maurier, an author my mum introduced to me as a young teenager. Mum is a huge fan of du Maurier's atmospheric, spine-tingling writing, and we've both read her books and together watched the films of those books. So, a huge thanks to Mum, for introducing me to *Rebecca*, 'The Birds', *Jamaica Inn* and all that wonderful, dark, literary suspense at an early age, which inspired my own writing.

Thanks also to my husband, Nick Watson, who travelled with me to Sicily, where we wandered the lunar landscape in the foothills of Etna. He's also accompanied me since on various volcano research trips, often holding out his hand from the edge of craters reassuring me that, 'Yes you *can* climb up here,' when I usually can't. Thanks for the faith, Nick!

A huge thank you to my wonderful editor, Victoria Haslam, for her inspiration and support from the very beginning, when we just had the seed of an idea. And when the edits are long and time is short, her positivity and sheer enthusiasm keep me going late into the night! Thanks also to Celine Kelly, who has worked closely with me on this book, made sense of my chaos, got what I was thinking and where I was going, and understood my characters even better than I did.

They say it takes a village to raise a child, and I think it takes a village to write a book, but there are so many people I should thank, I'd need to write another book to include all their names! But thank you to the Thomas & Mercer team for all their guidance and support, and to my family and friends for putting up with me – when my head is so full of a book, I'm in my own world – and not great company in the real world!

ABOUT THE AUTHOR

Photo © 2024 Nick Watson

Sue Watson was a TV producer at the BBC until she wrote her first book and was hooked.

Now a *USA Today* bestselling author, she has sold almost 2 million books exploring the darker side of life, writing psychological thrillers with big twists. Originally from Manchester, Sue now lives with her family and Cosmo the cat in leafy Worcestershire where much of her day is spent writing – and procrastinating.

Follow the Author on Amazon

If you enjoyed this book, follow Sue Watson on Amazon to be notified when the author releases a new book!
To do this, please follow these instructions:

Desktop:

1) Search for the author's name on Amazon or in the Amazon App.
2) Click on the author's name to arrive on their Amazon page.
3) Click the 'Follow' button.

Mobile and Tablet:

1) Search for the author's name on Amazon or in the Amazon App.
2) Click on one of the author's books.
3) Click on the author's name to arrive on their Amazon page.
4) Click the 'Follow' button.

Kindle eReader and Kindle App:

If you enjoyed this book on a Kindle eReader or in the Kindle App, you will find the author 'Follow' button after the last page.

Made in the USA
Middletown, DE
19 June 2025